LEGEND

ASHES OF AETHER

HOLLY ROSE

RED
SPARK
PRESS

ASHES OF AETHER

HOLLY ROSE

To my sister, for helping me to believe.

BELENTRA

Ruins of Ithyr

Nimira

LUMARIA

Aesari

Mithrys

Shalandril

FENYR WOODS

Olona Island

Verethia

Tarethel

Althira

Eldasil

ALANOR

Caelis

Talmira

The Shimmering Isles

WORLD OF IMYRIA

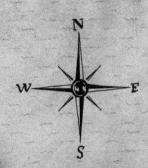

N
W · E
S

TALIĐOR

KRALAXXAS

Uldren Isle

ĐROMGAR

Odela
VALKA
Boldred

Zol Arrod

Arnvik
Jorga
Avrak

Đalry
Gerazad
JEKTAR

Lowrick

The Ghost
Woods

NOLĐERAN

Đul Kazar

Lenris Port

Esterra
SELYNIS
Nezu

Tuylon

Meran Island

CHAPTER 1

FIRE FALLS TOWARD ME. Blazing flames spread into ferocious wings. There's no time to escape.

I reach through the air and gather all the aether I can. Violet sparks crackle in my fingertips, and the magic amplifies as it joins with that which flows through my blood. Together, the power is great enough to fuel my spell.

I thrust out both hands, my palms facing the oncoming fiery blast. Despite the aether dancing across my fingers, I feel the sweltering heat. It's close enough to blister my hands and singe the edges of my cerulean adept robes.

But I will not be defeated. Not on my birthday.

"*Aquir'muriz!*" I shout. My voice rings through the empty arena and echoes off the highest stone seats.

The aether heeds my command. Violet sparks turn to swirling sapphires, and the spell blossoms into a shield of blue light. Flames lick at the edges and gnaw holes across the emerging magic.

My breathing slows to a halt. I fear it's too late.

But then my shield becomes corporeal. The sapphire light materializes into a whirlpool so violent it hides the raging inferno beyond.

Flames sizzle as they meet the tumultuous water. Steam billows through the arena, and water sprays out as my shield weakens.

I grit my teeth and fuel the wall with more power, willing for it not to disintegrate and leave me entirely exposed, but the defensive spell soon falls apart. Water splashes onto the smooth marble slabs beneath my feet, and the freshly made puddles glisten in the late noon sun.

The fiery wings are also gone. Not even embers remain.

Kaely tosses her mousy brown braid over her shoulder. An ugly sneer contorts the countless freckles splattered across her cheeks. Her eyes, violet like mine, smolder with relentless hatred.

We were friends once. That seems a lifetime ago, despite it being only last year. I don't know what I did to deserve her hatred. Surely breathing isn't a crime?

Her glare is so venomous, with magenta flames blazing in her eyes, that I think she may kill me—though we are only dueling in the arena as part of today's Combat Class.

My attention drifts from Kaely to our spectators. Archmage Lorette Gidston sits on the lowest row of stone seats, our peers gathered around her. Lorette's talon-like hands rest on her lap, and her expression is a mask of cool indifference while she watches us, as if we aren't trying to kill each other. She appears to be in her mid-thirties, but I know for a fact she is much older than that. Her platinum hair is scraped into a bun so neat not even a single strand strays from its place. While this is my second year as an adept—a mage in training—I've never once seen Archmage Gidston wear her hair down. I imagine she would look quite pretty with her hair falling loose across her face, softening her severe features.

Remembering that now is not the time to be scrutinizing the Archmage's appearance, I return my attention to Kaely. But I'm a moment too late.

"*Telum!*" Kaely commands.

A blast of raw aether hurls from her fingers and surges toward me far quicker than the fiery wings did.

I could counter her spell with another aether shield, but I doubt mine will be powerful enough to fend off the attack. Kaely is much stronger than me. The only reason my previous spell nullified hers is because I wielded the element of water against fire. Aether is not one of the four elements, so I can't adopt a similar strategy.

Since shielding isn't an option either, I focus on the spot a few paces from me, far away enough that I'll be beyond the blast's range. I close my eyes, doing my best to ignore the magic racing straight for me, and picture my chosen position. I draw aether into my palms and let it run freely through me.

"*Laxus!*"

At my shout, the teleportation spell claims me, and my body glimmers away into aether dust.

I fade too slowly.

As I slip through the folds of time and space, Kaely's blast slams into me. Pain rips through my shoulder, white-hot and blinding. Though it hurts, I'm lucky the blast caught me mid-teleport, or else the sheer force of it would have torn me apart.

I stagger from the teleportation spell, emerging exactly where I envisioned, and clutch my shoulder. No blood wells out, at least not externally, but the pressure of the blast will have probably ruptured my vessels, and my entire shoulder will be starting to blacken with a hideous bruise.

Kaely prowls toward me, and her footsteps shatter the tense silence enveloping the arena. The other adepts no longer murmur among themselves; their attention is entirely focused on our deadly duel.

She raises her arm, and aether gleams in her hand like a lethal torch. My stomach broils with acid as I guess at which spell-words she may next utter. I can barely straighten, let alone defend myself.

Is this how it will end? Am I to die on my birthday?

I don't know why Archmage Gidston hasn't intervened yet. I've never seen a duel taken this far. Maybe among magi, but not among adepts.

"*Gelu'gladis.*" Kaely's voice is both a sneer and a whisper. A promise of death.

Ice. She has chosen to end me with ice.

I can only watch as she stretches sapphire light into a sword. My heart pounds furiously against my rib cage as the frozen blade solidifies.

I squeeze my eyes shut and brace myself for the caress of death. But it does not come. Neither does the bite of the frozen sword.

"*Ignir'muriz.*"

My eyes snap back open. Archmage Gidston stands between us. A fiery shield encases her, and it blazes so brightly the amber light glints across the arena's marble.

Kaely's frozen sword dissolves as it touches the flaming shield. Disappointment descends over her expression as a dense shadow. Disappointment that she could not defeat me once and for all.

"That is enough!" Archmage Gidston booms, her shout tremendous enough to make the clouds tremble. Even Kaely flinches. "Your victory has already been earned, Adept Calton. If you continue, you will end up killing her."

Shame brands my cheeks, as scorching as the inferno Kaely hurled at me.

Kaely raises her brows in apparent surprise. "Reyna should be able to withstand my attacks. She is the Grandmage's daughter."

Her words might sound unassuming—respectful even—to everyone else, but I can hear the mockery in her voice. I clench my left fist. My other hand still clasps my shoulder. Through the cerulean fabric of my adept robes, I feel my skin throbbing where the blast struck. She was so close to killing me.

"Indeed," Archmage Gidston says, turning to me. "She is."

Her words are cold and pensive, and I can't tell what she's considering. Perhaps how unlike my father I am. When he was an adept at the Arcanium, he was known as a prodigy, while I am a useless and lazy adept.

"*Conparios.*" Magic bursts from the Archmage's hands and radiates out. When the light fades, a small vial remains on her palm. It's barely larger than her little finger, and frothy green liquid churns within like fluorescent slime.

As unappetizing as it appears, the sight of the healing elixir relieves me enough to straighten my posture. But I continue clutching my shoulder to suppress as much of the pain as I can.

"Catch, Ashbourne," the Archmage says as she tosses the vial to me. In the next breath, she mutters *ventrez* and a wind spell swirls from her fingers, blowing the small container across the arena and into my hands.

I tear off the cork, tip back my head, and deposit the entire contents into my mouth. The potion tastes like rotten eggs and has a lumpy texture that reminds me of liquified slugs, but I swallow it all in a single gulp and try to cough none up. Hopefully the potion will work quickly enough to banish my pain and minimize any bruising.

Archmage Gidston doesn't watch and instead turns to address the other adepts. "Now that the last pair have finished dueling, your lesson is over for today. You are all dismissed." She offers us no words of praise, but she never does. I'm yet to see the Archmage of Knowledge impressed with any of our performances.

The adepts scramble from their seats, and one by one they murmur *laxus* and disappear into clouds of violet light. Aether scatters across the arena and glitters in the wind.

Archmage Gidston follows them, likely teleporting back to somewhere inside the Arcanium. In addition to overseeing its daily running, she also calls it her home. She lives somewhere in the upper levels, but I don't know where exactly. That part of the Arcanium is banned to mere adepts. Actually, most of it is, aside from the teaching rooms and the library. While my father is the Grandmage of Nolderan, and arguably the most powerful sorcerer in the world, even I am forbidden from entering areas restricted to official magi.

When all the other adepts have teleported out of the arena, only three of us remain: me, Kaely, and Eliya.

Eliya bounds over to me with such speed she almost sends me flying back onto the stone floor, and her unruly crimson hair dances around her heart-shaped face. Fortunately, she brings herself to an abrupt halt before reaching me.

"Reyna!" she exclaims, clutching my shoulders and shaking me. "Are you all right? Are you hurt?"

I don't mention that her fingers are pressing deeply into my left shoulder, the one which was injured by Kaely's aether blast. The healing elixir hasn't yet kicked in. Maybe in ten more minutes it will, but I expect my wound to be tender for a few days.

"I'm fine," I mumble. If Kaely weren't here, I would be more honest. I try to stand tall and proud, but I'm somewhat hunched because of the injury.

Kaely lifts her chin, doing her best to look down at me. Only figuratively, though, since she is much shorter than me. Sometimes I wonder whether she hates me because I'm almost twice her height.

Our eyes lock together. I think she will say something, but she instead draws aether into her fingers and mutters *laxus*, fading away without another word.

Then only Eliya and I are left standing here, surrounded by the arena's towering walls and thousands of empty stone seats. Against its sheer size, I feel as insignificant as an ant. Perhaps I am. Today I was horribly defeated by Kaely and failed to put up a decent fight against her.

I let out a heavy sigh.

"It wasn't *that* bad," Eliya says.

"It was terrible."

"Well, it's not just you. None of us have ever gotten close to beating her."

I gaze over to where Kaely stood moments ago. Aether dust still swirls there. "She's so strong," I say wistfully.

If only I were as strong as Kaely. Then my father would not be ashamed that the only heir to the Ashbourne family was a sorry excuse for an adept. Maybe I would be a better sorceress if I tried harder and spent more time studying, but what's the point? Kaely will always be far stronger than me. I never understood why she took to hating me when we started at the Arcanium. I should be the one who hates her, since she represents all that I am not.

"Her father is the Archmage of Defense." I suppose Eliya is trying to reassure me with a reminder of that fact, but it has the opposite effect.

"My father is the Grandmage of Nolderan." The words taste like ash on my tongue. "And yet look at me."

"Don't think like that," Eliya says, grabbing my hand and squeezing it. "You'll make a great mage when you graduate from the Arcanium."

"But not as great as Kaely."

Eliya presses her lips into a grim line, clearly knowing that nothing she can say will convince me otherwise.

"Please try to smile, Rey-rey," she says after a pause. "It's your eighteenth birthday today. You shouldn't be sad on any birthday, let alone your eighteenth."

I try to smile, but it must look as forced as it feels since Eliya sighs. My fake smile falters, and I replace it with an expression which matches my sour mood.

I know I would be a better adept if I tried, but even if I pour my heart and soul into studying, it still won't be enough to defeat Kaely or to make my father proud. I've long decided that it's better by far to hide behind the mask of idleness than to have my lack of talent laid bare for the world to see. I can never meet my father's expectations, be the prodigy that he was, so I would much rather be a mediocre mage out of choice than because of fate.

At least I can say the reason she defeated me so horribly today is because I don't work hard enough.

"You can't let Kaely spoil your eighteenth birthday." Eliya swings my hand back and forth as she pleads me. "Think how gleeful she would be if she knew you were this upset."

"I'm not upset. I'm just angry she dared to take the duel so far."

It's a lie, and we both know it, but Eliya doesn't point it out. Her expression continues to silently implore me not to let Kaely ruin my birthday. Eliya is right. I shouldn't let Kaely make me miserable. Not today.

"Anyway," I say, "what are you doing tonight? No one's made any plans with me yet."

"Not even Arluin?"

Her question strikes a raw nerve. "No," I grind out, "not even him." When I saw him last night, he mentioned nothing about my birthday. Not a single thing.

"What about your parents?"

I huff a strand of long, dark hair from my face. "My father has important meetings until late tonight. So, I was thinking the two of us could do something instead? Something that involves getting really, really drunk."

Eliya shuffles uncomfortably, not looking me in the eye, and focuses on the marble floor. Her guilt is plain to see. "Um, as great as that sounds, I already have plans tonight."

"You . . . you already have plans." I do my best to ensure the words don't sound as bitter as they taste, but I'm not sure I succeed.

Eliya's shoulders sink. "I'm meant to be going to my uncle's house for dinner tonight."

"And you can't get out of it?"

She shakes her head, and my heart plummets. "No, I'm sorry. We arranged it weeks ago. I forgot it was your birthday until this morning."

I can't believe what I'm hearing. "You forgot it was my birthday." I turn away from her and squeeze my eyes shut, willing myself not to cry. First, I suffered a horrible defeat at Kaely's hands, and now it appears my best friend forgot my birthday. And she even has the audacity to tell me I should be happy on my birthday, especially my eighteenth one.

Maybe I'm overreacting, but her betrayal cuts deep.

"Please don't be mad at me," Eliya whispers.

"It's fine," I force out, waving my hand and trying to keep my words as steady as I can. "I'm not mad. Not mad at all."

My tone must not be very convincing since she says, "You are cross—I can tell. I'm really so sorry, and I promise I'll make it up to you."

I suppose I should say something, but I can't find the words. I stare at her in disbelief.

She wraps her arms around me in an apologetic hug, but I feel numb. The arena's stone walls loom over us, casting their shadows in every direction.

I manage to place an arm across her back, but that's all. As much as I don't want to hurt her feelings, she forgot my birthday.

She releases me from the hug, and I step back, unable to look at her. "I'll see you later," I say, drawing aether around myself like a blanket.

Eliya wrings her hands together, guilt visibly gnawing on her. At least she knows she has done wrong.

I close my eyes, picturing my home in as much detail as I can: the enormous gates, the luxurious gardens, the glistening stone walls of the manor itself. When the image is fully formed, I release the aether and let it spiral from my grasp.

"*Laxus!*" I say, and the teleportation spell washes over me.

I drift away, leaving behind aether dust to scatter across the empty arena.

CHAPTER 2

THOUGH I HAVE CAST THE spell thousands of times before, a part of me is yet to become accustomed to the way teleportation feels. In one moment you're standing on solid ground, and in the next you're drifting through the folds of time and space. It's as if you're floating through something more liquid than air but lighter than water. That substance is, of course, aether.

When teleporting a few paces away, the spell is over in the blink of an eye and the peculiar sensation is much less noticeable. But when traveling from one side of Nolderan to the other, the teleportation takes far longer, and I am shrouded in darkness for perhaps ten seconds. It isn't the same darkness as night, not even a moonless one. I suppose it's closer to being locked inside a deep cavern. Prior to learning this spell, I never knew absolute darkness.

When my teleportation spell is complete, the first thing I feel is the solidness of the ground beneath my feet and the stability it provides. The second thing I feel is the late summer breeze brushing over my cheeks. Even after fully materializing, I remain in darkness for several heartbeats.

Finally, violet light pierces the void. It sketches the enormous gates guarding our manor, complete with our family crest: a shield featuring two winged lions roaring at each other, their manes fanning out like wildfire. Our family is known for its special affinity to fire spells, earning us the surname Ashbourne. And I won't lie: Fire spells are definitely my favorite sort of magic. Our preference goes back a thousand years, when Nolderan was in its infancy. It's well recorded that an ancestor of mine, Alvord Ashbourne, invented *ignir'alas*, the spell of fiery wings which Kaely hurled at me during our duel. I hate that she has mastered the spell so perfectly, while mine is far from flawless. At least the inferno itself isn't lacking in ferocity.

The light drafts out the gardens beyond the gates and the tall chimneys of our manor. It also outlines the buildings behind me and the street I'm standing on.

When the aether finishes sketching the most intricate details of my surroundings, the darkness dissolves into a world of rich color.

I stride over to the gilded gates, and my attention falls onto the magnificent lion crest. Aether hums across the metallic bars, and the golden highlights shimmer like threads of sunlight. I place my hands on my hips and raise my head. The movement hurts a little less than before. It seems Archmage Gidston's healing elixir is finally starting to kick in.

"Reyna Ashbourne," I announce to the gates, my voice loud and clear.

The aether barrier flashes, and the gates swing wide open, recognizing my voice and permitting my entry. I step through, and once I'm on the other side, the gates clang shut behind me.

Rainbows of bright flowers decorate the gardens. My mother has tried many times to teach me the names of all the species she grows in our gardens, but I never remember any of them. Except for roses, tulips, and pansies—and maybe a few others I can't think of right now.

My mother plants the flowers herself, entirely by hand, and even uses a shovel rather than an earth spell. When I was younger, I sat on the grass and watched her labor and then asked why she didn't use magic since it would complete the task in a fraction of the time. She replied, "If we use magic for everything, then life itself will lose its magic." I didn't understand her words then, and I still don't. Especially since she doesn't even water our gardens by hand.

Enchanted buckets sweep up and down the flower beds, sprinkling droplets of water across the vibrant petals. Unlike the gates, which have their enchantment powered by Nolderan's Aether Tower, these buckets will eventually run out of magic and fall to the grass. The water inside them isn't conjured, either. That comes from the fountain at the center of our gardens.

Once my mother has painstakingly planted the flowers with her own hands, they are maintained by our reptilian servants. In case you're wondering, that isn't a metaphor. Our servants are quite literally reptilian. Though they might be closer to what one calls pets than servants, or perhaps something in between.

These creatures are known as faerie dragons and called the island of Nolderan their home long before my ancestors did. But they aren't like actual dragons. Rather than fire, they spew tiny balls of aether when agitated. They're also the size of a cat, with azure scales and amaranthine butterfly wings. Faerie dragons are easily domesticated since they will do absolutely anything for aether crystals, and conjuring aether crystals is effortless for magi, even for useless adepts like me.

As I walk through the gardens, one of the faerie dragons darts past me and almost knocks me over with the empty bucket it clutches in its tiny talons. I pause and watch as the faerie dragon continues to the fountain to refill its bucket.

The fountain is made from marble and is twice my height, with three tiers from which the water cascades. An ornate pattern is chiseled into the edges and reminds me of frills.

Once the bucket is refilled, the faerie dragon flies back to its colorful flowerbed. I hold out my palm, and though the gesture is small, the faerie dragon immediately takes notice. It lowers the bucket onto the path, and water sloshes out and spills over the sides, but the faerie dragon doesn't care. Its butterfly wings flutter as it swooshes over to me.

The faerie dragon hovers above my palm and lets out an impatient yelp. Greed glints in its jewel-like eyes, and its velvety maw nudges my fingers. Delicate antennae tickle my wrist.

Despite the abysmal day I've had so far, I can't help myself from laughing. "Are you really that hungry, Zephyr? Has my mother not fed you at all today?"

Though faerie dragons are unable to vocalize any syllables, they understand every word of our language. Zephyr bobs his head in the most unconvincing nod I've ever seen. Faerie dragons are notoriously difficult to tell apart since there's little variation in their size and shades, but I've never had any trouble distinguishing Zephyr from the rest of our reptilian helpers. His temperament always gives him away.

I know my mother likely fed our faerie dragons at lunchtime, but I humor him anyway. I draw aether into my palm, and Zephyr's scaly tail trembles with anticipation. Many might say that the magi are addicted to magic, but faerie dragons suffer from a far worse affliction.

"*Crysanthius*," I say, and the aether solidifies.

Zephyr swoops down, and his long pink tongue darts out like a frog's as he snatches all the crystals from my grasp. His tongue is extremely slobbery and leaves a thick layer of saliva coating my palm.

"Ew, that's gross, Zephyr!" I exclaim, wiping my empty hand on my robes. "Have you really no manners?"

He flashes me a toothy grin that reveals his tiny fangs. While I've never been bitten by a faerie dragon, I'm certain it would do more than sting.

Zephyr somersaults through the air as he returns to his bucket.

I roll my eyes. "Show off."

His tail flicks out as if to assure me that he heard the insult. His talons close around the handle of the bucket, and he darts back to his flowerbed, leaving me to continue through the gardens.

Arched windows line the sides of our manor and glitter like diamond panels in the late noon sun. I don't pause to gaze at them as I ascend the steps leading to the large doors of our manor.

They're gilded like the gates, and just as heavy. Since there's no enchantment over them, I have no choice but to heave them open. I would utter *ventrez* and shove them aside with a gale, but my mother would scold me if I ruined the paintwork.

With my injured shoulder, pushing the doors open is a considerable effort. I clumsily burst into the hall and nearly fall face-first onto the tiles.

There are several faerie dragons inside, all busy supervising the enchanted brooms and feather dusters. None turn to look at me. Those we allow to work inside are the most well-behaved. If Zephyr saw me stumble, he would throw me a smirk.

After regaining my balance, I make my way through the hall and pass the portraits of many long dead Ashbournes. Some offer me a cheery wave, while others blatantly ignore me.

I find my mother in the drawing room. She has a paintbrush in her hand, like usual, and is staring down the canvas in front of her. I'm certain she spends more time scrutinizing her artwork than actually painting, but that technique has somehow earned her the reputation of Nolderan's most illustrious artist. That's also how my parents met, apparently.

When my father was crowned the Grandmage of Nolderan, my mother was commissioned to paint his portrait for the Arcanium, and somehow they fell in love. I've never cared to learn more details than that.

Today my mother isn't painting portraits. She's instead painting flowers blooming across a dreamy, twilight landscape, and they rustle in a breeze I can see but not feel. A shooting star whizzes across the shadowy sky.

My mother is so focused on her painting that she doesn't notice me as I enter the room. I collapse on the sapphire chaise opposite her and let out the most dramatic sigh I can muster. That gets her attention.

Her eyes narrow as she takes in my disheveled appearance. "Darling, your robes are singed," she says and then returns to her painting.

My fingers claw into the chaise's velvet. It seems even my own mother has forgotten that today is my birthday. Or maybe she cares as little about me as both my best friend and my boyfriend do.

"Kaely nearly killed me today in the arena!" I blurt.

"Nonsense," she says, her eyes not leaving her painting. "Archmage Gidston would never allow such a thing. Besides, you said the same thing yesterday."

"No, I didn't," I protest. "That was last Friday when she swapped my Blood Mint for Fire Bloom during Alchemy, and the potion exploded in my face."

"And like I said, that was your own fault for not smelling the herbs first. Besides, are you sure Kaely was responsible? I know the two of you have had a strained relationship since starting at the Arcanium, but you can't blame her for your every mistake."

"It's far from a 'strained relationship.' She hates me! And I still don't understand why."

"I've explained this to you before," my mother says, swirling her brush across her palette as she mixes together navy and indigo paint. "Kaely is ambitious, as all adepts should be. Graduating from the Arcanium and becoming a mage isn't easy. She strives to be the best, and as the daughter of the Grandmage of Nolderan, you're her greatest rival. It's natural for you both to have grown apart by this."

That's a ridiculous reason to hate someone, but I keep my opinion to myself. I unfasten the first few buttons of my high collar and slide the cerulean fabric far down enough to reveal my injured shoulder. Even with Archmage Gidston's healing elixir, it's as bruised as I expected. Burst blood vessels lace my skin like black spider webs.

I thrust my index finger at my bruised shoulder. "Would you also call this a strained relationship?"

My mother's eyes drift over to me. Apparently the injury is severe enough for her to set down her paintbrush and palette on the nearest table. "Oh," she says, peering at my shoulder. "It seems she did try to kill you this time."

The calmness in my mother's voice would concern me, if not for the fact she's always like this. Through all my eighteen years, I can't recall a single instance of my mother raising her voice. I can also safely say that I inherited my volatile temper from my father. I suppose the Ashbourne temperament goes hand in hand with our preference for fiery spells. The other thing I inherited from my father are my spindly legs—though his are as stocky as they are long. When my mother and I are both standing, I dwarf her petite frame.

She perches on the chaise, and her slender fingers splay across my bruised shoulder as she examines it more carefully. My similarities with my father start and end at my height and temper. I seem to have inherited everything else from my mother. Like me, she has hair the color of the midnight sky on her current painting, and her face is long and oval.

"How did this happen?" she asks softly.

"Kaely struck me with a blast of aether," I say. We tend not to use the true names of our spells in conversation, lest the aether in our blood reacts with our words. "If I hadn't been in mid-teleport, I'd be dead."

She frowns at my wounded shoulder and then shakes her head. "I will ask your father to speak to Archmage Gidston. Training should not be this dangerous."

I give her a stiff nod. The reason Archmage Gidston didn't intervene earlier is probably because I'm an Ashbourne and she thinks I can endure more than I can.

My mother leaves the chaise and paces over to the oaken cabinet in the far corner of the room. It features paneled doors and drawers with brass handles and is decorated by floral flourishes carved into the wood. The upper part mostly consists of glass and displays the finest crystalline chalices we own. Most have been in the Ashbourne family for centuries, and my father tells me some are as ancient as Nolderan itself. If that's true, it would make them over a thousand years old. Thanks to the aether imbued in the chalices, they are resistant to shattering. As a child, I once came close to testing their durability, but my father stopped me before I could let the chosen chalice fall onto the hallway's tiles. He was so furious he couldn't bear to look at me for a whole week. If I brought up the incident now, even a decade later, he likely wouldn't speak to me for an entire day. That particular chalice belonged to his grandfather, so it is far from the oldest one we have inside our cabinet, but it is the most precious to him. My great-grandfather was a Grandmage of Nolderan, like my father, and he idolizes him greatly. Sometimes I catch him staring up at my great-grandfather's portrait when he thinks no one is looking.

My mother opens the topmost drawer of the cabinet and rummages through until she finds a round, silver tin. She returns to her spot beside me and unscrews the lid.

The salve inside is so red it looks like hundreds of crushed rubies. While Blood Balm is the name of this regenerative ointment, blood isn't an ingredient, and it's instead made from the leaves of Blood Mint. The balm smells far more pleasant than the potion Archmage Gidston gave me in the arena. Blood Mint is the most prominent note in its fragrance, being the active ingredient, and it makes the ointment smell like something between cool mint and spicy pepper.

She dips her fingers into the ointment and slathers a thick layer of glossy crimson across my shoulder. As vivid as the hue is, it doesn't stain my skin. My pores quickly absorb the balm, and if not for the sting spreading across my shoulder, I would forget it was there.

I hope that with both the healing potion and the regenerative balm, my recovery will be quick. Each time I look at the bruise, I'm reminded of Kaely and the defeat I suffered at her hands.

Once my mother finishes applying the ointment, she screws on the lid and sets the tin onto the nearest counter.

"Does Father still have meetings until late tonight?" I ask. "Or have they been canceled?" The hopeful note to my voice raises it a pitch higher.

To my dismay, my mother shakes her head. "We'll do something at the weekend to celebrate your birthday."

"Even Eliya is busy," I grumble. Apparently all those dearest to me care little about my birthday. At this rate, I'll be left to celebrate it alone with only a bottle of wine for company.

"Have you asked Arluin?"

"He's forgotten, too."

"What do you mean he's forgotten?"

"Last night he didn't mention anything about making plans."

"Well, why don't you find him and see if he's busy?"

"I suppose I'll have to," I say, sliding off the chaise and striding out the room. Though I'm annoyed at him for forgetting that today is my birthday, at least his company is better than none at all.

"Don't forget to change your robes," she calls after me. "And make sure you brush your hair!"

CHAPTER 3

Dusk has fallen by the time I leave my manor. I've swapped my singed robes for a sky-blue sleeveless dress. Blossoms climb the skirts, and a pink ribbon accentuates my waistline. A gossamer shawl drapes my shoulders, and dainty rose-colored slippers cover my feet, but they're hard to see with my skirts brushing the floor.

An illusion conceals the bruise on my shoulder. Other magi will be able to tell I've cast an enchantment over my skin, but they won't see it unless they dispel my illusion. And doing so is regarded as a terrible insult here in the Upper City of Nolderan, where magic is free to flourish.

I don't bother teleporting myself to Arluin's manor, knowing he won't be there. Other than sleeping, he spends little time inside his home. But he can hardly be blamed. If I lived in a big, lonely manor then I would also spend little time in it. He doesn't even keep faerie dragons and insists they are merely pests.

I instead teleport to the archway which marks the Arcanium's entrance. QUEL ESTE VOLU, PODE NONQUES VERA MORIRE is etched into the ancient stone. It's written in Medeicus, the language of aether and translates to: *That which is aether may never truly die.* When saying the phrase out loud, we prefer to use the common tongue, in case we inadvertently activate our magic. All our architecture features the Medeicus translation, however.

Beyond the arch, a lengthy path trails to the Arcanium. Statues of long dead magi tower on either side and cast long shadows over me as I pass beneath. Glittering violet crystals float along the path. They are much like the ones I fed Zephyr, though these are clustered together and housed in decorative silver hemispheres. They glow vibrantly with aether, acting as tiny streetlights.

The end of the path is marked by the statue of Grandmage Delmont Blackwood, Founder of Nolderan and the Magi. The plaque fixed to his podium reads exactly that, but I doubt there's anyone in the entire city who wouldn't recognize him. He has a long beard and bushy brows which the portraits of him inside the Arcanium depict as being the shade of black ink. He wears the magnificent robes that only Grandmagi are permitted to wear and clasps the same crystalline staff my father never goes anywhere without. The weapon is forged from aether, and its surface ripples with magic, though you can't tell that by looking at the statue.

I don't stare up at Grandmage Delmont Blackwood for long before following the flight of stairs which spirals around him.

The Arcanium itself is a sprawling palace of countless spires. Thick pillars form a portico, and illustrations are carved into the pediment atop it. They portray the Primordial Explosion: when aether exploded in the emptiness of time and space, forming the Heavens, the Abyss, and Imyria—the mortal plane of existence. Throughout my first year at the Arcanium, my tutors insisted on drilling the origins of the universe over and over during our classes, even though every child from magi families can already recite the tale by heart.

My footsteps echo through the portico as I pass the rows of pillars. The Arcanium's large doors are spread wide open, allowing the adepts and magi to pass through in a stream of cerulean and indigo robes. Since I've changed out of my adept robes for the evening, I'm a stark contrast to the rest of the crowd. The Arcanium is off limits to the ordinary people of Nolderan, but no one stops to question me. They all know my face, thanks to my father.

The inside of the Arcanium is as grand as its multi-pillared entrance and opens to a large, domed atrium. Thousands of aether crystals form the ceiling, and their dazzling light casts the chamber in a lavender glow. In the day, they shine even brighter with the sunlight reflecting off them.

There are a few faerie dragons inside the Arcanium, but they stay far from the crowds. They flutter across the ceiling, ensuring the sponges cleaning the crystals don't lose their magic and fall on anyone below.

With it being nightfall, most people are leaving, and it's a struggle to squeeze past everyone heading in the opposite direction, eager to return home.

On the other side of the atrium, there's an entrance which looks like a smaller version of the portico outside. When I reach it, I hurry down the plummeting staircase.

It's a long descent into the Grand Library of Nolderan since it was built far beneath the Arcanium itself, shrouding its secrets from the rest of the world. I use the bannister to steady my steps, and my hand skims over the polished whitewood.

The staircase splits near the bottom, and I bear right, mostly because of my shoulder. Otherwise it would make little difference which side I choose, since the stairs arrive at the same part of the library.

Bookcases span every wall and climb toward the high, vaulted ceilings. Their shelves are made from the same wood as the bannisters, and the ornamental flourishes gilded across their edges make them so regal they wouldn't look out of place inside a real palace. An enormous chandelier hangs at the center of the library's main chamber, and dozens of glassy arms spiral from it, but they don't hold candles. Aether crystals instead hang from the ends, and all are chiseled into multifaceted teardrops.

Even work-shy adepts like myself can appreciate the breath-taking beauty of the Grand Library of Nolderan.

My feet reach the last step of the plummeting staircase and meet the tiled floor. Black and white squares run diagonally alongside each other and form a chess board, though there are no playing pieces. With the chandelier's blinding light reflecting off the surface, staring at the tiles is like gazing at an optical illusion. I quickly avert my gaze to avoid being disoriented.

Beneath the chandelier lies a gleaming white desk. Like the other tables and chairs situated around the library, its legs are carved into wooden scrolls. Dusty old tomes are stacked on the desk, their leather covers battered and bruised from centuries of wear and tear.

An elderly woman sits there, binding the pages of each ruined book to new covers. Her round face reminds me of a tortoise's, and the wrinkles across her cheeks and brow are as deep as folded pages. Her snowy white hair forms wispy clouds around her globular face. A pair of too-small, black rimmed circular spectacles perch on her nose. She peers through them as she diligently works to heal each book piled on her desk.

The ancient librarian's name is Erma Darkholme, and fifteen years ago she was the Archmage of Knowledge before handing her title to Lorette Gidston. She's also the most terrifying woman I've ever had the misfortune of meeting and makes Archmage Gidston seem like a saint.

As busy as she is with repairing the Grand Library's most ancient books, she notices me as soon as I set foot upon the checkered tiles. She may be extremely short-sighted, but she has the ears of a bat. Her glassy magenta eyes snap up and narrow at me.

I freeze as if I've been caught in a game of blind man's bluff, and conjure the most amenable smile I can muster. I need no mind-link to read her thoughts. Her gaze is revealing enough. I know she's suspicious as to why one of the Arcanium's most indolent adepts would visit the library past dinnertime. My reputation is also far from clean, but I hold Eliya accountable for most of that. After all, it was her idea to skip our History Finals last year by filling our tutor's goblet with a Draught of Forgetfulness we concocted during Alchemy. We hoped it would cause our History tutor, Professor Rellington, to forget all about our examinations, but we brewed the potion incorrectly. Green boils sprouted across his face, and they lasted an entire month. He has never forgotten the incident, and neither has the rest of the Arcanium.

Erma holds my gaze for a moment longer before returning to her work. I don't doubt she's still watching me out of the corner of her eyes as I scurry across the library.

A few adepts gather around curve-legged tables, meticulously scribbling notes into their journals with fluffy white quills. I pay them no attention as I march toward the library's left wing, where Arluin normally sits.

The aisles sprawl out, displaying archaic books on every topic imaginable. Their colorful covers form a rainbow which contrasts the gilded whitewood bookcases containing them.

I soon spot Arluin's curly, raven-colored locks at the very back of the left wing and crouch behind one of the bookcases cutting through the chamber. He sits on a crushed velvet armchair, its cushions of a violet hue. His left hand curls around the ornate wooden arm, while his other holds open the current page of the worn tome he's reading.

One by one I withdraw the books sitting on the shelf in front of me, careful not to let their hardened leather covers scrape against the wooden shelves. But I suppose it makes little difference. Whenever Arluin's nose is stuck inside a book, his ears stop working.

A pile of books soon forms beside me, and my view to Arluin is clear. He still wears his cerulean adept robes, having not yet returned home since his lessons ended this afternoon. His uniform looks far more elegant on him than it does on me. His robes emphasize his majestic presence, while mine only serve to drown me.

I lean on the bookshelf, and it creaks under my elbow. I haven't yet forgiven him for forgetting my birthday, but I can't help myself from resting my head in my hands and peering at him.

His face is so serene while studying. Tiny lines of concentration crease his brow. From where I crouch, I have a side profile view of him. His nose is perfectly straight, and his jawline is bold. The black curls nestling atop his head appear even glossier with the glow of aether, and their softness somehow sharpens his features. If I weren't annoyed at him, I might have stared at him for hours.

The corners of my lips tug upward as a plan hastily forms in my mind. It would be unfair to say Eliya is responsible for all of my mischief.

I curl my fist as I draw on the aether buzzing through the air. The tiny particles of raw energy snap to my command, swirling between my fingers. The aether is fueled by that which already flows through my veins.

"*Ventrez*," I whisper quietly enough for only the magic to hear. As the spell-word is spoken, aether warps into air magic. A wind spell forms at my fingertips.

I flick my wrist and unleash the magic upon Arluin.

The conjured breeze swirls forth, growing in strength as it nears him. The wind spell sends his cerulean robes billowing out, and the book he's reading slams shut with a deafening thud.

He looks so astonished as he leaps onto his feet that a laugh escapes me. I remind myself I'm meant to be furious at him.

"Reyna," he calls out, whirling around as he examines the countless aisles. "I know it's you. There's no one else in the whole Arcanium—no, the entire city—who's as silly as you."

The bookshelf groans beneath my elbows. I spring away, but it's too late. The sound is loud enough to condemn me.

His gaze snaps over to my direction. His eyes are purple like all of us who practice aether, but his are among the most vibrant shade of magenta I've ever seen. Only my father, who is the most powerful mage alive, has brighter eyes than him.

"*Ventrez*," Arluin says before I can realize, summoning a wind spell of his own. The gale crashes into the shelf above me, and all the books topple over.

There's little time to leap away and stop them from smacking me in the face. I draw more aether into my fingers and envision the spot a few feet from Arluin.

"*Laxus*," I say, and the magic obeys my command.

In the next breath I'm safely away from the falling books, and they land onto the tiles with a tremendous clamor. I wince at the sound, knowing it won't go unnoticed by Erma.

While my teleportation spell is for the most part successful, I'm not exactly in the spot I intended. Instead, I'm much closer to Arluin.

He glances me up and down, his eyes dancing over the blue flowery dress I wear. Judging by the smile playing on his softly arched lips, he appears to be satisfied with his evaluation. His arm slips around my waist and pulls me nearer.

Now we're so close I can feel the heat of his chest as it presses against mine. Our lips are close enough to touch, separated by the thinnest thread of distance. My stomach flutters.

Though I've kissed Arluin a thousand times before, I long for more. Even if I were to kiss him every day for the rest of my life, it will never be enough.

We are both silent and still, the air around us thick with tension. Our breaths fall to the same rhythm, our gazes fixed on each other.

Arluin is the one to break our stare. He leans closer, his warm breath trailing across my neck. Though I wish it had instead been his lips, I shiver at his closeness.

"Reyna," he whispers into my ear, his lower lip grazing my lobe as he speaks, "have you cast an enchantment over me? Because you look far too bewitching." His arm wraps more tightly around my waist, and with his spare hand, he sweeps a strand of dark hair from my face. My skin tingles as his fingers brush my cheek.

With his words and the way he holds me, I can't help myself from arching into him. Then I remember he forgot my eighteenth birthday, and I'm supposed to be mad at him for it. Which I still am, of course. Even if he's currently holding me in the most distracting way.

I wrinkle my nose at him, but I must admit it's an effort not to grab his hair and kiss him as if we aren't in Nolderan's Grand Library. "You say that exact same sleazy line every time I make an effort to look pretty!" I definitely don't mention how it has the same effect every time he says it. "If you want to seduce me, you'd better try harder."

His gaze returns to my lips, and I immediately regret my words. Warmth bubbles in my stomach as his hand slides down my neck and traces my collarbone. I wonder whether his hands will slip even lower. "Then what if I tell you about all the indecent ways I'm think-ing of kissing you?" he murmurs into my neck, all but kissing the skin there. "Would that seduce you more?"

My body is screaming that yes it would, but I do my best to resist his charming words and teasing touches. Especially because we're in a library.

Clarity descends on me before I can forget my purpose in coming here.

"Do you even know what day it is?" I blurt.

He has the audacity to answer: "Tuesday?"

I slap him across the cheek. Not particularly hard, or else Erma will hear. That is, if the falling books haven't already alerted her to our mischief. I'm surprised she's not yet stormed over. She normally has by now.

"Tuesday?" I exclaim in a vexed whisper. "Tuesday! So, you really have forgotten then!"

I try to wriggle from his grasp, but there's no escaping his arms.

He wears an innocent expression on that captivating face of his. Now I wish I'd slapped him harder, even if it risks inciting Erma's wrath. "I honestly have no idea what you're talking about."

"It's my birthday—my eighteenth birthday! I can't believe you!"

"Oh yes," he says, "of course it is. How could I forget something as important as that?"

"I knew it all along!" I jab my index finger into his chest, but it hurts me more than him. "You really do care more about those books of yours than you care about—"

He silences my accusation with a chaste kiss. It might have tasted sweet if I weren't so furious with him.

Before I can scold him for the stolen kiss, he chuckles. "Don't be so silly. How can I care more about books when they don't look half as lovely as you?"

"So, you only care about me because you think I look lovely?"

He simply smiles at me. "And because you're the silliest person I know."

To anyone else, that might sound like an insult, but I know it's a compliment of deep meaning.

Once, when we were drunk in the dead of night, he confessed to how much he loved my silliness. He said it helps him forget all that has happened.

That he is an exile's son.

Though I very much wish to still be mad at him, his smile disperses the remnants of my rage.

I let out a sigh and sink into his arms, allowing them to support my weight. "You are the most awful boyfriend in all of Imyria."

"And the most dashing."

I roll my eyes at him. "Don't think I'll let you off lightly."

"Oh, I know. I expect to be groveling for weeks."

"I suggest you start groveling tonight."

"In that case, how about I take you to The Violet Tree and buy you all the wine you can drink?"

I flash him a triumphant grin. He knows me so very well—even if he did forget my birthday.

But before I can respond, footsteps thunder from behind. The sound ricochets through the vaulted ceiling.

"What do you two think you're doing inside my library?" Erma snarls, glaring at us through her small, circular spectacles.

If I were not preoccupied with leaping away from Arluin, I might have pointed out that this isn't her library. It isn't even my father's. It belongs to Nolderan.

"N-nothing," I stammer, my cheeks burning a crimson so vivid that my expression alone is evidence enough of the lie.

Arluin is a little less flustered than me. "We were just leaving," he says, hurrying over to the books lying heaped beneath the bookcase.

Erma's temples twitch as she examines him and the fallen books. "Good," she snaps, whirling around. "They had all better be returned to their rightful places, or else I will be informing Archmage Gidston of your insolence."

My shoulders sag with relief as Erma's purple robes disappear around the bookcases. While our position was rather compromising, this isn't the first time Erma has caught us—or other adepts—locked in amorous embraces.

"Come on," Arluin murmurs, gathering the books. "It seems we ought to get going."

CHAPTER 4

HAND IN HAND, WE LEAVE the Grand Library. The Arcanium's atrium is mostly empty now, and we stroll through the large, circular space.

We reach the other side of the chamber and pass the rows of pillars standing sentry outside the Arcanium's entrance. Floating crystals illuminate our path as we follow the staircase around Grandmage Delmont Blackwood.

When we're at the bottom, I turn to Arluin. "So, we're going to The Violet Tree?"

"Indeed, we are."

"And you really meant what you said about buying all the wine I can drink?"

"Of course."

"You know I can easily drink all your wealth in a single night."

"We'll see about that," he says with a laugh.

We continue through the Arcanium's grounds, passing the dozens of towering statues which line the path. Many depict my own ancestors since the Ashbourne family has produced the most Grand-magi throughout history. One day, my father will also likely have a statue erected here in his memory. I can't say the same about myself.

We slip beneath the archway, Arluin's hand still clasping mine, and step out onto the cobbled streets.

The buildings of Nolderan are all made from white granite, and the smooth surfaces appear silver in the dusky purple glow of the floating streetlights. Cobalt tiles ripple across the rooftops like waves, and they peak into perfect triangles. We turn left down Lenwick Street, the main road which winds through the Upper City and connects all the most important structures. It reaches to the very back of Nolderan, where the Aether Tower lies.

Day and night the Aether Tower hums with raw magic, fueling the city with power. It's connected to a network of several smaller spires and ensures the flow of magic through every street to maintain permanent wards such as the one enchanting my manor's gates. Larger wards, like the one covering the entire isle, prevent any foreign sorcerers from teleporting inside.

We turn onto another street and head to Revelry Row, where The Violet Tree is situated. Many of Nolderan's finest establishments can be found here. The Violet Tree itself is the city's most luxurious inn, and the food and wine they serve is exquisite.

The stars twinkle high above, and the shadows dance around us. Our walk is tranquil, or at least it is until we take a shortcut through the quieter streets and pass a faulty streetlight, its crystal flickering on and off. I can't remember the last time I saw one broken and squeeze Arluin's hand. He, however, seems unbothered by the sight of it. Even when we pass another one.

An uneasiness ripples across my skin like tiny shards of ice. Now the shadows are suffocating, and inexplicable dread coils through my stomach.

The air smells like death. Cold, lonely, and rotten.

And I am certain we are being followed. No—stalked like prey.

I stop.

"What is it?" Arluin asks. I feel his gaze on me, but I don't turn to look at him.

I spin around, searching for whatever it is pursuing us, but with many of the crystalline streetlights broken, it's almost impossible to discern anything amid the shadows.

Yet as I train my eyes on a narrow dark corner, I'm certain I can make out the silhouette of a hooded figure.

I tremble at the ominous sight. Arluin grips my hand.

"Something's there. . ." I whisper, not daring to raise my voice in fear of alerting the shadowy figure. "Watching us."

Arluin follows my gaze, squinting at the darkness. When I look back, the silhouette is gone.

"There's nothing there."

"But I saw someone—something."

Arluin pulls me in and kisses the top of my head. Even the caress of his lips doesn't banish the uneasiness crawling across my skin. "You must be imagining things. Don't tell me you've already started drinking."

I press my lips together. Perhaps he's right. There's no one there, nor any trace of them. Maybe the hooded figure was only a figment of my imagination. Yet I can't shake away the realness of the presence. How it felt like death whispering through the shadows.

"Come on," he says gently. "If we stand here all night, staring into the darkness, won't we end up wasting your birthday?"

I manage a small nod, and he leads me farther down the street. After a few paces, I glance back to where I thought I saw the hooded silhouette, but there's still no one there.

Only darkness.

With The Violet Tree being Nolderan's finest inn, it's also the most expensive. That's why I'm pleased Arluin offered to fund my drinking for the night. My adept's stipend is measly, and I've almost spent every penny this month. Arluin also receives a stipend from the Arcanium, though his is greater since he's a fourth-year student and is better able to help with brewing potions and conducting research than a second-year such as myself. But he doesn't need this small salary. After his father was exiled, being the only child, he inherited all his family's assets. That includes the Harstall's manor which is as splendid and ancient as mine, and also various business shares which have ensured him with a steady income during these past five years.

Revelry Row is bursting with life when we arrive. Men wear colorful silk tunics, heavily embroidered with metallic thread, while women wear dresses so extravagant they make my pale blue dress look dull in comparison. Though Arluin is still clad in his cerulean adept robes, he doesn't look too out of place. The few magi strolling the streets are also in their uniforms. Some are so proud of their robes I'm sure they never take them off. My father is one such example.

The Violet Tree is located at the beating heart of Revelry Row and has the same white walls and cobalt roof as any other building along this street. If not for the sign, it would be difficult to tell it apart from all the other inns and restaurants.

In the late summer breeze, the sign lazily swings back and forth from its steel pole. A violet oak is painted on the sign, and it glows against the dark background. The tree's leaves rustle in the wind, and it's enchanted with aether, like my mother's artwork.

The inn's door is a deep shade of mauve, and blossoms are carved into its wood. Arluin holds the door open for me, and I step inside.

For a long moment, everything is silent and still—so unlike the inn I always visit.

Convinced he's somehow taken me to the wrong place, I turn to him. But before I can say anything, a cacophony of voices erupts from the darkness.

"*Surprise!*"

The crystalline lights switch on, revealing the faces of everyone I hold dear. My mother and father both stand there, as do Eliya and the rest of my extended family. All of them are crowded into The Violet Tree's front room.

Aether dust sprinkles over me. I'm so astonished I don't look to see who it comes from. "I . . . I thought no one wanted to spend my birthday with me."

Behind me, Arluin clears his throat but says nothing as Eliya rushes over to me. Her hug is so forceful it irritates my injured shoulder.

"You have no idea how horrible I felt lying to you before! The look of disappointment on your face was so unbearable I almost told you everything."

"And it's a good job you didn't," my mother says with a sigh. "Or else weeks' worth of plans would have been ruined."

Eliya gives my mother a meek look as she releases me.

I turn to my father. He stands a head and shoulder above everyone else, and in his magnificent robes he looks as fearsome as Grandmage Delmont Blackwood's statue outside the Arcanium. He has also brought his crystalline staff with him. Only my father would bring Nolderan's most deadly weapon to a birthday party.

"What are you doing here, Father?" I ask, my brows knitting together in confusion. "What happened to all the important meetings you have until late tonight?"

The corners of his auburn beard tug up as he smiles. "Since my daughter's birthday is far more important, I canceled them all."

I laugh at that, though I doubt my father would have actually canceled his meetings. Most likely, he's managed to book a rare night off his duties. But if something dire does arise, he'll have no choice but to leave and see to it.

Dozens of tables and chairs are normally scattered through The Violet Tree, but tonight they're replaced by an enormous table which spans the entire length of the room. It's made from polished sandalwood, but you can only tell that by the double twisted legs since the rest of the table is covered with silver plates and crystalline goblets.

It takes me at least ten minutes to make it to the table, thanks to my aunts, uncles, cousins, second cousins, and relatives I'm not even sure are related to me. My father's side of the family is rather small, since he's an only child like me, but my mother more than makes up for it with her expansive family.

When we're all seated, servers bring over countless dishes of more foods than I can imagine—and these are just our appetizers. My parents have hired out The Violet Tree to throw a mighty banquet, most likely through my mother's charms and my father's reputation. And of course, our family's riches.

It seems the inn is still serving other guests this evening, however. A few patrons trickle in through the door, and the servers take them through to the back rooms. All look over at our banquet as they pass, and many stop to speak with my father. My father knows nearly everyone in the Upper City. How he can remember so many names and faces, I'll never know. His acquaintances all come over and wish me a happy birthday. While I suppose it's nice of them, it's also rather annoying since it stops me from eating my food and drinking my moon-blossom wine—an extravagant import from the elven lands which is infused with aether. We only drink it on special occasions.

Eliya sits to my right, and Arluin to my left. He talks about boring things with my father, like the research he's currently involved in. My father is as strange as Arluin in that he enjoys discussing such matters, and the two of them engage in one of the longest and dullest conversations I've ever heard. He doesn't blame Arluin for his father's mistakes, though he personally banished Heston Harstall from Nolderan. But I know he remains wary of Arluin, a part of him wondering whether one day he too will fall down the same path. It's by the slight reservation in his eyes that I can tell, but he's never said anything out loud to me nor has he objected to my relationship with Arluin. I don't doubt that he has many such conversations with my mother, though. It's probably because of her that he holds his tongue.

In between dishes, I chatter with Eliya about our Medeicus and Fire Magic tutors. Apparently several other adepts have spotted them looking incredibly familiar when out and about through the city over the past few weeks. It's a far more riveting topic of conversation than research.

By the time we finish eating, I am certain I've nearly finished an entire bottle of moon-blossom wine all by myself. I'm presented with a mountain of gifts, but unwrapping the colorful paper is an almost impossible task. I end up dropping the present from my mother and father. It falls onto the wooden floor with a thud. In my defense, it is a small box.

My entire family laughs.

"You're already really drunk!" Eliya exclaims beside me, unable to control her giggling.

"No, I'm not," I protest, leaning down to find the box beneath my feet. But it seems she's right since I fall off my chair. More laughter erupts across the table.

I tilt back my head and stare up at the arched ceiling. The walls spin around me in an awful bout of vertigo.

Arluin's face appears above me. Actually, I can see three of him, all his faces blending together where they meet.

"Do you need some help down there?" he asks, raising a brow at me.

His voice echoes in my ears, and it takes me a moment to understand his words.

I lower my gaze. "Maybe . . ."

Arluin kneels beside me and searches the floor for where the box landed. When he finds it, he scoops it up and helps me back onto my chair.

He hands it over, but I slide it back across the table to him.

"Can you open it?" I ask quietly. "I think I will drop it again if I try."

Eliya finds that question hilarious.

Arluin obliges and tears the red paper off the small square box. He opens it and presents me with a pair of diamond earrings. They are shaped like chandeliers, and I'm certain they would reach my shoulders if I put them into my ears.

"They're beautiful," I gasp, my fingers running across one of the diamond swirls.

When I look up, my mother is smiling. "I knew you would like them, darling."

"I do have impeccable taste," my father says. That earns him an annoyed look from my mother.

"These aren't the ones you picked, Telric," she says. "You wanted to buy Reyna the ugly set which looked like spiders."

My father scratches his chin, disturbing the thick auburn hair which sprouts there. "Are you sure?"

She sighs at him and shakes her head.

When at last all my gifts are unwrapped, I take to drinking once more. Arluin's eyes tighten as I lift my goblet to my lips.

"Are you really going to drink more wine?" he asks me.

"Of course. Why wouldn't I?"

"Because you've already drunk so much."

Eliya leans forward, joining the conversation. "Don't worry, Arluin," she says. "Me and Reyna are used to drinking until we pass out."

Arluin runs a hand down his face. "That's exactly what concerns me."

He has little say in the matter, however, and after another bottle of wine, I end up passing out. I'm not sure how long I'm unconscious, but when my eyes reopen, I see my mother and father leaving. The rest of the table is mostly empty now. Eliya hasn't passed out yet, though. I feel her patting my head. Why exactly, I don't know.

"Make sure she doesn't spend the night in a gutter," my father grumbles to Arluin.

"I'll look after her!" Eliya exclaims beside me. Maybe that was the reason for her patting my head.

My father doesn't turn to Eliya. Thanks to her, I have spent the occasional night sleeping in an alleyway.

"I'll help you take her back home," Arluin says. His arm wraps around my waist, preparing to lift me from my seat. I spring to life and shake him off.

"I'm not going home!" I object. "It's my birthday, and I haven't finished celebrating it."

Arluin sighs. I'm surprised he doesn't bother pointing out that I've spent most of it with my head on the table.

"That's the spirit!" Eliya claps her hands together. "Here, Rey-rey, drink some more wine!"

Much to Arluin's dismay, she passes me another goblet.

The moment the wine greets my lips, I black out again.

When I finally return to my senses, Eliya is long gone and Arluin is hauling me off my chair.

"Where's everyone gone?" I demand, this time not resisting as he lifts me. One of his arms is secured under my legs, while the other supports my back. The ground looks a lot farther away than it probably is. "Why did they leave so early?"

Arluin chokes out a laugh. "It's definitely not early."

"Oh," I say, blinking at him. In his arms, I feel like I'm floating. "Can I have more wine?"

"Not a chance."

I pout. "Why not?"

"Because you are very, very drunk right now."

"I'm only a little bit drunk."

Arluin doesn't seem to fall for that lie. He shakes his head and carries me toward the door. I let my head droop back. From this angle, the table is upside down. All the dishes and goblets are gone. And my gifts, too.

"Where are all my presents?"

"Your parents took them home," he says. "They had to make a few trips."

"Oh."

We come to the door. It's shut.

"Can you get that?" Arluin asks, his arms still full with me.

I reach for the door, but my hand is too far away and my fingers only find air. I use my foot instead and give the door a mighty kick. We barge out into the night and almost collide with the couple who are entering the inn. I throw back my head and laugh. I immediately regret doing so. It's more evidence that I'm drunk.

He flashes them an apologetic look, but it does little to soothe their scowls. Their angry expressions make me laugh harder. Arluin hurries away from them before I can add to the insult.

"Hey," I say when he comes to a stop. I prod his chest. "I just remembered something."

He peers down at me. "What did you remember?"

"That you didn't get me a present."

"I did."

Maybe he gave me his present when I blacked out. "Oh yes," I say with a big nod. "I remember now. It was a lovely . . . uh . . ."

His shoulders shake with silent laughter. "Reyna, I haven't given it to you yet. You asked me if I got you a present, not whether I gave it to you."

"Oh. Right. When are you going to give it to me then? You can't wait until tomorrow or it won't be a birthday present, will it?"

"I was intending to give it to you tonight. But now you're too drunk so it'll have to wait until the morning."

"I'm not too drunk."

He shoots me a dubious look.

"Please, Arly," I beg him. "I won't be able to sleep now. Not knowing what my present is will keep me tossing and turning all night."

"You were sleeping just fine on the table before."

I scrunch my nose at him. "I'm not waiting until the morning. Besides, why can't I be drunk for your present?" I don't add that all my other presents were given to me while I was drunk, but I do think it's a strong argument.

"Because," he simply says.

"'Because' isn't a reason."

"Reyna, I'm taking you home."

"No, I don't want to go home. I want to go to yours. I'll be good, I promise."

"You're never good," he says, kissing my cheek.

"If I go home with you, then at least you'll know whether I'm asleep or whether I'm awake drinking more wine."

He breathes a laugh. "All right. Point taken."

"So, that means we're going back to yours?"

"Yes."

"And you're also going to give me your present?"

"We'll see about that part."

I lift my head and commit to being on my best behavior. Perhaps then he'll let me have his present.

He's never made this much of a deal about presents before. Not even when he got me Mr. Waddles for my sixth birthday. Arluin chose him because ducks are my favorite animal and purple is my favorite color. Even twelve years later, Mr. Waddles still sits on top of my chest of drawers. He's not as fluffy as he once was, though.

Arluin has always gotten me the most thoughtful presents. That's why I'm dying to know what this year's will be.

He closes his eyes and draws aether around us.

"*Laxus*," he says, and we leave The Violet Tree behind in a glittering cloud of purple dust.

CHAPTER 5

WE EMERGE OUTSIDE THE GATES of Arluin's manor. Like mine, they're enchanted to prevent others from teleporting inside. The Harstall family crest features a serpent coiled around a sword like vines. Its forked tongue darts out, and I'm sure I can hear it hissing. But that could also be the aether humming across the tall steel bars.

"Arluin Harstall," he announces, and the gates swing open.

Arluin carries me through, and they clang shut when we're on the other side. I could have opened them myself, though perhaps not particularly well in my current state. As the current owner of this manor, Arluin has enchanted the gates to also recognize my voice and my name. But I doubt it would recognize my slurred speech.

While the architecture of his manor is as splendid as ours, the gardens are not comparable. The grass is wild and overgrown with weeds. When I used to visit as a child, the shrubs were perfectly clipped into lions and griffins and stags. Now they have all long lost their magnificent shapes.

The pond is just as neglected. Long ago, it was filled with pink lilies and shimmering fish. And many ducks, too. I always fed them lots of bread, much to his mother's delight. She loved baking.

Once, I accidentally dropped a large crust into the water and tried to fish it out. I leaned too far over and ended up falling into the pond.

Arluin had to pull me out. I thought he would laugh at me for it, but he never did.

I return my attention to him. His raven curls shine in the starlight. He's so focused on walking and not dropping me that he doesn't seem to notice me gazing at him.

"You can put me down now if you want," I say, feeling rather guilty that he's doing all the work while I'm doing nothing.

"I don't want to."

Since I'm quite comfortable, I don't argue with that.

He carries me through the rest of the gardens and up the few steps leading to the manor's double doors. Both have brass knockers, and twin serpents coil around each ring. Some of the black lacquer has peeled off the doors, revealing small patches of brown wood. I've pointed this out to Arluin many times, but he hasn't bothered to repaint the doors. There are no servants to do it for him, either. There hasn't been since Arluin's mother died. That was when his father, Heston, started delving into necromancy, though it took six years for him to be caught. It was his gray eyes which finally gave him away, along with the inability to draw upon aether. Dark magic consumed and corrupted it all.

The magi searched their manor and discovered the ancient tomes Heston stole from Nolderan's vaults, where forbidden relics are locked away beneath the Arcanium. It was easy for him to get hold of them, since he was the Archmage of Defense before being exiled and replaced by Kaely's father.

But I shouldn't be thinking about such awful things. Especially not on my birthday.

Arluin's hand shifts beneath my knee as he flicks his wrist.

"*Ventrez*," he says, and the conjured gale blows the doors wide open. This is why much of the paint has chipped off. He often uses his magic instead of pushing them open with his hands.

His grasp tightens around my legs, holding me more securely, and then he carries me through the doors. He doesn't bother shutting them behind us. There's little reason to do so. The enchanted gates ensure no one can trespass on his property. And since it's summer, the weather is mild.

His manor is far tidier inside. The tiles are so well polished that they gleam despite being cast in darkness.

"Can you get the lights?" Arluin asks, angling me toward the switches on the left of the doors.

I lean forward and feel the wall until my fingers locate the circular button. I push it firmly, and the chandelier switches on.

It's like the one hanging inside the Grand Library, but much smaller. Aether crystals droop from the arms. While there are far fewer crystals than the library's chandelier, they're more than bright enough to illuminate the hallway.

A deep blue rug sprawls out before us, and it stretches over to the spiraling staircases on the other side of the hall. Golden thread weaves through the rug, forming a hexagonal pattern. Arluin continues over it and ascends the stairs.

"You'd better not drop me," I warn him when we're halfway up. I glance back and see that it's a long way down. I don't look for long.

A smirk dances on Arluin's lips, and I wonder whether he's considering it. Or at least pretending that he is. But he instead replies, "I promise I won't."

We reach the top of the stairs without him dropping me, and we head straight into his room. The door was left ajar, so we easily burst through.

A mahogany bed takes up most of the space. Its four posters look like oversized candlesticks, and regal swirls are carved into every inch of the wood. White silk hangs from the frame and ripples with the delicate breeze blowing in through the open window.

A crystalline lamp stands on the counter beside the bed, and it looks like a standing chandelier. Zig-zagged wooden panels of assorted shades form the floor, and a crimson square rug featuring a paisley pattern lies in front of the canopy bed. It's set at a diagonal and appears diamond-like as we enter.

This has always been his room, even before Heston was exiled. It's a lot smaller than the master bedroom across the corridor, but Arluin can't bear to enter it, let alone sleep in there.

He sets me down on the bed and heads over to his wardrobe to hang his adept robes. The wardrobe is also crafted from mahogany, and the decoration carved into its panels matches the swirls running across the bed. I normally leave my robes hanging over the armchair in my room, but Arluin is much fussier than me about having wrinkles in his clothes.

I tilt my head over the edge of the bed and watch from upside down as he loosens the metallic buttons of his high collar. If he notices me staring, he doesn't look bothered. He finishes unbuttoning his collar and pulls the cerulean fabric over his head, revealing the hard planes of his torso. If he weren't so far away, I would run my hands over his chest. Maybe I will when he comes closer. Though with how much I drank tonight, he'll probably insist we go straight to sleep.

As he opens the wardrobe to hang his robes, I turn my attention to the grandfather clock standing in the corner. Thanks to the aether imbued in its springs, it perpetually ticks. According to its hands, it's currently quarter to twelve.

My birthday is almost over.

"Arluin," I lament. For dramatic effect, I let my arm flop over the side of the bed. "You need to give me my present before midnight, or else it won't be special anymore."

He shuts the wardrobe and turns around, his breeches still on. I watch him cross the room, and the bed dips as he perches on the edge beside me.

"Very well," he says.

"Really?" I exclaim, having expected him to refuse. I scramble up, but most of my weight is hanging over the bed, and gravity pulls me down. I'm unable to haul myself back up.

With a soft laugh, Arluin grips my waist and helps return me to a sitting position. Our faces are so close they're almost touching, and his warm breath caresses my skin. I would kiss him, if not for the fact I'm dying to know what my present is.

He reaches for my face, and his thumb sweeps across my cheek. "Reyna, I . . ." His shoulders are taut with tension, and hesitance clouds his expression.

The last time I remember him being this nervous was four years ago, when he confessed he no longer saw me as a friend. When he first kissed me.

I rise onto my knees so we're at the same height, wrap my arms around his tense shoulders, and kiss the top of his head. "What's the matter, Arly?" His dark curls muffle my voice. They're as soft as they look.

It occurs to me now that he might be using my drunkenness as an excuse. Whatever the gift is, he's worried about how I will react to it.

He hesitates. Then he draws in a shaky breath and holds out his hand. "*Conparios.*"

A jewelry box emerges from violet light. It's covered by midnight blue velvet and decorated with small flowers. His hands tremble slightly as he opens it.

Inside lies a silver, heart-shaped locket. Delicate roses are etched across its gleaming surface.

My breath catches in the back of my throat.

"Do you like it?" he asks with a frown.

"Of course I like it. Did you think I wouldn't?"

"It wasn't that," he says, lifting the necklace from where it lies. He mutters *evanest*, and the empty box disappears in a cloud of aether.

"Then why were you so nervous to give it to me?"

He lays the locket flat on his palm and glances up at me. "A memory crystal lies inside. I wanted to make a promise to you and have it forever recorded so you know my sincerity."

I sit back on my heels. "What promise?"

Arluin doesn't answer. He waves his hand over the locket, and it springs open to reveal a glittering crystal. "*Incipret.*" At his command, the memory crystal fills with a purple glow as it starts to record.

"Reyna," he begins, "I am a man who has nothing, who is nothing. I know I don't deserve you, but you mean everything to me. In this world, I have nothing else left."

I rest my hand on his cheek. "Arluin, please don't speak about yourself like this. You mean everything to me, as well."

He places his finger on my lips, hushing me. "I've loved you for as long as I remember. And it's only when I'm with you that . . . that I forget . . ."

That he is a necromancer's son. That he watched his father commit atrocities in an attempt to resurrect his mother.

Though I silently finish his sentence, he doesn't voice the words. And I don't expect him to. I hate the tortured look in his eyes as he relives his darkest memories. His father's most horrifying experiments.

I pull his finger from my lips and then kiss him, hoping it will banish the nightmares afflicting him.

But Arluin stares at the wardrobe. Even when my lips trail across his jawline and down his neck, he barely reacts to my touch.

Realizing my efforts are in vain, I kiss his nose and say, "Arly, we can't change the past. We can only shape the future."

My words have more effect. He snaps to life and clasps my face so tightly it's as if he fears I will slip away.

"Marry me," he gasps. "Please marry me, Reyna. I can't bear the thought of ever being without you."

My heart makes a giddy flutter. This must be the promise he wished to make.

"Of course I'll marry you," I say. "Who else would put up with my drunken antics?"

The attempt at a joke seems to go unnoticed. His expression remains serious.

"We'll marry each other after you graduate from the Arcanium. By then, I will have been a qualified mage for two years and will hopefully have a good career ahead of me—"

I brush a low hanging curl from his face. "You know I'd marry you tomorrow."

"Reyna, your father will never allow that. It would be too great a distraction from your studies."

"I'm eighteen now," I say with a shrug. "By law, I no longer require parental permission to marry. I'll come and live with you. I spend most of my nights here, anyway."

"I can't do that, Reyna. I'll be lucky if he even lets me marry you." He pauses, chewing on his lip. "Do you think he will?"

"Why wouldn't he?"

His shoulders sink. "Because of my father." His voice is so quiet it's barely audible.

"Arluin, you are not your father."

"Maybe you don't see the shadow of my father when you look at me, but everyone else does. Behind my back they whisper about how I will follow in my father's footsteps, how I too will become a necromancer. Even your father."

"No, he doesn't," I say, and hope he can't see through my lie. I know every time my father gazes upon Arluin, he is reminded of his oldest friend's treachery.

Arluin doesn't argue with me. A brief silence stretches between us. He glances down at the locket and finally says, "Anyway, this is the promise I wanted to make. I will marry you when we've both graduated from the Arcanium. I swear it."

Though I would rather marry him tomorrow than in three years, I protest no further. It doesn't matter when we marry, so long as we do.

"Then I will wear this locket every day, as my promise to you," I say. "And we'd better have the most extravagant wedding Nolderan has ever seen."

That brings a smile to his lips,. "If you want an extravagant wedding, then an extravagant wedding we shall have."

I return his smile.

"*Terminir*," he mutters. The memory crystal ceases to glow, and he closes the locket.

Arluin leans behind me and sweeps away my hair. He secures the locket around my neck, and his fingers tickle me as they brush over my skin.

When the necklace is fastened, he turns back to me and takes my hand in his. "I promise," he whispers, "I will marry you—"

I cut him off by pressing my lips to his. He is at first caught off-guard, but he soon reciprocates and kisses me back with as much vigor. Our lips move in time to one another's, and we kiss each other as though we are starved for air.

My fingers knit through his dark curls, and I use them to pull him closer. His hand slides up my waist, reaching higher until it comes to my breast. He kneads the soft flesh through the thin fabric of my dress, and a moan escapes me.

I shove his shoulders, and he falls into the scarlet sheets. I straddle him, my pale blue skirts pooling around us.

"It's late," he says. "And you're drunk."

I run my fingers across his chest, feeling the firm edges of his lean muscles. "You asked to marry me, and now it seems you don't want me," I tease.

"I never said I don't want you," he says, gripping my waist and hauling me off him. He sets me onto the sheets beside him and leans on his elbow, gazing down at me. His fingers trace my shoulder. "Just that it's late and you're drunk. Both of which are facts."

"I don't want to sleep."

"Then we won't sleep," he says, pulling down one of my sleeves and leaving half of my chest exposed to the cool night air.

He kisses me there—and then everywhere else. And as he promises, we spend most of the night making love to each other and very little of it sleeping.

CHAPTER 6

I wake with my head resting on Arluin's chest. Crimson brocade blankets spill over us, and our bare legs are tangled together. Sunlight filters through the open window and sharp shadows slice across the room.

His skin is warm beneath my cheek. My fingers trace lazy circles across his chest. One of his arms is tucked around my waist, holding me flush against him. Every now and then he lifts his arm, flicking to the next page of the book he's reading.

I tilt back my head to get a better look at the cover. But my temples scream in protest, and the pain is so piercing my sight blurs. A groggy fog descends over me. While I have experienced many a hangover, this might be the worst one yet.

I must have let out a small whimper of pain since Arluin asks, "Feeling the wine?" His lips twitch with amusement as he looks down at me. If I felt a lot less awful, I would slap him for his smirk.

"Yes," I grunt.

"Do you regret drinking so much?"

"No. Never."

Arluin lets out a gentle laugh and returns to his book.

I close my eyes again, feeling the steady rise and fall of his chest. With my ear pressed against his skin, I can hear the drum of his heartbeat. I try to focus on that rather than the pain shooting across my temples.

"If it's really that bad," Arluin says after a while, "I have a numbing potion in the top drawer." He gestures to the counter on his side of the bed. The crystalline lamp there casts a purple glow over the pages of his book.

"You could have said so sooner!"

"You needed to learn your lesson."

"There's no lesson to be learned."

He arches a brow at me. "You passed out. Several times."

"I only remember the once."

"And you were dancing on the tables with Eliya so loudly the servers were trying to usher you both out."

"I don't remember that."

"You don't believe me?"

"No, I do." Dancing on the tables is something I've done plenty of times before with Eliya, and considering how much my head hurts, it isn't surprising I don't remember it happening.

Arluin shakes his head as he puts down his book and leans over to the counter. He pulls open the top drawer by its birdcage handle and rummages inside until he finds a potion vial. It's as small as the one Archmage Gidston gave me yesterday in the arena, but this one is far more decorative. Gold swirls encase the glass, spiraling up to the top where they form a cap. The liquid within is as thin as water and of a shimmering lapis hue.

He passes it to me. The glass is freezing where the potion touches, but room temperature where it does not. I flip back the metallic lid and drink the entire contents in a single gulp. This numbing potion is called Ice Honey, and it tastes as sweet as its name. The frozen nectar slides down my throat, and I can already feel it working. It's one of the fastest acting potions—and also the most addictive. Small amounts relieve pain, but large quantities can freeze every muscle in your body—including your heart. Overdoses require immediate medical attention, and even then the chances of survival are slim.

"Thanks," I say, returning the empty vial to Arluin.

He places it beneath the crystalline lamp, and the vibrant purple light makes the gold swirls glitter. I lie back on his chest as he picks up his book and continues to read.

The burgundy leather cover is embossed with ornamental flourishes and is entitled '*The Arcane Art of Alchemy.*' I suppose he's reading it as part of his research project. The Arcanium is always trying to improve Nolderan's potions, particularly ones with undesirable side effects such as Ice Honey.

We lie there in a peaceful silence for several minutes. Then a terrible thought occurs to me.

"What day is it today?"

"Wednesday," he says, not glancing away from his book.

"What time?" I ask, bolting upright. The scarlet sheets fall from my shoulders, leaving my back vulnerable to the morning breeze.

He points to the grandfather clock ticking away in the far corner of the room. "One o'clock."

"My morning classes!" I swear under my breath. My tutors will report my absence, and then my father will know I've been skipping classes again.

Arluin chuckles and pulls me back onto his chest. "Don't worry," he says, his free hand brushing away the strands of hair which have fallen in front of my face. "I submitted letters of absence for us both last week."

I let out a sigh of relief and crawl back under the blankets. With my head resting on his chest, I stare at the silk drapes hanging from the bedframe. They dance back and forth in the light breeze. I listen to them rustling against the wooden floor, as well as the turning of pages as Arluin reads. My eyes drift shut, a heaviness falling over me. The Ice Honey has shifted my headache now, and the gentle sounds are like a lullaby.

But before sleep can claim me, Arluin says, "Reyna?"

My eyes flutter open. "Yes, Arly?"

He clears his throat. I realize he's set his book down on the counter. "I . . ." he begins, but his words falter. "There's something I need to tell you. I should have last night."

"What's the matter?" I ask, sitting up.

"If you change your mind about marrying me, I will understand."

"Arly, what are you talking about? Why would I not want to marry you anymore?"

Arluin leans back into the embroidered pillows and closes his eyes.

I weave my fingers through his and press our conjoined hands to my chest. "We already made a promise to each other. Whatever you feel you must tell me will not change that."

His throat bobs as he swallows hard. "I've never told you about this . . ."

"Is this about your father?"

He manages a slight nod.

"If it's too painful to say, then don't say it." I brush aside a dark curl and kiss the skin beneath.

"But you have a right to know what you'll be marrying." His eyes remain shut.

"Whatever this is, I will love you all the same."

He draws out a deep breath. I hear it shudder as it passes his lips. "Even if I am a monster?"

"You're not a monster, Arluin. I've told you so many times that you're not your father. Nor will you ever be."

Arluin shakes his head. "You don't know what I've done."

My throat dries as my racing mind tries to fill in the blanks. I suspect what he will say next, but I desperately don't want to believe it. Nor do I wish for him to see the resignation in my expression. I'm glad his eyes are still closed.

"Arly," I say softly, not trusting my tongue with anything else.

"I missed her so much, Reyna. I still do."

I know he's talking about his mother. I keep my mouth shut, hoping he will continue talking of his own accord. He does.

"He started studying necromancy the month after she died. At the time, I didn't know exactly what he was doing, only that he would bring her back and that I could never tell anyone, or else she would never return.

"The following year, he forgot to lock the door to the cellar. I followed him inside and I saw . . . I saw him bring a corpse back to life." He grits his teeth. "A human corpse."

I say nothing, barely able to breathe.

"It looked human, but it was closer to a wild, starved animal. My father only realized I was watching when the corpse rolled off the table and charged toward the dark pillar I crouched behind.

"My father incinerated it before it reached me. With the way it screamed, I thought all of Nolderan would hear. I was only ten and didn't understand necromancy was forbidden, but I knew what he had done was wrong. And yet . . . ."

Arluin inhales sharply, his nostrils flaring with the force, and he finally opens his eyes. My entire body is frozen, my face included.

"I asked him if I could help. If he brought back my mother, I didn't want her to be like that corpse. He explained to me that wraiths are the most sentient of undead, as the soul is left intact when they are created, whereas the souls of ghouls and wights are fragmented.

"He was aiming to bring her back as a wraith and have her possess her body. Normally undead rot, but if the magic is powerful enough, then they will not. Since my mother was buried in a crystal coffin like all magi, her body would still be intact. The problem he faced was that her soul was long gone, having dispersed into aether upon her death. With his experiments, he was trying to reconstruct the souls of those already long dead.

"He first taught me how to raise ghouls by reanimating dead rats. Did you know, Reyna, that the first spell I ever cast was that of dark magic? Not aether. I learned forbidden magic before I learned ordinary magic. And I didn't just practice on rats, either. Sometimes when I look in the mirror, I fear that dead, gray eyes will gaze back at me."

Then he falls silent. He stares up at me. I know he expects an answer, but I can offer him none.

He lowers his eyes, looking at the blankets around us rather than me. "Do you hate me now, Reyna? Now that you know what I've done? What I truly am?"

Maybe I should hate him, maybe I should fear him. But I feel neither and that's what scares me.

What he has told me . . . If my father knew, he would be exiled just like Heston. And my father was lenient with banishment. The punishment for practicing dark magic is death.

I wish Arluin had confessed none of this. Because now I don't know how I will face my father. I should immediately report all of this to him. Keeping Arluin's secret means betraying my father— betraying Nolderan. But I can't break Arluin's trust. I can't bear to see him exiled.

Or executed.

In that instant, I know my choice.

I rest my head on the pillow beside him. Arluin doesn't move. He stares at the ceiling.

"I don't hate you," I finally manage, my voice but a breath. He doesn't turn to look at me.

"You should," he insists. "I'm a monster."

"If you're a monster, then you'll be my monster."

That gets him to turn and face me. There's a tortured look in his magenta eyes. I reassure myself that if he were still practicing necromancy, they would not glow with such a vivid hue of aether.

I take his hand once more and hold it against my cheek. "You were young, Arly. You can't be blamed for any of it. This is your father's fault, not yours, and he has already been punished for it."

He hangs his head and whispers, "Is it wrong of me to miss him?"

I sit up again and wrap my arms around him. "He's your father," I say, resting my head on his shoulder. "The two of you are bound by blood. All that he has done doesn't change that. It's natural for you to miss him."

Arluin is still at first. Then his fingers find my hair, and he toys with the ends, lost in thought. I wish I could banish his demons, but other than by hugging him, I do not know how.

"Reyna," he says after a moment, "will you still marry me, despite everything?"

"Of course I will," I reply, kissing his cheek. "I promise I will still marry you, no matter what."

CHAPTER 7

EVEN BY THURSDAY AFTERNOON, MY hangover is yet to disappear. I took plenty of Ice Honey this morning, but it's long worn off, and I don't dare take more. Not if I want my heart to keep beating.

At least the nasty bruise on my shoulder has healed, and I no longer need to conceal it with an illusion. Yesterday I returned home at five o'clock, and my mother slathered more Blood Balm over my shoulder. I slept all evening and barely woke on time for my classes this morning. It was only thanks to her I did.

Throughout my History and Medeicus lessons, I sit with my head in my hands. I stare at my tutors as they prattle on, and though my ears hear their words, my mind doesn't register their meaning. My eyes might be open, but my brain is fast asleep. My tutors notice nothing out of the ordinary, however, since I rarely pay attention.

During Alchemy, it's harder to sit and stare into space due to the practical nature of this subject. Luckily, we're allowed to work in pairs, and Eliya brews the potion by herself. She's quite understanding of my current affliction, but I suppose that's because she played a large part in causing it.

"You're not actually still hungover?" she asks in a hushed whisper, leaning over our cauldron. Aqua liquid bubbles within.

We're supposed to be making a Potion of Water Breathing, and it looks just like the color of the ocean. While that sounds rather pretty, you probably wouldn't think so if you knew the three key ingredients: jellyfish tentacles, fermented sea kelp, and mackerel gills. The reagents must be boiled slowly before finishing the potion with a splash of water magic.

I don't look up at her and instead watch her wooden spoon stir the frothy mixture. "I don't understand how you're not. Did you even drink any wine yourself, or were you too busy trying to make me drink it?"

"Of course I drank just as much as you," she says, shaking her head at me. "Your parents were paying for the entire banquet, wine included, so I made the most of it."

I can't argue with that and dearly wish I had Eliya's remarkable tolerance for wine.

After Alchemy, we have Illusionary Class, and unlike the rest of today's lessons, I'm unable to sit there and do nothing.

Professor Donatus Nyton has stacked all the chairs and desks at the back of the classroom and has replaced them with dozens of mirrors. We are instructed to conjure an illusion of ourselves—a perfect replica. While we have practiced cloning flowers and food and animals, this is the first time we have ever crafted illusions of ourselves.

And it turns out replicating humans is the most challenging illusion of all.

I'm stationed at a golden, full-length mirror that sits before large, arched windows. They're pulled wide open to allow the summer heat to escape, but I'm sure the breeze is blowing more warmth into the stuffy classroom. I would conjure ice and use it to cool myself, but I'm otherwise preoccupied with sculpting my illusion. It's nearly impossible to concentrate with the heat.

Eliya, who stands before the mirror on my left, lets out a sudden laugh. "Koby!" she exclaims to the adept next to her. He's a cheery, round young man with a mop of brown hair. "Look at your nose!" She points at the illusion he's made of himself.

The clone is nearly perfect—aside from its nose almost being the same size as its hand. Its ankles are also bent at an odd angle. The illusion doesn't twitch and looks more like a life-sized doll than a living person. Even if its nose and ankles weren't strange, no one would be fooled into thinking it's the real Koby.

"As if you're doing a better job, Eliya," he says.

"You just watch," she tells him. Intrigued to know how her next attempt will fare, I stop the illusion I'm conjuring to look at hers.

Eliya draws aether into her fingers and gazes into the mirror opposite her. "*Speculus!*"

The magic swirls out and settles between her and the full-length mirror. The purple cloud swells, forming the silhouette of a person. When the light fades, an image of Eliya remains.

Except it isn't entirely like Eliya. It has the same crimson hair and heart-shaped face. But it's several inches taller, and there's a large discrepancy between its breasts and Eliya's. It's hard not to notice the size difference. I wonder if Eliya is joking with this attempt, since the illusion looks like it will topple over from the front-heavy weight.

"See," Eliya announces, gesturing to the illusion. "Look at how perfect mine is."

Poor Koby doesn't know where to look. His round cheeks immediately flush.

I let out a gentle cough. "Eliya, don't you think—"

She turns to me, placing a hand on her hip. "Don't I think what?"

"Well, the illusion looks rather stretched." I figure that's the safest way to say it's much taller.

"No, it doesn't."

I decide not to press that point.

"And uh . . ." I try to gesture in the direction of the clone's breasts. With how red Koby already looks, it's probably best not to shout that particular word.

She frowns at me. "What?"

"You know . . ."

Apparently she doesn't know. So, I have to be more creative. I nod to my chest and then to the illusion's.

She finally understands. "They are that big!"

I cast her a dubious look.

"You're just jealous," she insists. While I can't deny I'm envious of Eliya's curves, I'm very certain they're not over-exaggerated like her illusion's are.

"All right, I'm just jealous," I say, holding my hands up in defeat. If not for this splitting headache, I wouldn't have surrendered so quickly.

Eliya flashes me a triumphant grin and points to my mirror. "It's your turn, anyway."

I didn't realize we were taking turns and go to explain that I can't concentrate because of the heat and my headache, but then I notice Professor Nyton standing behind us. He's a tall, thin man, and it's a wonder I didn't notice him sooner. His arms are folded across his chest, and he peers at us through his monocle.

I really hope he didn't hear our conversation about Eliya's breasts.

I'm left with no choice but to turn to my mirror and gather aether into my fingers. I focus on my reflection as best I can: the oval shape of my face, my dark brows which pinch together in concentration, and the sunlight reflecting off my long hair. When I'm satisfied that I've captured every detail, I release my magic.

"*Speculus!*"

The aether spills out and forms my illusion. It's identical in every way, like my reflection has sprung from the mirror. The clone's unblinking eyes stare back at me.

A slow clap sounds from behind. "Splendid work, Ashbourne. Truly splendid. Though we should expect no less from the Grand-mage's daughter."

Most of my tutors see me as the lazy student I am. A few are somehow convinced I'm a genius. Professor Nyton is one of the latter. But I suppose I am better at Illusionary Class than Alchemy or Medeicus. It isn't as boring, and I spend less time asleep.

Professor Nyton continues his lap of the room and watches the other adepts as they replicate themselves. The twins—Jaron and Braedon Trindell—are doing an especially good job, no doubt because the two boys are used to staring at identical versions of themselves. But Professor Nyton doesn't marvel at their illusions. Not like he did with mine.

When he's out of earshot, Eliya scoffs at me. "Yours is only good because you spend too much time in front of the mirror."

If we weren't in class, I would splash her with a water spell for that. Actually, I'm tempted to do it anyway. Professor Nyton would probably let me off lightly for it, especially if it were just a small splash.

My expression cracks into a wide grin. "Now look who's jealous."

She just wags her tongue at me and waves her hand, dispersing her illusion. Then she sets to work at creating a new image of herself, this time shorter and less voluptuous.

I return my attention to my illusion. It still gazes straight ahead with its unblinking eyes. Though I've succeeded in creating a perfect replica of myself, the next step is to make it mimic my every move.

In the mirror, I catch Kaely glaring at me. Her fists tighten, and so do her clone's. It seems she is ahead of me yet again, having already mastered the next stage of the spell.

Yet when Professor Nyton passes her, he spares her no more than a glance. And that only fuels her rage.

While I don't hate Illusionary Class, I'm glad when it ends. It's our final lesson of the day, and I can't wait to crawl back into bed.

Eliya's arm links with mine as we cross the Arcanium's atrium and step through the portico which leads outside. When we pass the rows of pillars, she turns to me and says, "So, did you like the locket?"

With a frown, I glance down. The necklace is hidden beneath the high collar of my robes. "From Arluin? How did you know?"

"He asked me if I thought you'd like it," she replies, as we descend the staircase which spirals around the statue of the Founder of Nolderan, "but I told him it would be too plain for your taste. He looked quite sad when I said that, though, and I felt pretty bad. But I changed my mind when he told me what he planned. Anything too fancy would distract from its purpose."

"Oh," I say. "I didn't know he asked you about it."

She stops in front of Grandmage Delmont Blackwood. It feels like he's scrutinizing our every move, but that's silly since these statues can't move. "So?"

"So what?"

She grabs both my arms. "What did you tell him? He proposed to you as planned, didn't he?"

I scan across all the adepts leaving the Arcanium. First-years and second-years finish at three o'clock, while the upper years have classes until later this afternoon. There's still plenty of people around us, however. Eliya may not shun Arluin for his father's crimes, but many others do. Though I suppose after what he told me yesterday, his father's crimes are also his own.

I don't dwell on that thought.

I give Eliya a pointed look and say, "He didn't propose to me. He promised to marry me."

"Isn't that the same thing?"

"He didn't get down on one knee, so that means he didn't propose."

She looks unconvinced. "Anyway," she continues eagerly, shaking my arms, "what did you say? You promised to marry him too, right? I swear if I'm not your Maid of—"

"Promised to marry who?" Kaely asks, marching down the last step.

I grimace inwardly. This is exactly why I wanted to avoid having this conversation in public.

"That's none of your business," Eliya snaps before I can speak.

"Did you have a nice party the other day?" Kaely asks me, ignoring Eliya. "I was heartbroken to learn I received no invitation."

I tighten my jaw. "And I was just as heartbroken to receive no 'Happy Birthday' from you. All I received was a nasty bruise."

Kaely tugs on her braid, pulling it to the front. "I hope it's healing well." She flashes me a smile that doesn't meet her eyes. "How's that necromancer of yours doing? I wondered what you were both up to yesterday when neither of you showed up for your lessons." I don't want to know how she found out Arluin didn't attend any classes yesterday. It's concerning she would go to such lengths to find out something like that.

"Again," Eliya says with a glare, "that's none of your business, Kaely." She shoots me a pleading look, silently begging me to leave.

Eliya is right that we should go, but I can't tear myself away just yet. "Arluin is no necromancer," I hiss.

Only after I speak do I realize that may no longer be true. Not after what he told me yesterday. But practicing a few dark spells years ago doesn't make him a necromancer, does it? His eyes still glow with aether. That means he's still a mage, or at least one in training.

I hope Kaely doesn't notice my hesitation before I add, "With how frequently you discuss necromancy, I fear you may be the true necromancer here."

Kaely lets out a sharp laugh and shakes her head. "Reyna, it wasn't my father who was banished for practicing necromancy. For digging up coffins and experimenting on corpses. Does your father approve? I mean, Heston was his closest friend, so maybe your relationship with Arluin doesn't disgust him."

"My relationship with Arluin doesn't concern you."

Kaely releases her braid and tosses it over her shoulder. She steps closer to me, malice glinting in her eyes. "I would wager your father doesn't mind that you're a necromancer's lover. After all, he allowed Heston Harstall to walk free when the punishment for such crimes is death."

"Kaely!" Eliya's eyes widen with horror. "You shouldn't speak of the Grandmage like that!" She tugs my wrist. "Come on, Reyna. Let's go."

I let her pull me away, and we start down the path lined by the many towering statues of long dead magi. But we only manage a few strides before Kaely calls, "*Laxus!*"

In the next instant, she appears in front of us, blocking our way. Before either Eliya or I can utter a single word, she continues her taunts. "I've heard you're frequenting the necromancer's manor more often these days."

"You've taken to stalking me now, have you?" I growl back. "What in the Abyss do you want with me, Kaely?"

"You misunderstand me. Are we not friends?"

"We are not friends," I grind out. "Not anymore."

"As saddened as I am to know you feel that way, I've always seen you as otherwise. I'm only looking out for you, Reyna. And with each day that passes, I'm becoming more concerned for you."

I cross my arms. "That's your pitiful excuse for obsessing over me?"

"I simply wanted to remind you to take your contraceptive potions with great care. If you have children with Arluin, then they will surely follow in their father's and grandfather's footsteps."

I stare at Kaely, my mouth hanging agape, unable to believe what I'm hearing.

"How dare you!" I roar when the shock of her words has worn off.

My patience with Kaely is quickly wearing thin. How I long to wipe that smirk off her freckled face.

I lunge for her, but Eliya grabs my shoulders and spins me around. "Ignore her," she pleads. "She's not worth it. If you allow yourself to be riled by her words, then you'll only give her the confrontation she wants."

I close my eyes and exhale deeply. Eliya is right. Kaely isn't worth wasting another moment on. She doesn't deserve even my anger.

I give Eliya a nod, and we pass around Kaely. But she refuses to let us leave so easily.

"Do take care he doesn't impregnate you with an undead fetus, Reyna!"

I halt.

Blood drums in my ears, deafening me. It boils through my body so furiously I think I will burst.

"What's the matter?" she asks me with a delighted laugh. "Scared he already has? Have you found out whether it's a baby ghoul or a baby wraith yet—"

My magic possesses me. Aether sparks in my fingers, and the fury in my veins rises to a crescendo.

"*Ignira.*" As the spell-word escapes my lips, I barely recognize my voice as my own.

The crackling flames are as loud as thunder. A ferocious fireball forms in my hands.

I unleash it upon her.

Other adepts shout, and so does Eliya. But their cries are distant, as though I'm hearing them through a stone wall.

"*Aquir'muriz!*" Kaely calls, conjuring a water shield before the fireball slams into her. The barrier withstands the attack, and droplets splatter across the stone path.

Magi charge forth, grabbing my arms and restraining them behind my back. I struggle to free myself but don't dare use any magic against them.

The corners of Kaely's lips curl into a vicious smile. When I try to breathe, it feels as if steel encases my chest.

I have made a horrible mistake.

Kaely taunted me into lashing out, and I have given her exactly what she sought. Using magic to strike other adepts or magi, unless instructed during classes, is prohibited by Nolderan's laws.

I should have heeded Eliya's warning.

This time, my father will be furious.

CHAPTER 8

ARCHMAGE LORETTE GIDSTON PACES BEFORE her desk. Her footsteps are muffled by the narrow, rectangular rug spread across the wooden floor. The yarns are weaved into a geometric pattern of reds, yellows, oranges, and browns, depicting the colors of fall.

The books lining the back shelves are arranged in alphabetical order, and each spine is perfectly aligned with the next. A small chandelier laden with aether crystals hangs from the ceiling and casts violet light over us all.

I stand to the left of Archmage Gidston's desk, restrained by the two magi either side of me. Even if my arms weren't secured behind my back, I wouldn't try to escape. Running would be futile, and foolish. It would only worsen my inevitable punishment.

Kaely stands across from me. When I lift my head, our gazes lock together. The corners of her mouth curl into a savage smirk, eager to see me punished.

Beside Kaely is her father, Archmage Branvir Calton. He's bald, with a beard the same shade as Kaely's braid. His bushy brows pull together in a deep crease, and his fists are tightened at his side. When his eyes sweep over to Kaely, she swaps her expression to a facade of fear, as though she is the victim.

I don't hide my glare, though I know it will only further condemn me.

In all my eighteen years, I've never known anyone to be more a snake than Kaely.

To think I once called her a friend.

I tear my attention from Kaely and scan across the few other adepts brought here as witnesses. Eliya is among them, as well as Koby.

My best friend's eyes are filled with worry. When Eliya catches my gaze, she presses her lips together in gentle reassurance, as if everything will be fine.

But it won't.

I've broken the city's laws. Adepts who commit such crimes are often expelled from the Arcanium, deemed unfit to become magi because of their volatile temperaments. This is why Archmage Gidston is unwilling to deal with the matter without my father present.

Now I can only hope that my father, despite his fury, won't subject me to such harsh punishment. This is the first time I've used my magic to strike another adept outside of the arena. And it isn't as if Kaely didn't deserve it.

Surely they won't expel me for a single mistake?

"Archmage Gidston," Branvir says after a while, "we've been waiting for almost an hour for the Grandmage to arrive. Perhaps we should begin without him?"

Lorette pauses her pacing. "No," she replies, "we cannot proceed without the Grandmage being present. Even with two Archmagi, this matter is far too delicate."

I can't bear to look at either of the Archmagi. If I were not the Grandmage's daughter, my crimes would be long judged by now. I would already be expelled from the Arcanium.

Branvir doesn't protest again, and so we continue to wait.

My palms are hot and sticky, and my racing mind imagines a thousand different ways this trial could go. Even muffled by the carpet, Archmage Gidston's footsteps drum in my ears to the rhythm of impending doom.

The walls spin around me. I struggle to keep myself upright. I don't know how much longer I can bear this excruciating wait.

But then the doors finally swing open, and my father strides in.

Though the room was quiet before his entry, now it falls completely silent—as if no one dares to even twitch in the Grandmage's presence. His magnificent robes storm around him and gold thread flashes through the indigo fabric like bolts of lightning.

My father comes to a stop before Archmage Gidston. He stands less than an arm's length away from me, but he doesn't turn in my direction. Nor does he glance at me from the corners of his eyes.

It's as if he can't bear to look upon his disgrace of a daughter.

"Archmage Gidston," he says, resting the end of his crystalline staff on the carpet, "if you will explain this matter. And swiftly. I must soon return to Tirith's ambassadors."

"Yes, Grandmage." Lorette folds her hands behind her back and straightens. Her eyes drift between Kaely and me. "This afternoon, shortly after the second-years finished their classes for the day, Reyna Ashbourne was seen attacking Kaely Calton with a fireball spell."

Only now does my father's head snap toward me. "Is this true?" His temples pulse with barely controlled rage. "Or do you dare to deny Archmage Gidston's words?"

"Yes, it's true I struck Kaely with a fireball spell but—"

My father raises his hand before I can explain, wordlessly silencing me.

A lump swells in my throat. I swallow, but it doesn't shift. I stare at the carpet to avoid looking at the disappointment on his face.

"The perpetrator confesses to her crimes," my father says, his tone painfully neutral. "For what reason did you call me here, Archmage Gidston? I believe both you and Archmage Calton should be more than capable of addressing this incident."

"Of course," Lorette replies, bowing her head. Her platinum hair doesn't move with the motion, the bun too tightly bound. "However, as it concerns your daughter, I thought it best to settle this matter with you present."

"While Reyna may be my daughter, she will be treated no differently to any other adept of the Arcanium."

Branvir huffs his agreement, while Lorette's shoulders stiffen with tension.

"Since Reyna is found guilty," Lorette says, "we must agree on the punishment she is to receive for breaking Nolderan's laws by using her magic with the intention to harm another." Her voice reveals little of her thoughts. It almost sounds like hesitation, but I'm not sure whether it's born of reluctance or apprehension.

"Is the punishment for such crimes not expulsion?" Branvir interjects.

Both my father and Lorette turn to face him, their expressions unreadable.

Will my father agree to expel me from the Arcanium? Will he allow me to be the first Ashbourne in generations to fail to graduate as a Mage of Nolderan?

Maybe he will disown me to prevent me from tarnishing our family's legacy.

My breathing is shaky, and my vision blurs. I may not be the most studious adept, but becoming a mage is my destiny.

I bite back the tears welling in my eyes—thick, heavy, and painfully bitter. I can't cry here. Not in front of my father, and certainly not in front of Kaely, who would take much delight in seeing how weak I am.

"The severity of the punishment depends on the specific circumstances of the incident," Archmage Gidston states. "Furthermore, this is the first time Reyna has committed such an offense, and no one was harmed by it."

My lips part. The tears freeze in my eyes before they can spill onto my cheeks.

I think she might be defending me. Though she let Kaely beat me horribly in the arena, she's arguing on my behalf. Even when my own father is not.

Is she doing this because I'm the daughter of Grandmage Telric Ashbourne, or because I'm Reyna?

"No one was harmed?" Branvir exclaims. A few adepts flinch at his shout. Koby is one of them. "My daughter could have been killed!"

"While your concerns are understandable," Lorette replies, her words as cool and precise as ice, "it's unlikely that Kaely would have been killed by a mere fireball. As the Archmage of Knowledge, the Arcanium falls under my jurisdiction. I know the capabilities of every adept in my charge. Kaely is one of the most talented second-years, and that is evident from her performance in the arena."

It seems Archmage Gidston is far more calculating than I realized. Though Branvir was moments away from exploding in a fit of rage, his wrath is pacified by the praise she offers Kaely.

He shifts his weight and scratches his brown beard. "Hm, perhaps that is true. But Reyna Ashbourne should not be let off lightly. It's fortunate my daughter is so talented, or else this incident could have proven disastrous."

"Again," Lorette responds, dipping her head, "your concerns are understandable. I can assure you that she will not escape lightly." She pauses and glances across at my father, her eyes tight with wariness. "I am of the opinion that suspension would be the most fitting punishment."

Hearing her words lifts some of the weight from my shoulders, and my exhalations come out steadier.

Suspension—I can live with that. It doesn't mean expulsion. And hopefully it won't mean disownment, either.

"For how long?" Branvir demands.

"I believe a month would be sufficient. What do you think, Grandmage?"

My father is silent, a contemplative frown etched deep into his brow. Before he can respond, a shout comes from behind.

"This isn't fair!" Eliya exclaims, her fists balled.

Everyone turns to Eliya. My father's expression grows sterner, while Archmage Gidston's fills with irritation.

"Adept Whiteford," she snaps, "you will remain silent. Or else you too shall be disciplined for speaking out of turn, especially while in the presence of the Grandmage of Nolderan."

But Eliya isn't so easily deterred.

"Archmage Gidston," she begins, placing her hands on her hips. "Was I not brought here as a witness? Does that not mean I have the right to recount what I saw with my own eyes and heard with my own ears?"

"Eliya Whiteford, I will not tell you again." Lorette's tone is glacial. "While it is true that you were summoned here as a witness, we no longer require your account since the perpetrator pleads guilty. There is no debate to be had, for this judgment has already been made—"

My father raises his hand. "Archmage Gidston, why don't we see what the girl has to say?"

Eliya bows her head, her crimson hair cascading over her shoulders. "Thank you, Grandmage."

"But be quick about it," he continues. "As I said, I must return to Tirith's ambassadors, and I do not wish to keep them waiting."

"Yes, Grandmage."

"Then speak your piece, Adept Whiteford," Lorette says. "Why is it you believe Reyna is undeserving of this punishment? Do you instead believe she is innocent?"

"No, Archmage Gidston," Eliya replies. "It's true that Reyna struck Kaely with a fireball spell, and I do agree she must receive some punishment for that."

I arch a brow at her, wondering whether she's even on my side. I'm quite content with a month's suspension, and I dearly hope whatever Eliya says won't worsen my punishment. Though I wouldn't be aggrieved if they decide to extend the suspension to three months.

Archmage Gidston folds her arms. She's not a particularly patient woman, and it's clear Eliya is testing her limits. "If you agree that Reyna is guilty and that she should be disciplined for her actions, then what more do you wish to add? As the Grandmage has already said, he has far more pressing matters. We should not waste anymore of his time."

"All I wanted to point out is that no one's bothered to question why Reyna struck Kaely. Like you said, Archmage Gidston, this is the first time Reyna has ever committed such an offence. And I, as the primary witness, can assure everyone in this room it was not without good reason." When Eliya finishes speaking, she glances at me. Determination burns brightly in her eyes.

Determination to see justice be dealt.

I return her expression with a wry smile. If I am to be punished, then Kaely ought to be as well. It's time she learns she can't spout whatever she pleases without fear of retribution.

"And what was that reason, Eliya?" my father presses.

"Kaely insulted Reyna. Several times. She refused to leave us alone."

Branvir turns to Kaely. "Is this true?"

"Of course it's true," Kaely says, her voice unshaken by Eliya's claim. "Reyna and I had a disagreement, and it's inevitable that during an argument, one may say words they later regret." She steps toward me and lowers her head. "If you took offense by what I said, Reyna, then I truly am sorry. I don't wish for ill feelings to fester between us. We have, after all, been friends for so many years."

I grit my teeth. It's almost impossible to hold my tongue. To prevent myself from screaming how much I hate her. How the two of us are not and will never again be friends.

Not after all the unforgivable words she has spoken.

"Such misunderstandings are not uncommon," Archmage Gidston says. "However, this does not justify violence. Regardless of Reyna's reasons for attacking Kaely, I believe the punishment for her offenses remains fitting. And if we are all in agreement, then this incident is also resolved."

I can bite my tongue no longer. I loathe how Archmage Gidston dismisses the incident as petty bickering. How Kaely will emerge unscathed. While I will be punished.

"It wasn't a simple misunderstanding," I seethe. "I did nothing to deserve the way Kaely spoke to me. Should magi be allowed to go around, spouting whatever awful words they please without fear of retribution? Is that the city—"

"Silence!"

The room stills at my father's shout. His attention remains on the tidy bookshelves behind the desk. He doesn't turn to look at me as he speaks.

"Magi should act as model citizens for Nolderan," my father asserts. "Their words should be chosen out of wisdom and not out of malice, and they should certainly not strike down others due to their ill-temper. What Archmage Gidston says is fair. There are no reasons that can justify your actions."

"You weren't there!" I know losing my temper will prove them right, but I can't contain my rage. "You didn't hear what she said! About Arluin, about Heston, about you. She claimed the reason you spared Heston from death is because of your previous friendship with him—"

"I think you remember incorrectly, Reyna," Kaely interrupts, her lips twitching. I can't tell whether it's the hint of a smirk or a snarl. "I never said the Grandmage spared Heston because of their friendship."

I wrestle with the magi still gripping my arms, but they don't relent. If my fists were free, I would use them to shatter Kaely's disgusting expression.

That was my ultimate mistake. I should have struck her with my fists instead of my magic. They probably wouldn't even suspend me for that. Most likely, a stern talking to by Archmage Gidston is all I would receive.

And hitting her would be so much more satisfying.

If only I thought it all through before unleashing my magic.

"You insinuated it," I spit. "Even if you didn't say it outright, you mocked Arluin and my father."

"And also she insulted you, Reyna," Eliya adds, her nose wrinkling. "Kaely, don't think I've forgotten that comment about undead fetuses—"

"That is enough!" my father booms, his voice reverberating through the small room.

It is safe to say I inherited my short-fused temper from my father, and not my mother.

Heston's betrayal plagues his heart even to this day, and his resulting wrath is terrifying.

"Leave us!" he roars. "All of you!"

Everyone is so taken aback by his sudden outburst that no one moves.

"Leave! I will deal with my daughter myself!"

On his second shout, the room springs to life. The doors swing open, and all the adepts brought as witnesses spill out. None wish to face the fury of Grandmage Telric Ashbourne. Even the magi restraining me leave.

With my arms now free, I roll my shoulders. The motion does little to relieve the cramp.

Eliya lingers longer than the rest. Her gaze meets mine, and her brows knit with concern. I know she is reluctant to leave me at my father's mercy, but there's nothing more she can do. She has no choice but to follow the others through the doors.

Though the room has mostly cleared, five of us remain. Aside from my father and me, that includes Lorette, Branvir, and Kaely.

Branvir's eyes narrow at the double doors, and he harrumphs, his disdain thinly veiled. I know he doesn't like my father much. Thirty years ago, when the previous Grandmage retired, Branvir was one of the few candidates in line to take his position. The following decade he also ran for Archmage of Defense, but Heston Harstall was instead appointed. It was five years ago, when Heston was exiled, that Branvir was finally promoted. But I think he would much prefer to be the Grandmage of Nolderan than the Archmage of Defense.

Thanks to all the aether humming through our veins, magi live at least twice as long as normal humans—sometimes even longer. My father will reign over Nolderan for the most part of another century. By then, Branvir will be nearing retirement himself.

Maybe this is another reason Kaely hates me. Because my father outranks hers. And because he will never have the chance to become the Grandmage.

Branvir doesn't dare to directly defy my father, though. That would cause him to lose his position. And being the Archmage of Defense is better than being nothing.

"With all due respect, Grandmage—" Branvir begins.

"I shall deal with my daughter," my father snaps. He turns to Kaely and glares at her, not bothering to hide the flames burning in his magenta eyes. She has the sense to flinch at his fury. "I also suggest you deal with yours. Matters which concern the safety of Nolderan and the magi should not be spoken of so lightly."

Branvir opens his mouth, and I wonder whether he'll argue with my father. Maybe to say that Kaely isn't entirely wrong. That Heston should never have been spared from execution.

Instead, he seems to change his mind and bows his head. "Indeed, such things should not be spoken of so lightly." He glances at Kaely, his eyes sharpening. "I can assure you that the two of us will have a thorough discussion concerning this matter."

My father gives him a curt nod, and Branvir starts over to the door. Kaely trails behind him. She doesn't turn, but I know if she dared, she would shoot me a venomous glare.

Now only Archmage Gidston remains, aside from my father and me.

"Lorette," he says as she too leaves, "I will inform you of Reyna's punishment when it is decided."

"Of course, Grandmage." Without another word, she steps out of her office and closes the doors behind her.

My father and I stand there in silence for a long while. He stares out of the arched windows, clasping his crystalline staff. Archmage Gidston's office is situated inside one of the Arcanium's highest spires. It can't compare to the vastness of the Aether Tower, but you can still see the entire city from up here.

Cobalt tiles ripple across the rooftops below, and Nolderan's walls stand proudly at the edges of the city. Beyond them lies the thick cover of trees, surrounding Nolderan like leafy clouds. They quickly turn into the deadly drop of steep cliffs. Then there are only sapphire waves, stretching on for hundreds of miles. From the docks in the Lower City, however, you can see the coastline of the mainland on the horizon.

I doubt my father is simply gazing out at the sea because he enjoys looking at it. Most likely, he's watching the lull of the waves in an attempt to soothe his rage.

What he's contemplating, I dread to discover. Is he considering worsening the punishment Archmage Gidston suggested? Will it be a longer suspension, or will it be something else entirely?

Maybe he's deliberating over the decision to disown me.

It seems I fidgeted at that awful thought since he finally speaks. "You will no longer see him."

"No longer see who? Archmage Calton?"

He must take my genuine confusion as sarcasm, since he whirls around with a face reddened by anger. "Arluin! You will see him no more!"

"Arluin?" I repeat, leaning on the desk. "What has Arluin got to do with any of this?"

"Your feelings for him have made you lose all sense! Made you stupid enough to strike a fellow adept!"

"Fine," I hiss. "Blame Arluin for this. Even though the reason I lost my temper is because of what she said about both of you."

His temples twitch. He says nothing. It seems he doesn't quite know how to respond to my brazen words.

"Don't think I don't know exactly what you're doing."

"And what is it you think I'm doing?" My father doesn't raise his voice. I've pushed him so far beyond anger that he's lost the ability to shout.

"You're using this as an excuse to stop me from seeing Arluin. And you can try," I sneer, "but it won't work. We're already promised, he and I."

"You're what?" he bellows.

"Promised," I say, my lips curling. "It means we are to marry."

My father whirls back to the window. His breathing is so loud I think all of Nolderan will hear it. If he spends another moment looking at me, he'll probably kill me.

He can lecture me about losing my temper, but he's no better himself.

"You don't care at all, do you?"

"I don't care about what, Father?"

"About our family. About being an Ashbourne. Is becoming a mage another joke to you, Reyna?"

I throw back my head and let out a hysterical laugh. "Now you're saying that because I love Arluin, I don't give a damn about our family? About graduating from the Arcanium? Maybe I will fail on purpose. Just for you."

His shoulders quake with rage, like a volcano moments away from eruption. It's a wonder the entire room hasn't yet exploded into flames. From either of us.

"What did I do to deserve such a disgraceful daughter?" he mutters, asking the waves far beyond that question. Not me.

I answer, anyway.

"Then don't let me disgrace you any longer, Father. Disown me. I know you're considering it, so go ahead and do it."

I don't know why I said any of that. I don't actually want him to disown me. Maybe that's why I said it, because I want to hear him say he won't. That however disgraceful I may be, he won't disown his only daughter.

"Is that . . ." he begins, but the words extinguish in his throat. "Is that what you want, Reyna?"

There's pain in his voice, and I hate hearing it. I already regret my words.

He turns to look at me, but now it is I who cannot face him. My gaze falls to the carpet. "Of course it's not what I want," I mumble.

"Then why would you say it?" he asks, his voice softening.

"Because that's what you want."

He draws out a long sigh. "It isn't what I want."

"It's not?"

"No, it's not."

We descend into silence. Both our tempers no longer blaze, but smolder quietly like embers.

"Then what do you want?" I ask. My voice is hushed, not daring to disturb the tentative peace budding between us.

"I want you to graduate from the Arcanium."

"And you don't want me to marry Arluin?"

"I never said I don't want you to marry him."

"But you don't, do you? You don't want me to marry the son of the man you exiled. Like everyone else, you misjudge him for his father."

Again, I hate what Arluin admitted. I fear it makes me a liar.

But it isn't Arluin's fault his father led him astray. He was young. How can he be blamed?

I will never tell my father the truth. I will take his secret to my grave. Arluin doesn't deserve banishment. Nor death.

"No, Reyna, this has nothing to do with Arluin's father. I would say the same regardless of whom you're planning to marry. You are too young, and marriage will only serve to distract you from your studies."

"I never said that Arluin and I are getting married soon. We might have promised to marry each other, but he insisted we marry after I graduate from the Arcanium."

The last of my father's rage slips away. His shoulders relax, no longer trembling with molten fury. "I see. Good."

"So, does that mean I'm still allowed to see him?"

"He remains a distraction from your studies."

"No, he doesn't. Arluin studies harder than every other adept in the entire Arcanium, just to prove he isn't like his father. That he doesn't deserve the way people fear and shun him. Ask Archmage Gidston if you don't believe me. And if you want to blame someone for distracting me from my studies, then blame Eliya. After all, we spend most of our time laughing and gossiping. But you're not cruel enough to stop me from seeing her, are you? Not that you could, since we have the same classes every day."

My father shakes his head and takes to staring out the window once more. I hope the fact he's lost for words means I won this argument.

"There's also the matter of your punishment," he says after a pause.

"It's fine. A month's suspension is fair. I did launch a fireball at Kaely, after all."

He scoffs. "Not a chance. You will certainly not be receiving a month's suspension from your studies."

"Why not? I'm guilty."

"I know you're guilty."

I frown at him. Not that he can see it. He still faces the arched window.

"Reyna, you forget that I am your father and that I know exactly what you're thinking."

"And what's that?"

"You're looking forward to having a month off from your studies and doing nothing at all."

"No, I'm not."

He turns to me and raises a bushy auburn brow. "If you insist on lying to me, I will worsen your punishment."

"Fine," I huff. "I may have been looking forward to some time off from my studies."

He gives a satisfied nod and then returns to the window. "That is why suspension would be an ill-fitting punishment. Fortunately, the one I have in mind is far more appropriate."

My heart dips. If it isn't expulsion or suspension, I'm scared to imagine what it will be. "What punishment?"

"Community service," he says, his mouth quirking. "At the library."

CHAPTER 9

THOUGH MY FATHER SAID HE must swiftly return to Tirith's ambassadors, he now has no problem with marching me to the Grand Library himself. It's as if he doesn't trust me to deliver myself to Erma Darkholme.

I can't possibly think why that would be.

He leads me out of the office and down the central spire. The winding staircase is so narrow there's not enough room for people to pass simultaneously. Flickering aether crystals are fixed to the walls like sconces, but their pale light fails to illuminate the entire spire.

The steps spiral down so far I can't see their end. The ornate rail is all which prevents me from tripping and plummeting into the unending darkness.

At the sight of the Grandmage, the magi ascending the stairs halt. They step aside, leaning into the walls to make room for us, and bow their heads in deference to my father. If it weren't for his position, I'm sure it would take us far longer to reach the bottom.

The antechamber we arrive in is high-ceilinged and dozens of portraits decorate every inch of the room. Like the paintings of my ancestors inside my manor, they are enchanted with aether, and the magi within the frames seem very much alive. All are dressed in their purple robes. Some wave at us, while others are far too busy reading their tomes.

Many elaborate benches lie beneath the portraits, and a group of adepts sit on the leftmost ones. First-years, I think. When we enter they're giggling and gossiping loudly, but they all fall silent as my father strides past. Apprehension initially clouds their magenta eyes, but it soon changes to intrigue upon noticing me. The entire Arcanium—perhaps even the whole city—will have already heard what I did. How the Grandmage's daughter launched a fireball at the Archmage of Defense's daughter, right in front of the Founder's statue. I don't doubt these first-years will start chattering about it as soon as we're out of earshot.

The antechamber leads to the Arcanium's atrium. Aether crystals glitter high above, twinkling in the late noon sunlight. The faerie dragons assigned to the Arcanium aren't polishing the ceiling today. Instead, they are supervising the enchanted brooms as they sweep across the polished marble floor.

The Grand Library lies opposite us, and my father marches toward it. Like on the stairs, the magi passing through the atrium pause to dip their heads at my father. He returns a brief nod, but his attention doesn't leave the library's entrance.

We descend the long, steep staircase, and bear right as it splits at the bottom.

Like usual, Erma sits at her gleaming white desk. Today she is stamping books and comparing each title to a long list. These tomes are especially old, judging by their torn pages. Most likely, enchanted quills have replicated their text into new copies, and she's marking the old books as being withdrawn from the library.

Erma doesn't look up as we approach. She just continues stamping away at the pile of books. But with her impeccable hearing, I don't doubt she knows we're here. Only Erma Darkholme, who held the title Archmage of Knowledge for almost one hundred and twenty years, is bold enough to ignore my father. After all, it is he who should show her reverence. Erma would have been in charge of the Arcanium when he was studying here.

For a long while, Erma says nothing. She simply dips her stamp into a pot of crimson ink and presses it onto the first page of each book.

My father finally lets out a gentle cough. I suppose it's unfitting for the Grandmage of Nolderan to be ignored by a mere librarian. A few adepts cast us curious looks. But that could also be because they've heard about me attacking Kaely.

"Erma," my father begins, "I have a matter which only you can resolve."

"Yes, yes, what is it?"

"It is regarding my daughter, Reyna."

Erma looks up. Her eyes narrow at me—no doubt recalling the other day when she chased Arluin and me from the library.

I do hope she doesn't start complaining about that in front of my father.

"I have already heard of this matter." She uses her stamp to gesture at the adepts huddled around a table in the far corner. "They all burst into my library as soon as their lessons finished, shouting to each other about how the Grandmage's daughter struck another adept with a fireball. The ruckus I had to deal with because of this incident!" She shakes her head, and strands of wispy white hair drift around her like clouds. "What is it then, Telric, that you require me for?"

"To oversee Reyna's punishment."

"What punishment is she to receive?"

"For the next month, she is to act as your assistant and help with any tasks you require completing. She is expected to help you every day after her lessons until nightfall, and from dawn to dusk on Saturdays and Sundays."

It's all I can do not to groan. I hadn't expected him to be lenient with my punishment, especially not after the argument we just had, but this is going too far. I will be exhausted every day for the next month and have no time to myself.

"If you find she does not arrive promptly at these times, disappears unexpectedly while working, or does not conduct herself in the appropriate manner, then I will see to it the consequences she suffers are far worse."

I'm certain those words are meant for me rather than Erma, though his attention remains on her. I peer at him, but his expression offers no clue as to what my alternative punishment might be.

If I behave inappropriately, will I receive the punishment Archmage Gidston suggested? A month's suspension? That's doubtful, since he knows it wouldn't bother me in the least. But I can't think what else he might have in mind.

I flash Erma a smile. It's probably best to do as she says. And to avoid annoying her too much.

"Leave her to me." Erma's icy glare fixes on me. "I will see to it that she's kept busy."

"Thank you, Erma," my father replies, stepping away from the desk and turning to me. He pauses, examining me carefully, as if he expects me to wreak havoc upon the Grand Library. "Be sure to stick to the times I have outlined. Or else, the consequences will be dire."

"Dire as in suspension? Or expulsion?" I know I risk his wrath for asking, but I can't help it. I need to know what's at stake. In case I accidentally sleep in too late on a Sunday morning. Or something else of the sort.

My father doesn't deign to answer the question. Without another word, he storms up the stairs.

Now I am left at Erma's mercy.

Hopefully she won't make my life too difficult. While she has scolded me plenty of times, she scolds many adepts every day. Surely she doesn't bear a personal grudge against me?

Any hope I had is dashed when she points to an enormous stack of books. It towers so precariously I think it may topple over if I breathe too suddenly. And if that happens, Erma will make me pick them all up. I approach with caution.

"These books have been left out by good-for-nothing adepts like yourself," she says, giving her current tome a particularly forceful stamp. "Each one needs returning to its rightful place."

I do my best not to grimace. Putting them all away will mean countless hours of running around the Grand Library. But if I show any sign of reluctance, she will assign me far worse tasks. Like reorganizing the topmost shelves.

Since resistance will worsen my sentence, I give Erma the most enthusiastic nod I can muster. "Yes, ma'am!" With that, I scoop up the books lying at the top of the towering pile.

"Get to it then," Erma growls.

I don't hesitate and set to work before she can bark out another command.

I glance down at the first book in my arms. '*The Origins of Medeicus, the Arcane Language of Magic, by Alward Brayton*' is scrawled onto its cover in cursive script.

I scurry over to the right wing of the library which contains books concerning the languages of Imyria. Besides Medeicus, the Grand Library is home to books on the different Elvish dialects of Lumaria, Alanor, and Fenyr Forest; the human languages of Selynis, Valka, and Tirith—though the latter's is also known as Common; and the Orcish tongues of both Jektar and Dromgar. Even the holy language of the Selynian Priestesses is featured in our books.

The only language which can't be found inside the Grand Library is Abyssal, the dark tongue of demons.

But long ago, our shelves would have been filled with grimoires of forbidden magic. Over a thousand years ago, when Nolderan was first established, the original magi hadn't shied away from practicing dark magic.

That was until the Lich Lord arose, a former Archmage of Knowledge. His quest to eradicate all life from Imyria almost succeeded.

Since then, Nolderan has strictly forbidden all forms of dark magic.

Or at least, that's what my History tutors have spent the last two years lecturing me about.

I scan across the nearest bookshelves, looking for where this one on Medeicus is supposed to go, but I only find books on Orcish and Elvish here.

My search takes me deeper into the Grand Library's right wing, and I pass a book with beautiful illustrations painted onto its cover. It depicts the shadowy trees and ever twinkling stars of Lumaria, the land of eternal night where the moon elves dwell.

I set aside the three heavy books I'm carrying, and my fingertips trace over the artwork. Even my mother would be jealous of the artist who painted this cover. With how lovely these illustrations are, I can only imagine how breath-taking Lumaria is itself.

Unfortunately, I have yet to visit. The Magi of Nolderan have little to do with the elven continent of Belentra, despite the moon elves having taught the first magi how to wield the aether in the air and in their blood. Our broken relationship with Lumaria is because the Lich Lord was once an Archmage of Nolderan and they blame us for his crusade against the living. My History teachers mentioned that the relationship between Nolderan and Lumaria became strained after that.

While my father receives ambassadors from all over the world, including even a few orcish Stormcallers who come from the lands beyond the three human kingdoms, I have only heard of him meeting one Lumarian ambassador.

It was five years ago, shortly after my father banished Heston for practicing necromancy. I suppose that's what Lumaria wanted to discuss, especially since they distrust us after what happened a thousand years ago.

I sneaked inside the Arcanium—a bold move considering this was long before I became an adept—and waited outside my father's meeting room all day for a glimpse of the Lumarian ambassador. She stood so tall that she dwarfed even my father. Her dusky purple skin shimmered like crystals, and her long silver hair billowed like streams of moonlight.

And her eyes were nothing like ours. Her eyes shone much brighter, her iridescent irises glowing with blues and purples. Her appearance captivated me so greatly that I forgot I was supposed to be hiding. My father scolded me for sneaking into the Arcanium, but

I didn't regret it. Glimpsing a moon elf for the first time was more than worth suffering his fury.

Footsteps sound from behind, snapping me from my daydream. I glance back, but I can't tell whose they are. Nonetheless, I retrieve my stack of books from the nearby shelf. Just in case it's Erma, already checking on my progress.

I peer at the books in my arms. The cursive letters of *'The Origins of Medeicus'* stare back at me.

I swallow. I've not yet returned a single book, and there are dozens to work through. If I don't hurry, Erma will soon be informing my father of my idleness. And then I will be granted a punishment far worse than assisting Erma or being suspended for a month.

Whatever that might be.

The books on the history of Medeicus, the language of magic which magi speak to invoke their spells, lie at the far end of this aisle.

I tilt back my head and examine the highest shelf. The books are arranged alphabetically, and authors with surnames beginning with 'A' and 'B' can be found at the very top. There's a gap between two tomes which looks the same width as this book's spine. Since I can see no other such gaps, that must be where this book lives.

I lift *'The Origins of Medeicus'* in one hand and balance the rest of the books in my other. "*Atollo.*"

Violet light envelops the book and raises it to the very top shelf. The magic fades as the book slots into place.

I watch it for a moment, hoping that my spell was accurate enough and that the book won't lose balance and come tumbling down.

It doesn't.

I turn on my heel and continue on, traveling to the next section of the library.

Though I return the next two books faster than the first, I soon realize a more efficient method is required. Or else it will take until midnight to tidy away all the other books.

I return to the Grand Library's main chamber and set to work with categorizing the stack of books. The steady thud of Erma's stamp sounds behind me. I half expect her to complain that I'm wasting time, but she doesn't.

When I finish organizing the tomes, I gather as many geographical books as I can carry and hurry over to those shelves.

There are now far more adepts inside the library. That must mean the fourth-years, whose lessons run until six o'clock on Thursdays, have finished for the day.

My lips pull into a smile as I weave in and out of the aisles, distributing the books as quickly as I can. Arluin will be here shortly, and at least gazing at him will make this punishment more bearable. Provided that Erma doesn't catch me staring at him.

But it isn't Arluin I first find.

Just as I turn a corner, I almost collide with Kaely. I nearly drop the books I'm carrying, half from surprise and half from fury.

I can't have been here for more than an hour, and yet Kaely has managed to locate me.

Didn't she go home with her father? Wasn't he meant to lecture her about not making light of necromancy?

I suppose I should expect nothing less from Archmage Branvir Calton.

Kaely's lips distort into an ugly sneer. "So, it's true. They've not even suspended you."

"Kaely," I hiss, my fingers clawing into the leather covers of the books. "What are you doing here?"

"I'm also an adept of the Arcanium. Is it a problem if I visit the library after lessons?"

My jaw tenses. She's not planning to continue taunting me, is she? Hasn't she already caused enough disruption today?

"You may go wherever you please," I grind out. "But stay out of my way."

"Or what? You'll strike me with a fireball again?"

While I can't use my magic against Kaely, I can whack her over the head with the heavy tomes I'm holding. That wouldn't break any of the city's laws.

But it would mean Erma reporting my unruly behavior to my father. On the very first day of my sentence.

I can't afford to lose my temper for a second time today.

"Just leave me alone, Kaely," I snap, pushing past her. But like earlier this afternoon, she refuses to let me go so easily.

"You should have been expelled from the Arcanium for your crimes!" Kaely calls after me, daring to raise her voice to a level that will enrage Erma.

I halt and turn back to Kaely. A vicious scowl distorts her freckles.

"You were bold to strike me with your magic in broad daylight," Kaely jeers, "and there were dozens who witnessed it."

"Just as they witnessed the insults you hurled at me."

Her nose wrinkles in disgust. "The reason you were spared is because you're the Grandmage's daughter. It seems I'm the only one who can see this injustice."

"Even now you continue to spew hatred." I cling to the books I carry, not trusting my hands to stray from their leather covers. I can't allow my anger to burst free again. "Kaely, what have I done to deserve the way you treat me?"

"You're the Grandmage's daughter," she blurts, her fists tightening. "You're lazy and useless, and you're not a good sorceress. Yet to everyone else, especially our tutors, you're someone special. But it's only because of your father. He's the Grandmage, not you. Why do you deserve such reverence? You haven't earned the right."

I shake my head in disbelief. "So, this is the reason you hate me? Do you think it was my choice for my father to be the Grandmage of Nolderan? Do you think I can help how others treat me? If it bothers you this much, then the next time anyone praises me, I'll tell them they should instead praise Kaely Calton because she can't control her irrational jealousy. Actually, no. I doubt even that would suffice. How about I ask my father to disown me and take you as his daughter instead, since you can't bear the fact that I'm the daughter of the Grandmage of Nolderan and you're not?"

A deep shade of crimson paints Kaely's face. Fury blazes in her magenta eyes. If she came here to goad me into losing my temper again, then she has failed greatly. If only my mind and my tongue were sharper earlier this afternoon.

"Reyna Ashbourne," she spits, "I have never known anyone to think more highly of themselves. Your arrogance disgusts me."

"My arrogance disgusts *you*? Have you not looked in a mirror lately? I think you'll instead find that your arrogance outshines every-one in the entire city."

"You—"

"That's enough," a male voice calls.

Too focused on Kaely, I didn't hear any footsteps approaching. When I turn, I see Arluin behind us. Frost shrouds his expression. The muscle at his jaw twitches as he meets Kaely's eyes, refusing to give her even an inch of ground as their stares lock together.

"Arluin Harstall," Kaely chides, her stare unrelenting as she speaks, "what a surprise. It seems you have your dog on a tight leash, Reyna."

"Leave us," Arluin hisses through his teeth. While my fury burns like wildfire, his is stone cold.

"You don't scare me, *necromancer*."

Arluin steps closer to her, his expression still frosty. I doubt even Kaely will succeed in melting it. I've never seen him lose his temper.

But there's a darkness in his eyes which makes me tremble. All I can think about is what he confessed to me yesterday. About the magic his father taught him, the crimes he himself has committed, and the secrets I swore to take to my grave.

Kaely's shoulders jerk back as he approaches. She would never admit it, but there's fear in her gaze. Whatever I can see in Arluin's expression, she can see it too.

"What are you going to do?" Her tone doesn't reveal her unease. It's as brash as always. "Kill me and raise me from the dead, just like your father reanimated corpses from graveyards?"

"Yes," Arluin breathes, mere inches from her. His voice is so quiet it's barely a whisper. "That is exactly what I will do. I'll kill you and bring you back from the dead as a mindless ghoul, forced to obey my every command while the very flesh rots upon your walking corpse."

Biles creeps up my throat. Especially as his face twists into an expression so wicked even Kaely's pales in comparison.

He terrifies me.

It's an awful thing to admit. That the boy I love, the boy I will marry, frightens me so much that a chill rattles through my bones.

I shouldn't be thinking this. I shouldn't fear him like everyone else. But I feel only horror.

Kaely stumbles back. A strangled noise escapes her throat as she stifles her fear. She whirls around, searching for witnesses. But aside from the three of us, only the books heard Arluin's terrifying words.

"You . . ." Her voice quivers. "You wouldn't dare. You would be banished. Just like your father. Or worse."

Arluin arches a brow. "What makes you think I fear banishment? Or even death? Do you dare test me?"

Kaely draws in a shaky breath. She opens her mouth, but no sound comes out.

Never have I seen her lost for words.

I should relish in her fear. But I feel only dread.

"You're still standing here?" Arluin sneers. "You wish to become my undead pet?"

Kaely stares at him, her eyes wide with horror, as if she can't believe what he's saying. When Arluin's lips curl into a wicked smile, she turns and flees without hesitation.

I gaze at the empty spot where she stood. I can barely breathe. Fear still imprisons me. I must banish it. Or my reaction will hurt him.

But I don't know how to shake away the dread coiling through my stomach.

Arluin draws closer to me. I try not to shudder as he takes my hand. As his thumb brushes over my cheek.

"I just heard what happened this afternoon," he murmurs. "I'm sorry I didn't come sooner. Are you all right?"

I can only manage a stiff nod.

I am a horrible person. He stepped in to defend me, is worried for my sake, and yet I can barely stand the feel of his touch.

I force myself to meet his eyes. Magenta. They are magenta, and not the color of death.

He must see the fright in my expression since his fingers leave my cheek. His hand releases mine.

"You're scared of me." Arluin takes a step away, his throat bobbing as he swallows. "Aren't you, Reyna?"

A wave of guilt crashes into me, and I shake my head hastily, the gesture likely too forceful to look sincere. "No," I lie, "I'm not scared of you."

Arluin heaves out a breath and runs his fingers through his loose, dark curls. "I didn't mean what I said to Kaely. I heard rumors of what she said this afternoon, and with the way she was talking to you now, I just . . ."

"I know," I say, not meeting his eyes as I reach for his hand. I focus on his fingers and the way they feel against mine. "I know. It's all right, I promise." I hope he can't hear the trepidation in my voice and that my words sound more convincing than they do in my head.

"I'm sorry," he whispers, his shoulders sagging.

And I am sorry, too. But I don't tell him that. Because it would mean admitting my fear.

I close the distance between us and wrap my arm around him. I press my head against his chest, staring down at the hardened leather covers bundled in my other arm.

Arluin returns my hug, and we remain like that for a long while.

He's not a monster. I know he's not. If he were a monster, how could his embrace be so comforting?

His fingers curl around a stray strand of my hair. "What time will you finish working for Erma?"

"By nightfall. But I doubt she'll let me leave until I've finished returning all the books."

"I was going to study for a few hours, so I'll wait until you finish."

"I'll stay at yours tonight," I say, wanting to return the atmosphere to normal.

His lips brush the top of my head in a soft kiss. I give his hand a squeeze before we break away, and I return to the task of tidying away the stack of books.

CHAPTER 10

RETURNING ALL THE BOOKS TAKES me several more hours, and we don't leave the Grand Library until long after nightfall. The Arcanium is mostly empty now, though we pass a few magi as we cross through the atrium.

We step beyond the pillars at the Arcanium's entrance, and the night breeze washes over my cheeks. Having spent far too long inside the library, the cool night air feels refreshing.

Our hands entwined, we wind down the spiraling stairs and continue past the statues lining the path out of the Arcanium. When we reach the archway with the words QUEL ESTE VOLU, PODE NONQUES VERA MORIRE etched into its stone, we come to a stop. Arluin pulls me nearer and closes his eyes, conjuring aether in his fingers.

Before he can finish casting his teleportation spell, I tug at his arm.

"Let's walk back," I say.

"Aren't you tired?" he asks. "Erma had you running around the entire library."

"She had me running around so much I can't even feel how tired my legs are. My head is the most tired. Hopefully some fresh air and a gentle stroll will wake me up enough to cook. I can't even remember when I last ate today."

"I'll cook."

I snort. "How? You can't cook."

"I can."

"Your cooking tastes awful."

"It tastes fine to me."

I cast him a dubious look. "Then not only am I worried about your cooking skills but also your taste buds."

"There's nothing wrong with my cooking, nor with my taste buds."

"Fine," I say with a shrug. "I'll cook for myself and you can cook for yourself when we get back. How's that?"

Arluin presses his lips together and hesitates for a terribly long moment.

I flash him a triumphant grin. "See? You prefer my cooking."

"Though I can't deny the fact you're a superior cook, that doesn't mean I'm incapable of cooking."

I shake my head. And he calls me stubborn.

"Come on then," I say, pulling him through the archway. "Tell me what's left in your pantry, and I'll think of something nice to cook us both."

As we continue along the cobblestone road and turn left down Lenwick Street, Arluin tries to remember what he has left in his pantry. His memory is excellent with useless facts such as what years various kings died, but it's awful at holding essential information such as what food he has.

But our conversation is soon cut short.

Halfway back to Arluin's manor, I once again feel the same suffocating presence I felt two nights ago.

I stop, my breaths ragged. I squeeze Arluin's hand tightly, my knuckles whitening with the strain.

"What is it?" he asks as I whirl around, frantically seeking the source of this terrifying presence.

Finally, I find it.

A hooded silhouette stands amid the shadows of a darkened alleyway.

"There!" I hiss, pointing at it. Maybe I should act more cautiously, but this time I'm determined for Arluin to see the figure. To prove it isn't a figment of my imagination.

The shadowy being lingers long enough for Arluin to glimpse it. His shoulders stiffen.

Then the silhouette is gone.

We both stare into the shadows where it disappeared. Neither of us says anything, our minds too wrapped up in our own thoughts.

"Who would be stalking us like this?" I mutter after a long pause. "It can't be Kaely, can it? From what she said earlier this afternoon, it sounded like she's been following us around."

Despite my words, I'm not convinced it's Kaely. She looked petrified of Arluin's threats, and this presence feels like that of dark magic.

I shiver.

Arluin releases my hand and scratches his chin as he thinks. "You could be right. Maybe she seeks retribution for how I threatened her." But I hear the note of doubt in his voice.

"Maybe she's following us around in the hope she'll find something to wield against us?" I say.

I pray that it is Kaely. Because if it isn't her, I dread to think whom it may be.

Arluin's fists tighten.

I know what he might be thinking. And I hope with all my heart he's wrong.

"To determine whether it's Kaely or not," he continues, "we will need to investigate further."

I suck in a sharp breath, staring into the darkened alleyway once more. "You want to follow them?"

Arluin doesn't answer. He clenches his jaw and strides into the shadows. Leaving me alone.

Though he's only a few steps away, the air grows much colder. I pull my cerulean robes tighter around myself and hurry after him.

I know it's foolish to chase phantoms, but I doubt it's wise to remain here by myself. Staying by his side is far safer. He is, after all, one of the most talented adepts in the Arcanium.

His footsteps ring out across the cobblestones. I wince at the sound. If his intentions are to ambush the mysterious figure, he isn't going about it the right way.

The streets grow narrower and darker. We race deeper into the tangle of alleys which sprawls through the Upper City. Too focused on trying to keep up with Arluin's furious pace, I almost fall over a stack of discarded crates. With how weather-worn the wood is, it seems they've been left out for some time. I don't stop to inspect them, though. Arluin is already turning the corner ahead. I sprint faster so he doesn't disappear from my sight.

His furious pace continues until we reach the end of that next street. Our path forks, and he glances around in search of the hooded silhouette.

I open my mouth, wanting to persuade Arluin to cease this pursuit and return to his manor before we're led any deeper into Nolderan's alleyways. But before I can speak, he's already off, running down the street to our right.

"Arluin!" I call. He doesn't seem to hear me.

Grimacing, I hurry after him.

One day he really will be the death of me.

We soon reach a circular sewage grate that has been cast aside. Arluin stands before the dark hole, peering into its depths.

"They wouldn't have gone down there, would they?" I whisper.

Arluin raises his head and examines the dark alley ahead of us. I don't want the shadowy figure to reappear but if it does, I would prefer for it to emerge from behind the corner. I dread the thought of going down into the sewers.

But no matter how much Arluin stares at the dark streets around us, the silhouette does not appear.

His attention returns to the sewage grate, and his expression hardens into steel.

"Please tell me you're not planning on going down there."

If the hooded figure disappeared down there, it can't be Kaely following us. She would never lurk in the sewers.

Going down there would be madness.

"I need to look," Arluin murmurs. "I need to be sure."

"You need to be sure of what, Arly?" I ask, my fear heightening. "We have no idea what's down there. We need to return to the Arcanium now. My father is probably still with the ambassadors. We'll tell him a cloaked figure has been following us. That the presence surrounding them can only belong to a dark sorcerer."

Arluin stares into the sewers, inhaling deeply. Then, before I can stop him, he leaps into the darkness.

I grit my teeth, glancing around at the shadows. If the hooded figure didn't disappear into the sewers, then I don't want to be left standing here. Maybe they're planning to strike me right now, seizing their opportunity while I'm separated from Arluin.

I curse him under my breath.

For such a seemingly clever man, he really is so stupid.

Rather than jumping straight into the hole, I slide over the edge and use the metallic rungs to steady my drop. My feet meet the stone beneath.

A putrid smell fills my nostrils. It's hard not to gag.

"*Iluminos*," Arluin says. A brilliant orb of aether spreads from his fingers. It floats above us, illuminating our surroundings with its dazzling light.

We stand on a narrow platform cut into the stone. It overlooks a canal of water which ensures sewage and rainwater run out to sea.

"There's nothing here," I whisper. Despite how soft my words are, they echo throughout the tunnel. "Come on, please, let's head back to yours."

"Don't you hear it?" Arluin asks, closing his eyes as he listens.

I fall silent and strain my ears as I try to discern anything but the rush of water.

"What—" I begin but stop. Because I too finally hear the noise coming from deeper in the sewers.

It's a rumbling. No, a growling. And it doesn't sound like it comes from only one being.

My pulse quickens. "Please," I beg him. "Please let's just go."

"There's something down here."

"I know. That's why we'll immediately report it to my father. We're adepts, not magi. We should let those who are more experienced deal with this."

But he only ventures farther into the sewers, the floating orb illuminating his path.

I follow him for a few strides, dread growing with every step until it becomes too much. Even if Arluin is a talented sorcerer, I have no idea what lies ahead of us. And whether we will be outmatched.

We must turn back now, before it's too late.

But Arluin refuses to listen to me. I will have to leave him here, though I hate the thought of abandoning him. My father needs to know something dark and rotten dwells within Nolderan's sewers.

I turn and race back to the hole we came through. This part of the tunnel is cast in darkness now that Arluin's orb has drifted away. I glance back, wanting to tell him that I will meet him at his manor. Hoping that he will see sense.

But then, the shadows hiss. They swirl and obstruct my path. From them, the hooded silhouette emerges.

I take a step back.

Darkness pours out, thick and heavy like foul smoke. When I draw in a breath, the air suffocates me.

"Where do you think you're going?" a man demands, his voice frighteningly familiar. Before I can respond, or teleport to safety, he raises his hand. "*Vorikaz.*"

Dark magic flings toward me. Obsidian chains wrap around me so tightly I fear they will snap me in half. I struggle beneath the bindings, but my arms are pressed into my sides and I can't move them at all.

Nor can I use any magic.

I can feel aether humming in the surrounding air, but it refuses to answer my call. The obsidian chains sever me from my magic.

"*Laxus!*" Arluin cries, appearing between us. Aether blooms in his palms as he prepares to unleash an attack on the hooded figure. "Release her at once!"

"Or what?" the man taunts. His deep laugh rumbles around us, echoing down the endless, dark tunnel.

Arluin's heels dig into the stone beneath, refusing to yield. But before he can release his magic upon our enemy, the shadows shift, spinning into clouds of darkness.

From them, a dozen more figures appear. Humans, orcs, and elves form their ranks. All are clad in black robes, and the same terrifying presence oozes from them.

Arluin can't defeat them all. Even if I were not bound by these chains, the odds of success would remain impossible.

A group of dark sorcerers lurk in Nolderan's sewers and threaten the safety of our city. My father must be alerted immediately. Before it is too late.

"Go!" I cry to Arluin. "Teleport to the Arcanium. Tell my father. Now!"

Arluin doesn't heed my words. The aether in his hands shines brighter, moments away from unleashing a spell upon our enemies.

But fighting them is futile.

"He looks the spitting image of you, my lord," says an orcish woman. She stands to the right of the hooded figure. Her skin is ashen green, and her white hair is woven into many long braids.

"He does?" the hooded man replies. "I've always seen more of his mother in him."

Horror hits me like a sudden blow to the chest. I can't breathe.

My legs betray me by giving way, and I tumble to the ground. Stone strikes my knees, and sharp pain jolts through them.

I stare up at the hooded figure, praying against all sense that I am wrong.

Shock too slams into Arluin. His eyes widen, and his mouth falls agape. The aether in his hands fizzles out and returns to the dark air. His shoulders tremble as the man strides toward him.

He throws aside his hood. The illumination orb high above shines over his face.

He shares Arluin's dark curls, though silver dusts his hair, and their bold jawlines are identical.

There is no denying their blood relation.

A cruel grin stretches across Heston Harstall's face, and his gray eyes gleam. "You are much taller than I remember, my boy."

CHAPTER 11

"Father," Arluin gasps.

A draft blows through the sewers. It carries with it the stench of death and decay.

"I have waited years for this moment," Heston says. "For our reunion."

The grimy walls sway. Numbness washes over me. I no longer feel the stone slabs digging into my knees.

Heston has returned. And he brings with him a cult of necromancers.

I know not what they plan. Only that they will doom my city.

Dark magic erupts from Heston's hands. "*Vorikaz.*"

Obsidian chains fling at Arluin. They bind him as tightly as they bind me.

"What are you doing?" Arluin exclaims. He writhes against the chains, desperately trying to shake them off, but they constrict. A sharp exhalation shudders through his lips as the chains give his chest a forceful squeeze.

"Taking precautions. Though I have missed you greatly and have thought of you every day, I fear you may not have missed me in return."

Arluin doesn't reply. But I know he missed his father. He told me that much yesterday.

I don't know whether Heston can see through Arluin's expression. His gray eyes rake over Arluin as he tries to discern his thoughts.

A sudden bout of courage ignites in my heart. Before fear can snuff out the small flame, I force myself to confront Heston.

"What do you want?" I demand, hoping my words sound stronger than they do in my head. "Why have you dared to return to Nolderan when my father exiled you? When he made it clear that if you were ever to return, he would execute you on the spot?"

Heston tears his attention from Arluin and scrutinizes me instead. I try to conceal my fear with an icy mask, but it begins to crack as his cruel eyes bore into mine. "To see my son. All fathers share the same grief over being separated from their children. Your father is no different. And this is the greatest weakness of the Grand-mage of Nolderan." The edge to his voice tells me he intends to exploit this weakness.

I shrink back, but there's nowhere to run. Not with these heavy chains and the dozen necromancers looming over me.

Blood thrums in my ears, urging me to fight with the only weapon I have left. My words.

"If you so much as lay a finger on me, my father will see to it you die a painful death, Heston." I spit his name with all the disgust I can.

"You already said he would execute me simply for breathing Nolderan's air, girl. What difference does it make if he will kill me, regardless?"

I have no retort. Not that one would improve my current situation.

I am bound with chains and cut off from my magic. So far beneath the streets, no one would hear if I scream. No one but Heston and his necromancers. And Arluin, who is as helpless as me.

If Heston decides to kill me right now, there's nothing I can do to save myself.

I stare up at him, trembling beneath the chains. I wish I could stop. But I can't.

"Don't look at me like that," he chides. "Tonight, you will serve an invaluable purpose."

"W-what purpose?" I hate how my lower lip quivers. But I'm no longer in control of my body. Fear shackles me more tightly than the obsidian chains.

"You will see," he simply says. The malice in his eyes fills my heart with dread. I don't know how it continues to beat. Especially so frantically.

I pull my gaze from Heston and look across to Arluin. He stares at his father as if he's seeing a ghost. His face is the color of bone.

He fears his father, and what is to come. Just as I do.

We should never have ventured down here. We should have gone straight to my father. If we had, we wouldn't be bound by Heston's chains, our magic cut off from us.

Nausea crashes into me. Have our actions already doomed Nolderan?

"I believe that's enough reunions for one day," Heston declares, turning to his necromancers. "We still have a city to sack and a Grand-mage to slay."

My father.

I barely hear the responding sneers. The drum of blood deafens my ears. Saliva tastes like ash in my mouth.

If Heston threatens my father with my life, I fear what choice he will make. And what Nolderan's fate will be.

Heston gestures to his necromancers, and two step forth. They haul me onto my feet and shove me farther through the tunnel. I feel weightless, as though I'm drifting over the stone.

As though I'm no longer here.

We enter deeper into the sewers, toward the growling. I think I know what it belongs to, but I don't dare to admit it—not even in my own mind. Because thinking that thought would make it real.

I edge closer to Arluin, though that's difficult with the necromancers escorting us. But I get close enough.

His head is lowered, his shoulders sagged in defeat. He must feel my gaze on him since he turns to me.

Fear and guilt cloud his magenta eyes. "Reyna," he murmurs so quietly I barely hear him over our footsteps, "I am so sorry."

At first, I don't know how to respond. This is his fault. If we hadn't come down here, we wouldn't be captured by Heston.

But I'm also to blame. I knew what a stupid idea it was, yet I followed him all the same. I should have immediately teleported myself back to the Arcanium. I should have left him. Nothing awful would have happened to him. Heston would never hurt his own son.

Or at least, I think he wouldn't.

Nonetheless, I squeeze my eyes shut and say, "This isn't your fault."

When I dare to reopen my eyes, his shoulders are taut with tension. "I won't let him hurt you."

All I can manage is a small nod. It isn't that I don't trust the sincerity of his words, it's just I know he's speaking from his heart and not his head. Heston's spell prevents us both from casting magic. And our arms are too tightly bound to wield a knife against him.

There is nothing either of us can do.

The growling becomes louder. As does the rattling of bone against stone.

Finally, we arrive at the source of the noise.

The sewers swarm with hundreds of corpses. Some are skeletal, without even a lick of flesh on their bones. Others are half-decayed, and the rotten smell of death wafts from them. All their eye sockets are empty, aside from the shadows swarming within.

The guttural growls, the clattering of bone—it all proves too much.

I double over and vomit across the stone. The sick splashes onto the robes of the nearest necromancer. His nose wrinkles at the sullied hem. He's a sun elf, evident by his pointed ears and golden hair. His tanned skin is sallow, however, and his eyes aren't bright like the few sun elves I've seen strolling the streets of Nolderan.

The elven necromancer looks at me from above his hooked nose and snarls, "Get a move on." He shoves me forth before I have the chance to compose myself.

Heston comes to a stop before his horde of undead and raises his hand. The rabble falls silent and still at his command. Hundreds of empty sockets stare back at him, awaiting his orders.

"Grizela, Virion," Heston calls. The sun elf who escorted me steps forth, as does the orcish woman with braided white hair. "It is time."

"Yes, my lord," they answer, bowing their heads.

"When you have completed your task, return here."

The two of them disperse into shadows. Dark magic hurls through the sewers swifter than any wind spell I can conjure.

"The rest of you," Heston continues, "take your positions. Wait for the signal and then direct the undead to begin their rampage. Raise all the fallen and rejoin us north of Lenwick Street. We need the numbers to take the city."

The remaining necromancers obey his orders, each taking a portion of their forces with them. Some undead remain behind with Heston.

"Impressive, isn't it?" Heston says to Arluin, when all the necromancers are gone. "I must admit, stealing corpses from graveyards without the magi noticing was no small feat."

I want to tell him that he's monstrous, that his wicked plans will never succeed. But I can't. I can do nothing but stare at the horde of shambling undead.

Arluin says nothing. He too watches the masses of decayed corpses.

Heston's patience quickly thins. "Do you have nothing to say to me, boy?"

Arluin pauses. He inhales sharply. "You left me." His tone isn't accusatory. It's flat and hollow, devoid of emotion.

"I was exiled. What choice did I have?"

"You could have taken me with you. Instead, you left me here to be shunned."

"Is that what you wanted?" Heston asks. "To leave behind everything? Everyone?"

Arluin says nothing. I feel his gaze drift over to me.

"That's what I thought," Heston mutters.

Explosions roar high above. They come from somewhere in the distance. The Lower City.

My stomach churns.

Heston's mouth twists into a cruel grin. "And so it begins."

Before either Arluin or I can demand to know what the necromancers have done, Grizela and Virion emerge from the shadows.

"It is done, my lord," says the orcish woman. "The magi and their guards are rushing to the Lower City to control the fires raging through the streets."

"Then we make our next move." Heston turns to me and sneers. "Time to pay my old friend a visit."

He grabs my shoulder and drags me through the crowd of undead. I try to resist, but he only pulls me more violently.

As we pass the mangled corpses, I keep my eyes lowered to the stone floor. But the rotten toes and skeletal feet are almost enough to make me vomit again.

"What of this one?" Virion calls to Heston.

"Leave my son down here. Bind him to a rock if you must."

"Again you abandon me," Arluin spits.

Heston halts.

"Let me help, Father."

At his words, my blood chills.

Arluin doesn't really want to help his father, does he?

When I turn to him, I hope to see something in his expression which indicates his words are a ploy to earn his father's trust. To enable our escape. But I see nothing. Only tempered ice.

The threat he paid Kaely echoes through my mind. That he would kill her and raise her corpse, just as his father taught him.

What if he meant every word he said?

"Help?" Heston scoffs. "How would you help?"

"You said you need the numbers," Arluin says. His eyes remain cold, not betraying his true thoughts. "You know I can raise the dead. Let me help."

Heston's hand tightens around my shoulder. "Are you prepared to betray the one you love?"

Arluin's gaze meets mine. Silently I beg him not to do this. Not to follow in his father's footsteps. His eyes soften. But only for a heartbeat. Then they freeze once more.

His attention returns to his father. "You are my blood," he says. "This city has shunned me since you left, and I care little for it. Allow me to play a part in its destruction. Don't turn your back on me again."

Heston watches him for a long, careful moment. Arluin stares back at him, unflinching.

"Very well," Heston says. He waves his hand and the obsidian chains around Arluin crumble away, freeing him. Dark magic returns to the shadows. "Do not make me regret this."

"I won't, Father."

CHAPTER 12

Heston shoves me through the sewers. Arluin follows close behind, while Grizela and Virion lead the clamoring undead. Our path is lit by the ghostly white light radiating from Heston's hand. The shadows dance around us as the spell flickers.

We soon reach a sewer grate larger than the one he lured Arluin and me down. Heston comes to a stop and peers at the metallic plate above us. He extinguishes the light, and darkness descends over us.

"*Arisga*," Heston commands.

A bolt of dark magic slams into the sewer grate and throws it aside. The metallic plate clatters as it shudders into a nearby wall. I examine the steel rungs leading up to the surface. Maybe Heston will release me from the obsidian chains so that I can climb up to the streets. If he does, maybe I can try to run or teleport away.

But Heston grants me no such chance. He grips my arm.

"*Farjud.*"

Shadows consume us. When I glance down, I can no longer make out my physical self beneath the cloud of darkness.

In the next instant, we are rushing through the air.

Solid ground greets my feet. The shadows fade away to reveal Nolderan.

We are deep within the side streets winding through the Upper City. Few lights shine through the windows at this late hour, and most folk will be tucked in their beds, oblivious to the threat looming over them.

Arluin appears from the hole next, the two necromancers behind him. Then the undead scramble out, piling on top of each other as they fight to enter the realm of the living.

"Grizela, you take that road," Heston says, pointing to the street which veers to the left. "Virion, take the other."

The two necromancers wordlessly follow his command and lead the undead through the streets, beginning their destruction of Nolderan. With their dark magic, they tear through the magical enchantments which secure houses. The ghouls are free to pour inside, their ravenous hands outstretched as they search for the living.

Screams erupt through the night. Grizela and Virion weave in and out of the houses, raising the corpses inside. The undead rampage ahead, leaving a trail of fresh bodies for the necromancers to reanimate.

It doesn't take long for the horde of undead to double in size.

So many lives will be lost tonight. If the undead are not stopped soon, this could mean the end of the magi.

Of Nolderan.

Heston watches his undead storm the streets. When the path has cleared, he urges me onward.

In the distance, fire rages through the Lower City. Smoke billows into the sky and suffocates the stars. Even when Heston drags me down several streets, his undead destroying everything in their path, I find no guards. They must still be focused on containing the destruction sweeping through the Lower City, unaware of the real danger.

By the time they realize, it will be too late. Heston's army will already be of an unimaginable size.

The streets widen as we approach Lenwick Street. The Arcanium's spires peek through the cobalt roofs.

Is my father inside? Or has he too been summoned to the Lower City to deal with the fires?

"*Gelu'tempis!*" a mage cries to our right.

A blizzard of frozen needles rains over us.

"*Ekrad!*"

Heston draws the shadows over us, forming a shield and preventing the blizzard from reaching us. When the mage's attack subsides, he releases the shadowy barrier.

Arluin steps forth. Aether swirls in his fingers. It crackles, spreading into ice.

I can't let him do this. I can't let him condemn himself.

If he chooses this path, he will become as monstrous as his father.

I open my mouth to scream, but no sound comes out. Terror mutes my tongue.

Arluin shapes the ice into a sword. "*Gelu'gladis!*"

He unleashes the frozen blade.

The mage draws aether into his fingers. But it's too late.

Arluin's icy sword strikes him through the chest.

The mage falls onto the street. Blood wells around the chunk of ice lodged inside him. He gurgles and chokes as he desperately tries to tear the frozen blade from his chest.

The life in his eyes soon fades. As does the magenta glow of aether.

The buildings spin around me.

If Heston wasn't gripping my shoulder and holding me in place, I would have collapsed onto the street along with the mage.

Arluin killed him.

Horror strangles me. I choke in its grasp.

When I finally tear my gaze from the corpse and look at Arluin, his face makes my blood curdle.

His expression remains indifferent. He has killed, and yet he does not care.

I can no longer believe this is an act. The Arluin I know is no murderer. He would never kill just to earn his father's trust. How can he stand there with such an icy expression? Has he killed before? Is that another secret he has never confessed to me?

He gathers the shadows into his hands—the same shadows his father wields.

"*Arka-joud*," he hisses. Dark magic pours over the mage's corpse.

I scream until my voice falters. Until my throat is raw and broken.

Arluin is a necromancer. As wicked as his father.

All along, I was blind to the truth.

The shadows wash over the mage's corpse. They gouge out his eyes and replace them with orbs of darkness.

The mage's fingers twitch first. Then he sits up. His head hangs limply as he stares at the ice piercing his chest. The surrounding blood has dried and blackened.

The corpse stands. He peers at his new master with his unblinking shadowy orbs.

"Go," Arluin commands. "Purge the living from these streets. Do not stop until all are dead."

The fallen mage turns and joins the rest of the undead as they rampage through the streets. He doesn't attack with his hands and teeth like the other ghouls. He conjures bolts of darkness and hurls them at any in his path.

Pride plasters across Heston's expression. "A wight? How impressive. I feared you would fail to raise a mere ghoul, let alone a wight." Heston grins. "You will prove a greater asset to our cause than I expected, my boy."

Arluin dips his head.

I don't look at him again.

Grizela and Virion soon rejoin Heston, and the number of undead with them has tripled. They march down the road and turn onto Lenwick Street.

More necromancers gather here. Together they have turned a hundred ghouls into an army so large I fear Nolderan stands no chance against them.

Many wights now fight the magi alongside the ghouls. They return the bolts of frost and fire with bolts of darkness. And when the magi fall, the necromancers raise them as another wight to fuel their army of the dead.

Heston remains at the rear of his onslaught. As does Arluin, raising so many ghouls and wights that I'm certain his eyes will turn from magenta to gray at any moment.

The magi surround the undead, slowly pushing them back. Hope surges in my chest. Maybe Heston won't win this fight. Maybe Nolderan will stand strong.

But that hope soon falters.

Heston releases my shoulder and strides into the sea of corpses.

"*Arka-kyrat!*" he shouts.

Shadows sweep over the fallen, magi and undead alike. As the dark magic touches them, each rises once more.

Even if the magi defeat a ghoul, Heston and his necromancers reanimate it—unless it was burned to ashes. Attacking the undead is futile. The only way Nolderan will succeed is if the necromancers fall. But the magi concentrate their attacks onto the foes nearest them, not onto the necromancers who remain far behind their undead minions.

Hands grab me, spinning me around.

I lift my head to see Arluin. As I look at him, I can only think of all those he has killed. All those he has risen from the dead.

After what he has done, how can he gaze at me with such softness?

Aether blooms in his hands. He closes his eyes and presses his index finger to the center of my forehead.

"*Mundes.*"

His spell cleanses the dark enchantment Heston cast on me. The obsidian chains wither away, returning to the shadows from which they were made.

I blink, unable to believe that he has freed me. That though he wields dark magic and has killed so many innocents, he has decided to save me.

Was this all an act? Did he resort to these measures so that his father would drop his guard? So that he would have this single chance to free me?

I want to believe that's the case. But I can't shake away the horrors he has committed.

Concern and fear fill his eyes. Fear for me.

Despite all he has done, gratitude blossoms in my chest.

"Go!" he whispers, just as Heston turns and witnesses his betrayal.

His father bellows with rage and merges with the shadows, charging straight for us.

I stumble back, my hands clasping Arluin's tightly.

"Arly," I gasp. I can't let go of him. If I do, I may never again hold his hand.

"*Rivus!*" Heston snarls.

Dark magic surges toward us.

"*Muriz!*" Arluin calls, forming a barrier of aether around us. The shadow bolt slams into the wall. He grits his teeth, desperately holding the shield in place. "Reyna, go!"

I know I must go, but I fear what will happen to Arluin. How his father will punish him for this treachery.

Arluin glances at me from over his shoulder. Desperation strains his brow.

Heston stalks nearer, anger blazing in his gray eyes. If I hesitate for a moment longer, I will be unable to escape. Arluin's efforts will be in vain.

I draw in a shaky breath and turn my back on Arluin, fleeing down the nearest alley. My heart pounds as I run. Blood thunders in my ears.

"After her!" Heston barks.

Shambling footsteps hurry after me. As do guttural growls. I don't look back to see what ghastly creatures Heston has sent. I run as fast as I can, unable to pause long enough to mutter *laxus* and teleport to safety.

I reach the end of the narrow street. But before I turn the corner, I hear a cry of pain.

Arluin.

My pace falters. I glance back. Heston looms over him, shadows encasing them both.

I don't have time to stop and see if he is moving—whether he is alive. The ghouls and wights are almost upon me.

I break into a sprint once more. Tears spill onto my cheeks, blurring the alleyway. I run so hard that breathing burns my nose and my throat.

I can't slow, not unless I wish for Heston to capture me again. To serve as my father's undoing.

Neither can I allow Arluin's sacrifice to be for nothing.

I choke at that last thought and pray that I'm wrong, that Heston would not kill his only child. The reason he turned to necromancy was to revive his wife. Surely a man who can't let go of his loved ones will be incapable of killing his son, no matter how much the betrayal may infuriate him.

I tell myself that over and over as I run. Yet I cannot shake away the fear snaking through my mind, threatening to extinguish any hope for Arluin's survival: The Heston who has returned to Nolderan is not the same Heston who was exiled five years ago, and there's no telling what a man as wicked as him will do.

The footsteps of the undead draw closer. And louder. Fatigue sears through my legs. Though I tire, the restless undead do not. Their strides quicken, gaining on me.

I will not last much longer.

If only there was enough time to teleport away before the ghouls reach me. Maybe I can cast a fireball but in my haste, it would be weak. Then what will I do when they are upon me and I'm unable to cast a second spell as their decaying hands wrap around my neck? As their teeth rip through my flesh?

The street opens to the main road. I suck in a breath. The air scolds my throat. It feels like swallowing venom. Ahead, a crowd of magi fights the undead. If I can reach them before my pursuers catch me, maybe I will stand a chance of survival.

Drawing in air and forcing my legs onward is becoming increasingly difficult. I don't know how many more steps I can take. I glance back to see how close the undead are.

Their gnarled hands are mere inches from me.

I return my attention to the path ahead. But I am too slow. One cobblestone is broken and juts out. When my foot meets it, I am thrown off balance.

I slam into the ground. My shoulder hits it first, the one Kaely injured. It isn't fully healed yet, and the resulting pain is excruciating. Though trying to move is unbearable, I force myself to do so.

But the undead are already upon me. And there is no time left to run.

CHAPTER 13

THE UNDEAD STALK TOWARD ME. Their strangled groans sound almost like sneers.

"*Muriz!*" I cry. Aether wraps around me.

The ghouls crash into the barrier. Ravenous growls echo through my shield. I hug my knees, staring up at the decayed faces.

I am trapped, surrounded by a horde of undead that seeks to return me to Heston. And that's if I'm lucky. Maybe they will misinterpret his command and return my half-eaten corpse to him.

And Arluin . . .

I squeeze my eyes shut, lowering my head.

I fear his fate, and whether I am soon to follow him.

A shadow bolt slams into my shield.

My gaze snaps up. Three wights stand behind the ranks of ghouls. Each utters *rivus* in its unnatural voice, and their calls reverberate off the narrow stone walls. A barrage of shadow bolts hurls at me.

My shield won't hold off their attacks for long. Cracks are already emerging in the crystalline barrier, and it shudders from the bolts of dark magic. Aether dust scatters into the wind.

Then the shield splits apart, falling around me.

And I am left entirely exposed.

I crawl back. The ghouls advance. Scraps of blood and flesh lie between their teeth and under their nails.

I gather more aether, preparing to blast the ghouls nearest me and praying I can also fend off the wights. But before I can, a shout comes from behind.

"*Ignira!*"

Flames surge forth, taking the shape of an enormous fireball. The spell skims over my head, singeing my hair with how close it sweeps. It slams into the ghouls.

The blast gives me enough time to scramble off the ground and return to my feet. I sprint to my savior, my breaths ragged.

It is my mother who stands there. Her long dark hair and magnificent magi robes flutter in the wind. She raises her hands, weaving aether into a wind spell. "*Ventrez!*"

A gale throws the undead back.

"Mother!" I choke out, clasping her hands when I reach her. Fresh tears burst from my eyes.

"Reyna!" She clutches me, pulling me into a hug. "Are you hurt?"

I shake my head. Though I'm not physically hurt, the images of Arluin raising the dead, of him falling at his father's hand, wrack through my heart. And I fear I will never repair.

"Thank the Heavens," my mother mutters, holding me tighter.

Our embrace is short-lived. The undead climb back onto their rotten feet and lumber toward us. Their blood-curdling howls echo through the night.

My mother pushes me behind her. I peer at the undead beyond, feeling more like a helpless child than a second-year of the Arcanium.

"*Gelu'vinclair!*" Frost swirls from her fingers and spreads across the street, covering the ground like a thick blanket. The ice winds upward, wrapping around their legs and freezing them in place. The ghouls snap their yellowed teeth at us, but the frozen shackles prevent them from taking another step closer.

Though my mother's spell renders the ghouls harmless, the wights remain a threat. They call out *rivus* in their guttural voices and launch shadow bolts at us.

"*Tera'muriz!*" The ground obeys my mother's command and rises into a wall of stone. Her earthen shield absorbs the volley of dark magic.

Then she snaps her fingers. "*Tera'quatir!*"

The stone wall shatters. Rock rains over the undead.

The spell crushes many of our enemies, but more close in from behind.

With my mother fending off the wights ahead, I whirl around to deal with the new threat.

"*Quatir!*" I cry. An explosion of aether rips through the air, slamming into the ghouls. It provides me with enough time to cast my next spell.

"*Ignir'alas!*" Flames spread from my fingers. They stretch into the scorching wings of a phoenix. The spell sweeps into the night and crackles through the dark air.

Then it descends at a terrifying velocity.

Fire roars. Smoke billows. Ash blows through the evening breeze as the flames obliterate the ghouls.

I glance back at the alley where the undead pursued me. They too burn from my mother's conjured flames. Even the wights.

It seems fire works best against these ghastly creatures.

My mother grabs my hand. She pulls me down the road, toward a large crowd of magi.

But we only manage a few strides before the air hisses to our right.

Heston appears from a cloud of shadows. Fury burns in his gray eyes.

"*Ekrad!*" he snarls.

Darkness spins from Heston's fingers. It warps into a towering wall and cuts us off from the group of magi.

Heston's mouth curls into a heinous smirk. "Mirelle Ashbourne. It's been a while."

"Heston." Aether dances in my mother's palms, ready to strike. "You will pay for what you have done."

"Will I now?" Heston barks out a laugh. "And who will I answer to? Nolderan has all but fallen, and its Grandmage will soon share the same fate."

"You're gravely underestimating my husband. Your vile magic will never stand a chance against him."

"You put too much faith in one man, my dear. What will he do when the lives of those he cares for most are at stake? I will force his surrender without needing to cast a single spell."

"If only Narla could see you now," my mother says, gritting her teeth, "what a monster you have become."

"Then it's a blessing she can't see me now." He raises his hand. Darkness gathers. "*Rivus.*"

A shadow bolt hurdles toward us. My mother draws aether into her grasp. "*Telum!*"

Her attack meets Heston's. Aether and darkness explode, ripping through the air. The resulting gust almost throws me off-balance. Both spells annihilate each other, and their remnants dissolve into the atmosphere.

Before my mother can conjure her next attack, Heston hisses, "*Gavrik.*"

A murder of crows envelops us. Shadowy birds swoop from all angles. Their caws pierce through my ears. Razor-sharp talons and beaks tear at our robes, seeking blood and flesh.

We use our magic to blast the phantom crows with aether and flames. Until finally, the spell is shattered.

We emerge from the cover of darkness with tattered robes and scratched faces. But the attack inflicted no fatal injuries on either of us.

"*Muriz!*" my mother yells.

Aether encases me. The barrier is as thick as the Arcanium's ancient stone walls.

I press my hand to the shield. Magic hums furiously beneath it. Beyond the barrier, undead stalk toward my mother.

"Your father," she gasps between shouting *ignira* and battling the ghouls nearest her. "You must tell him Heston is here!"

I swallow, the strained note in her voice hard to bear.

She is greatly outmatched. And if my father doesn't arrive soon . . .

I banish the thought. I can't let fear distract me.

I close my eyes and exhale deeply, focusing on my breathing. Aether sparks in my fingers.

Creating a mind-link works similarly to teleportation. The difference is that I must instead imagine the person I wish to communicate with in meticulous detail. I learned this spell recently, and I failed many times during practice.

I can't fail now.

I first imagine my father's magnificent robes and the golden thread running through the indigo fabric. Then I add his auburn hair and beard which ripple around his face like a lion's fiery mane, and also a deep crease in his brow as he frowns at me. Finally, I complete my image of him with the vivid glow of his magenta eyes and the crystalline staff he always clutches.

"*Aminex* Telric Ashbourne," I whisper when I finish painting the mental portrait of my father.

I hold my breath, fearing that maybe my magic hasn't worked. Or that maybe my father hasn't heard my call above the chaos raging through Nolderan.

But after several long heartbeats, he finally replies.

"*Reyna?*" His voice echoes through my mind.

"*Father!*" I exclaim, without the syllables physically leaving my lips. Conversation via a mind-link flows as easily as thoughts, heard only by those it's cast between.

"*Where are you?*" His words are hurried. To answer my call, he would have needed to clear his mind, just as I did. And that means he cannot fight the undead while our mind-link is being channeled.

"*With Mother. Heston—he's here!*"

"*Where is here?*" comes his frantic response.

"*Somewhere along Lenwick Street. North. I came through an alley. I think—*"

Before I can offer more information, a scream shatters my concentration. The mind-link falters.

A shadow bolt pierces my mother's chest. The veins in her neck blacken and throb as the poisonous magic seeps through her blood. Her eyes bulge from their sockets, blood-shot and swollen.

"Mother!" I leap onto my feet and push against the aether shield. But it refuses to move. No matter how desperately I try to rush to my mother's side.

Her hand reaches out for me. Then it falls.

Swollen eyes stare at me. She doesn't blink.

I slide down the aether shield. I don't feel the impact of the ground.

Heston steps over to where my mother lies.

"*Arka-duat.*"

A stream of shadows floods into her nostrils, filling her corpse with dark magic.

My forehead presses into the barrier. My fingers dig into it.

The shadows darken. They swarm upward and form a figure which resembles my mother.

A wraith hovers above my mother's body. Its features are identical to hers, except it is born of shadows and not flesh and blood.

"I only need one of you to render Telric helpless," Heston says. "And this way he will know the consequences of failing to surrender."

I crawl away, my eyes not leaving my mother's spectral form. My back hits the other side of the aether shield, preventing any further retreat as Heston and his undead stalk toward me. The spell my mother cast to protect me now hinders my escape.

I shove my shoulders into the solid wall, hoping it will give way beneath my weight. The energy continues to hum. No cracks show. Panic overwhelms me.

Shadow bolts smash into the shield. They come from Heston and his wights. And my mother too, or at least the wraith of her.

Stiff fingers claw at the aether barrier. Ghouls surround me from every angle.

I conjure what flames I can, knowing fire magic is the most effective against the undead.

My shield shatters.

The ghouls advance. I open my mouth, but there's no chance to speak any spell-words.

"*Ventrez!*" a voice rings out from high above.

A wind sweeps under my feet, lifting me from the ground before the ghouls can reach me.

The gale blows me up onto the cobalt roofs and gently sets me down beside the Grandmage of Nolderan.

My father clenches his crystalline staff with both hands, his knuckles ivory white. The veins in his forehead throb, and his shoulders quake with rage.

His wrath is so ferocious I fear flames will sweep from him without him speaking the spell-words, and that they will be born of a fury so wild, they will obliterate even me.

Though his magical presence is terrifying as he stares down at Heston, the undead and my mother's corpse, I cling to it like a blanket.

"Mother," I choke out, my body wrought with grief.

He places a hand on my shoulder. "Stay here." Then he releases me and raises his staff. "*Muriz.*"

Aether swirls out, covering me with a dense shield. Despite the immense energy humming around me, I know this spell cost my father only a fraction of his strength.

"*Laxus.*"

In the next instant, he appears on the streets below, standing opposite Heston. His teleportation spell is complete before I can blink.

"*Muriz,*" the grandmage mutters again. This time aether sweeps across my mother's body, protecting her from further violation. He swallows hard, staring at her body beneath the aether shield. His hand trembles from both grief and wrath.

"Heston," he growls, "how dare you return to Nolderan."

"I missed my boy," Heston says with a shrug.

I clench my fists. Fresh tears well within my eyes. All I can see is Heston standing over Arluin. I still don't know whether he is dead or alive.

"What you have done . . ." My father inhales sharply. "My wife—your crimes are unforgivable. There's no retribution great enough for your evil. Even the Abyss has no place for one as heinous as you."

Heston laughs. "I really am terrified, oh mighty Grandmage. How do you expect to save your city when you couldn't even save your wife?"

My father lets out a roar of fury, which turns into the word *ignira* halfway through.

Flames rush toward Heston. He raises his hands, and the shadows shift around him in a shield. "*Ekrad,*" he whispers.

His wall of darkness is wide enough to protect himself and the undead nearest him from the scorching flames. But the fireball doesn't collide with Heston's shield. It continues past and slams into my mother's wraith.

Fire rages across its shadowy form, eating away at the darkness. The wraith lets out a piercing shriek. Though the scream is unnatural, I hear the traces of a voice which sounds like my mother.

I squeeze my eyes shut, unable to watch as the fire consumes her and sends dark magic scattering through the air like soot.

When I finally dare to reopen them, the wraith is gone.

My father's jaw tightens. His gaze lingers on my mother's unmoving face.

"I *spared* you," he spits, turning back to Heston. "The punishment for your crimes should have been execution, but I instead exiled you. And this is how you repay me?"

"You expect me to be grateful for what you did?" Heston snarls. "You banished me. You stole everything from me. Tonight you finally tasted the bitterness of loss, and you cannot bear it?" More dark magic gathers in his hands. "*Rivus.*"

A shadow bolt surges toward my father. The wights nearest Heston imitate the attack, and a volley of darkness rushes at him.

"*Ignir'muriz.*" A wall of fire erupts around him, absorbing the attacks. The dark magic shrinks back.

My father drums the end of his staff against the ground. The sound thunders through the street and echoes off every wall.

"*Ignir'quatir.*"

The flames explode, blazing toward the undead.

Heston only has enough time to shout *ekrad* and conjure a shield to defend himself, leaving the rest of his undead exposed to my father's attack. The fire consumes their decaying bodies. Thick smoke blows into the air, as does the smell of charred, rotten flesh.

My father's spell is so fearsome it leaves the cobblestones streaked with charcoal.

Though Heston's shield protects him from the brunt of the blast, it throws him off-balance.

"*Tera'vinclair,*" my father calls before Heston can retaliate. The street rumbles. A shock wave charges forth. When it reaches Heston, the ground lifts and encases him in stone chains.

The necromancer roars with fury as the earthen manacles bind him to the street. He draws the shadows into his fingers, but before he can utter any spell-words, my father unleashes more flames upon him.

"*Ignir'alas.*"

Fiery wings sweep up, gaining velocity in the air. Then they crash down to Heston, who is unable to defend himself.

He screams as the ardent flames engulf him, as they lick the flesh from his bones. Beneath the fervid amber light, his silhouette struggles against the earthen restraints. But the shackles do not relent. Neither does my father.

"*Ignira.*"

An enormous fireball rushes from my father's hands and obliterates whatever remains of Heston.

His dying shrieks ring through the night. I fall to my knees. The hard cobalt roof tiles slam into me.

Though this monster murdered my mother, I can't bear to listen to him burn.

But he soon falls silent. Then there's only the crackling of flames.

And Heston Harstall is dead.

CHAPTER 14

FOR A LONG WHILE, I just stand there, gazing down at the streets below. It could be minutes or hours that pass. The firm ridges of the cobalt tiles dig into my knees. But I feel no pain. Numbness spreads over me. Ash whirs around me. The smell of death fills my nostrils.

A vague thought arises in the back of my mind: I'm likely breathing in Heston's incinerated remains. The realization should nauseate me. But I feel nothing. Not disgust. Not rage. Not even grief.

Just emptiness. Like I'm no longer here. Like the images racing through my mind are only ghosts of a nightmare I dreamed.

My father steps toward my mother's unmoving body. He waves his hand, and the aether shield around her disappears. As does the one encasing me.

"*Laxus,*" I breathe, my voice coarse and broken.

The teleportation spell washes over me and transports me to the street. My father stands ahead of me, and as I watch him fall to his knees, it feels as though more than a few feet separate us. As though I'm peering at him through a clouded window. I want to step toward him, but my legs refuse to oblige.

His crystalline staff drops from his hand. It falls onto the cobblestones. The clatter rings through the street. And over and over through my mind. Beneath it, I can scarcely hear the death and destruction beyond. Fires simmer in the Lower City. Before, they were raging infernos. Now they are flickering embers, their amber glow streaks the night sky. The unnatural howls of the undead sound in the distance.

But this street is silent and still. Just like my heart, my mind.

"Mirelle!" he chokes, cradling my mother in his arms. Anguish rolls down his cheeks. Somewhere far in the depths of my mind, it occurs to me this is the first time I've seen my father cry. And it only makes me hollower, until I can no longer feel the ash dancing over my face.

Like a statue, I stare at my father as he grieves, the shattered pieces of my heart unable to grieve with him. Unable to even feel guilt for failing to do so.

Dawn pierces the darkness, bringing with it a new day. Golden rays blaze through the sky, igniting the clouds. It's as if the Heavens are enraged by the horrors wrought upon us last night.

Footsteps sound from down the street. My father slowly raises his head as they approach. My neck is too stiff to move, so I turn my eyes in their direction.

Archmage Branvir Calton marches toward us. A dozen magi follow him.

Branvir comes to a stop before my father. Shock flashes across his face as he notices my mother's body.

No one says anything. Not my father, not Branvir, not any of the magi with him. A morning breeze sweeps over us. It brushes through my hair, sullied and knotted by last night's chaos.

Archmage Calton finally breaks the silence. "Grandmage," he says, dipping his head. "We have managed to capture two of the necromancers. They have been secured for questioning."

"And the others?" My father's voice is shaky, far from his usual strength.

Branvir hesitates. "We have so far been unable to locate them."

"Find them," he growls. "Then incinerate them all."

Branvir's gaze turns to me. "And the boy?"

"What boy?" my father demands.

"Heston's boy. It is reported that he raised the dead alongside the necromancers."

Arluin.

Fear penetrates the hollowness like a knife. My heart, which was so frozen it barely beat, now pounds furiously in my chest.

My father looks at me. "Is this true?"

I say nothing, lacking the strength to lie. But I refuse to condemn Arluin with my words. There must be something in my gaze that gives me away, since my father's face turns to stone.

"Kill him too," he grinds out. "Kill every last one of them."

Branvir's eyes return to me. I meet his stare. Our icy gazes lock together.

I must find Arluin before he does. Whether he is dead or alive, I do not know, but I will not let anyone harm him.

He saved me. And yet they would execute him for it.

Branvir's nostrils flare. I know he can see it in my expression, what I intend to do. My father must see it too. He sits upright, horror filling his magenta eyes. Horror that I would seek to save the son of his enemy.

I grit my teeth and pull aether into my grasp. It flickers like purple flames, fueled by my frenzied heart.

"Reyna!" my father shouts, his voice thick with worry. Worry for me or for what I will do, I don't know. Nor do I have time to contemplate it.

I must find the boy I love. The boy I have sworn to marry, no matter what.

"*Laxus!*" I cry.

And before any of them can stop me, I fade into aether.

Blood pounds in my ears like relentless drums of war. But the war upon Nolderan is already over. Now only a few undead remain, and magi blast them into smoke and ash with conjured flames.

A sea of bodies stretches before me. They are of varying states of decay and mutilation. A thousand dead faces stare at me.

Everything spins.

I think the ground might be rushing toward me, but I refuse to let it win.

I force myself to remain upright and wade through the depths of death. I try to avoid the bodies, but I still feel the softness of flesh and the brittleness of bone beneath my boots. The sensation threatens to collapse me, but I cannot save Arluin if I allow myself to faint.

I must find him. Quickly, before Branvir and his magi track me here. I must ensure he escapes Nolderan.

And if he is dead . . .

No.

He can't be dead. We made a promise to each other. He wouldn't break it.

I arrive at the alleyway where Heston's undead pursued me. I come to a halt upon the spot where Arluin freed me, where he fell.

I scan across the lifeless faces, but I don't see Arluin's. Nor do I see his raven curls amid the mountain of corpses.

I try farther along the street. But even when I search the street after that, I still find no sign of him. Neither dead, nor alive.

I remain there for a while, staring down into the stream of bodies.

I should feel relief at not finding Arluin's corpse. But I only feel hollow. As hollow as I felt while gazing down at my mother's broken body.

I don't know where he is, and I have no proof of his fate. And it is the not knowing which threatens to break me.

I must find him. Whatever it takes, I must.

With the street swaying around me, I stagger toward the nearest heap of bodies. Then I begin the task of rolling them away. Each and every one. Not caring how their too-cold skin feels against mine. My mind is bursting from the seams with one single thought: that I must find Arluin. No matter what.

I roll aside an elderly lady, her unseeing eyes staring up at the approaching dawn. Beneath her lies a boy, no older than ten. Dried blood trails across his cheek. Bites mangle his arms. Bone glimpses between the torn flesh.

I don't linger on him. Because I next spot dark curls.

"Arluin!" I gasp, reaching for him. I pull with all my strength, willing for him to part from the mass of bodies. He comes loose and rolls to me.

My stomach clenches. I think I may vomit. But I don't. I can't.

I turn his head toward me. The dark curls fall away—

To reveal a face that looks nothing like Arluin's. The man's brown eyes gaze up at me. Unblinking. His nose is too hooked to be Arluin's, and he's at least a decade older.

The tension in my stomach slips away. I slump back onto the bloodied street.

For a moment, I was certain it was him. And now I'm grateful it is not. Even if it means another man lies in his place. Another loved one snatched from someone else.

If he isn't here, amid the stream of corpses flowing through the street, that means he is alive. And if I don't find him before my father, before Branvir, before the Magi, he will be killed.

I squeeze my eyes shut and block out the noises drifting through the street: the guttural howls which grow fainter and fainter, the crackling of flames which now sounds like distant whispers. Aether flutters through the wind, and after all the magic used and the lives lost last night, the air is even more abundant with it. I draw the humming energy into my fingers.

Then in my mind, I paint Arluin in as much detail as I can. His glossy curls that look as though they're carved from onyx, his magenta eyes, his bold brows, his soft chuckle as he laughs at something I said.

When his portrait is achingly vivid, I release my spell.

"*Aminex* Arluin Harstall."

I wait. And then I wait a moment longer. But there is no response.

I try the spell again. And again. Yet no matter how many times I try, the only voice in my mind is my own.

If he's alive, why would he not respond? Why would he let all my frantic calls go unanswered?

Unless his silence means that he's dead. And that the reason I can't find him is because his body has been reduced to ash.

I sit there huddled on the street, surrounded by countless corpses. My entire body trembles. Cold sweat drips from my skin.

The sun rises higher in the morning sky. Its bright rays bask the white walls of Nolderan in a golden glow, and it makes the cobalt roofs ripple like sapphire waves. A new day is upon us, yet I remain chained to the night before. The events play over and over in my mind, an inescapable echo of the past. I watch as Heston murders my mother and raises her as a wraith. I watch as Arluin reanimates the dead before falling himself.

I would give anything to forget it all, to rid my mind of the ghastly images which haunt me.

And then the unbearable truth slams into me. I choke, suffocated by the terrifying realization.

My mother is gone. I will never again watch her paint.

And Arluin is gone, too. I may never know his true fate.

Tears burst from my eyes, bitter and heavy with anguish. It's as though a dam has burst apart. Before, my heart was numb, unable to grieve, unable to feel anything. But now I feel everything all at once.

Pain pierces through my heart like a dagger. My chest feels like it's being torn from the inside out. My breaths come out as sharp gasps as I struggle to breathe.

A part of me considers falling back onto the street with the corpses and letting exhaustion consume me.

I hear footsteps. I think it may be Branvir and his magi, having tracked me down in the hope I will lead them to Arluin.

But Arluin isn't here. I'm not even certain whether he lives.

I don't turn to look as the footsteps continue pacing toward me. As they pound furiously against the street, breaking into a sprint.

"Reyna!"

It is neither Branvir nor my father's voice which calls my name. It is Eliya's.

She shouts my name again. I still don't move. She slides down beside me on the ravaged street. She pulls me close, and blood coats her hands as she clasps me. Grief blurs my sight, but I see the crimson stains blemishing my cerulean adept robes. It isn't my blood. I don't know whose it is.

Eliya says nothing as she hugs me. Though we sit amid this horrifying stream of dead bodies, she doesn't flinch. Last night, she probably witnessed enough terrifying images to haunt her for an entire lifetime. Just as I have.

"They're dead," I croak out. By now, the sun shines upon us with its full radiance. "They're both dead."

Eliya pauses, stroking the back of my head. I can barely feel her fingers. "Who's dead?" Her voice is little more than a whisper, as though she can't bear asking such a terrible question.

I stare down at my blood-stained fingers. At first, words fail me. "My mother," I gasp, my heart thudding as I relive her death. "And Arluin . . . I think he . . ."

Eliya doesn't respond. She hugs me tighter.

We stay there for a while. The summer sun shines gloriously upon the street. I scarcely feel its warmth across my cheeks. The gentle heat begins to bake the bodies around us. Magi and guards soon appear, clearing away the ruins and corpses which litter the streets.

After some time, Eliya helps me to my feet. Her arm secures my balance. If not for her, I would have already fallen back into the stream of bodies. In fact, I wouldn't have stirred at all.

"Come on," she says softly. "Let's get you home and cleaned up. Sitting out here on the street won't do you any good."

I know she's right. Staying here will achieve nothing. I will only get in the way of those who are clearing the streets and trying to return Nolderan to a state of normality.

But I don't want normality. It would mean accepting that my mother, that Arluin, are both gone. I would rather stay out here on the streets, dwelling on what has already passed. Because I can't bear the bitterness of the present and would rather keep on rejecting it.

Despite all this, I let Eliya guide me away—if only because I lack the strength to resist. I am but a fallen leaf flowing down a stream, allowing the water to take me wherever it pleases.

Eliya draws aether into her hand. With her other, she clasps my arm.

"*Laxus,*" she says and then we drift into the wind.

We become one with aether, floating through the folds of time and space—through the fabric of reality. But since I already feel weightless, I don't really notice the sensation.

My manor manifests before us. The elaborate gates stand tall, no different from any other day. The two winged lions on my family crest roar at each other as they always do.

I hate how normal everything looks. That my manor is untouched by the destruction which wrought through the city and the darkness which murdered my mother.

"Reyna," Eliya mutters, nudging my shoulder. It's only now I realize that the enchanted gates won't open for her and that we have stood here for some time.

I squeeze my fists. I don't feel the sharpness of my nails against the softness of my palms. I could be drawing blood, and I would not know.

"Reyna Ashbourne," I force out. Each syllable is a tremendous effort. Yet I heave them all out, and the aether shrouding the gates glistens in response. They swing wide open, and Eliya guides me through.

She leads me along the path which winds through our gardens. I hate the colorful flowers blooming everywhere. The pansies, the tulips, the primroses, the marigolds—I hate them all. They are too vibrant, too cheery.

They remind me of my mother.

The faerie dragons sweep up and down the gardens, ensuring the enchanted buckets thoroughly nourish each flower. It's as if nothing has changed—as if my mother is alive.

But she isn't. Heston killed her. He raised her from the dead with his vile magic. My father destroyed her ghost.

A sob wracks through my body. Eliya can urge me no further.

She lets me stand there for a while, as I cover my face with my hands so I don't have to look at my mother's bright and beautiful garden. I weep into them.

Finally she nudges me forth, and I'm so lost my body complies. I vaguely see Zephyr fluttering over to us. His head tilts to one side as he silently asks what's wrong, why tears streak my cheeks.

"Not now, Zephyr," Eliya mutters, waving him away.

But the faerie dragon doesn't leave. He watches as we climb up the manor's stairs. His violet wings beat back and forth.

Eliya opens the doors and helps me inside. Zephyr glides through behind me. Too busy helping me through the hallway, Eliya doesn't shoo him away.

We pass paintings as we ascend the staircase. Many are my mother's, and they depict quaint landscapes and delicate flowers. I can't bear to look at them and keep my gaze fixed on the steps. My fingers curl around the polished bannister, and I use it to haul myself up. Zephyr's wings flap behind us.

She guides me through to my room and sits me down on my bed. Zephyr perches next to me.

Lavish golds and creams decorate my room. The cabinets are all gilded with flourishes, and an embroidered rug stretches across the marble floor. Eliya presses the switch beside the door, and the aether crystals high above flicker on. Their brilliant light makes the threads weaved through the rug shimmer like sunlight.

I stare blankly at the rug.

Eliya says something and then leaves. Since I don't catch her words, I don't know where she's going.

Zephyr nestles into me, his head resting in my lap. His amaranthine eyes stare up at me, quizzical yet concerned.

I tentatively run my fingers across his head, just between his antennae. His azure scales are smooth and cool beneath my skin. The motion is more soothing than I expected, so I stroke him again. Zephyr growls softly, his forked tongue flicking out with contentment.

His eyes shut, and we remain like that until Eliya returns.

She carries a porcelain bowl and sets it onto the counter beside my bed. Her eyes scan across the crimson stains which mar my robes. "Let's get you out of that."

I give her a small nod, but don't rise. I stop stroking Zephyr, however. He lifts his head and peers at me.

"Zephyr, you'll have to move," Eliya says. "Reyna can hardly get changed while you're sitting on her lap, and she can't sleep in those robes, can she?"

He doesn't move. At least not at first.

Eliya glares at him until he slides from my lap and onto the silken sheets beside me. He rests his head in his talons and sulks at her.

She pays him little attention as she helps me out of my robes. Sweat and blood makes the fabric stick to my skin, and removing them takes several minutes. She finds a loose nightgown in my cabinet and helps me change into it. The material is silken like my blankets, but plainer and complete with thin straps.

I try to crawl into bed, but Eliya stops me.

"You'll get blood all over your sheets," she says, lifting my hand and inspecting the dried blood which coats my skin. "Let me help you wash it off."

Eliya leads me to the counter where she placed the porcelain bowl and gathers aether into her hands. "*Aquis*," she says. Water splashes from her fingers. She finds a cloth in the top drawer and dips it into the conjured water. After wringing it out, she sweeps it across my hands and face. The water is lukewarm as it glides over my skin. Some of the blood dissolves quickly. Other patches are so stubborn she has to scrub until my skin is so red and raw I think it may bleed and undo her hard work.

When I'm free of blood and dirt, Eliya lets me climb into bed. I wrap the blankets around myself and shiver. She casts me a pitiful look, but it soon falters as she yawns. I doubt she slept much last night, either. Guilt wrenches through me.

I don't know what she suffered from the attack—who she may have lost. And yet here I am, so weak and pathetic that she has to do everything for me.

"Did . . ." I begin, but my voice breaks. "Did you also lose . . ." Consumed by my own grief, I don't know how to ask such an awful question.

Yet Eliya seems to understand my meaning. To my relief, she shakes her head. "No," she replies. "No one."

A pang of envy plucks at my heart. The emotion vanishes as quickly as it appears. Though it's brief, I feel terrible for feeling it.

It isn't that I wish she lost anyone dear to her. It's just that I wish I were like her: that I hadn't lost both my mother and the boy I love in a single night.

"I'm sorry, Reyna." She scoops me into another hug. Her tears dampen my hair. "I'm so sorry that all this happened to you."

I don't hug her back. I stare at the tall mirror in the far corner of the room. Through it, I watch her hug me and wonder whether she feels guilt over losing nothing while I have lost so much.

I know I should tell her she has no reason to apologize. She didn't steal Arluin and my mother from me. That was Heston. He's the one to blame. But since he's already dead, what use is there in hating him for it?

And maybe my father also holds some of the blame. The punishment for practicing dark magic is execution, yet he spared Heston. If he instead executed him all those years ago, none of this would have happened.

Except Arluin would likely hate him for it. But my mother would be alive.

I let out a deep breath. In the mirror, I can see how broken I look. My skin is deathly white, and the rings around my eyes are so dark they appear bruised.

Eliya finally releases me and steps back, wiping her cheeks with her sleeve. "You should rest. As we all should."

I only nod, still unable to summon words to my lips.

Her gaze trails across to Zephyr, who is crawling up the bed to my side. "And you should come along as well," she says to him. "Reyna needs to sleep."

The faerie dragon buries himself into the blankets next to me. He watches Eliya out of one eye, daring her to move him.

"Don't think I don't know what you're doing."

Zephyr shuts his other eye in response.

"You're just being nice so Reyna feeds you more aether. But she really needs to sleep now, so you'd better not bother her."

His tail twitches.

Eliya pulls the embroidered curtains together, blocking out the sunlight, and she turns off the aether crystals on her way out. "Sleep well, Reyna," she mutters, closing the door behind her.

Then we are cast in complete darkness.

Zephyr nestles deeper into my side. I stare up at the shadowed ceiling, once more watching as Heston murders my mother. As he breaks Arluin with his wicked magic. Each time, I break a little more with him.

Gentle snores come from Zephyr beside me, and while it seems impossible at first, his sounds eventually lull me into a deep sleep.

CHAPTER 15

FIRE BLAZES THROUGH THE SKY, *and thick, black smoke shrouds the moon and stars. The smog clogs my throat as I try to breathe.*

The flames roar through the streets, ravaging all they touch. A large chunk of rock hurls toward me. I dart underneath, just as it comes crashing down. The sound booms through the street and rings through my ears. I don't stop to glance back at the heaped rubble. I just keep running.

My feet are bare, and I wear my thin nightgown. I sprint through bloody puddles. Crimson droplets splash up at me, staining the pale silk of my gown. Even though my feet and my ankles are slick with blood, I don't pause.

Heston—I must find him. Before it is too late.

Rain falls on me. But it isn't water which splatters over my shoulders. It is blood. The blood of all the lives lost tonight—all the lives that will be lost if I don't stop Heston before he claims everything and everyone.

Stiff fingers reach for me. Rotten claws grab my ankles and tangle through my hair. I shake them off and continue running.

I find no one else alive as I hurry through the streets. Only piles and piles of bodies, the undead feasting on their flesh. I almost vomit at the sight of a ghoul gnawing on a severed arm, but I can't stop for even a single heartbeat. I must keep running and running until—

The street opens to the Upper City's square. An enormous fountain lies at the center, as it always does. A mermaid perches on the top tier. Each marble bowl is carved into the shape of a clam. Stone benches are strewn around the fountain.

The square is empty. Except for Heston. He has my mother. He presses an obsidian dagger to her throat. The blade is serrated, and dozens of skulls are etched into the handle.

I halt. I stare at Heston, and my mother. There's a pleading look in her magenta eyes.

"Reyna," she whispers. "Go, please! Leave me."

Heston laughs as he draws the dagger across her skin and slices through her neck.

Blood gushes out like a waterfall. Her eyes widen, watching me until the very last moment when she slams into the ground. Then she doesn't move.

I scream until my throat is raw—until I can scream no more.

When I raise my head, it is no longer Heston who looms over her body and clasps the bloodied blade.

It's Arluin.

"Arly," I gasp, staggering toward him. I've searched all over the city for him, and yet here he is, standing right before me.

He doesn't respond. He grips the obsidian dagger and gazes down at my mother and the puddle of blood spreading around her. A wicked smile curls on his lips. I choke at the sight, but he doesn't turn to me. It's as if I've become invisible in this scene. As if I don't belong.

Then I notice his gray eyes, the same shade as his father's. Cold and dead: the mark of a dark sorcerer.

He is a monster, just like his father.

I shiver with horror and wrap my arms around my chest. My fingers become sticky with the blood coating me—the blood which the Heavens wept.

Footsteps sound from behind. I whirl around. It's my father.

His violet robes billow in the wind. Once magnificent, they are now sullied with blood.

"Father!" I shout, but he doesn't seem to hear me. He marches to Arluin.

"You," he snarls, aether crackling like lightning in his hands. "I will execute you like the vermin you are."

"No!" I scream, racing forth. My heart pounds to the same frantic rhythm as my feet. They slap against the slippery street, and I skid. The balls of my feet burn with the friction from the edges of the jagged stones.

But I don't reach my father in time to stop him.

"Telum!" he cries, unleashing a blast of aether from his fingers. He hurls it at Arluin.

My gut twists.

Arluin will die.

Even if he has become a monster, he is still the boy I've always loved. The boy who betrayed his own father to save me.

"Farjud," Arluin calls before the spell reaches him, melding with the shadows.

He slips through the blast as though it's merely air and not pulsating magic. His cloud of shadows penetrates the aether, and he materializes on the other side, inches away from my father. Now there is but a slither of air between them.

Arluin raises his obsidian dagger. He plunges it through my father's chest.

"This is for my father," he hisses as he twists the blade.

Pain shoots through my heart. It feels as if he has also stabbed me.

I scream loudly enough for Arluin to finally notice me. He turns and smiles. It isn't a smirk or a sneer. Just an ordinary smile.

And that makes it even more terrifying.

"Reyna," he says, stepping toward me. He holds out his bloodied hand.

I stumble back, tripping over my feet. But I don't hit the street.

I fall through the darkness of my grief.

There is no end. I keep tumbling through the emptiness until it finally claims me.

I jolt awake, my murderous heart thundering in my chest. How it does not explode and end my life, I do not know. In that moment, as I am lingering between the state of sleep and wakefulness, I think it will.

My skin is soaked. Not with blood like in the nightmare, but with a cold sweat. My breaths come out like gasps as I desperately suck in all the air I can, my lungs starved from all my screams. The scratchiness of my throat tells me I wasn't only screaming in my dreams.

Zephyr sits up and looks at me with his amaranthine eyes. They glow in the darkness. I stroke his head, and he settles back beside me, nestling in the silken sheets. I steady my breathing to the rhythm of my fingers running over his azure scales.

From across the room Mr. Waddles, the stuffed purple duck Arluin bought me for my sixth birthday, stares back at me. For several beats I glare at it, considering whether I should leap from my bed and throw it out the window. But I don't. The images I just witnessed were nothing more than cruel dreams. Not memories. They weren't real, and they never will be.

Arluin is gone, and I don't know whether I will ever see him again, except for in my dreams. And I hope I never again dream of him, because I hate how my treacherous heart twists him into a monster that he is not.

Instead of hurling Mr. Waddles out the window, I murmur *ventrez* and blow him into my lap. His lilac fur is patchy in many places.

As a child, I took him everywhere with me. That means he suffered much damage over the years, and some of his stitching has come loose. But I will never throw him away. Even when he is thread-bare, I will still cherish him. He's one of the few things I have left of Arluin, other than my memories.

And his locket.

I set Mr. Waddles on the pillow beside me and reach for the locket hanging from my neck. Since Arluin gave it to me, I haven't taken it off. That was only three days ago, and yet it already feels like an eternity has passed. In one night, everything has changed. My entire world has been torn asunder.

Now my mother is gone. Never again will I be able to watch her swirl her aether-imbued paints across her palette and bring mystical landscapes to life. Never again will I be able to turn to her when I am hurt. I must spend the rest of my life without her.

That single thought is enough to send fresh tears streaking down my cheeks. Their flow is obstructed by the dried ones from when I wept in my sleep.

My fingers run across the locket, feeling the edges of the silver heart. It is warm from being pressed against my skin. I consider opening the locket and allowing the memory crystal inside to play. But I decide against it, knowing that I will be unable to bear listening to the promise we made to each other only three nights ago. That we would marry when we have graduated from the Arcanium.

Now that seems an impossible thought.

Even if Arluin is alive, he can never return to Nolderan. Not after his father murdered my mother, not after he wielded necromancy against the magi. I'm certain he planned it all along, to ensure Heston lowered his guard long enough to free me. And though he became a monster to save me, my father will never accept that—will never believe it. As soon as he sets foot inside Nolderan, my father will execute him where he stands. He will burn him with the same flames he used to destroy Heston.

And that, all of that, is only if he lives. Because I can't be certain that he does. But if I allow myself to believe he is dead, then I will truly break.

I release the locket, and it falls back into the hollow of my neck. I lift Mr. Waddles and cradle him to my chest, lying my head back onto my pillows. My breaths are slow and steady, and the toy duck rises and falls to the same beat.

I gaze up at the shadowy ceiling, and once more, my nightmares arise. I feel a blade twisting through my heart, and I move Mr.

Waddles to check if the phantom knife is there. But there is nothing. My skin is intact beneath my nightgown. It's my grief which causes the sharp ache.

Realizing that my dreams will only further torment me, I slip from beneath the sheets and pace across the room to my cabinet. Zephyr doesn't stir, having already fallen back asleep, and my footfalls are soft. He will probably wake soon and demand aether crystals. Maybe Eliya is right about him, but I appreciate the company.

I return Mr. Waddles to the top of my cabinet and grasp one of the entwined handles, pulling open the middle drawer. I find a satin robe inside, and I wrap the pale fabric around my nightgown, securing it with the thin belt. Then I pad out my room and head downstairs.

My fingers trail across the bannister as I descend the staircase and use it to support my weight. My body is fatigued, and each step is a great effort. It's as though I haven't slept for even an hour, but the waning light filtering through the stain-glass windows tells me it must have been several. And that's assuming it is still Friday.

I find my father downstairs in the hallway. He is gazing up at one of my mother's paintings. This one depicts Nolderan's waves against a midnight sky, and a braided golden frame crowns the seascape. Her brushstrokes form dark waves of varying shades of deep blue and green, and sea foam powders the crests. The full moon shines high above, and the waves reflect the starlight. Like all of my mother's artwork, it's enchanted and appears more like a window than a painting. The sea rises and falls to a steady rhythm, and it laps against the shore. The pebbles stir as the waves meet them.

Judging by how stiff my father's posture is, it seems he has stood here for a long while. He doesn't stir as I come to a stop behind him and stare up at the painting as well. We stay like that for several minutes until he finally speaks.

"This was always her favorite," he murmurs so quietly that at first, I think he's talking to himself.

I give him a feeble nod. Though since his back is turned to me, he won't be able to see the gesture.

I already knew it was her favorite; she told me herself many times. It's why we display it at the very center of our hallway.

"It was the first one she painted after you were born," he continues, his gaze still fixed on the lulling waves. "That's why it was her favorite."

The way he talks about my mother, as if she is already long gone, fills my heart with more pain. I don't know how much more it can take. As I stare into the rolling waves, I watch her die all over again.

My weeping must be loud enough for my father to hear, since he turns and pulls me into a hug. I can count on one hand how many times my father has hugged me. Unlike my mother, he isn't particularly warm. Only his temper is.

Yet now he hugs me all the same, and it's clear in the way he embraces me that he needs the comfort as much as I do. I can also tell from his blood-shot eyes and ashen skin that he feels as broken as me.

"I'm sorry, Reyna," he says after a moment, his voice so laden with regret it sounds breathless. "I'm sorry I couldn't save her." He leaves many words unspoken, but I hear them all: that he is sorry he could not destroy Heston in time, that he is sorry he did not execute him five years ago, that he is sorry his mercy murdered my mother.

I say nothing. I know it isn't truly his fault, yet I can't bring myself to speak. I just stand there crying, my weight resting entirely in my father's arms.

After a while, when my tears stop falling, my eyes drift over to the arched window across from us. The sun slowly sinks into the horizon, casting us all in darkness.

"I'm sorry, too," I say.

My father frowns at me. "For what?"

"I forgot to go to the library and help Erma today. I'll go tomorrow morning and assist her all day. I promise I won't forget again."

To my surprise, my father shakes his head and hugs me tighter. "No, Reyna," he says, the words breaking as they leave his mouth. "You don't need to. You never need to again."

CHAPTER 16

MY MOTHER'S FUNERAL IS HELD on Sunday. Though I slept through all of Saturday, I appear no more well-rested as I stare into my mirror. My oval face appears narrower than usual, my cheeks sunken. Over the past three days, I have eaten nothing. Last night, I tried to eat but the first bite left me nauseated and I ended up returning to bed. My eyes, despite having spent most of this time closed, are puffy and swollen.

I wear a black lace gown that may have been beautiful if I were not wearing it to my mother's funeral. If she were here, she would insist on me using an illusion so I don't walk through Nolderan looking like a hideous wraith. And maybe I should, but I feel too fatigued to cast a single spell.

I leave the mirror as I am—with my long, dark hair barely brushed—and descend the stairs to the hallway. My father is waiting for me, his attention drifting across my mother's paintings as he paces back and forth. This morning, he wears black brocade robes with ornamental silver buttons decorating the high-collar. I can't remember the last time I saw him wearing anything other than his Grandmage's robes.

I've kept him waiting for some time, but he doesn't comment on it. He pushes open the grand doors of our manor, and we wordlessly step outside.

Even though my mother is gone, the faerie dragons still tend to our magnificent gardens. On Friday, I couldn't stand the sight of the brightly colored flowers, but today I stop and stare at them all. I can almost see my mother planting each with her own hands. While the flowers will bloom for a long time, thanks to the faerie dragons, they will eventually wither away.

"I'll plant them," I whisper. My father pauses and turns to the bed of violet pansies I'm staring down at. "Without her, our gardens will soon grow bare. So, I'll plant the new flowers when these ones die."

He is silent for a short while and then nods slowly. "She would like that," he mutters. The rushing fountain almost drowns his soft words. "She would like that very much. If her gardens were to wither away, she would blame us for not taking better care of it."

We stand there for a while longer before continuing to the enchanted gates at the end of our gardens. Since we are approaching from the inside, they swing open without either of us needing to command them.

The gates close behind us and then my father clasps my shoulder. He gathers aether into his other hand, and it's only now I realize he has left our manor without his staff. Today is one of the few occasions he ever has.

"*Laxus*," he says, and the manor fades away.

The pale purple light sketches the Upper City's cathedral. The needle spires stand tall and proud, and the many stained-glass windows depict the gods.

Though we aren't particularly religious here in Nolderan, Grandmage Delmont Blackwood was from the Kingdom of Tirith, where they worship the ten major gods. The magi do acknowledge the existence of the Caelum—beings of pure light energy who originate from the Heavens. Legend says they once walked our world before Meysus the Wise separated Imyria from the Heavens and the Abyss. While we believe in the gods, we do not revere them like we revere aether—the origin of everything in the universe. Including both the Caelum and Malum, since light and dark magic formed from the splitting of aether during the Primordial Explosion.

The cathedral's spires sway above me, and I am thankful for my father's arm as he guides me up the white stone steps and through the arched entrance. Like with the archway at the Arcanium's entrance, the words QUEL ESTE VOLU, PODE NONQUES VERA MORIRE are etched into the otherwise smooth stones.

As I reach the cathedral's final step, I glance back over my shoulder. A low white wall marks the cathedral's perimeter, and beyond that lies a crowd of somber and tearful faces. I don't recognize any of them; they aren't gathered here for my mother. Most likely, they await the funeral which will follow my mother's. I've been so wrapped up in my own grief that I almost forgot my father and I are not the only ones who have lost a loved one. Heston's evil has scarred all of Nolderan.

I turn back to the Cathedral's entrance, my neck stiff and slow with the motion, and then step forward and through.

Inside, the vaulted ceilings reach so high that my breaths seem to echo through them, let alone my footsteps as we walk through the hall. Hundreds of wooden pews stretch before us. Their ends are carved into ornate detailing. All the pews are filled, save for the one at the front where there's still room beside my aunt and my cousins. Beyond the sea of pews, the cathedral opens to a high domed chamber. The gods are painted onto the curved ceiling and are imbued with aether, making them seem as real as all the people gathered on the pews.

Meysus the Wise, God of the Moon, sits on a crescent moon. He has a long white beard which swirls like smoke and wears midnight black robes embroidered with silver thread. He flicks through the thick tome he is reading. It is Meysus which Tirith venerates the most, though they pray to all the ten major Caelum.

On the opposite side of the chamber is Zelene, Goddess of the Sun. Her skin is deep amber, and her hair and eyes shine brilliantly with golden light. The white skirts of the single shoulder dress she wears flutter around her legs. She holds the sun in her hands, high above her head. The Mother Goddess is worshipped fervently by the people of Selynis, and it is said she is the one who shaped humans from clay and breathed life into us.

On the eastern and western sides, Aion the God of Wind and Navis the God of Sea stand opposite each other. A great eagle perches on Aion's shoulder, while Navis clutches an enormous trident. The rest of the chamber's domed ceiling features the remaining ten gods: Iara the Goddess of Music strums a lute, Tyronis the God of Thunder strikes his hammer and calls down lightning, Avris the Goddess of Dreams slumbers on a cloud beside Meysus the Wise, Ranthir the God of Love aims an arrow with a heart-shaped head, Thela the Goddess of Hunt throws her spear at deer, and Vetia the Goddess of Luck jingles her coin purse.

Beneath all the gods lies my mother's coffin. Like the Arcanium's atrium, it is formed from crystallized aether. It's of a pale purple hue, and the surface glimmers as the light reflects across it. The crystal is translucent enough that I can make out my mother's shadow through the sides.

The sight of her, vague though it may be, brings me to a sudden halt. We are halfway through the cathedral now, and everyone turns to look at me, but I barely notice them. All I am aware of is the strained rhythm of my heart.

I stare at her crystal coffin for so long that the cathedral spins around me. My father catches me before I fall, though it's only afterward that I realize I was falling. He helps me to the front right pew, where my aunt and cousins have left room for us.

On our way, we pass Kaely and her father—as well as Eliya and the rest of her family. The other two Archmagi are also gathered here: Lorette Gidston, Archmage of Knowledge, and Krasus Lanord, Archmage of Finance.

I slide down onto the pew beside my father. The wood is cool and smooth beneath me. As solid as the bench is, I feel no more stable than I did on my feet, and I dig my fingers into the edges to prevent myself from teetering over.

For a long while, no one dares to say anything—not so much as a hushed whisper. We all stare at the crystal coffin in the center of the chamber. My sight blurs and then there are three coffins: one for my mother, one for my father, and one for Eliya. And maybe I should imagine one for myself too, because I fear my heart will cease beating at any moment, suffocated by grief.

My gaze trails up to where the Goddess Zelene is holding up the sun. Golden petals scatter around her. It's as though they are made from sunlight.

She created us, and we are supposedly her children, but it's impossible to see her as a loving mother. If she cared for her creations, why would she allow us to suffer? Why would she create humanity with a capacity for such evil?

But Zelene, or at least the enchanted painting of her, doesn't answer my questions. She continues staring up at the sun above her head, her gossamer skirts twirling around her.

There's no afterlife, either. Though Selynis would have you believe otherwise. We magi know better. Upon death, souls disperse into the energies they are made from and return to the atmosphere. Only the most powerful sorcerers can hope for their souls to remain intact enough to become aether spirits drifting through the world. Perhaps some of Selynis's priestesses burn so brightly with light magic that their souls transcend to the Heavens upon death and become immortal saints. But that is merely conjecture, since Nolderan has neither proved nor disproved the fate of Selynis's priestesses after death.

As for my mother, it's unlikely fragments of her spirit remain in the world. Heston warped the aether in her soul into dark magic, and my father obliterated the resulting wraith. All that remains of her now is her paintings and her gardens.

"We gather here today to commemorate the life of Mirelle Ashbourne," a priest begins, pulling my attention from my thoughts. His voice echoes through the grand hall. Light magic radiates from him. He wears white robes decorated with golden thread.

"And to commit her into the hands of the gods," he continues.

The finality sends fresh tears streaming down my face, and I consider shouting that none of the gods care about us mortals. They are locked away in their Heavens. Only for priests and priestesses might they spare a second thought.

They certainly don't care that my mother is gone.

I barely hear his next words, too busy trying to control my weeping so that it doesn't echo through the cathedral's vaulted ceilings and disturb everyone else listening to his speech. I vaguely hear him talking more of the gods, of aether and light, and of how my mother had been a kind and brilliant woman.

My blurred gaze fixes once more on my mother's crystal coffin. In the shimmering surface, I see Heston standing over her body, her veins throbbing as poisonous dark magic chokes the life from her. And I see myself helpless to stop him from murdering her and raising her as a wraith.

If only I weren't so weak. If I were stronger—as powerful as Kaely—then I would have been able to fight Heston with her. We would have held him off long enough for my father to arrive. And then my mother would still be alive.

I can blame Heston for her death, even my father for not executing him five years sooner, but I can't deny that I also had a hand in her death.

If only, if only—there are so many *if onlys,* and yet I cannot change the past. I must accept what I have done. That my weakness killed my mother.

My father rises, and as I feel the shift of his presence, I notice that the priest has finished speaking. My father gives a speech, of how he met my mother when she painted his portrait upon his succession as Grandmage of Nolderan, of how she scolded him so many times to sit still. His words twist the dagger already piercing my heart.

Eventually he falls silent once more, tears streaking his cheeks. I doubt he is aware of them. The Grandmage of Nolderan would never normally allow himself to cry in public, to show that weakness. He is too proud for that. But what use is there for pride when my mother is dead?

The priest continues to speak of gods who care not for us, and he offers more prayers to them and her memory. Only his final words penetrate my ears: "That which is aether may never truly die."

If I were not choking on my tears, I may have laughed at what a half-truth that is. Yes, aether can never be destroyed—that part is not inaccurate. But what Nolderan's favorite maxim fails to mention is that aether can be warped into dark energy, while the reverse is impossible. When my father destroyed my mother's wraith, the dark energies consisting of her soul scattered through the world.

She is dead in every sense of the word. The saying does not apply to her.

That is why when everyone bows their head and mutters it back, I cannot bear to do so. It would be a lie upon my tongue.

Soon my father ushers me from my seat and guides me to the center of the chamber where my mother lies. I feel like a piece of string trailing behind him.

We come to a stop before her crystal coffin. The lid is half open, revealing my mother's pale face and the vibrant flowers she clasps to her chest. Though crystal coffins preserve bodies and my mother's appearance hasn't deteriorated over the past few days, I hardly recognize her face. The expression she wears is too still. She looks more like a doll than a person.

I grip the edges of the crystal coffin, and my tears fall within. Aether vibrates beneath my fingers.

This is my fault. If I were not so weak, I wouldn't be looking down at my mother's corpse.

I don't know how long passes before my father pulls me from the coffin. I stagger back and stare up at the gods and goddesses. Silently I curse them for their cruelty.

The truth is clear. The mighty Caelum care not for us mortals, and there is little use in praying to them for salvation. We can only believe in ourselves and our own abilities. I can pray over and over to them, but the only way I can protect those I love most is with my magic.

And that is why, no matter the cost, I will become the most powerful mage Nolderan has ever known—even more powerful than my father.

Never again will I allow those I love to be stolen from me.

THREE YEARS
LATER...

CHAPTER 17

AETHER RUSHES THROUGH ME. I am deaf to all but the magic singing through my blood, begging for release.

I focus the energy into my fingertips. The storm of aether crackles. With the sheer force pounding through my body, even the arena's towering walls fail to make me feel small.

I am power. I am fury.

"*Folgos,*" I hiss.

The aether sparks into lightning. It thunders from my palms and darts across to where Kaely stands.

"*Laxus!*" she calls, teleporting away before the lightning reaches her.

My spell continues onward and collides with the barrier surrounding the arena. The lightning bolt fizzles out. If not for the enchantment, our magic would have long destroyed our audience.

It isn't only our class that watches us; many of the lower years perch on the edges of their stone seats, intently watching our duel. Fifth-years sparring on their final day at the Arcanium makes for a remarkable performance. Next week, we begin our Mage Trials. We are almost magi.

I turn, searching for Kaely's new position. I find her behind me.

"*Speculus!*" she calls.

The aether in her hands spins out into two clones. Now three identical Kaelys conjure magic.

"*Gelus!*" they cry in unison, flinging large shards of ice at me. Each is shaped into a frozen arrowhead.

The two frost bolts conjured by her clones contain only a fraction of her power. But they will still hurt if they strike me.

I weave aether into fire magic. "*Ignir'muriz.*"

Flames roar in my hands. I pull them around myself in a blazing shield.

The three frost bolts crash into the fiery wall. The ice hisses. Water splashes across the stone slabs. Steam billows through the arena.

My shield remains strong. I shape the flames into a mighty fireball. "*Ignira,*" I snarl.

Three years ago, I was disciplined in Archmage Gidston's office for striking Kaely with this same spell. Now the Archmage watches us through narrowed eyes, her hands folded across her lap, as though she doesn't realize that the two of us are aiming to kill each other.

This fireball might be the most ferocious one I've ever cast. Since my mother died, I have worked tirelessly to hone my skills and master all the spells I know—as well as the advanced magic I've learned more recently. Even my father would be proud of this fireball.

My lips curl. Fear glistens in Kaely's eyes—in the eyes of all three of them. But the fleeting emotion vanishes as swiftly as it appears.

"*Aquis!*" the three Kaelys shout together.

A water blast shoots from their fingers and meets in the middle. Then their attack gains momentum and charges at my fireball.

The two spells collide with each other at the center of the arena. Though water holds a colossal advantage against fire, my fireball is fueled with immense power, and that makes our attacks equal.

Magic roars. The force flings back both Kaely and me. Her mirror images dissolve. The blast is so thunderous I don't hear myself slamming into the ground. Nor do I hear Kaely's thud.

The resulting haze is so thick I can barely see her across the arena. But the hatred in her eyes burns vividly enough to penetrate the dense steam.

In our third-year finals, I scored the same mark as her. And last year, I *beat* her. By ten whole marks across all of our classes. To achieve that, I had to study day and night, and my father was so very pleased by my dedication to my studies. I even scored the highest in our year.

That's why she hates me more than ever. She can no longer say I'm undeserving of our tutors' praise. Now I might actually be better than her.

At least with written examinations. I've yet to beat her in a duel.

That's why I must defeat her today. Once we graduate from the Arcanium and become magi, I may never again have the opportunity to duel her.

And if I can't beat Kaely, how will I ever protect those I love from monsters like Heston?

I scramble back onto my feet. Through the smoke, I scarcely make out her doing the same.

But before either of us can unleash another spell, aether radiates from the center of the arena. Archmage Lorette Gidston emerges from the cloud of violet light.

Our duel is over before the real fight can begin.

"That is enough." The Archmage's crisp voice rings through the arena. "*Ventrez.*" She conjures a wind spell and uses it to blow away all the steam.

With the fog cleared, Kaely glares at me, every ounce of the loathing in her heart unveiled. I glare back at her with as much bile, my own expression as disdainful as hers.

If Archmage Gidston notices our murderous scowls, she doesn't comment on them. "Excellent work, both of you."

Neither of us responds. We continue glowering at each other.

Lorette turns and scans across the other fifth-years sitting in the audience. "Trindell, Varsley—you're both up next."

Koby stands, as does Jaron.

But Archmage Gidston shakes her head at Jaron and says, "Not you. You've already had your turn in the arena." She gestures to the other Trindell twin. "On your feet, Braedon."

The two of them teleport down to the arena.

Kaely and I hold each other's glare for a moment longer. Then she scrunches her nose and murmurs *laxus*, teleporting back up to the stone seats. I do the same, appearing on the stairs at the end of Eliya's row. My fists curl as I stride over to where she sits.

"What's the matter?" she asks as I slump down beside her.

My jaw hardens. "Nothing."

She arches a brow at me. "Really? You don't look mad at all."

I lean back, the stone wall of the row behind digging into my shoulders, and I blow out a breath. "I didn't beat her."

"Your match was a draw."

"Drawing with her isn't the same as winning."

"Why are you so focused on beating her? Three years ago, she was completely wiping the floor with you. Look at how far you've come. Now you're her equal."

"I don't want to be her equal."

"Then what do you want, Reyna?"

I want to be better than her. So much better. Even as an adept, my father would have easily defeated someone like Kaely. And yet I've never come close to beating her.

If I can't defeat even Kaely, how can I become as powerful as my father? Three years ago, I swore to become mightier than him in order to protect those I love. As it stands, how can I ever hope to achieve that?

But I tell Eliya none of this. I turn to where Kaely sits on the opposite side of the arena, and I continue glaring at her. Not that glaring will help me defeat her.

At the end of the day, we gather inside the Arcanium's hall. Three enormous chandeliers hang from elegant ceiling roses, and aether crystals dangle like raindrops from the spiraling arms. Their light has a purple tint and makes the white herringbone tiles of the floor appear lilac.

Natural light filters in through the many arched windows lining the hall, and they are tall enough to reach from the floor to the embellished ceiling. Plum velvet drapes are tucked beside the windows, held in place by tasseled, golden cords.

Since the lower years have spent the past few weeks completing their written examinations, the hall is filled with square drop-leaf tables. They are carved from oak—as are the matching chairs—and all feature twisted legs.

Every adept of the Arcanium is present; there's nearly one-hundred and fifty of us in total. With there being far more adepts than desks and chairs, many are crowded around the walls.

Fortunately, Eliya and I arrived early enough to claim seats next to each other. We sit two rows back from the front, behind the adepts who arrived even earlier. That includes Kaely, who sits on the frontmost row. I glare at her mousy brown braid and the back of her cerulean robes, but it is far less satisfying than glaring at her freckled face.

Archmage Gidston sits on the dais, and her eyes rake across every adept of the Arcanium. Her chair is oaken like ours, but grander. Floral details are etched across its arms and legs. Beside her stands many of our tutors, their hands clasped behind their backs.

When every last adept has arrived, she finally addresses us all.

"Today marks the end of the Arcanium's 1694th Year," she declares, her words carrying to even the furthest corners of the hall. "This year, we have witnessed many outstanding achievements. Such as Quella Hyers, who obtained full marks in every examination she completed last week."

She gestures to a student sitting in the row ahead of me. The girl stands, and everyone claps.

When we fall silent, the girl returns to her seat and Archmage Gidston continues her speech.

"And also, Artus Milford who, despite being only two marks off failing last year, has now emerged as the top of his class."

Another student rises from his chair, and the entire hall showers him with applause. His achievement is quite remarkable. When I put little effort into my studies, I never came close to failing. To now be the top of his class, he must have worked even harder than me. I suppose the fear of almost failing and being thrown out of the Arcanium probably had much to do with that.

He sits back down, and Archmage Gidston continues praising various adepts. A second-year is also commended for their performance during Combat Class, while a fourth-year is applauded for their work with an Alchemy research project. None of us fifth-years are mentioned, however. Not until the end of her speech.

"And now we must applaud our fifth-year students for all their hard work over the last five years."

We fifth-years get to our feet, and the rest of the hall applauses us.

"However, their time as adepts is not yet complete," Archmage Gidston continues when we return to our seats. "Next week, they will begin their Mage Trials. In order to graduate from the Arcanium, they must prove they have the required strength of heart, mind, and magic. We wish them all the luck with their trials and the bright futures ahead of them."

CHAPTER 18

"NO MORE LESSONS," ELIYA SINGS as we pour out of the hall with all the other adepts, "ever again!"

We come to a stop at the center of the Arcanium's atrium. The aether crystals which form the domed ceiling glisten in the late noon sun.

"You do realize this means you'll have to get a job soon?" I say.

"Why would I need a job? My father's apothecary makes so much money that he doesn't need to work. I'll just inherit his business."

"You'll have to share it with your brother," I point out. Eliya's brother is six years younger than us and is due to start at the Arcanium next year. Which I suppose is next month now, since we're already in December.

"Even if I have to share it with Wynn, there will still be plenty of money for us both—" She cuts herself off as Koby walks past, and she grabs his shoulder, spinning him around. "Hey, Koby! Do you want to come to Flour Power with Reyna and me?"

"Sure—" he begins.

"When did we decide on that?" I interject. "I need to go to the library."

She rolls her eyes at me. "Why do you need to go to the library on a Friday evening?"

"I need to find a book."

"What book?"

As we speak, Koby's head snaps back and forth between the two of us.

"*Concerning Conflagration and Combustion* by Alvord Ashbourne," I reply. "I need to improve my fire wings spell."

"Your fire wings spell is already great," Eliya says. "Besides, don't you have a copy in your manor? What about the original one old Alvord wrote?"

I shake my head. "The original manuscript was taken to the Vault centuries ago for preservation. That's why I need to go to the library and find a copy before our Mage Trials."

"You won't need a fire spell on the Trial of Heart."

"I'll definitely need it for the Trial of Magic."

"The Trial of Magic isn't until Friday."

"I need to study it this weekend. I'll be too tired in between the trials next week."

Since the three of us are stopped in the center of the atrium, many adepts flash us annoyed looks as they wind around us. Eliya pays them no attention and heaves out a sigh at me.

"Can't you go some other time? The library will still be here in the morning. Go and get your book tomorrow."

"And the bakery will also still be there in the morning."

"But it won't be our final day at the Arcanium in the morning, will it?"

I press my lips together, unable to argue with that.

"Lorea! Blake!" Eliya calls over to more adepts in our year. "We're heading to Flour Power now. Do you want to join us?"

Lorea is as tall as me, with dark skin and ebony hair bluntly cut to her shoulders. Blake is almost half her height, and he has short strawberry-blond hair and nearly as many freckles as Kaely.

"Sure," Blake says. Lorea nods. Both of them start over to us.

"Great," Eliya replies. "Now help me convince Reyna not to go to the library and to come with us instead."

"Why do you need to go to the library?" Lorea asks, peering at me.

"To study?" My response comes out sharper than I intended.

"You seem to do a lot of that these days," she says.

Eliya snorts. "Too much."

I turn to Koby for support. He only shrugs.

"Maybe you should take a break," Blake suggests, unhelpfully.

"Fine, fine," I say, throwing my hands up in surrender. "Let's go to the bakery first, and then I'll go to the library later."

Eliya purses her lips, probably deciding whether to tell me to get the book tomorrow, but she leaves it at that.

"All right then!" she says. With that, she bounds out of the Arcanium, and we all trail after her.

When we reach the street beyond the Arcanium's archway, we each mutter *laxus* and teleport ourselves to the bakery.

Like all the buildings of Nolderan, Flour Power has a cobalt roof and walls built from white granite. The door is painted powder blue and has paneled windows. Through them, I see cake stands filled with colorful treats. Lace trim decorates the edges of each tier.

It's only when my teleportation spell is complete and the aether has faded away that I remember which part of the Upper City this bakery belongs to.

Glancing over my shoulder, I see the alley where Heston's undead pursued me—where my mother saved me. And I'm certain I currently stand upon the very spot where Arluin fell. But when I look down, the cobblestones beneath me are no different to any of the others. Since that fateful night, I've visited this part of the city several times. And it always leaves me shaken.

The bakery's gleaming windows spin around me. I barely notice as the others open the door and head inside. The tinkling bell chimes over through my ears.

"Reyna?" Eliya asks. A frigid wind blows over us, and she pulls her cerulean robes tighter around herself. "Are you coming inside?"

"Coming," I murmur. I tear my feet from where they stand and follow her inside with everyone else.

The others have chosen to sit at a circular mahogany table with curved legs. A lacy tablecloth covers its surface. There are only two empty chairs left. Both face the windows and have a clear view of the alley beyond.

For a moment, I consider asking Lorea to swap with me, since her back is to the window. But then I wordlessly slide onto the chair beside Eliya. Explaining why I don't want this seat would mean reliving those horrors. Over the past three years, I've tried to bury the nightmares as deeply as I can. But now, being here, so close to where everything happened, all those terrifying memories are violently bubbling to the surface.

The locket around my neck suddenly feels as heavy as a string of bricks. I clasp at the fabric of my robes, feeling where the locket lies beneath.

Not once have I taken it off. Nor have I opened the locket and watched the memory recorded within. Arluin's promise echoes through my mind. His words are loud enough to drown out the conversation around me.

There has never been any sign of him. To this day, I don't know his fate.

We never found a body but if he's alive, why has he never tried contacting me? I know he can't return. My father and the Archmagi would have him executed the moment he sets foot inside Nolderan. But surely if he's alive, he would try to see me again. Or at least let me know he isn't dead.

After all, we made a promise to each other. The proof of it hangs around my neck.

A sharp nudge pulls me from my thoughts.

I turn to Eliya and blink.

She gestures to Mrs. Baxter who stands before us. "Reyna, what are you having?"

Mrs. Baxter is the owner of Flour Power. She bought this property six months after the necromancers attacked. I can't remember what this building was before she took it over. Perhaps it was a tailor's, or maybe a quill and ink shop.

She's a plump lady who wears the same flowery, pastel apron and bright smile every time I visit her bakery. Her pale blue eyes mark her as being neither a mage nor a descendant of the founding families. She uses no magic in her baking, but her cakes are the most delicious I've ever tasted. My mother would have liked her. Especially since she always went on about how we shouldn't use our magic for everything.

"Um," I begin, chewing on my lip.

As lovely as Mrs. Baxter's cakes are, I've lost my appetite. With the bitter lump swelling in my throat at the thought of Arluin, I don't know how I'll swallow a single bite. And then Mrs. Baxter will think I don't like her cakes. I suppose I could say I'm not hungry, but then Eliya will want to know what's the matter. And I don't feel like explaining to her right now, especially not while the others are around. Though we've been in the same classes for the past five years, I'm not particularly close to any of them. It's Eliya who is friends with them.

"I'll have the same as you," I quickly say to Eliya.

Thankfully, no one comments on my hesitation.

"Would you like cream with it?" Mrs. Baxter asks.

I have no idea what I'm ordering. But I can't say that without revealing how distant I've been.

In the end, I just nod.

"All right," Mrs. Baxter says, turning away. "I'll get everything plated up for you now."

When she leaves, the others carry on talking. I tune them out and stare into the alley across the street.

All the images of that terrible night come rushing back so vividly I can hear the growling of ghouls and smell the putrid stench of their rotting flesh. The mahogany chair wobbles beneath me, and now the thought of eating cakes and cream—or whatever else I ordered—almost makes me vomit all over Mrs. Baxter's floor.

Then, as everything is spinning around me, I'm certain I glimpse Arluin's raven curls amid the alley.

I blink and sit up.

But when I stare into the alley again, I can only see the long shadows that the late noon sun is casting across the street.

Was he there? Or did I imagine him?

Then I'm thrown back to the moment where I was rummaging through all the dead bodies, desperately trying to find him.

My breaths come out as gasps. I bolt from my seat, no longer caring what the others think.

"Reyna!" Eliya shouts after me.

I don't stop. I continue through the bakery and shove open the powder blue door. The bell tinkles overhead. I keep running. All the way across the street, until I reach the alleyway.

The shadows loom over me. Several moments pass.

But Arluin doesn't appear. Not even when I squeeze my eyes shut and will for him to step from the shadows.

It seems he was never here at all.

"Reyna!" Eliya shouts again. Her hurried footsteps chase me.

I glance back to see her racing toward me. Then I return my attention to the shadows and grasp the locket beneath my robes.

She stops behind me. "Reyna, what's the matter?"

"I thought I saw something," I whisper, not turning to her. I don't want her to see my disappointment. "But it seems I was wrong . . ."

"What are you talking about? What did you see?"

If I explain that I thought I saw Arluin, that I think of him every day, then I fear I'll rip open the stitches holding together the broken pieces of my heart.

She reaches for my hand and squeezes it. "Come on, let's go back inside. Mrs. Baxter just brought the cakes over."

With how horribly my stomach is churning, I know I won't be able to eat anything. "I think I'll head home," I say. "I don't feel too good."

"How come?" she asks with a frown. "What's the matter?"

"I've probably caught a cold. It's the season for it, I suppose."

Her frown doesn't abate. I know she doesn't believe me. At least not entirely. "Well, make sure you take a healing potion as soon as you're home."

"I will." I hold out my hand. "*Conparios.*" My coin purse emerges from violet light. It's of a pink and gold satin brocade, complete with a decorative metallic clasp.

Eliya shakes her head before I can open my purse. "Don't worry about that. I'll eat your slice."

"Are you sure?"

"Of course I am," she replies. "Make sure you look after yourself. Our first trial starts on Monday, so don't forget to take that healing potion."

"I won't forget. I promise."

She gives me a wave and then heads back into the bakery, her crimson waves floating behind her.

My gaze returns to the shadows. I stare at them for several minutes more, a question weighing on my mind.

What if I didn't imagine Arluin at all?

CHAPTER 19

WHAT I SAID TO ELIYA was a lie. I don't teleport home. Instead, I teleport back to the Arcanium and head to the library.

The Grand Library of Nolderan is as it has always been. Nothing has changed over these past three years. The enormous crystalline chandelier is as dazzling as ever, and the checkered tiles still disorient me as I reach the last step of the long staircase.

There are few adepts inside the library, which is fortunate because Eliya would be hurt if she found out I lied to her. Guilt gnaws at me, but I shake it away. She is better off with Koby and the others rather than someone who sees ghosts wherever they go.

Erma Darkholme sits at her desk beneath the chandelier. Today, she's flicking through an old tome. I don't stop to look at which it is. Her gaze rises as I pass her desk, and she peers at me through her dark-rimmed spectacles. They sit so far down her nose it's a wonder they don't topple off.

"What are you doing here?" she demands.

"I came to find a book."

"Hm," she simply says. I turn away, but she continues speaking before I can leave. "Haven't you adepts finished for the year?"

It seems even Erma is discouraging me from studying. Maybe Eliya is right to be worried about me. Maybe I am going mad.

I doubt Erma's words are spoken out of concern for me. Her only concern will be whether she has a break from us adepts over Yuletide.

"Yes, Professor Darkholme," I say, dipping my head. "We finished today."

"Then why not wait until January when your studies resume?" Her eyes narrow with suspicion. She hasn't forgotten my mischievous ways during my first two years at the Arcanium.

"My studies won't continue in January, Professor Darkholme. I'm a fifth-year student, so today is my last day as an adept of the Arcanium. My Mage Trials start on Monday."

"Ah," she says, her attention returning to her old tome. "I see."

I continue through the library, and this time Erma doesn't stop me.

The book I seek, *Concerning Conflagration and Combustion*, is located on the Grand Library's second floor, along with the other tomes dedicated to fire magic. During my third year, I studied this book to improve my fireball, but I didn't make many notes on the spell for *ignir'alas*, which Alvord Ashbourne famously invented five hundred years ago.

I take a right turn and ascend the narrow, winding steps. They aren't as numerous as the ones leading into the library, and I soon reach the second floor.

The shelves containing books on fire magic are located at the far end, so I weave through the sprawling aisles until I arrive at that section.

I come to a stop before the bookshelves. Like all the others, their edges are gilded and they stand at five times my height.

Concerning Conflagration and Combustion perches on the highest shelf, exactly where I remember. Its burgundy leather spine sits between two smaller books, and its title and 'Alvord Ashbourne' is scrawled onto it.

I imagine holding the book in painstaking detail: my fingers brushing over the smooth leather cover and the gold leaf ornamentation glistening in the violet light of the nearby aether crystals. When the book is concrete in my mind, I speak the spell-words. "*Vello* Concerning Conflagration and Combustion *per* Alvord Ashbourne."

A glittering cloud swirls up to the topmost shelf. My magic locates the book, secures it, and then drifts down, depositing it in my hands.

I tuck the tome under my arm and return to the winding stairs.

But I only manage a few strides.

From the corner of my eye, I glimpse a flash of cerulean, and I pause, peering down the aisle. Another adept stands at the far end. He has dark curls. And his frame looks so very familiar . . .

My heart skips a beat. I hurry toward him, my frantic footsteps ringing throughout the library.

I go to shout his name, but my lips barely part before he turns.

And when he does, I realize that he isn't Arluin. His face is too round, too soft, and his nose is too pointed. His curls aren't raven black, but deep chestnut. From the other end of the aisle, his hair looked much darker.

"Um," the boy begins, "can I help you?" He looks at me like I've gone mad. Maybe I have.

Wherever I go, I see Arluin. Today isn't the first time I've imagined him, but it has never been this frequent. Maybe it's because our Mage Trials are around the corner, and my mind is haunted by the promise Arluin and I made. That we would marry when I graduated from the Arcanium.

"I . . ." My throat closes around my words, but I force them out as best I can. Or else, I will only make myself look more foolish. "I thought you were someone else."

I'm glad he turned before I could shout Arluin's name, because everyone knows who the traitor's son is. Now I can only hope he doesn't ask who I thought he was. Maybe I could give him Koby's name. He probably doesn't know Koby well enough to know that he looks nothing like him.

Fortunately, the boy doesn't ask.

"Oh," he says. "You're Reyna Ashbourne, right?"

"Yeah."

"That's amazing."

"It is?"

"You're the Grandmage's daughter."

"Yeah," I say again, hoping my voice doesn't sound as bitter as it does in my head. Is my father all people see when they look at me? Will I forever live in his shadow? "I am," I add, in case my initial response sounded as short as I think it did.

"What's it like having the Grandmage as your father?" he blurts and then seems to remember that we're both strangers. "Oh, I shouldn't ask something like that. You don't need to answer if you don't want to."

"It's fine," I reply. It isn't as if other adepts haven't asked me the same question a thousand times before. Though that was mostly in my first year at the Arcanium. "I suppose it's like having any other father," I say with a shrug.

The boy doesn't seem content with that response.

"Maybe he has higher expectations for me than most?"

He appears a little more satisfied with that. "Your Mage Trials are next week, aren't they?"

"They are."

"I bet you're nervous about them."

I smile and try to make it not look like a grimace. "A little. Anyway, I should get going." Most of all, I don't want to get caught by any other adepts. Hopefully, he won't tell anyone he's seen me here and Eliya won't find out I lied to her.

"Oh, of course," he replies. "Good luck with your Mage Trials next week."

"Thanks," I say.

With that, I turn and head back to the winding steps.

When I return to the central chamber, Erma is still reading the same book. She looks up as I place *Concerning Conflagration and Combustion* on her desk.

"I would like to borrow this one for two weeks, please."

Erma scans over the cover and then reaches across her desk for the ledger, opening it to the current page. The current date, Friday 2nd December 1694, is scribbled across the top. The rest of the page is split into a table with five headers: *Title, Author, Name, Duration,* and *Returned*. She dips the nib of her quill into her pot of ink and writes out all the information onto the next empty line in the table. She leaves the cell for *Returned* blank.

"*Concerning Conflagration and Combustion* will be of use in the Trial of Magic," she says as she returns her quill to its golden, bell-shaped holder. Her name is etched into the gleaming surface. "Particularly on the second round."

"That's what I was thinking. I was hoping to improve my fire wings spell before then."

"Best of luck with the trials," Erma says, to my surprise. Until now, I didn't know that she could even manage a single nice sentence.

I retrieve *Concerning Conflagration and Combustion* from her desk and turn to the steep stairs leading out of the library.

"And do remember, there are no second chances. If you fail even one trial, you will never become a Mage of Nolderan."

As if I needed that reminder.

Nonetheless, I force a smile. "Thank you, Professor Darkholme. I will do my best to ensure that I do not fail."

CHAPTER 20

IT'S LATE WHEN MY FATHER comes home. Though for him, ten o'clock on a Friday night is rather early. Some nights he doesn't return at all. He would never admit it, but I'm sure he sometimes falls asleep at his desk. His office is on the highest floor of the Aether Tower.

I'm currently sitting in the drawing room, studying *Concerning Conflagration and Combustion*. Taking notes is difficult thanks to Zephyr, who has mistaken my desk for his bed. I tried to move him, but he started spewing balls of aether at me. In the end, I decided to share the desk and work around him. I don't know why he likes it so much. Surely a hard, wooden surface isn't comfortable?

The only blessing is that he doesn't snore too loudly.

My father peers around the door. "You're home? And . . . studying?"

I don't tell him that he's the third person who has commented on my studying habits today. "Why wouldn't I be home? It's ten o'clock."

"It was your last day at the Arcanium, wasn't it? I thought you and Eliya would be celebrating until the early hours of the morning."

I wonder if Eliya and the others left their celebrations at Flour Power or if they continued inside taverns. Another pang of guilt sweeps over me, but I brush it aside. I wasn't lying when I said I wasn't feeling well. Except I have a sickness of the heart, rather than the body.

"I wasn't in the mood for it."

My father is the last person I want to discuss Arluin with, especially after he ordered Archmage Calton to execute him. Since then, neither of us have mentioned it. I suppose we both know how the other will react, so we seem to have silently agreed it's something best left forgotten.

He gestures to the book lying on my desk. "What are you studying?"

"*Concerning Conflagration and Combustion,*" I say, holding up the burgundy cover. "I want to improve my fire wings spell."

"I passed Archmage Gidston earlier in the Arcanium. She spoke highly of your abilities during Combat Class today."

I shrug as I place the book back onto the desk.

"What's the matter?"

I stare at Zephyr's shimmering scales rather than my father's face. "Nothing."

I wonder whether he will press the matter, but he doesn't.

"Aside from your fire wings spell, are you ready for your trials next week?" he asks after a short pause.

"What choice do I have but to be ready?" If I fail my trials, I will tarnish my family's legacy and shame my ancestors like Alvord Ashbourne, whose book lies on my desk.

"Indeed." Maybe once he would have spoken that word as a sigh, frustrated by my lack of discipline. But now I can't tell what emotion laces his voice.

I feel his gaze on me for a few more minutes. The drawing room would be silent, if not for my flicking of pages and Zephyr's slow, gentle breaths.

"Well," my father finally says, "I'll let you get to it."

"I left you some food in the kitchen," I say. That meal was made with my magic, of course. My mother would be disappointed to know the two of us do nothing by hand these days. My father is too busy working, and I'm too busy studying.

"Excellent, thank you." With that, he steps out the room and leaves me to continue examining *Concerning Conflagration and Combustion*.

I end up falling asleep with my head on the book. I jolt awake and frantically inspect the pages to see whether I've crumpled them. If there's even a single wrinkle, Erma will bill me an extortionate amount to have a new copy bound.

Last year, I spilled a few drops of mulberry juice onto the book I was studying for our midterm examinations. In my defense, the specks were tiny, though they were a vivid shade of purplish-red. She charged me half of my monthly stipend.

Once I'm certain the pages are free from creases, I shut the tome quietly enough not to wake Zephyr and lean back in my chair. My attention drifts over to the brass clock hanging over the fireplace. Its black serpentine hands point to twenty past three.

I almost fall off my chair with surprise. I didn't realize I slept for so long.

I rise and gently push the chair under the desk. Despite my carefulness, Zephyr's eyes flutter open. He yawns, revealing rows of tiny ivory fangs. I leave the drawing room and head upstairs. Zephyr follows me.

I pass my father's room. No light filters through the narrow crack beneath the door, so I do my best to prevent the floorboards from creaking under my weight. My father is a light sleeper, and at three in the morning, I'm in no mood to deal with his crankiness.

When I arrive at my room, I close the door softly behind me. Zephyr darts over to my bed and claims the center.

"You know I'll have to move you," I hiss. "How do you expect me to get into bed with you right there in the middle?"

Zephyr opens an eye and stares at me. I glare at him until he crawls over to the left side of the bed.

I drape my cerulean robes over my golden armchair and pause. I only have one more week of wearing them. If I pass my Mage Trials, I will be bestowed with the violet robes of the magi.

And if I fail, I will wear neither adept nor magi robes for the rest of my life.

I pace over to my cabinet and pull out a nightgown. I change into it, switch off the crystalline chandelier, and slide into bed beside Zephyr. His azure scales are so luminous that they are visible even in the darkness.

The shadows swirl as my vision adjusts to the lack of light. I close my eyes and keep them shut for a long while, but no sleep finds me. Even the softness of my bed doesn't lull me into slumber.

I grasp the locket around my neck and run the silver heart between my fingers.

What if I didn't imagine Arluin standing there in the alleyway?

All my foolish wishes weigh heavily on my heart. The darkness shifts, and I find myself staring up at the ghost of his face.

I reach for the lamp beside my bed and switch on the aether crystals. But there's no one else here. Only Zephyr and me. My cerulean robes stare back at me from where they hang over my armchair.

I don't try to fall asleep again. With all the onerous thoughts playing on my mind, it would be pointless.

I switch off the lamp and climb out of bed. On my way out, I grab the velvet cloak hanging on the back of my door. Zephyr doesn't stir as I leave.

The corridor beyond is dark, and I use the walls to help me navigate back to the stairs. When I near my father's room, I tip-toe past. Not only do I fear his grumpiness at being awoken, but also him demanding to know why I'm creeping out at three in the morning.

Actually, it might now be closer to four o'clock, but I don't peer into any of the rooms downstairs to check the clocks. I continue through the hallway, passing all my mother's paintings, and out the grand doors. I close them behind me carefully.

On the other side, the golden lion knockers stare at me with suspicious, metallic eyes. I turn away from them and start through the gardens.

Moonlight shimmers across the satin petals of the blooming flowers, and the fountain at the center flows to a steady rhythm reminiscent of gentle rain.

My warm breaths form a small cloud as they meet the frigid air. Frost powders the grass and glistens in the starlight. A sharp chill claws over my arms. I clasp my velvet cloak tighter around myself and wish I picked a thicker one. The stones are like ice beneath my bare feet as I traipse over them.

"*Calida,*" I murmur. A flame sparks within, warming me from the inside out. Now when my toes touch the stone, the ground feels no colder than my bedroom floor. Nor do I feel the wintry breeze gliding through my cloak.

The aether enchanting the tall gates glows brightly through the shadowed gardens. When I reach them, they swing open in a shrill, metallic clang, and the sound ricochets through the night.

I wince and glance back at the manor. No light switches on. If my father heard the sound, then he has ignored it, likely thinking it came from someone else's manor farther down the street. Thankfully, the gates close more quietly than they opened.

I step out onto the dark street. There's no one around to wonder what the Grandmage's daughter is doing out in the dead of night, barefoot and dressed in her nightgown. Before anyone can appear from around the corner, I mutter, "*Laxus.*"

A violet cloud enshrouds me, and I fade into the night.

I emerge outside Arluin's manor.

Dark iron gates greet me, as does the serpent coiling around the blade on the Harstall's family crest. The gardens were neglected when Arluin lived here, but now they're entirely out of control. The weeds have grown so tall they strangle the trees.

Though Arluin has distant cousins, none of them have claimed this place. It seems they want no connection at all with Heston or his manor.

After the necromancers and their undead were defeated, Branvir and a group of magi searched the manor. I don't think they found anything, and if they did, I heard nothing about it. The eventual fate of this manor will be demolition, but my father is yet to issue that order. And I don't think he will for a very long time. He can't bear to utter a single word about Heston.

Over the last three years, only I have visited the manor. This isn't the first sleepless night that I've teleported here.

I take another step toward the gates. The protruding edges of the cobblestones dig into the soft undersides of my feet.

"Reyna Ashbourne," I say to the enchanted gates. They remember my name and swing open.

Passing through the wild gardens isn't easy. Overgrown roots jut out, and brambles spiral across the path. A few thorns nick the back of my calves. I stop and curse them under my breath. The brambles are sharp enough to draw blood, and a few drops dribble down to my ankles.

"*Ignira,*" I breathe, launching a fireball at the thorns which dared to attack me.

The brambles crumble into ash as my flames touch them. I turn on my heels and continue to the manor's entrance, trying to avoid being stabbed by more thorns.

The brass twin viper knockers are rusted, and most of the paint has peeled off the doors. Large, wooden patches streak across them. When I push open the doors, they creak so violently I fear they will fling off their hinges and crash into me. Luckily, they don't.

The blue rug spread through the hallway is so filled with dust that it appears gray. Cobwebs hang from the ceiling like enormous fishing nets. I push past them and ascend the spiraling staircase.

The steps groan beneath my weight, no longer used to being walked upon. As I come to the top of the stairs, I pause and stare at the door to the master bedroom. Heston's face and the image of him being burned to death by my father's flames flashes through my mind. His tortured screams ring through my ears.

Clenching my fists, I force myself away and continue toward Arluin's room. The door is still left ajar from the last time I was here.

Musty air chokes me as I enter. For three years, the windows have remained shut, and the room is suffocated. The curtains are tucked away, and moonlight streams through the grimy windows, silvering the edges of all the furniture inside the room.

Ticking comes from the corner where the old grandfather clock stands. Thanks to the abundance of aether imbued inside its springs, it will likely last another fifty years until it falls silent and still.

I pad over the zig-zagged wooden panels forming the floor, and my feet soon meet the crimson square rug lying in front of the canopy bed. My heels sink into the plush threads. I reach for the nearest mahogany bedpost and my fingers curl around it, feeling every peak and valley of the ornate design carved into the wood. My attention settles on the scarlet quilt. Dust motes blanket it like snowflakes. It feels like only yesterday Arluin carried me up here and promised to marry me.

Exhaling deeply, I leave the post and settle onto the edge of the bed. The mattress dips with my weight.

I sit there for a while, my fingers running across the silk brocade sheets and disturbing the dust. My gaze sweeps around the room, taking in every aspect: the aether crystals hanging from the ceiling, the paneled wardrobe still filled with Arluin's clothes, the crimson curtains held beside the arched windows by matching tiebacks.

When I finish absorbing every detail, I reach for the silver locket around my neck. My hands tremble slightly as I unclasp it.

I pinch the delicate chain between my fingers and dangle it. Like a pendulum, the silver heart swings back and forth. It takes several moments to fall still.

I want to believe with all my heart that Arluin lives. That there's hope the two of us will meet again, even if we can never be together.

But if he is alive, why wouldn't he try to contact me? Why wouldn't he let me know he survived his father's attack?

I need closure. But I fear I will never find the answers I seek.

The silver heart blurs as tears well in my eyes. I brush them away and place the locket flat on my palm.

I gaze down at it, hearing the echo of the words within. I've never once opened it. I feared doing so would cause our promise to lose its sacredness. To become truly impossible.

But that thought is nearly laughable. It's already impossible. How can Arluin keep his vow when he's not here? When he might be dead?

And so, I do what I've contemplated doing for three years. I open the locket.

Aether pours out. It sketches the scene of the memory it recorded. The two of us are shown in magenta light. The crystal even captured the brocade detailing of the sheets beneath, though the fabric is painted in a purple glow.

"*Reyna,*" Arluin says, "*I am a man who has nothing, who is nothing. I know I don't deserve you, but you mean everything to me. In this world, I have nothing else left.*"

Upon hearing his voice, I choke out a sob. He sounds so distant, but it's still him.

This is another reason I didn't dare to open the locket. I knew I would be unable to bear the sound of his voice. A part of me considers shutting the locket before old wounds are ripped open. But I don't. The wounds are festering, anyway.

In the memory, my hand reaches up and rests on his cheek. "*Arluin, please don't speak about yourself like this. You mean everything to me, as well.*"

He places his finger on my lips. I wish I could feel his touch—for me to be sitting there beside him instead of my ghost. I hardly recognize her as being me. Her eyes are too bright, too filled with hope. She doesn't know that this night will be one of her last with the boy she loves.

Would this memory be any different if I'd known what destiny planned for us?

"*I've loved you for as long as I remember,*" Arluin's voice continues. "*And it's only when I'm with you that . . . that I forget . . .*"

That he is a necromancer's son.

If only he were someone else's son. Then all this wouldn't have happened. Then we might still be together.

The locket weighs heavily in my palm. I don't know how it doesn't slip from my grasp and fall to the floor.

I watch myself kiss him, watch how still he is within my embrace. Maybe he suspected that our time together was reaching an end and that this moment would be one of our last. Maybe that's why he decided to record this memory.

"*Arly,*" I say when I finish kissing him, "*we can't change the past. We can only shape the future.*"

My words sound nothing like my own. All I want is to change the past. To change it so that we can be together, so that my mother is alive. Maybe if I'd immediately reported my suspicions to my father, everything would be different.

Or would it? Would fate still have torn us apart?

"*Marry me,*" Arluin gasps. In the vision, he clasps my face. "*Please marry me, Reyna. I can't bear the thought of ever being without you—*"

I don't wait to hear my response.

I slam the locket shut, and the delicate metal shudders from the force. My shoulders tremble as I stare at the silver heart in my palm. I squeeze my fist shut, and the locket digs into my skin.

I fall into the silk sheets. The mattress reverberates with the impact. Dust fans into the air and swirls in the moonlight. I gaze up at my hand, the locket concealed within. I let out a heavy breath. It leaves my lips hoarse and uneven.

I wish for him to return, even if that's a selfish wish. If he's caught here in Nolderan, no amount of pleading will save him from my father's wrath. But I need to know the truth. I can't spend the rest of my life with a gaping hole ripped through my heart.

I need to know that he's alive. That he didn't die to save me.

I refuse to believe I'm the reason he is dead.

I bring my knees up to my chest and stare at the fine silk drapes hanging from the mahogany bed frame. My breaths reach them and they ripple slightly. I squeeze the locket tighter in my hand and cradle it to my heart in a silent prayer. To whom, I'm not sure. The gods certainly aren't listening.

We swore a promise to one another, and I'm clutching the proof of it in my fist. I can't help the foolish hope that he may come back, as impossible as it may be.

My eyes flutter shut. The ghost of Arluin's face drifts through my mind, gently lulling me to sleep.

That night, I dream of passing my Mage Trials and him returning to Nolderan.

To marry me, just as we promised.

CHAPTER 21

RELENTLESS WINDS WAIL IN MY ears. They tear at my hair, and the strands become long, slender blades which slice across my cheeks. Overhead the Aether Tower's enormous orb of energy hums, powering all of Nolderan's magical needs.

I pause on the very top step leading up to the tower and scan across the city beneath. The cobalt rooftops appear even smaller than they do from Archmage Gidston's office in the highest spire of the Arcanium; the Aether Tower is at least thrice its size. I can see all the waves as they tumble across the sea and the dark silhouette of Talidor's coastline crowning them.

While I've never known myself to have a phobia of heights, a dizzying bout of fear crashes into me. The city below spins. We're so high up that we must be within the clouds.

My breaths are labored from the countless steps leading up here. I'm certain Eliya and I were walking up the spiraling staircase for at least an hour, though it feels an eternity. My legs are numb from fatigue. It's hard to believe ascending the tower isn't part of the trial itself.

And it's even harder to believe that Eliya is undeterred by the strenuous climb. She bounds ahead to the edge of the platform. The way she leans over and points below makes my stomach lurch. All I can hope is that a sudden gust of wind doesn't blow her off before the Trial of Heart begins.

"Look!" she exclaims. "I can see my house from all the way up here. Even the pond in our garden!"

How she can see such details from this height, I have no idea. Even when I squint, I can't make out much more than rippling cobalt roofs and the streets weaving through them like a network of spider-webs.

I take a step nearer and force a smile. "How wonderful."

She's too busy marveling at the world below to notice the dry-ness in my tone.

We aren't the first adepts to arrive. The Trindell twins are already present, and they both lean against one of the tower's curved stone spires. Blake is also here, along with a few others.

Koby appears behind me. His cheeks are bright red, and he seems even more out of breath than I was. When he reaches the last step, he doubles over.

"By the gods," he groans. "I didn't think those stairs would ever end."

"Nor did I," I reply. "And we still have an entire trial to complete."

He straightens and wipes his brow. "Don't remind me. Hopefully, I'll manage to catch my breath before Archmage Gidston arrives."

I start to respond, but Eliya calls me.

"I can't see your house, Reyna!" she shouts, leaning dangerously far over the platform. "Maybe it's because yours is on the street right beneath us?"

I take a few strides closer and hesitantly peer at the city below. With the winds battering into me and threatening to blow me over the edge, every instinct screams at me to run back down the stairs. Even if it would take an hour to reach the bottom.

But I don't. If I refuse this trial, I will never become a mage. I only have this one chance to prove my worthiness.

And if I fail, I will shame the Ashbourne legacy and disappoint my father.

I ignore my fear and stay right where I stand.

"Maybe it's that," I say.

"And look at how small the Arcanium is," Eliya continues, pointing at the distant spires. "Isn't it crazy since it's actually so big?"

I follow her gaze across to where the Arcanium lies beneath us. Even the tower containing Archmage Gidston's office seems so low down. The looming statues which guard the entrance are little more than dots.

But my assessment of the Arcanium is cut short. Purposeful footsteps stride toward us. I glance back to see Kaely approaching. The wind tugs on her braid.

She scans over my face, and her lips twist with smugness. Whatever she sees in my expression delights her. "Morning, Reyna," she says, stopping a few paces short of Eliya and me. "You look awfully pale today. It wouldn't be the height getting to you, would it? That would be such a shame, since your father can't help you now, can he?"

At her words, the other adepts gathered atop the Aether Tower fall hushed. Koby's mouth hangs agape. I don't know why everyone is so shocked. Maybe it's bold of her to confront me right before our first trial, but this is Kaely. She probably hopes to work me up into such a fury that I strike her with a fireball the moment Archmage Gidston arrives and disqualify myself from the Mage Trials. She would take great pride in being the reason I failed to graduate from the Arcanium.

Maybe she succeeded three years ago, but I'm no longer that same person. I won't lose my temper. Not when it means putting everything at stake.

The other adepts are silent. They glance between Kaely and me, awaiting my response.

Eliya steps between us, no doubt fearing that I will lose my temper and destroy my entire future.

"Why don't you just mind your own business and leave Reyna alone? Everyone is anxious to begin our first trial. The last thing anyone needs is for you to pick a fight with Reyna."

The other adepts nod their agreement, but none dare to directly oppose Kaely. Only Eliya is willing to involve herself in an argument between the daughters of the Archmage of Defense and the Grandmage of Nolderan.

Kaely's gaze rakes across the other adepts. When she finds no allies, she turns on her heel and storms over to the other side of the tower.

I blow out a breath and run my fingers through my hair. With the fierce winds slamming into us, it does little good in tidying the tangled locks.

"Can you believe she tried that stunt right before our first trial?" Eliya grumbles.

I shake my head. But I'm far from surprised by Kaely's behavior. She will stop at nothing to ensure my failure. If there's an opportunity to sabotage my trials, she will seize it.

Before Kaely can decide to march back over and taunt me again, Archmage Gidston arrives.

She steps from a cloud of violet light. The violent winds blow the aether dust through the air.

I'm not the only adept who stares at her in disbelief. Here she is, teleporting straight to the top, while we all had no such luxury. The wards surrounding the tower prevent anyone but official Magi of Nolderan from teleporting inside. The Aether Tower isn't the only area restricted to adepts. The Vaults are another, where Nolderan's most dangerous artifacts are stored far beneath the Arcanium. Only Nolderan's most senior magi are permitted inside.

"It appears everyone has arrived," Archmage Gidston says, scanning over us all. "Good. Then let us delay no further." She continues to the platform's edge.

Eliya and I step away and line up with the other adepts. She stands to my left, and Koby to my right. His fists clench as he visibly braces himself for the trial. Eliya appears much more relaxed. She looks like she's waiting for an order at Flour Power rather than waiting for the Trial of Heart to begin.

"The past five years of your education at the Arcanium will culminate in these three Mage Trials," Lorette declares. "Making it this far is an achievement itself. Many struggle to complete the grueling years of training as an adept.

"Now, as you should all be aware, the Mage Trials consist of three separate trials: the Trial of Heart, the Trial of Mind, and the Trial of Magic. Today, you are all to undertake the first trial and prove whether you have the courage and faith required of a mage. To prove that you will not waver in the face of any danger. To prove that you will serve Nolderan with the utmost dedication and obey the orders of the three Archmagi, and the Grandmage himself, without hesitation."

She gestures to the city below. Her indigo sleeve ripples in the roaring winds. "As for your first trial, I'm sure you can guess what is expected of you."

I swallow at that.

I've heard rumors of what the Trial of Heart entails. Namely, jumping off the edge of the Aether Tower. I dearly hope my suspicions are wrong, but the glint in her eyes suggests otherwise.

"While the task is simple, it is not for the fainthearted." She holds out her hand. "*Conparios.*" A plain feather appears. It is of a tawny color with white spots along the tip and most likely originates from a quail.

She pinches the feather between her fingers and holds it high for us all to see. "One by one, you will leap from the Aether Tower with nothing but this feather. And I must stress that I mean nothing else, not even your magic. Casting even a single spell is forbidden on this trial. Choosing to use your magic means demonstrating a lack of faith, and you will fail this trial."

I stare out at the sea of cobalt rooftops. My legs feel wobbly. I hope I'm not visibly shaking, or else Kaely will be pleased to see my fear.

Despite the terror snaking up my spine, I have no choice but to place my faith in Archmage Gidston and the Trial of Heart. Because failing this trial means failing to become a mage.

"Are there any questions?" Lorette asks.

Koby fumbles for a moment. Then he hesitantly raises his hand.

"Yes, Adept Varsley?"

"Um," he begins, chewing the inside of his cheek, "if we are forbidden from using our magic, how will we survive the fall?"

Further down the line, some adepts murmur. I suppose they're wondering how we will avoid certain death. That's also what I would like to know.

"Answering that question would defeat the purpose of this trial," Archmage Gidston replies. "However, I can reveal two things. Firstly, that if we allowed all our adepts to fall to their deaths, then Nolderan would be in very short supply of magi. And secondly, that if you ensure you hold the feather at all times, then you will be in no danger. I cannot say more than that, nor can I reveal the specific mechanics of this trial. You must all have faith."

"What if we let go of the feather?" Koby asks. "By accident, I mean."

The Archmage gives him a pointed look. "Don't let go of it."

His throat bobs as he swallows.

"If you would like to forfeit, Adept Varsley, then you are welcome to do so. However, you will fail your Mage Trials and will be unable to graduate from the Arcanium. The same goes for anyone else who lacks the faith to complete the Trial of Heart."

Koby quickly shakes his head. "No, Archmage Gidston. I don't want to forfeit."

"Good," she says, her gaze returning to the rest of us. "Then if there are no further questions, we shall begin. Who would like to go first?"

No one steps forth. Aside from the howling wind, there's only silence. Maybe if nobody volunteers to be the first person to leap, Archmage Gidston will pick someone herself.

Behind my back, I cross my fingers and hope she doesn't choose me. If I see someone else jump and not die, it will go a long way to bolstering my faith in this trial.

Before Lorette can select anyone, Kaely raises her hand. Tension slips from my shoulders. She's only volunteering herself to prove how much better she is than me, but for once I'm grateful for her arrogance. I really didn't want to be the first one to leap off the tower.

"Adept Calton, you wish to go first?"

Kaely's lips pull into a calculating smile. Her expression makes my heart skip a beat. Whatever she is planning, I'm not sure it has anything to do with her going first.

"Actually, Archmage Gidston, I was wondering whether I could make a suggestion?"

"What suggestion do you wish to make?" Lorette asks.

"I was thinking that it would be the most fitting for Reyna to go first, since her father is the Grandmage of Nolderan. I'm sure I'm not the only one who wants to see how it's done."

My stomach sinks with dread. Everyone's eyes are on me. I grit my teeth, willing for my apprehension not to show.

I'm probably not the only one who noticed Koby's fear, but he can afford to show such weakness. His father isn't the Grandmage of Nolderan. He isn't being constantly measured against impossible expectations. And not just the expectations imposed on him by others, but also the ones he imposes on himself.

To my dismay, whispers of agreement ripple through the other adepts. They are almost inaudible over the violent winds, but I hear them anyway. Even Koby nods his head. It's all I can do not to glare at him for hanging me along with everyone else. If I do, I will reveal how much this trial terrifies me. They will all think me weak. And I refuse to ever again be weak.

Because the cost of weakness is death.

Eliya is the only adept who doesn't fervently nod her agreement. Unlike the others, she isn't thinking of how my going first benefits her. She clenches her jaw and doesn't even try to hide the glare she flashes Kaely.

"Adept Ashbourne," Archmage Gidston says to me, "would you like to go first?"

Since she has asked, I suppose I could decline. But that would mean admitting my fear. And maybe she would interpret my refusal as forfeiting this trial.

That's a risk I cannot take.

I paint the most courageous expression I can muster on my face and hope that it convinces me as much as everyone else.

I can do this.

I am the Grandmage's daughter, and a descendant of Nolderan's most powerful family. My heritage must count for something.

And, as Archmage Gidston said, this trial is arguably easy. All I need to do is hold the feather, jump off the tower, and ignore the instinct to save myself from falling with my magic.

I suck in a breath and say, "Of course I would love to, Archmage Gidston. I'm honored that Kaely would request for me to go first."

I must appear calm. Or Kaely will know how much she's riled me.

"Excellent," Lorette says, holding the feather out to me. She gestures for me to come forth.

Eliya squeezes my hand and whispers, "Good luck!"

I return her gesture with a thin smile and start over to Archmage Gidston. When I reach her, I take the feather from her grasp.

The feather itself is unremarkable. I hold it high and examine it with great care, but I detect no magic within the feather—just the residue from when she summoned it.

I'm not certain how an ordinary feather will ensure my survival, but I can only cling to it and maintain my faith in this trial.

"Are you ready to begin?" Archmage Gidston asks.

My gaze drifts beyond the feather to the city below. Soon I will be plummeting toward those cobalt rooftops and pointed spires. My stomach tangles into a thick knot.

I don't look at Archmage Gidston as I nod. The gesture is stiffer than I expect, and I hope no one can see the tension in my neck and shoulders.

"Then you must now jump from the tower," she says. "And do not, under any circumstances, release the feather."

The moisture drains from my mouth at the warning, and my throat is left parched. All I can imagine is the quail feather slipping from my grasp and leaving me to tumble to my death.

I'm glad my back is to all the other adepts. I'm certain the blood has drained from my face, casting me a sickly pale shade. I keep my attention fixed on the city beneath, so that Archmage Gidston can't see the true extent of my horror.

My fingers grip the quail feather. Faith. I just need to have faith that Archmage Gidston won't let me die, that the feather won't slip from my fingers. As long as I keep hold of it, I won't fall to my death.

I hope.

"And if you are having any second thoughts—"

Knowing that I've delayed long enough, I don't let Archmage Gidston finish. Before she can ask me whether I'd like to forfeit the trial, I throw myself off the tower.

The winds are quick to embrace me. They slam into my cheeks. The cobalt rooftops and deadly spires rush toward me. My gut clenches. I think I might be screaming into the wind. But they roar so loudly that they drown out my voice.

A sudden gust shoves me to the right. The impact catches me off-guard, and the quail feather almost slips from my grasp. I clutch it with all the force I can. My survival depends on it.

The wind spins me over and over as I tumble through the air. A painful ache fills my ears from the changing pressure.

Gleaming spires hurdle toward me, threatening to impale me like enormous spears. I'm falling faster than my mind can process it. A moment ago, they seemed so far away. Now they are so close.

One spire draws sickeningly near. I squeeze my eyes shut, unable to watch as it surges up to meet me. I wonder whether I will feel any pain before the spire rips me open.

Panic shoots through me like bursts of lightning. My magic screams at me to save myself. To teleport to safety.

But I ignore every instinct. I can only place my faith in Archmage Gidston. Using my magic means failing.

And I can't fail.

The spire skims past. I open my eyes a heartbeat later. By then, it's already high above. And the street is almost upon me.

People below are going about their daily business, unaware that I'm plummeting toward them. Toward my death.

The ground is only a few feet away.

I'm going to die.

I scream. But no one seems to hear me. I'm too panicked to check if the quail feather is still clutched in my fist, or if I lost it on the way down.

Magic boils in my veins. With death so near, it's almost impossible to ignore its desperate plea. Aether snaps to my fingers. The image of my manor's gates and the lion crest on them flashes through my mind.

But before I can utter *laxus* and teleport away, aether explodes around me. The blinding light swallows me. I no longer feel the wind whipping me. Magic thunders in my ears and makes them ache.

When I next blink, I'm standing at the very top of the Aether Tower, in the exact spot I stood prior to jumping.

My legs buckle beneath me. I don't know how I manage to stay on my feet. I grasp my wobbly knees, willing them to steady, and rapidly breathe in and out. My eyes trail across to the city below. Knowing how close I'd been to death almost makes me vomit. Thankfully, I don't.

"Congratulations, Adept Ashbourne," Archmage Gidston says. With the ringing in my ears, her voice sounds distant, though she stands less than a few feet away. "You have successfully passed the first Mage Trial, the Trial of Heart. Today, you have demonstrated the faith and courage required of a mage."

Right now, I feel anything but courageous. All I want is to teleport home and curl up in my bed. I take a moment to process the rest of her words. That I passed, even though I was so close to using my magic and forfeiting my trial.

With my body in shock from the closeness of death, I'm incapable of feeling triumph. I stay there at the edge for a while, doubled over and gasping for breath. I'm surprised she doesn't usher me away.

At least I'll never again need to jump from the Aether Tower. This is certainly an experience I don't intend to repeat.

When I straighten and force my trembling legs to walk away, Archmage Gidston turns to the rest of the adepts. "Who would like to go next?"

Eliya's hand shoots up. "I'll go!" she exclaims, darting forth and swiping the quail feather from my fingers.

Before Archmage Gidston can say anything, Eliya leaps from the tower. Her crimson hair spills around her.

With widened eyes, I stare down at her descending form. There isn't even a trace of fear inside her eyes.

And that either makes her the most courageous person I know, or the most foolish.

CHAPTER 22

I STUMBLE OUT OF THE Violet Tree, almost tripping over the low step and flying into Eliya. She laughs and grips both my arms, steadying me in place.

The icy evening breeze slams into my cheeks, somewhat sobering me. I tilt back my head and peer up at the darkness veiling the sky. The clouds are as dense as smoke, and specks of snow whir through the wind. Some gather on my lashes, and I blink them away. The crescent moon peeks from the cover of clouds and illuminates the heavens with its silvery rays.

My vision blurs. Then there are two moons staring down at me.

I rub my eyes until my sight returns to normal. Tonight, I drank much more wine than I intended. I was hoping to get up early tomorrow morning and take some more notes on *Concerning Conflagration and Combustion*, but I doubt I'll wake before noon. Coming to The Violet Tree wasn't my idea, though. It was Eliya's.

When we were descending the Aether Tower after the Trial of Heart, Eliya suggested celebrating our success with a few glasses of wine. I declined when she first asked and reminded her that we still have two more trials to complete this week. But she only insisted our next trial isn't until Wednesday and we have all of tomorrow to recover. Having no argument to that, and still feeling awful for leaving her at the bakery on Friday, I ended up agreeing.

The thought of the next trial fills me with dread. Archmage Gidston said the Trial of Heart is arguably the easiest of the three, and that involved a near death experience. Two adepts failed this morning. Each teleported away before Archmage Gidston could summon them back to the top of the tower. Now our class of twenty adepts is down to eighteen.

I'm also not entirely sure what the Trial of Mind involves, aside from it assessing whether we adepts have the cleverness required of magi. It also apparently takes place in a maze far beneath the Arcanium, though I'm uncertain of the accuracy of those rumors. While studying Alvord Ashbourne's old tome probably won't help me pass the next trial, it's better than sitting around and doing nothing while my anxieties gnaw on me.

"What should we do now?" Eliya asks, interrupting my thoughts. She murmurs *conparios* and summons her crimson coin purse. She shakes it, but only the rustling of velvet fills the night. Not the clinking of silver. "That last bottle we ordered emptied my purse."

My own purse is just as empty. With Yule around the corner, I've already spent a lot on buying presents for New Year's Eve. And tonight, I also burned through the last of my stipend.

"Well," I say with a shrug, "I suppose if we're out of money then we'll have to head back for the night."

Eliya pouts. "But it's not even nine o'clock!"

"It's the week of our Mage Trials. We should get an early night so we're well rested for Wednesday. The Trial of Mind will involve more than jumping off a tower."

Eliya grabs my arm and swings it back and forth. "Reyna," she grumbles, drawing out both syllables of my name, "when did you get so old and boring?"

"We *are* twenty-one now, in case you've forgotten."

"Age is just a number, especially when you're a mage who will live until like two-hundred."

"We're not magi yet. We still have two more trials to pass. And drinking so much that we sleep through all of tomorrow and still feel groggy on Wednesday morning certainly won't help with that."

"But we won't feel groggy on Wednesday morning if we sleep through all of tomorrow."

I shake my head at her. "Anyway, we don't have any money left. How are you expecting to get more drinks? By flirting with rich noblemen?"

"That isn't a bad idea." Her lips stretch into a wide grin. "But I have an even better one in mind."

I know I shouldn't ask, since it will only encourage her, but curiosity gets the better of me. And the wine is also likely to blame. "What is it?" I ask, folding my arms and bracing myself for whatever maddened idea Eliya's crazy mind has conjured.

"We'll solve our money problem like old times!"

"What are you talking about?"

"Have you really gotten so old and boring that you don't remember the mischief we got up to as first-years?"

"Oh," I say, now realizing what she means. "Absolutely not."

"Why not?"

"Because we're fifth-years who are soon to become official Magi of Nolderan and should know better than to break the law."

"It's only my uncle we'll be stealing from," Eliya replies. "It isn't illegal if it's from family."

"I'm pretty sure stealing is illegal no matter who you're stealing from. Besides, he's your family—not mine."

"We've never been caught before."

"And what if we're caught this time? We would be in so much trouble that Archmage Gidston will probably disqualify us from the Mage Trials."

"Why would we get caught now? We're better at magic than when we were first-years."

"You never know what may happen."

"Fine, fine," Eliya says, waving her hand dismissively. "Let's go home and miss out on the enormous shipment of moon-blossom wine my uncle just received this evening."

"Moon-blossom wine?"

"Mm," she says and pulls me along the road. "Doesn't matter now though, since we're going home."

"Wait." I tug my arm from her grasp, and she comes to a stop. "Has he really got loads of moon-blossom wine?"

"That's what I just said. An enormous shipment of moon-blossom arrived earlier this evening, and we're going to miss out on it. Think about all the aether swirling inside every sweet, sweet drop. Drinking plenty of moon-blossom wine would ensure our bodies are fueled with magic for Wednesday's trial. It's such a shame we're going home."

"Fine," I say, heaving out a sigh. "You win."

Eliya beams triumphantly at me. "I knew you would eventually come to your senses."

The offer is too tempting to turn down. Moon-blossom wine is like liquid gold poured into a bottle, and certainly costs as much. Only the moon elves of Lumaria brew it, so we have to import it from the elven continent of Belentra.

Long ago the magi tried cultivating moon-berries, the aether-infused fruit which flowers into the precious blossom, but they never had any luck. Lumaria is situated upon more nexuses—clusters of ley line intersections—than Nolderan, and even imbuing the soil with aether isn't enough for the moon-berry trees to grow. Maybe it's because the plant prefers the eternal night of Lumaria. Unfortunately, we don't have our own equivalent aether-filled fruit.

Most people can't afford moon-blossom wine, and those who can only drink it on special occasions. Such as New Year's Eve.

When we started at the Arcanium, Eliya and I regularly drank moon-blossom wine, thanks to Eliya's uncle. We only ceased our exploits when he became suspicious over his mystery thieves and tripled the security of his warehouses.

I hope he's dropped his guard over the past four years.

"To your uncle's warehouse, then?"

Eliya's grin widens. "Let's go."

Eliya's uncle, Garon Whiteford, is unequivocally the richest man in all of Nolderan. While he possesses no aptitude for magic and was never selected for adept training like Eliya's father, he more than makes up for it with his trading expertise. Whatever goods you want from the three kingdoms, or even from Belentra, Garon can get them for you. He holds shares in at least half of all businesses in Nolderan: from taverns to barbers to tailors. Even those he hasn't invested in owe him many favors. And most importantly, he's the key supplier of moon-blossom wine here in Nolderan.

While a merchant as illustrious as Garon lives in the Upper City, his warehouses are situated away from his own residence and lie along the docks: the perfect location for receiving his latest shipments.

Eliya and I emerge from a cloud of violet light. The gentle sea breeze rustles through my hair, and the smell of salt wafts into my nose. Behind us, ships of all sizes sit docked at the many wooden piers traipsing out to sea. There are huge galleons carrying silks from Selynis, and there are also small fishing vessels which have not long returned from their evening haul.

In the shadowed horizon, far beyond the slumbering ships, mountains from the mainland of Talidor rise above the sea's tumultuous surface.

Ahead of us are the vast stone buildings of the Warehouse District. Eliya takes the lead, starting down the street and gesturing for me to follow her. Garon's storehouses are clustered together, and they are some of the largest in Nolderan.

The buildings loom over us, and their towering height blocks out the night sky. No specks of snow are visible down these narrow streets.

Our hurried footsteps sound tremendously loud against the silence. After a few strides, I glance back over my shoulder. I'm not sure why I do, since we are yet to break any laws, but I can't shake away my paranoia. If we are caught, the consequences will be dire.

This is such a stupid idea. Why did I agree to it?

My pace falters. Eliya immediately notices. She frowns at me.

"What's the matter?" she hisses.

"What if we get caught?"

She shoots me an exasperated look. "We've already been through this. It's only my uncle. I promise it'll be fine."

I press my lips together. "You're sure?"

"Very sure."

I hesitate for a moment longer. Before I can change my mind and teleport home, Eliya grabs my arm and pulls me deeper into the Warehouse District.

A few blocks later, Eliya stops behind a corner and peers around it. The warehouse Garon uses to store his liquor is up ahead, but she doesn't take another step forth.

"What is it?" I whisper.

"My uncle," she mouths. "He's here."

"Maybe we should go back."

Eliya continues to stare at the street around the corner. I can't see past her.

"What's he doing?"

"Talking to someone," she says, turning back to me. "And his workers are all carting out moon-blossom wine. Lots and lots of it."

"There will probably be none left for us," I murmur.

"Let's wait until they're gone. Then we'll see how much is left."

Knowing she won't leave without first searching her uncle's warehouse, I don't bother arguing with her. Hopefully, we won't get caught for trespassing a warehouse already emptied of moon-blossom wine.

I close my eyes, straining my ears to make out what the muffled voices are saying.

"Alric!" Garon shouts. "Be careful with that! If even a single bottle is broken, I will have to deduct it from your wage."

"Yes, sir," comes the meek reply. Rickety wheels roll over the cobblestones. I suppose the sound belongs to the carts which Garon's workers are using to distribute the moon-blossom wine.

Minutes stretch into what feels like hours. I lean against the stone wall behind me and fold my arms. It takes an eternity for the voices to quieten and for the footsteps to fade away.

"They just shut the doors," Eliya says. "We should be good to go now."

"Is there anyone left?"

"I can only see one of his workers. But we'll need to be quick. In case they come back."

"And you're sure we won't get caught?"

"Stop worrying so much," she says, shaking her head at me. "Right, let's not waste any more time. You deal with the worker. I'll get the doors open. We'll grab all the bottles we can and then make a run for it."

I only nod.

"*Conparios*," Eliya says. A dark cloak appears from a cloud of aether. She drapes it over her shoulders and pulls the hood over her crimson hair.

I do the same, and when both our identities are concealed, Eliya dashes beyond the safety of our corner. I hang back a few paces and watch as the worker, who is busy tidying a stack of crates, notices Eliya rushing toward Garon's storehouse.

He opens his mouth, either to shout for guards or to demand to know what she's doing, but no words have the chance to escape his lips. Aether swirls in my fingers.

"*Somnus*," I mutter, my words barely brushing the evening breeze. Though I speak quietly, it's loud enough for my magic to answer my call.

Violet light drifts over to the worker. It seeps into his nostrils as he inhales.

He blinks lazily, and his movements slow as my spell tightens its grasp over him. Then his eyes finally close.

In the next breath, he tilts over and falls face-first onto the street, snoring loudly. I pause for a few beats, ensuring he's definitely fast asleep, and then hurry after Eliya.

How long his slumber will last depends on two factors. Firstly, how much aether I used to fuel the spell. Since I cast it quickly, I didn't power it with an awful lot. Secondly, it depends on how much aether flows through his blood. The greater his affinity for magic, the more he will resist my spell.

With some luck, he will remain asleep for several minutes. That should be long enough for us to get in and out of the warehouse.

Up ahead, Eliya fiddles with the warehouse's gigantic lock. She wiggles a thin metal pick inside it. Magic is of no use. The building is heavily fortified with defensive wards, and even the slightest tremor of magic will set off the city's alarms. That means we can only resort to ordinary methods to break into the storehouse.

Fortunately, Eliya is an expert at lock-picking. Her father keeps his most treasured potions inside large chests with similar locks, offering Eliya plenty of opportunity to practice over the years. Somehow, her father has never caught her breaking into his chests and borrowing his potions.

It takes less than a minute for Eliya to burst the lock open. The internal springs click into place. She glances back and flashes me a smug grin. Then she tears the padlock from the wide wooden doors and shoves them open, revealing the contents of Garon's storehouse.

Barrels of ale and crates full of rum line the stone walls. We waste no time rummaging through them and head up to the second floor, where Garon keeps his more expensive liquor. The bottles here are from world-famous breweries, indicated by the fancy script on their labels. Many crates of moon-blossom wine lie at the back, and the dusky liquid sparkles in the low light.

"I can't believe how many bottles he has in here!" I exclaim, sifting through for the most expensive wine. The labels are written in Elvish, and while I can't read it fluently, I can recognize their alphabet well enough to identify which are from Twilight Hill—the finest winery in all of Lumaria.

Eliya picks up several bottles with the same labels, filling her arms with wine. "Yule is only a few weeks away. I suppose he's hoping to make a good profit off moon-blossom wine this year."

Once we have gathered all the crystalline bottles we can carry, we hurry back down the wooden steps.

Just as we reach the lower floor, I see another worker kneeling beside the sleeping one, frantically shaking him. Worst of all, he's shouting loudly enough for his voice to echo through the entire street.

I curse and bolt out the warehouse, Eliya close behind. As if on cue, a patrol of guards appears from around the corner. They glance between us and the two workers. The bottles of moon-blossom wine bundled in our arms are incriminating enough.

The guards don't hesitate before charging straight for us.

CHAPTER 23

WE RUN, AND THE GUARDS give chase. I clutch the wine tightly as we flee through the Lower City. We turn street after street, hoping to lose our pursuers. Exhaustion makes our breaths ragged, and rawness burns down my throat and into my chest. But I press on at full speed.

No matter what, we can't get caught. Not when it means being disqualified from the trials and never becoming magi.

We reach a dead end. I grit my teeth, examining the wall. The guards' hurried footsteps sound a few streets away. Maybe we'll have enough time.

"Let's teleport," I say. "Now."

"To the cliffs?"

I give her a hurried nod, already gathering aether into my hands. I visualize the cliffs lying far beyond the city walls, at the very edge of our island. "*Laxus,*" I call. As does Eliya.

Just as we unleash our magic, the guards appear at the end of the street.

Fortunately, they are too far away to interrupt our teleportation spells, and we vanish before their eyes.

In the next heartbeat, the blinding light fades into shadowy cliffs. The moon silvers the crests of the waves rolling beneath, and the evening breeze rustles through the surrounding trees. With our arms still full of wine, we continue higher up the grassy mound and collapse at the top.

"Thought they nearly had us there," Eliya gasps, setting her bottles down on the grass and wiping the sweat from her brow.

"That's because they nearly did," I retort. "I thought you promised everything would be fine."

"We weren't caught, were we?"

"We were worryingly close."

"But we weren't actually caught, and that's what matters." She tears the cork off the bottle closest to her and lifts it to her lips.

I watch her for a moment and shake my head, but I don't continue the argument. I reach for a bottle and sip on the moon-blossom wine inside. The elegant sweetness washes over my tongue, every drop oozing with magic.

There really is nothing better than moon-blossom wine. And this stash might be worth almost getting caught.

"Wouldn't it be nice to be a moon elf?" I say, shaking the crystalline bottle either side as I muse over it. The dusky liquid swirls within and glitters in the starlight.

"What makes you say that?"

"Well, moon-blossom wine will be much cheaper in Lumaria since it won't need importing. And if I lived there, I could grow my own moon-berry trees and make my own wine. I could even start up a winery."

Eliya leans forward, her eyes gleaming. Some of her wine splashes out of the bottle. "If I had my own Lumarian winery, I would drink it day and night. I would have so much I could bathe in it."

"You wouldn't be able to sell it if you bathed in it."

"I just wouldn't tell any merchants about that part."

"What if they found bits in it?"

Eliya narrows her eyes. "Are you saying I'm dirty?"

"Maybe," I say with a shrug.

"*Aquis.*" Water splashes from Eliya's fingers. It soaks me from head to toe.

My mouth falls agape. I stare down in disbelief at my drenched dress. A chilling wind rolls over me, far icier now that I'm soaked through. "I can't believe you just did that!"

"And I can't believe you just called me dirty," she says, a smile twitching on her lips. "Serves you—"

Before she can finish, I call out *aquis* and return the favor. My water spell splashes over her, and then she is as drenched as I am.

We both burst into laughter. But it isn't funny for long, because now we're both soaked and shivering. My teeth chatter. If we weren't magi in training, the chill would spoil our evening. Luckily for us, the problem is easily fixed by speaking the spell-word *calida*. Warmth sparks within, and I can no longer feel the chill. The heat radiating from my skin dries the fabric of my clothes.

We soon return to drinking our moon-blossom wine, and it doesn't take long for us each to finish a bottle and crack open another. With each sip, more aether courses through my bloodstream.

"Reyna?" Eliya says after a moment.

I glance up at her. "Yeah?"

Her fingers play around the top of her crystalline bottle, and she chews on her lower lip. She looks stuck for words. Eliya never hesitates to speak.

"Are you sure you're all right?" she finally asks.

"What do you mean?"

"You didn't seem yourself the other day."

My heart skips a beat. I hope she hasn't found out I visited the library after leaving the bakery. "On Friday?"

She nods.

"I had a headache."

"I don't believe you."

I flinch.

"At least, not entirely. I don't think it was just because you had a headache."

I lean back onto the grass. "Then what do you think it is?"

"I don't know," she says with a sigh. "It's just after you went, I remembered that street was where I found you three years ago, when you were . . ."

When I was searching the heaps of bodies for Arluin.

She doesn't say those ghastly words. They linger between us, nonetheless.

She puts down her bottle and takes my hand. "If you want to talk about it, I'm here to listen."

I lower my head, unable to meet her gaze. I know I should probably talk about everything with her. It's been so long, and yet I've not spoken to anyone about what happened that night. I doubt it's healthy to keep such awful things bottled up, but trying to speak about it feels like a monumental task.

"I . . . I never found his body," I whisper. My words are so quiet I don't know whether they reach Eliya over the roaring wind. "I have no idea whether he's dead or alive. And I don't think I'll ever know the truth."

Eliya squeezes my hand. The small gesture grants me a sudden burst of courage. My caged emotions bubble and overflow, spilling from my lips.

"If he's alive, why has he never come back? Why didn't he at least let me know that he isn't dead?"

"Reyna," Eliya says softly, "if he's alive, after the crimes he committed, he can't return. And I think it's best he never does."

"I know," I reply, swallowing down the bitterness swelling in my throat. "My father would have him executed. That night, he ordered Archmage Calton to burn them all. Even Arluin. I know what fate awaits him here, but I miss him so very much."

Eliya releases my hand and presses her lips together. Her reluctance is clear. Whatever she intends to say next, I know I won't like to hear it. But I don't stop her from speaking. "Reyna, he's a necromancer. During the attack, he sided with his father. He murdered innocents and raised them from the dead."

"You weren't there," I grind out, my fingers curling around the neck of my bottle. "Heston captured me and planned to use me against my father. The only way Arluin could save me was by earning his father's trust. And to do that, he had to resort to using necromancy. If he hadn't made those choices, the entire city would have likely fallen."

"You're right, I wasn't there. But how did he know how to wield dark magic?"

"His father taught him," I say, picking at the decorative label of my bottle. I don't look up at her as I speak. I fear what I'll see in her expression.

But I hear the betrayal in her words all the same. "You knew about it?"

"He only admitted it after promising to marry me."

"I can't believe you didn't tell me about his father teaching him necromancy."

I hate the hurt in her voice. "It was Arluin's secret to tell, not mine."

"But you're my best friend."

"If anyone else had found out, Arluin would have been exiled. Or killed."

"You didn't trust me?"

"No, I just didn't want to burden you with such a terrible secret. And he only told me a few days before everything happened."

Eliya gives me a stiff nod. She doesn't press the issue any further and sips on her wine.

I stare down at my bottle instead of drinking from it.

Would things be any different if I had told her Arluin's secret? If I'd told my father?

I shake my head. Telling anyone wouldn't have stopped Heston's attack. It wouldn't have stopped him from murdering my mother. All that would have changed is Arluin being unable to rescue me. Then I probably would be dead, along with my mother. And I don't want to even imagine what Nolderan's current state would be.

"Anyway," Eliya says, "I guess it makes sense."

"What makes sense?"

"Why you've been so down lately. There's a part of you that's wondering whether he will come back, isn't there?"

My shoulders sag. "Is it wrong of me to hope that he will? Even though he is a necromancer? Even though it will mean certain death for him?"

Eliya shifts closer and pulls me into a fierce hug. "It isn't wrong of you to want that," she whispers. "You still love him. And you've loved him for a very long time. But he can't come back. You know that, don't you?"

"I know," I mutter.

We stay like that for some time. The waves crash into the rocks far below, and the frigid wind howls. With the warmth radiating from us both, we don't feel the chill. Snowflakes powder our hair.

"Come on then," Eliya finally says, releasing me from her embrace. "Let's go home."

The crescent moon has drifted far through the sky, still shrouded by the heavy clouds. I'm uncertain what time it is, but I know it must be late for Eliya to suggest returning. Or maybe she suggested it because I'm such awful company tonight.

I gaze at the unopened wine bottles scattered all around us. "What should we do with these? If I take them home, my father will be suspicious as to where I got them from. As will yours."

"We can bury them here," she replies, tapping her chin in thought. "And then after we pass our final Mage Trial, the Trial of Magic, we can come back here to celebrate."

"All right," I say and stagger up onto my feet. The world sways around me. While sitting down, I didn't realize how tipsy I was. But now that I'm standing, I notice the full extent of all the wine I drank this evening.

"*Tera*," Eliya mutters, and green light swirls in her fingers. She directs it to the grass, and her magic carves out a hole. The layers of mud float a few feet above, surrounded by a vivid green glow.

I'm grateful Eliya took charge of digging the hole. If I tried, I would probably carve through the entire cliff. Wine makes magic far less precise. Especially if you slur the spell-words and your magic thinks you mean something else.

While Eliya collects the unopened bottles and deposits them inside the hole, I gather the empty ones and murmur *ventrez*, blowing the evidence off the cliff. I take care to say the spell-word with as much clarity as I can. Thankfully, nothing unexpected happens.

I don't see where the wine bottles land. Since I hear no smashing, the waves must have devoured them.

Eliya lowers the layers of mud back into the hole. When the earth is returned to its rightful place, the emerald glow fades. There is no seam in the grass to show where Eliya dug it up. It looks like it was never disturbed.

"All done," she declares, brushing her hands together. "Time for us to head back, then. Will you be fine teleporting yourself home?"

"You definitely drank more than me tonight. It should be me asking you that question."

"We both know I can handle my wine better than you," she says with a wink. "But anyway, I don't want to leave you here by yourself if you're not feeling well."

"I feel fine."

"You know what I mean."

"It's been three years. I can handle it."

"All right," she says. "Make sure you don't study too much in the morning."

I breathe a laugh. "I promise I won't."

She draws aether into her hands. "Night then, Reyna. Sleep well."

"You too," I reply, just as she mutters *laxus* and disappears into violet light.

Aether dust scatters through the wind and swirls with the snowflakes.

With a deep breath, I gaze up at the crescent moon. My fingers play with the silver locket hanging around my neck.

Eliya is right. If Arluin is alive, it's probably best he never returns. Because I fear I would forsake my future, my father, just to be with him.

I know I must put the past behind me. I can't spend the rest of my life wallowing over what happened three years ago. But I don't know how to banish the grief which haunts my heart.

I draw out a sigh. Standing out here all night will do me no good.

Closing my eyes, I gather aether into my fingers and picture the towering gates outside my manor. I imagine them so clearly that I can almost see the two lions roaring at each other on our family crest.

When the image is concrete, I whisper *laxus* and unleash my magic. I fade away into the night, leaving behind a cloud of glittering purple light.

Yet when I emerge from the teleportation spell, brine wafts into my nose.

I open my eyes. The tall gates of my manor are nowhere to be seen.

I let out a groan and blink several times, praying that I'm not actually looking at the ships anchored in the harbor. But no matter how much I rub my eyes, the piers don't morph into my home.

Fantastic.

I slap my forehead. It seems I mis-targeted my teleportation spell, no doubt because of the wine. The only consolation is that my mistake hasn't meant a trip deep into the sea. That has apparently happened to a few magi before.

Not daring to try teleporting again in case it lands me beneath the waves, I break into a sprint and hurry through the Lower City.

The streets are almost empty at this late hour. A few drunken sailors stumble out of taverns and call over to me. I ignore them all and keep my attention fixed on the road ahead. Fortunately, they don't bother me with anything more than a few slurred shouts.

Since my manor is located at the far end of the Upper City, my journey home is a long one. The streets are shadowed, and only the radiance of the floating aether crystals stops me from tripping over the uneven stones. The buildings seem to sway as I run. I grimace. If only I'd targeted the spell more carefully. I was certain that the image was clear enough in my mind, but apparently not.

It takes me a long while to reach the steps leading up to the Upper City. By then, my pace has slowed to a jog. With everything spinning around me, I'm not sure whether I'll manage the rest of the way home. Not wanting to spend the night sleeping in an alleyway, I force myself onward.

But it seems Vetia, the Goddess of Luck, really isn't on my side tonight.

A force slams into me. It sends me flying back onto the cobblestones. The impact bruises my limbs, and I graze my palms from trying to break my fall.

Wood splinters, and the cart I crashed into topples over. All the bottles inside smash onto the street. Red wine splashes out like blood and soaks me.

Dazed, I stare at the debris.

Footsteps hurry toward me.

"Are you all right?" a low male voice asks, nudging my shoulder.

Still disoriented, I blink a few times until my sight refocuses. I tilt back my head and turn my attention upward.

A very handsome stranger gazes down at me.

CHAPTER 24

WE STARE AT EACH OTHER, neither of us saying anything. The night breeze tugs on the fine, golden strands of his wavy hair. A hint of fair stubble dusts his jawline, and his emerald eyes glisten in the radiance of the surrounding aether crystals. I've never seen such a vibrant shade of green.

His gaze breaks away from mine, and he scans over the rest of me. I follow his eyes as they sweep over my torn sleeves and the grazed skin peeking from beneath.

He seems to remember himself then and jolts back to life. He reaches for my hand, which is scraped from the uneven stones. "Here," he says. "Allow me to help you up."

I don't protest as he takes my hand and guides me back onto my feet. Lightning sparks from our conjoined fingers and surges up my arm. It's as though magic is pounding through my body, but I know this energy isn't aether. Yet it feels like sorcery, nonetheless.

His doublet is of scarlet satin, with a filigree pattern entwining the cuffs and the high collar. Beneath it he wears dark breeches and polished black boots which reach his mid-calves. He appears to be a few years older than me—certainly no more than five—and stands only a few inches taller. His fingers are also callused, which is unexpected since his clothes suggest he is of nobility.

"Have we met before?" I blurt, the words out of my mouth sooner than I can realize. I immediately regret them. He must already think me an idiot for gawking at him, let alone for asking him such a ridiculous question. Of course we have never met before today. How would I forget those striking emerald eyes?

Fortunately, he doesn't mock me for the question. He only blinks at me. His fair lashes are long enough to make even Eliya jealous.

"No," he says. "No, we have never met."

Unable to withstand the intensity of his gaze, I lower mine and focus on the cobblestones beneath. Thousands of tiny glass shards glitter around us like fallen stars. Puddles of blood-red wine streak across the street.

"You're hurt," he says, examining the scrapes on my arm. My eyes drift over the wreckage surrounding us. I notice the labels of his smashed bottles: *Ruberra* and *Sanguilus*. While they are both nowhere near as expensive as moon-blossom wine, they certainly aren't cheap.

"All your wine! I'm so terribly sorry—"

"Don't be," he says, cutting me off. "They're only wine bottles. They don't matter."

"But so many are broken!"

"And you are injured." There's a softness to his voice, which makes me shiver. I do my best to stifle my reaction to him.

"I'm fine," I say, pulling my arm from his grasp. He lets me go.

His perfectly straight brows pinch together. They're as golden as his wavy locks. "Are you sure?"

"They're just shallow scratches. With a bit of Blood Balm, I'll be healed within a few hours."

The handsome stranger says nothing. He continues to stare at me with that piercing gaze of his, making me feel increasingly uncomfortable. I suppose I could bid him good night and continue on my way, but I don't. I could tell myself it's because I feel guilty over smashing so many of his wine bottles, but I would be lying if I said it has nothing to do with the way I feel inexplicably drawn to him.

"Where were you taking your cart?" I ask.

"Oh," he says, scratching the back of his head and disturbing the golden locks which tumble from there. "Back to my tavern."

"You own a tavern?"

"I do," he replies. "The Old Dove."

"Oh, I know that one. Isn't it a few streets away from The Violet Tree?"

"Yeah, on Fairway Avenue."

"So, you must be the new owner who bought the place a couple of weeks ago?"

"That's me."

"My friend and I have been meaning to visit. The last owner was too shrewd to hire enough staff, so you would always have to wait hours to be served."

"I have heard that the previous management left much to be desired," he says. "We're closed tonight, since it's a Monday, but why don't you stop by tomorrow and see what you think of the service under my management?"

His offer almost sounds like a business affair, but there's an edge to his voice which suggests this is more than a friendly invite. Maybe I'm imagining that he's flirting with me.

"Sure," I say, even though tomorrow night will be the night before our second trial. "I would love to visit."

We stand there awkwardly. Then I remember that I was asking about his cart.

"Do you need any help with your cart?"

His gaze sweeps across to it and lingers on the broken wheels. He doesn't look as concerned as I expected him to be, and I'm relieved he isn't too annoyed at the current state of his cart. And his wine, since most of the bottles are smashed.

"I can use my magic to help you bring it back to your tavern."

"Are you sure?"

"It's my fault they're broken," I reply. "It's only right that I help you bring the unbroken ones safely back to The Old Dove."

"It's my fault for not swerving the cart away fast enough."

"It's hard to maneuver carts quickly, so you can hardly be blamed."

"But—"

"Just let me help you."

"All right," he says. "If you insist."

I step closer to the cart. "*Ventrez.*"

A wind spell rushes from my fingers. It blows the cart up from the street and hovers at shoulder height.

"Lead the way," I say.

With a nod, he strides down the street. I follow, blowing the cart in front of me and taking care not to let any more bottles fall and smash.

On the next corner we pass a few people, but no one stops to gawk at our levitating cart. They mostly ignore it and continue their laughter as they stroll past. In a city full of magic, where the streetlights themselves are floating crystals, such a sight is unremarkable.

"You know," I call over to the golden-haired stranger, "I don't think I caught your name?"

His pace falters, and he falls into step beside me. "Nolan." He holds out his hand, but I flash him a strained smile and gesture to the floating cart I'm focused on. He lowers his hand and hastily adds, "Nolan Elmsworth."

"Well, it's lovely to meet you, Nolan Elmsworth. Though I do wish it hadn't been because I broke all your wine."

"You didn't break them all." He points to the remaining bottles in the cart.

I breathe a laugh. "True enough."

Nolan doesn't ask for my name, but I decide to volunteer the information.

"I'm Reyna," I say. "Reyna Ashbourne."

"It's my pleasure to meet you, Reyna."

He doesn't mention my father. I can't remember the last time I introduced myself to someone and they didn't ask about Grandmage Telric Ashbourne. But I'm not complaining. It's a relief to not be in my father's shadow, for once.

"Most people ask about my father when they meet me," I tell him, anyway. "I think you might be the first who hasn't."

"He's the Grandmage of Nolderan, isn't he?"

"Yeah, he is."

"I only moved here a few weeks ago when I bought the tavern. I did have an inkling that you shared his surname, but I wasn't sure if I remembered correctly. I hope I didn't offend you."

"No, not at all," I reply. "I just thought it unusual that you didn't ask me about my father. But it makes sense since you're new here. Where are you from?"

"Tirith."

"Tirith is rather large."

"I'm from Dalry. Does that satisfy your curiosity?"

"For now."

"I suppose that means you will have more questions for me later?"

"Perhaps. Though I have yet to think of them."

He chuckles at that.

Fairway Avenue is the next street along, and The Old Dove lies five doors down on the left. A white dove with a monocle and a walking stick is painted onto its wooden sign.

I slow my pace as we near the tavern, guiding the cart with great care. If I smashed Nolan's windows as well, then that would probably be enough to make him mad. Especially since they're so immaculate. With how gleaming they are, it looks like they were cleaned earlier today.

Nolan pulls out a key and jiggles it inside the lock until it yields. He swings open the door and holds it wide as I direct the cart inside.

I set it down at the center where there's plenty of space away from the tables and chairs.

The Old Dove looks much like I remember from when Eliya and I visited last year. Due to how long it would take for our drinks to arrive, we tended to avoid this one.

Wooden beams run along the cream ceiling. Each round table features a small aether crystal. All are switched off, and the room is blanketed in shadows. Moonlight spills in through the polished windows, bright enough that I can discern most of the tavern's interior.

A counter lies at the far end of the room. Behind it, the stone walls are decorated with shelves containing barrels of ale, bottles of wine, and dozens of tankards.

Nolan flicks on the switches beside the door, and the aether crystals hanging from the center of the ceiling ignite, washing us in dazzling purple light. The tabletops glint with the radiance.

"Right then," I say, turning to Nolan. I point to the broken cart heaped at my feet. "What are we doing with all these bottles?"

He gestures to the door next to the counter. "We'll put them all inside the cellar, along with the rest of the wine and ale down there."

"Sure," I say, bundling up several bottles into my arms. Nolan grabs the rest, and I follow him into the cellar.

The wooden door groans as he opens it, and we start down the few stone steps. We enter a small room that is barely large enough to fit the countless barrels strewn around. Two large racks are propped against the back wall, filled with bottles of assorted wine. Nolan begins to fill the gaps with the wine he carries, and I do the same.

Once we're done, we head back up the steps and Nolan shuts the door behind us.

"Well," he says. "Thank you very much for your help tonight."

"It's the least I could do, seeing as it was my fault your cart broke and your bottles got smashed."

"And I am to blame for your injuries," Nolan replies. "So, I think we can conclude we're both equally at fault."

"I'm not that injured."

"You look rather injured to me."

I glance down at my arms. It's my right one which is the most battered, likely because I used it to break my fall. On closer inspection, it's in a worse state than I thought. I suppose all the moon-blossom wine I drank this evening is responsible for numbing the pain. The scratches are deeper than I realized.

"They're just minor wounds," I insist.

"They'll still need cleaning."

"They'll be fine after a bit of Blood Balm."

"And you will manage to clean your injuries and apply the salve to them yourself?"

I hadn't considered that part. If my father is home, he will probably be asleep. While I might manage the task myself, it would take longer than letting someone else do it. And I would likely make a racket loud enough to wake my father. Then he would be furious over being awoken in the middle of the night, and also that I drank so much during the week of my Mage Trials.

On second thought, allowing Nolan to help me with my injuries seems the wisest choice. And he isn't wrong that we are both to blame for our collision. I've repaid my debt—or at least partially—by helping him to carry back the unbroken wine bottles. I suppose it's only fair he repays his debt by assisting me with my injuries.

"Fine," I say, huffing out a sigh. "If you really won't take no for an answer, then I guess there's no harm in letting you help me with them."

"Good." Nolan takes my uninjured arm and guides me to the nearest table. He pulls out a chair and helps me sit. I consider telling him it's my arm which is wounded and not my legs, but I decide against it since he's just trying to be nice.

"Wait here," he says, turning to the stairs. "I'll get the tin of Blood Balm and a bowl of water."

The steps creak as he ascends them, and then I hear his footsteps above the ceiling.

Nolan returns downstairs a few minutes later, with a tin of Blood Balm in his hands, and starts over to the wooden counter at the far end of the tavern. He rummages through the shelves until he locates a clean cloth and a ceramic bowl.

"You don't need to find any water," I call over to him. "I'll use my magic to conjure some."

Nolan nods and carries the items over to me. He sets the bowl and the tin onto the table.

"*Aquis*," I say. Water splashes into the bowl and fills it entirely. Tendrils of steam swirl from the bubbling surface. I hope I didn't make it too hot.

Nolan helps me roll my sleeve up to my shoulder, exposing the wounds. They look worse than they feel. Not that I trust my senses right now. I keep the fabric held in place as he sloshes the cloth inside the bowl and soaks up all the warm water. When enough has absorbed, he wrings out the cloth and glides it across my skin.

I flinch.

"I thought you said the injuries weren't bad," he says, a light smirk playing on his lips. It's only now I realize how close he is. Lightning pulses in the little space between us, and I lean back slightly to avoid it.

"The water's hot."

He dips his finger into the bowl, and the surface ripples. "It's only lukewarm."

"Fine," I say, scrunching my nose. "The scratches might be a little deeper than I thought."

He doesn't dwell on his victory and sets to work with swiping the damp cloth over my wounds and cleaning them.

When he's done, he reaches for the tin of Blood Balm and opens it, revealing the glossy crimson contents. The scent of cool mint and spicy pepper wafts into the air.

He presses his fingers into the balm, leaving an imprint, and smears the substance across my scratches. I jolt as he traces over my skin, and this time I'm glad to have the excuse of the Blood Balm stinging me.

Once all the scrapes are slathered in ointment, I roll down the fabric of my sleeve. Nolan screws the tin's lid back on.

"Thanks," I say.

"No thanks is needed," he replies. "We are both to blame for what happened tonight. It was only right that I helped you with your wounds, since you helped me with my cart."

"I'm sorry again about all your wine."

"Don't be," he simply says.

We fall into a silence. Nolan's attention turns to the window behind me, while mine drifts over to the bowl of warm water. I watch the tendrils of steam wafting out as I try to think of something suitable to say, but my mind has become devoid of words.

"It's very late," Nolan finally says. I suppose commenting on the time is as good as anything, especially since I could think of nothing myself. Pointless conversation is certainly better than tense silence.

"Yeah, it is." I would love to extend my response, but I don't know how. All I can think of is to say it's dark, but I doubt that would further our conversation.

"If you need to stay here for the night, you're more than welcome to do so."

I whirl around, my mouth hanging agape. "You want me to stay for the night?"

Nolan cringes at my expression, his dimpled cheeks tinging with crimson. "I didn't mean it like that. I was just thinking that with your arm being injured and it being so late . . . And there are several spare rooms upstairs."

"Oh."

Now it's my turn to redden. I can't believe I interpreted his words like that.

"I drank a lot of wine tonight," I tell him, though I'm not sure it's a good enough excuse.

He laughs. "It's fine. It's my fault for not realizing how that would sound."

"No, that was definitely my fault."

We pause again. Nolan breaks it before it stretches on for too long.

"Anyway," he says, "the offer stands. But I will completely understand if you would rather not."

I hate how there's a part of me that wants to spend the night with Nolan—

In his tavern, I mean. In one of the guest rooms.

Before I can lose good sense, I swiftly reply, "Thank you for your kind offer, but I will have to decline. My Mage Trials are taking place this week, and I really should head home. If my father learns I've been out drinking all night during such a critical time, then he will be furious."

"I understand."

The chair legs scrape against the tiles as I stand.

"Wait," he says as I turn to leave.

I stop and glance back at him. "Yes?"

"I was wondering when I could see you again."

"You want to see me again?"

His lips tug into a soft smile. "Only if you would also like to see me again."

"Yeah," I say, the words spilling off my tongue before I can realize, "I would like to."

"Then will you come by tomorrow?"

"My second Mage Trial is on Wednesday morning, so I won't be able to stay for too long. But I'm sure I could spare an hour or two."

"Great," he breathes, "then I look forward to seeing you tomorrow."

Dizzying warmth sweeps over me. My knees feel like soft clouds beneath me as I stare into his mesmerizing emerald eyes. The distance between us feels too small, despite us being farther apart than before.

"As do I," I whisper.

Our gazes hold. My heart thumps with anticipation.

Before this moment can last a heartbeat longer, I tear myself from where I stand and hurry out of his tavern. Only when I am outside, with the chilly night air biting my cheeks, do I realize that I didn't bid him good night.

CHAPTER 25

A BARD'S MELODIOUS VOICE CUTS through the busyness of the Upper City's square. Though the crowds are bustling this morning, everyone stops to listen to her lute and her captivating voice. The fountain at the center of the square trickles in the background.

I swing my legs back and forth from the bench I sit upon, watching the bard serenade her audience. The bowl at her feet is already brimming silvers, and I even spot a few gold coins thrown in there.

One gold coin is enough to cover the annual salary of a well-paid dockhand. Or at least, I think it is. Since I've never held that job role myself, I can't be certain of their exact income. But what I do know is that this bard would never receive this kind of money down in the Lower City. Here, we are just a stone's throw from the Arcanium, and plenty of nobles pass by. To those who are as rich as Eliya's uncle, a gold coin is nothing compared to the talent of this bard.

Apparently she only started playing here last week. And according to the murmurs amid the crowd, she worked as a barmaid in the Lower City prior to her newfound fame. Already she must have earned a fortune. I can't deny that I'm envious. Unfortunately, I'm unable to play a single instrument. Nor can I sing. Now I realize what a mistake that is.

Since I'm long out of my monthly adept's stipend, all I can offer the bard is applause between each song. I wish I could offer her more, seeing how her gentle music is doing wonders for my headache.

When I woke up, my temples were filled with excruciating fire. I took a large dose of Ice Honey to numb the pain, but it has worn off. And I don't dare to take any more.

Moon-blossom wine really is strong. And I drank so much of it.

I clasp my head in my hands. Even the thought of alcohol nauseates me. Right now, I don't intend to drink another drop of wine ever again.

All I hope is that I will have recovered by tomorrow morning. Or else raiding Garon Whiteford's warehouse will prove to be a very costly mistake.

Too busy nursing my headache and listening to the bard's silvery voice, I don't notice Eliya sliding onto the bench beside me.

"You look worse for wear," she chirps, startling me.

I look up at her and groan. "Do I honestly look that bad?"

"Oh yes," she replies. "You should have fixed yourself with an illusion before heading out."

I sigh. Compared to me, she looks well-rested. But I suspect that's only due to carefully conjured illusions. With how much Eliya drank last night—which was even more than me—she should look dreadful.

I should have probably done the same and hidden my awful appearance with illusions. But the headache made it impossible to concentrate on casting any spells. Clearly Eliya has a higher pain threshold than me.

"Remind me to never again agree to one of your plans," I grumble, rubbing at my temples.

"Why?" she asks. "Didn't you have fun last night? Isn't the headache worth it?"

"No," I growl. "And neither is it worth the mess I've gotten myself into."

Her magenta eyes sparkle with curiosity. "Mess? What mess?"

"After you left, I miscalculated my teleportation spell."

"You didn't accidentally teleport yourself right into the middle of the sea, did you?" she asks, choking on a laugh.

"No, but nearly. And it was far worse than that."

Eliya taps her chin as she contemplates all the possibilities which might have befallen me. "Did you teleport yourself into the sewers and get covered in waste?"

"No, but that probably would have been far less messy."

"Just tell me," Eliya demands. "I'm already out of ideas."

"I teleported myself to the docks."

"That doesn't sound too bad. Not like teleporting yourself into the sea or the sewers."

"Yes, but when I was sprinting home, I ended up crashing into someone because I wasn't looking where I was going."

Eliya frowns. "That still doesn't sound terrible."

"He was wheeling a cart full of expensive wine back to his tavern, and I smashed most of his bottles."

"Oh, I see," she replies. "You're right, that doesn't sound great. I bet he was furious. Listen, I'll talk to my uncle about it. Nearly everyone owes him a favor. I'm sure he will be able to convince this man to leave you alone. Even if he has to replace the bottles you broke."

"No, no," I say swiftly, "that isn't the problem. He wasn't annoyed about the wine. Not even in the slightest."

"I'm confused. If he isn't angry at you, what is the problem? How have you gotten yourself into such a mess?"

"Because he wants to see me tonight," I mumble. "And I agreed."

"You're still making no sense. If he isn't mad at you, then why would he—" She cuts herself off, realization illuminating her face. "Oh, I get it now. He likes you and asked you out on a date. That's what it is, isn't it?"

"He didn't ask me out on a date."

"Didn't you say he wants to see you again tonight?"

"Yes, but it's not a date."

"It sounds like a date to me."

"No, he just asked if I would stop by his tavern tonight."

"Hm," Eliya says suspiciously, scrutinizing my expression. "Is he handsome?"

"I don't remember. I was drunk, thanks to you."

"Well, he must have been handsome if you agreed to meet him again."

"I miscalculated my teleportation spell, so I wouldn't place too much trust in my judgement last night."

"Do you remember what he looked like?"

"He was around my height with wavy gold hair and very green eyes."

"And when you say *his* tavern, do you mean he owns it?"

"Yeah, he does."

Eliya sucks in a deep breath and fans herself, despite the frigid winter air. It looks like it's trying to snow again, judging by the thick gray clouds swarming in the heavens. "I'll have him if you don't want him."

"You've never even met him."

"He sounds handsome. And he owns a tavern. What more can a girl want?"

I roll my eyes at her.

"And I still don't see why it's such an issue. If you don't want to meet him, then don't."

I stare down at my hands. "Well . . ."

"You're not sure whether you want to go?"

"I don't know," I mumble.

"What do you mean you don't know?"

"It was dark. And I was drunk. Maybe he's hideous."

She narrows her eyes. "I think you're making up excuses."

"Why would I be making up excuses?"

Eliya hesitates. "Because . . ."

"Because of what?"

"Because of Arluin," she whispers.

I swallow and turn away from her. My attention settles onto the bard who is still playing her lute for all those gathered in the square.

I can't deny Eliya's words. Last night, after the tipsiness wore off and I crawled into bed, an overwhelming wave of guilt crashed into me. Guilt over flirting with Nolan, over agreeing to meet him tonight. The emotion is so irrational that I don't know how to explain it to Eliya. Arluin has been gone for three years. He might even be dead. Why can I not let go of him?

Eliya places her hand on mine. I clench the edge of the stone bench so tightly that my knuckles whiten. "Reyna," she says softly. "It's been three years."

"I know," I reply, my words cold and dead.

"Do you think . . ."

"Do I think what?"

She bites her lip. Whatever she intended to say, she seems to have decided against it.

A few tears escape my eyes and trace down my cheeks. I hurriedly wipe them away with the back of my sleeve. "Sorry," I mutter.

"For what?" Eliya asks.

"For this."

She pulls me into a hug. "You never need to apologize for being upset, silly. What sort of best friend would I be if I were mad at you for crying?"

I give her a slight nod but remain silent.

"Why don't you stop by his tavern tonight?" Eliya says after a moment, releasing me from her embrace. She lifts my hand from the stone bench and squeezes it. "Since it isn't a date, what's the harm in meeting him again?"

I can think of no answer to her question, other than betraying Arluin's memory. How can I move on from him so soon? Three years is nothing compared to the eighteen years I knew him.

After our conversation last night, I know exactly what Eliya thinks of him. Like everyone else, she believes him to be wicked. But he freed me. And I refuse to believe that using dark magic to save me makes him monstrous.

"I'll come with you," Eliya says, "and if he's as hideous as you fear he might be, then we'll run straight out. How's that?"

I close my eyes and let out a heavy breath. I wish I could explain to her how all this makes me feel. I wish I could make her understand.

"What if you don't go tonight and you spend the rest of your life wondering what you missed because you were too busy holding onto the past?"

I can't argue with her. What she says is the reason I've not entirely ruled out visiting The Old Dove tonight. There was an inexplicable connection between Nolan and me. Gazing at him made my pulse quicken. And he appeared to be as dazed as me.

But all of that could have been down to the moon-blossom wine. To know, I need to meet him again.

And if I don't, will I regret it?

I already knew that I couldn't go on like this, wallowing over Arluin for the rest of my life. Maybe meeting Nolan signifies the start of a new chapter. I think that's what terrifies me the most.

But, as Eliya says, what's the harm in us visiting The Old Dove? It isn't as if I'll be going alone. And if I change my mind, I'm sure Eliya would happily flirt with him and divert his attention from me.

"All right," I finally say. "Like you said, what's the worst that can happen?"

"That's the spirit!" She leaps to her feet and pulls me up with her. "Come on then, let's go! But first we need to get you properly dressed to impress Mr. Handsome-Tavern-Owner!"

CHAPTER 26

Glimpsing my gaudy appearance in a nearby window, I turn to Eliya and grimace. "I look ridiculous," I say for what must be the tenth time. At the very least.

For a start, the midnight blue dress is barely thick enough to keep the wintry chill at bay. And the cut is straight across my shoulders, exposing them to the night.

Then there's my hair, which Eliya has weaved into an excessively fancy updo. If only she let me wear it down. I'm still considering pulling out all the pins when she's not looking. But if I do, she will be furious, and Eliya's rage isn't a pretty sight to behold. I definitely don't want to be on the receiving end of it.

So, I press on through the streets in this ridiculous dress, doing my best not to shiver. With how thin the fabric is, I suggested teleporting us both to The Old Dove and avoiding the chill. But Eliya wanted to walk so she can see exactly where Nolan's tavern is located. I tried to explain it's the tavern which had the awful service, but she insisted that she didn't remember. I think she just wanted me to suffer.

"Don't forget we have our second Mage Trial in the morning," I warn as we turn the corner and step onto Fairway Avenue. "We can't stay too late tonight. Nor can we drink more than a few drops of wine."

"I know, I know," Eliya mutters under her breath. "You've already said so five times."

"I mean it. One drink all night. Nothing more."

"Yes, yes," she says, waving her hand dismissively. She won't admit it, but I know she is already scheming to get her hands on more than just one drink. Though we both spent all of our stipend last night at The Violet Tree, Eliya's father was kind enough to top hers up. Mine didn't, however. If my father knew I was heading to a tavern on the night before the Trial of Mind, he would flay me alive.

That's why we need to be back early. And sober.

When we arrive at The Old Dove, Eliya pauses outside the door and peers at the white dove painted onto the swinging sign. Three men burst out, and we step aside to let them pass.

"You know," Eliya says once they're gone, "I haven't been here in years."

"Nor me. Well, at least not until last night."

"Let's hope this handsome new owner knows how to treat his customers properly."

I clamp my hand over Eliya's mouth and glare at her.

"What?" she demands, her voice muffled by my palm. She grabs my wrist and yanks my hand away, freeing her mouth. "It's not like I said you thought he was handsome."

The two people passing by shoot us curious looks.

"You'd better behave."

"I'm always on my best behavior," she says, mischief glinting in her eyes.

I groan. Bringing her here was a terrible idea.

"What's his name, anyway?"

"Nolan Elmsworth," I say, my voice hushed in case anyone overhears.

"Even his name is handsome!" Eliya remarks far too loudly. "Well, let's see whether his face measures up to the rest of him." With that, she shoves the door open and strides inside. I trail after her.

It's busier than I expected, with many of the round tables full. There are six staff in total, including Nolan. He's behind the wooden counter, chatting to a man and pouring ale from a nearby keg.

His hair is fair and tousled like I remember from last night, and his eyes sparkle like vivid emeralds. There is only one thing the moon-blossom wine caused me to forget: He looks far more handsome than I recall.

I lower my head as he passes the filled tankard across to the man and hope he hasn't caught me staring at him. Warmth tinges my cheeks, incriminating me.

My pace must have faltered since Eliya grips my arm and drags me to the empty table in the corner. Last night, every table was gleaming beneath the aether crystals, but now this one is sticky from the ale spilled across it.

When we are sitting down, Eliya leans over the table, careful to avoid dipping her sleeves into the patches of ale. "Don't tell me that's him!" Again, her voice is much louder than I would prefer.

"Which one?"

"The one behind the bar!" she exclaims in a half-whisper. "I can't believe how gorgeous he is. He practically looks like a god walking among us mere mortals. How could you think he might be hideous?"

"I drank a lot of moon-blossom wine."

"Imagine if I hadn't talked you into coming here tonight. Look at what we would have missed out on!"

I raise a brow at her.

"What *you'd* have missed out on, of course," Eliya quickly corrects herself.

"If you're really that interested in him, I can introduce you."

She wags a finger at me. "Not so fast. Don't think I don't know what you're doing."

"And what is it you think I'm doing?"

"Trying to wriggle out of this."

"No, I'm not."

"Go and talk to him then."

"What?" I blanch. "I can't just walk up to him!"

"Of course you can. We're in his tavern, and we're here to drink. So, hurry up and place your order."

"The Trial of Mind is tomorrow, and we aren't here to drink. Why don't we come back another time?"

"Not a chance. I spent hours making you look pretty."

"I look ridiculous."

"Come on, Rey-rey. If you end up marrying him one day, think how grateful you'll be."

"By the gods, Eliya! Marriage? You're getting quite ahead of yourself."

"I'm just being prepared. Who knows what might happen?"

"Definitely not that."

"Fine," she says. "When he gives you the night of your life, then you'll be grateful to me."

"Eliya!"

"What? Now don't tell me that's unlikely to happen. He looks like he would be good in bed, too."

How exactly she's come to that conclusion, I have no idea. Nor do I wish to know.

I bury my head in my hands. If I weren't red before, I certainly am now.

"What's the matter with you?" she asks.

"Your behavior is the matter."

"I never knew you were such a prude."

"I'm not."

"When was the last time you had sex, anyway?"

"We are not having this conversation here!"

"Why not? A tavern is a perfectly good place to discuss such matters."

I bolt up from my seat, fearing she will find a way to worsen this conversation. "Give me the money," I say, holding out my hand. "I'll get the drinks." Right now, I would do anything to shut her up. Even approaching Nolan is preferable to continuing this discussion.

Eliya grins triumphantly at me. "*Conparios.*" Her velvet coin purse appears in her hands. Metal clinks as she chucks it over to me. I catch it clumsily.

"What do you want?"

"Wine. Any will do."

With a deep breath, I head toward Nolan's counter.

Soon I will become a Mage of Nolderan—provided I pass my trials, of course. That means I can order drinks from a bartender. No matter how handsome he may be.

Despite my silent words of encouragement, my hands are shaking by the time I reach him. What if I imagined him asking me to come here tonight? What if he doesn't recognize me?

I clutch Eliya's crimson coin purse tightly and hope he doesn't notice my trembling.

As soon as he finishes serving his current patron, he sweeps over to me. His head tilts to one side as he studies me.

A silence lingers between us. His emerald eyes lock with mine. Everyone else melts away. Even Eliya.

I don't dare breathe, worrying it will come out as a sudden gasp. His gaze is so intense that sparks of lightning pulse through my nerves.

With how potent this energy is, I wonder whether he too can feel it.

I break our stare to glance back over my shoulder. Eliya is watching us. When she catches my eye, she pretends to drink from an imaginary goblet.

That's right. Drinks.

I turn back to Nolan. His eyes haven't strayed from me. My breath catches in the back of my throat. Surely he doesn't gaze at all his customers like this?

"I . . ." Words fail me. I clear my throat and try again, this time with more force. "I was wondering whether I could have two goblets of white wine, please."

"Will it be *Vedemia, Jasone,* or *Enti Adega?*" he asks, his eyes remaining fixed on me as he speaks.

"Um, *Vedemia,* please."

"For both of you?"

"Yes, please."

Only now does his gaze leave me. He reaches behind him for two goblets and a bottle of *Vedemia*. He pulls out the cork. Before I can wonder whether he remembers me, he asks, "How's your arm doing?" He tilts the bottle over the goblet nearest him, and the bubbly liquid flows within.

"Better," I reply. "Thanks for asking."

Nolan inclines his head in a slight nod, while I inwardly curse myself. Why can't I think of anything better to say?

He finishes pouring wine into the first goblet and reaches for the other. "Reyna Ashbourne, wasn't it?"

I grin widely at him remembering my name, and probably end up making myself look like a fool. But I suppose I shouldn't be surprised he remembers me, since he was sober. Or at least, I think he was.

"Yes, and it was Nolan, right? Nolan Elmsworth?"

"Indeed, it is," he replies, popping the cork back into the bottle.

He's almost finished serving me, and so far all we've discussed is my arm and our names.

As Nolan turns to place the bottle of *Vedemia* back onto the shelf behind him, I glance over at Eliya. She shoots me a thumbs-up. I'm sure if she actually heard our conversation, it would instead be a thumbs-down.

And if she knew how little progress I've made, she would kill me.

"So," I say as he slides the two goblets toward me, "how much will that be?"

"Nothing," he replies.

"Nothing? How can wine cost nothing?" Unless you steal it from Garon Whiteford's warehouses, that is.

"It's on the house."

I gawk at him, having no idea how my terrible flirting has caused him to buy drinks for us. Well, not exactly to buy drinks since he owns all the alcohol here. But free drinks, nonetheless. "You're sure?"

A smile dances on his lips. It makes my heart flutter. "Why wouldn't I be?"

"Because I already cost you a fortune in wine last night." Eliya would clip me round the ear and tell me I should just graciously smile back, lest he decides to charge us for the drinks.

"I can think of far worse reasons to crash a cart full of wine," he says.

Is he flirting with me? Or am I imagining it? This time I don't have a single drop of wine to blame my imagination on.

A blush spreads across my cheeks, and I dip my head before he can notice. Like a bumbling fool, I almost spill the goblets over as I reach for them. Fortunately, Nolan steadies them in place, preventing a disaster.

"Thank you," I mumble as I turn away. With my words spoken so softly, I don't know whether he hears them.

I start back over to Eliya and my wobbly legs threaten to spill the wine all over my dress. At least it's only white wine. After several strides, I begin to think of better responses. Such as that I can also think of far worse reasons to be crashed into. If I'd said that with a coy smile on my lips, I might have actually gotten somewhere.

But am I even trying to get anywhere at all?

I don't look Eliya in the eye as I sit opposite her. Gingerly, I slide one of the metallic goblets across to her.

"Well?" she demands, drumming her fingers against the table.

"Well, what?" I ask, quickly lifting the goblet to my lips so that it covers most of my face. I keep it there for as long as I reasonably can.

"How did it go?"

I take several long sips of wine before I have no choice but to set it back down and face Eliya. "Um, well. I think?"

Eliya narrows her eyes, clearly unconvinced.

"He gave us free drinks," I say.

She leans back in her chair, folding her arms. Surprisingly, she has not yet touched her wine. "Good. What else?"

"He asked about my arm."

Her eyes narrow a little more. Clearly that wasn't the response she was hoping to hear.

"He remembered my name."

"And?"

"And . . ." I tap my lower lip, which is moist from the wine gathered there. "And that was it."

Eliya's forehead meets the table with a thud. I glance around to see if anyone is staring at us. Luckily, no one is. Not even Nolan.

"You absolute idiot!" she roars. The wooden table thankfully muffles her voice. "By the gods, you're a lost cause."

My shoulders sag, and my fingers toy with the fine details engraved into the bottom of the metallic goblet.

"Right well," Eliya continues, sitting up in her chair and taking a long sip of wine, "since you've ruined tonight's plans, we have no choice but to come back here tomorrow."

"Can't we just brush this off as incompatibility?"

Her temple twitches. "No," she growls into her wine. "I know you like him. Or else you wouldn't have stood there, blushing and gawking at him like a fool."

"Was I really?" I ask with a groan.

"Don't worry," she replies. "He was especially smiley while talking to you, so I can tell he also likes you."

"That wasn't what I was worrying about," I mutter. Still, her words send my stomach somersaulting. And a part of me hopes her assessment is accurate.

"Anyway," I say a moment later, "does this mean we can go now?"

"Fine. But we're coming back here tomorrow night." She gives me a pointed look.

We drink the rest of our wine. Eliya finishes hers in mere minutes. She drinks it as though it's water.

"You're so slow," she complains, gesturing to my goblet. In my defense, only a small amount remains.

I push the goblet over to her. "You drink it then."

She does and finishes it in a single gulp. Then she gets to her feet. "Right then. Let's go."

I stand from my chair and follow her through the tavern. We weave past the surrounding tables as we head to the door. But I only make it halfway across the room before a hand snags my wrist.

I turn to face Nolan.

Now that there isn't a counter between us and his fingers are wrapped around my wrist, the rush of energy is as overwhelming as I remember last night.

"Reyna," he murmurs, "can I borrow you for a moment?"

Enthralled by his emerald eyes, I find myself nodding.

Nolan leads me farther back into the tavern, just behind the stairs. Here, we are out of everyone else's earshot.

I stare at him, losing myself in his mesmerizing gaze. I barely notice as he begins to speak.

"I know you said you needed to leave early because of the Trial of Mind in the morning, but I was hoping you would stay a little longer. We didn't get much of a chance to speak tonight."

I swallow, glancing down at his leather boots.

"If I offended you before, then I do apologize."

"Why would you have offended me?" I ask.

He opens his mouth but then closes it, seeming to have nothing to say. I feel terrible. He's probably worrying about how I abruptly left after he said that he could think of worse reasons to crash a wine cart.

"I wasn't offended," I say quietly. "I just didn't know how to respond."

I suppose when in doubt, honesty is always the best policy.

A light smile twitches on his lips. He takes a step closer. "You weren't sure what to say?"

I try to step back, but the wall behind me prevents me from moving any farther away. Any thoughts of escape die when he closes the distance between us so much that I can feel his warm breath against my cheeks. The air pulses with vigorous energy. With anticipation.

My hands are clammy, and my heart thumps wildly in my chest. I hope it isn't loud enough for him to hear.

"You ran away so quickly," he continues, his eyes tracing over my face, "that I didn't have the chance to ask you something."

At first, my voice fails me. Fortunately, it comes rushing back before I can yet again make myself look like an idiot. "What is it you wish to ask me?"

He pauses. Many heartbeats pass between us. Then he finally asks, "What are you doing on Thursday evening?"

"Nothing," I reply. "Aside from sleeping early so I'll be well rested for my final trial. Why do you ask?"

"I was wondering whether you would like to join me for dinner?"

I blink, momentarily taken aback by his question. It's hard to believe he's asking me this. That this isn't some cruel joke.

"Yes," I breathe, before sense can return to me, "yes, I would love to."

"Great," he says with a smile. "Then meet me here at six o'clock on Thursday evening."

"Won't you be busy working?"

"I have enough staff to handle things for a few hours."

"In that case, thank you."

"For what?" he asks.

"For inviting me to dinner."

"And thank you for accepting my invitation." He steps away, and I suddenly realize how cold it is without him so near. "Best of luck with your trial tomorrow."

I thank him again and start toward the door. Eliya is waiting there, a curious look spreading across her face.

When we burst out of the tavern, she turns to me and exclaims, "You'd better tell me exactly what just happened. Every last detail!"

And so, I tell her everything.

CHAPTER 27

ARCHMAGE GIDSTON LEADS US DOWN a dark, steep staircase. Aether crystals glisten along the walls, illuminating the steps ahead of me. I can see little beyond that, aside from the back of Eliya's head. Everything else is lost to the shadows.

With the passage being so narrow, we're forced to walk in single file. My palms skim across the coarse stone walls as I try to maintain my balance. When we first started down here—the South Western exit of the Arcanium's atrium—there was an ornate metallic banister to guide our way. But now we are so far underground that the smooth steps have turned to jagged rock and I stumble over them.

Thousands of steps lie between us and our trial, just like with the Trial of Heart. At least this time, the stairs are going down.

Eventually, we reach the end.

A vast cave stretches out before us. Aether crystals protrude from the walls, bright enough to illuminate every inch of the chamber.

Archmage Gidston strides to the stone altar at the center. An enormous hourglass floats above it. Instead of sand, aether dust fills the lower bulb, and an ornate golden frame houses the glass.

"Today, you will all undertake your second Mage Trial, the Trial of Mind."

No one dares to breathe as Lorette speaks. Down here, there's no wind. When she pauses, an unnatural silence fills the cave.

"These tunnels form an underground maze beneath the Arcanium," she continues, gesturing around us. Aside from the stairs, there are five exits. Only darkness lies beyond them.

She points ahead at the largest exit, the one directly opposite the stairs. "Though the tunnels are long and winding, they all converge back to this chamber, and you will have an hour to return. If you cannot escape the maze within that time, you will fail your trial. As this is the Trial of Mind, you must use your wits to solve the many magical obstacles which will stand in your way."

If I pass today, I will be one trial away from graduating the Arcanium and becoming a Mage of Nolderan. Though I do not know what obstacles await me inside this maze, I know many adepts fail this second trial. Especially compared to the first. I can't be one of those adepts. I can't fail.

Archmage Gidston's eyes narrow as she scans across us. "Do you all understand what this trial requires?"

We answer her question with nods. Except for Kaely. She raises her hand.

"Yes, Adept Calton?"

"What if we meet other adepts inside the maze?" Kaely asks. "What are the rules for interacting with peers?"

I clench my jaw. I have little doubt she is wondering whether the two of us will cross paths. And if we do, whether she will be permitted to strike me.

A few adepts murmur at Kaely's words. But they're probably more concerned about what it means for their trial, rather than if it allows them to attack their rivals.

"That is a good question," Lorette says. "Though you will each start from different entrances, many of the tunnels overlap, and it is inevitable some of you will meet each other inside the maze. As this is a Mage Trial, the usual rules of the Arcanium do not apply. Whether you choose to see a fellow adept as a friend or as a foe is entirely your discretion."

Wonderful. Not only do I need to worry about the magical obstacles scattered throughout the maze, but also Kaely, who will look for every opportunity to attack me and to ensure I don't pass this trial.

The corners of Kaely's lips curl with vicious satisfaction.

I do my best to ignore her murderous expression, but a terrifying thought snakes through my mind.

If the Arcanium's rules don't apply on this trial, then does that mean Kaely wouldn't be punished if she killed me?

Nausea sweeps over me. Today, failure isn't my only concern, but also death.

"Are there any other questions?"

No one speaks or raises their hand.

"Good," Archmage Gidston says. "Then we will begin."

Her indigo sleeve flutters as she gestures to the exit on the far right. "Reyna Ashbourne, Lorea Bayford, Keion Bridwell, Kaely Calton, and Myron Dalston. The five of you are to follow me to your starting positions. The rest of you are to wait here." With that, she turns and marches into the tunnel.

"Good luck," Eliya whispers.

"You too," I say with a brief smile and then hurry after Archmage Gidston and the other four adepts.

The passage is narrow, like the stairs. Since there are no aether crystals in here, Archmage Gidston murmurs *iluminos* and conjures an orb of dazzling light. Though it's bright enough to light our path, the uneven ground remains shadowed. I take each step with great care, careful not to crash into Myron, who's in front of me.

"Feeling nervous?" Lorea hisses from behind.

"Yeah," I reply, glancing back at her. "A bit. You?"

"Just a little."

We soon arrive at another chamber, this one smaller than the previous. Five more tunnels surround us. All are shielded with aether. The humming barriers are so thick I can't see the path beyond.

"Reyna Ashbourne," Archmage Gidston says, pointing to the first tunnel on our left. "You will start here. Please take your position."

I do as she instructs and make my way over to the first tunnel. The barrier's surface ripples and swirls, bursting with magic. Even this close, the path ahead is obscured.

"Lorea Bayford." Archmage Gidston gestures to the next tunnel, and she continues to work clockwise until she has allocated everyone else's starting positions.

"A thunderclap will mark the start of the trial," she says, once we are all waiting before our designated tunnels, "and the aether barriers will fall. Your hour will begin at that precise moment. I wish you all the best of luck on this second trial."

With that, she heads back into the main chamber.

"Good luck, Ashbourne," Kaely sneers when Archmage Gidston is gone. "You're going to need it."

More focused on passing the Trial of Mind, I ignore Kaely and don't bother with a retort. As I stare at the aether barrier ahead of me, I feel her glare burning into me, but she says nothing else.

Archmage Gidston's voice echoes from down the tunnel as she leads the next group to their starting locations. I can't decipher the names since she's muffled by the cavernous stone walls, but I know Eliya can't be among them. Her surname is Whiteford, so she will be in the last group, along with Koby.

Another moment passes.

Then I hear Archmage Gidston taking the third group of adepts over to their starting locations. There will only be one more group after this.

Gravel crunches beneath another adept's boots. My nerves are so taut that I spring to action, convinced the trial has begun. But the aether barrier still hums in front of me, barring my path. I place my hand flat against it. The magic vibrates beneath my touch. Its tingling is so intense it feels like tiny needles are pricking my palm. I jolt back.

Archmage Gidston announces the final group. Her voice fades as she leads them away.

Any moment now, the trial will begin.

My heart pounds with anticipation. Adrenaline spikes through my veins. The trial hasn't even begun, and I already feel as though I will burst apart. The wait drags on, and I begin to wonder whether the trial will ever begin, or if we will be waiting forever and—

Thunder booms. It comes from everywhere, ringing out so loudly the cave walls tremble.

A crack follows. The aether barrier shatters. But it doesn't fall like glass. It dissolves into glittering dust and scatters into the shadows.

The Trial of Mind has begun.

I plunge into the darkness. The aether barrier repairs behind me, preventing my retreat. My footsteps drum wildly against the stone path, but I only manage a few strides before I come to a halt, realizing that I can't see anything.

"*Iluminos.*" My magic explodes into a brilliant orb. Its rays penetrate the shadows. The end of this path is just a few yards ahead. If I'd continued much longer, I would have collided with the wall. The tunnel forks into two paths. I glance down each, but both are shrouded with darkness. I can't tell them apart. From where I stand, they look identical.

There is no way to know which path I should take.

With a deep breath, I turn right and pray I made the right decision.

My illumination orb hovers above as I run. It casts a shadow over me, and my silhouette sprints on the wall beside me. This path leads to several more turns, and I choose each at random. Soon I worry I'm heading in circles, blindly charging through this maze of tunnels.

My path splits into three. I halt.

If I am sprinting in circles, I'm wasting precious time. I have only one hour to complete this trial, and I don't know what obstacles will hinder me.

I must think of a better way to navigate this maze. A way to recognize whether I've ventured down each path before.

Frowning, I scan over the bumpy ground, hoping to find something of use. If only I had string, or maybe seeds, to scatter across the stone. Then I could mark my path.

An idea strikes me.

"*Gelu*," I mutter and press my palm to my boot. Ice swirls over the sole.

I return my foot to the ground. When I stride forth, frost glitters where my boot was. Hopefully, the icy footprints will last long enough for me to navigate the maze.

I continue through the tunnels, now choosing each with more confidence. But I soon run into my frozen footprints, and I curse under my breath. It seems I was definitely going in circles before I covered my boot with ice.

I trace back my tracks until I find the turning which set me into this loop, and I choose an alternative path.

My boots pound against the rocky floor. Too focused on running, I barely notice the flash of fair hair to my right.

I pause, glancing in that direction.

Myron stands there. His magenta eyes fix on me. Recalling Archmage Gidston's words, I swallow.

He isn't one of the best adepts in our year—far from it. But I don't wish to waste time fighting him. Yet if he decides to strike me first, I will have no choice in the matter.

Aether blooms in my fingers. Just in case he makes his move.

Our gazes hold for a moment longer. I wonder whether he will propose another option: to ally together and use our wits to solve the obstacles scattered throughout these tunnels. I've hardly ever spoken to him during our five years at the Arcanium, and he's one of the quieter adepts in our year, but such an alliance would be beneficial for us both.

Deciding he would have struck by now if he intended to fight, I let the aether in my hands fizzle out. I open my mouth to call over to him, but he turns and flees in the opposite direction. His cerulean robes disappear around the corner.

I roll back my shoulders. It isn't as if I needed him. An alliance would have benefited him more than me.

Knowing I've wasted several precious moments, I pick up my pace as I hurry through the tunnels. Though my icy footprints tell me I'm not going in circles, I still worry whether I'm taking the wrong path through the maze.

The stone walls open to a cave. Ornate braziers sit at each corner, and a large one lies at the center. I scan over the metallic structures and then notice the door on the other side. It blends so perfectly with the walls that, if not for the faint lines marking its edges, I wouldn't know it was there.

I stride through the cave and over to the door. Then I shove it with all my might.

To my dismay, the door doesn't so much as creak.

I grit my teeth and try again, but it's still no use.

Realizing brute strength won't work, I murmur *ventrez* and conjure a wind spell, hoping a gale will blow aside the door.

Again, it has no effect.

With a sigh, I turn to the braziers. It was foolish to expect that force alone would open the door.

What I'm meant to do with these braziers, I have no idea.

I study them for a while longer. Braziers are usually filled with fire, so does that mean lighting them will open the door?

While I doubt it's that simple, I suppose there's little harm in trying. And maybe even a failed attempt will lead me closer to figuring out what I need to do. There's no point standing here and staring at the braziers while time is ticking away.

"*Ignis*," I say and send flames into each of the five braziers.

My conjured flames dance in the braziers. I hold my breath, hoping I've somehow overcome this obstacle—unlikely though it may be.

But then the flames surge up, leaving the braziers behind. They gather into a roaring inferno. Fire rushes toward me.

"*Aquis!*" I shriek.

Water blasts from my palms and crashes into the flames. It sends them spilling out into the chamber. The remnants of the fireball collide with the stone walls, charring them.

If I had been a moment slower, I would be nothing but ash right now.

Shock strangles me. I double over and gasp for breath until I recompose myself.

I turn to the braziers again and study them more carefully. Clearly lighting them isn't the solution.

I sigh and lean back against the charred wall behind me. Since this first attempt nearly killed me, I'm hesitant to try again. The next attempt could mean death.

But I also can't waste any more time.

I need to think of something clever. And fast.

I scan over the room, wondering what else I can try. I hope to find a hidden clue somewhere—maybe a riddle—but I find none. Only plain stone walls surround me. The room is empty aside from the five braziers.

Though my last attempt failed miserably, I remain convinced I must somehow light them to unlock the door. But if not fire, what else?

My eyes narrow at the center brazier. It's larger than the rest, indicating its superiority. There must be a reason.

Think, Reyna. Think.

I chew on my lip, desperation clouding my mind, and squeeze my eyes shut. I can hear ticking in my ears. But thinking about the time will only distract me and waste more minutes. I need clear thoughts. Not panicked ones.

My gaze trails across to the door. If only I could blast it open. Though the wind spell failed miserably, what about aether? After all, it's far more powerful than the four elements—

That's it!

The largest brazier must represent aether, while the four smaller ones represent the elements. Maybe that means I must light the center brazier with aether.

I draw on my magic and watch it swirl in my fingers. A part of me fears I will be wrong yet again. That this attempt will fail and the spell will retaliate.

But if I don't try . . .

Before I can change my mind, I whisper, "*Volu.*"

The aether follows my command. Violet light drifts to the center brazier and settles within. My jaw tenses as the aether flickers, and I pray my guess is right.

Several moments pass. More aether whirs in my fingers, ready to conjure a shield in case the magic inside the brazier strikes back at me.

But nothing happens.

The violet light remains within the brazier.

Hope soars within my chest. It worked!

I turn to the other braziers. Fire, water, earth, and air must go inside each. But in which order? Placing the wrong element inside the braziers will cause my magic to retaliate.

Water defeats fire, and fire defeats air. Because of that, I'm certain water and air must go on either side of fire. First, I need to decide which brazier to place fire inside. And if I choose wrongly, I risk my magic striking back.

But if I don't try, I'll never pass this trial. I've already wasted too much time here. I need to open this door as soon as possible. Or I won't make it out of this maze before the hour is up.

At least I will be prepared if my magic retaliates again. Since I'm only lighting one brazier, rather than five, there will be fewer flames to hurl at me if it does.

"*Ignis,*" I say, sending flames toward the nearest brazier.

For a moment, they hover there. Then they charge for me.

But I am prepared and cry out *aquis*, meeting the spell with a blast of water. Since these flames are less potent than the previous ones, my water spell easily douses them. Tendrils of steam pour out. I wave them away, clearing my view.

I try the brazier to my right. This time, the flames stay right where they are. Their amber light flickers inside the brazier.

I grin.

Two down, three to go.

Now I need to decide where to place water and air.

I stop before the flame-filled brazier and glance at the ones in the adjacent corners, unsure of which to pick.

In the end, I choose the left brazier. "*Aquis.*"

Water magic splashes over to the brazier. It hovers there. I ready myself to summon an earthen shield in case I've guessed incorrectly.

But the magic remains within the brazier.

I guessed correctly.

I turn to the brazier on the right. "*Ventrez.*"

Air magic flutters to the brazier. Knowing that the choice must be correct—after all, fire defeats air—I don't bother summoning flames to my fingertips.

White light shines in the brazier. I start over to the final one.

"*Tera.*"

Earth magic springs from my fingers and fills the remaining brazier with emerald light.

Magic hums. Green, red, blue, and white beams fire at the center brazier. The aether inside explodes. Violet light shoots out and strikes the stone door.

Rumbling echoes through the small room. The door rolls upward, revealing my path.

I sprint straight through.

CHAPTER 28

BEYOND THE DOOR, MORE DARK walls greet me. I turn corner after corner, my frozen footsteps indicating whether I'm heading in circles. I don't know how long has passed since the trial began. I'm certain it can't be more than half an hour, but I might be wrong.

My pace is frantic as I navigate through the winding tunnels. My breaths burn my nostrils, and my lungs greedily gasp for air. But I can't slow. If I do, I will fail.

A force crashes into me. It sends me flying into the stone wall behind. I steady myself and spin around, aether humming in my fingers. Whether they're a friend or a foe, I don't know, but I will be ready for either case.

"Ow," whines a female voice. She clutches her shoulder where we collided. Curly red hair sweeps out as she turns to me.

"Eliya!" I exclaim, grabbing her hand. While the backs of my arms hurt from where they slammed into the wall, it appears Eliya took more of the force from our crash. "Thank the gods it's you!" For a moment, I feared it was Kaely.

"Of course it's me." She rubs her shoulder. "Why do you have to hurt so much?"

"Don't run into me, then."

She wrinkles her nose at me. "You're the one who ran into me. Besides, don't you have a streak going for running into people?"

"Technically, I ran into the cart and not Nolan," I correct. "Anyway, we don't have time for idle chit-chat. Not when the clock is ticking away."

"Don't you mean the hourglass?"

I roll my eyes at her.

We hurry through the tunnels. After a few strides, Eliya glances back and gestures to the icy footprints behind us. "What a genius idea," she says in between panting. "Why didn't I think of that?"

"Thanks," I reply.

Eliya's illumination orb hovers over us, as does mine. Both our silhouettes run alongside us. Our furious footsteps and ragged breaths fill the darkness beyond.

Several turns later, we reach our next obstacle.

The path opens to a sitting room, with crimson sofas, oaken shelves filled with books, paintings of wondrous landscapes, and a crackling fireplace. The other half of the room is a perfect reflection of it.

I step toward the mirror and press my hand against it. From its cool touch, it seems to be ice rather than glass. If it is, then maybe fire will work against it.

Hopefully my magic won't retaliate against me, like it did with the braziers. At least I have Eliya here.

"Be ready to conjure a water shield," I tell her.

"What—"

Before she can finish, I weave aether into fire magic and unleash it upon the mirror. "*Ignira!*"

Flames swarm from my hands and slam into the frosty reflection. Fire licks at the ice and drops spill across the wooden floor. A hole emerges, revealing a tunnel that continues through the maze.

Just as I go to step through, the mirror freezes again. The path vanishes.

At least my magic doesn't return with a vengeance.

"Maybe it'll work if we both try?" I suggest, turning to Eliya.

She casts me a dubious look. "Somehow, I doubt it will."

"What's the harm in trying? If it works, we'll have broken through quickly. And if not, we'll just have to put our heads together and figure out how to solve it."

"Fine," Eliya says with a sigh.

The two of us conjure flames and cry out, "*Ignira!*"

Two fireballs slam into the mirror. This time the ice melts quicker, and the resulting hole is larger.

I dive toward it. But as I draw near, the mirror freezes.

"Maybe we shouldn't try that again," Eliya snorts. "In case next time you lose your fingers."

I don't turn to her as she speaks. Instead, I glare at the mirror. Like the door with the braziers, force won't break it, no matter how much magic fuels our spells.

"How do you think we can solve this one, then?" I ask.

Eliya taps her chin as she thinks. "Well, the only other obstacle I've faced so far was a door with a riddle on it."

"What did it say?"

"*What runs around the city, but never moves?*"

"Roads?"

"That's also what I first thought," Eliya replies. "But apparently that's wrong."

"Streets?" I try again.

"Same thing. And don't try guessing paths, either."

"Sewers?"

"Still wrong."

"I give up," I say with a shrug. Besides, we currently have a far more urgent matter to deal with. "What was it?"

"Walls, of course! Because walls run *around* the city, whereas roads and sewers run *through* the city. That's why they don't count!"

"Ah, I see."

Eliya shakes her head at me. "And here I was thinking I was bad at riddles. You're actually awful at them!"

"Thanks." I gesture to the surrounding room. "Now, how about you put your amazing riddle skills to use and figure out how we can solve this puzzle?"

"Right, right," Eliya says, scanning across the room and the mirror.

I take to searching our surroundings. I move aside the books on the shelves and lift the round, embroidered pillows which lounge about on the crimson sofas, hoping to find a clue hidden somewhere. Maybe a scrap of paper with a riddle or instructions written on it. But I find nothing. Not even when I pick up the book resting on the mantelpiece. It's a biography of Nolderan's founder, Delmont Blackwood. The pages are old and dusty.

"Wait," Eliya says as I go to return it to the mantelpiece.

With the book still in my hands, I turn to face her. "What?"

"That's it!"

"What's it?" I ask.

"Look, look!" she exclaims, bouncing up and down. She points to our reflection in the icy mirror.

"Where?"

"Look at the table in the mirror."

I do as she says. My gaze falls onto the reflection of the low table. On it lies the same book as the one in my hands. But in the reflection, I clutch only air.

"I see," I reply. "Since this book differs in the mirror, it must have something to do with how we need to solve this puzzle. But what do you think we're supposed to do with it?"

"Maybe we need to place it on the table, just like it is in the mirror?"

I do as she suggests. Nothing happens.

With a groan, I lift the book. But this time, my reflection is also holding it. I pause, frowning at myself in the mirror.

"I think we did something," I muse, turning back to Eliya. "When I first picked up the book from the mantelpiece, I wasn't carrying it in the mirror. Now after placing it on the table, my reflection is also holding it. So, that means we must have done something right. But what I don't understand is why it's still not letting us pass?"

"Maybe there are other items out of place? What if we need to match them all to the reflection?"

"That could be it."

We search high and low through the rest of the room, comparing every item with its reflection.

I check the shelves again. This time, I notice a few books out of order, so I rearrange them to match the mirror. Meanwhile, Eliya moves the candle on the cabinet to the mantelpiece, just as it appears in the reflection.

A crack rumbles behind us. The mirror shatters.

"*Muriz!*" I cry. Aether encases us both. Shards of ice fling at us. The edges of each are sharp and would tear us to shreds, if not for the aether shield.

When the barrage of frozen shards ceases, I let the aether shield fizzle out. The way is clear, and ice crunches beneath my boots as I stride into the tunnel. Eliya follows me.

The wooden floor returns to coarse stone. After we pass the frozen debris, I notice that the icy magic on my boot has faded away.

"Wait," I call to Eliya, who is sprinting on ahead. "I need to enchant my boot again. The spell has worn off."

"All right," she says, coming to a stop.

I lift my foot and press my palm to the bottom of my boot. "*Gelu.*" At my command, frost envelops the sole. Now when I walk, my footsteps once again mark the stone path with ice.

"Right," I say, jogging over to Eliya. "Let's go."

We hurry through the endless tunnels, retracing our footsteps if we end up doubling back on ourselves. By now, we must be well over halfway through the trial—maybe forty minutes. But it could be more than that. Maybe fifty minutes have passed, leaving us with ten minutes to navigate through the maze. Perhaps only five remain.

And I'm uncertain how far we are through the maze. Maybe we will reach the end at any moment. Or maybe we are heading deeper and deeper into the tunnels.

I do my best to ignore those thoughts of failure and focus on the path ahead. At least I can be certain we aren't going in circles, thanks to my—

"*Ignira!*" a shout booms to my left.

A fireball hurls toward us.

"*Aquir'muriz!*" I hastily throw a water shield in front of Eliya and me. She does the same, reinforcing our defenses.

The fireball slams into our shields. I grit my teeth and channel more magic into the spell so that it holds the relentless flames at bay.

Through our combined efforts, the fireball is extinguished. Steam fills the tunnel.

Through the haze, it's hard to identify who attacked us. I can only see their blurred silhouette and the illumination orb floating above them.

But there is only one adept arrogant enough to attack the two of us together, to risk their own future just to sabotage mine.

"*Ventrez,*" I mutter, waving my hand. A wind blows down the tunnel, dispersing the steam and revealing the adept who stands there.

Kaely.

CHAPTER 29

Kaely's braid flutters in my conjured breeze. Malice burns in her magenta eyes.

She seeks to destroy me once and for all.

"Is now really the time for this?" I spit.

Kaely strides through the tunnel and closes the distance between us. "Now is the only time for this. To settle our debts and ensure that someone as undeserving as you does not become a Mage of Nolderan." Her gaze snaps across to Eliya. "But you may go. Continue through the tunnels, pass this trial. I have no quarrel with you."

Eliya's jaw tightens. "That's a shame. Since I have a quarrel with you."

Kaely snorts an unhumorous laugh. "So be it."

Aether sparks in her fingers. In the next heartbeat, it turns to earth magic, swirling like gaseous emeralds inside her palms.

"*Tera!*" Kaely calls, her voice echoing through the shadows. The green light slams into the ground a few paces ahead of us. It burrows into the stone and digs out an enormous chunk. A chasm is left in its wake. Kaely raises the rock high into the air and hurls it at me.

But aether is already blooming in my fingers. I weave it into air magic. White light whirs in my hands.

"*Tempis!*" I shout.

My wind spell rushes forth to meet the boulder. The violent vortex slashes through the rock like a storm of daggers. Pebbles rain on us as my magic erodes the boulder and reduces it to rubble.

Before Kaely can launch another attack, Eliya takes the offensive. "*Gelu'gladis!*"

Ice shoots out from Eliya's fingers, forming a frozen sword.

"*Ignir'muriz!*" A wall of flames wraps around Kaely, preventing Eliya's icy attack from reaching her. The fire licks the frozen blade until it's nothing but droplets. The remnants spray across the tunnel's walls.

"*Ignir'quatir!*" Kaely roars.

Her fiery wall explodes. The flames spread out in all directions. The inferno scorches the surrounding stone walls and hurdles toward us with as much rage.

I barely have enough time to process the rushing flames, let alone conjure a shield. I cry out *aquir'muriz* and do my best, converting aether to water magic as swiftly as I can.

The resulting defense is paper thin. The flames blaze through it as though it's merely air.

Boiling heat slams into me. I collide with the ground. The back of my head strikes the stone first, and pain jolts through me like white-hot lightning. But that pales in comparison to the flames which threaten to gnaw on me until I am nothing but ash.

"*Aquis! Aquis!*" I scream, desperately trying to extinguish the fire engulfing me.

It takes two blasts of water before the flames die down and I can roll away. The embers at the front of my robes are snuffed out as I press my chest against the cool stone and suffocate them.

Footsteps ring out as Kaely approaches. I struggle to push myself upright. Specks of darkness scatter across my vision. Agony courses through the back of my head.

My cheek presses against the coarse stone as I turn to look at Eliya. She seems to be faring better, probably because Kaely aimed her attack at me. Though Eliya was also flung off her feet, the flames were more merciful to her. Her robes are singed, but she staggers upright and manages to stand. Unlike me. My arms fail to even push me into a sitting position.

Kaely halts before me. Smugness distorts her expression. "And here I thought you might actually put up a fight—"

"*Telum!*" comes Eliya's cry.

A blast of aether flies from her hands.

"*Muriz.*" A powerful shield encases Kaely and absorbs Eliya's blast. "*Quatir.*" The shield erupts.

Aether surges toward Eliya. She cries *tera'muriz* and hastily shapes the ground into a barrier.

But when the explosion slams into her defense, the earthen shield shatters. Pebbles fling out. Some scatter across me.

Eliya stumbles back, unable to defend herself from Kaely's next spell. "*Gelu'vinclair.*"

Frost spreads across the floor, thickening as it reaches Eliya's feet, and shackles her in place. The icy chains spiral up to her knees and then to her chest, rendering her firmly rooted.

All I want is to leap onto my feet. To face Kaely and prove I am not this weak. But my flesh is raw from the flames and my muscles protest at every movement. As does my head, which is rapidly plummeting into oblivion.

Eliya opens her mouth to cry out another spell. But before she can, Kaely calls *laxus* and teleports across the chasm she created. She appears in front of Eliya.

Kaely tears off the violet ribbon securing her braid and wraps it around Eliya's mouth. Her brown hair unravels in thick waves. She knots the ribbon in place. Now all of Eliya's spell-words are muffled. No magic springs to her fingers.

Eliya scowls at her, rage blazing in her expression. Kaely tilts her head as she studies her, amusement glinting in her eyes.

She doesn't spend long staring at Eliya, though. She soon turns to me, a venomous sneer plastered across her face.

"Even two against one, you cannot beat me. You are this weak, and yet you believe you deserve to become a Mage of Nolderan?"

My nails claw against the coarse stone, cracking from the force. A desperate growl escapes from the back of my throat. I barely recognize it as my own. It sounds too pathetic to belong to me.

"Look at you," Kaely continues with a dark laugh. "You're so useless I didn't even need to break a sweat to defeat you and your friend. Yet all of our tutors favor you. Even Archmage Gidston. How can they possibly think someone this weak is better than me?"

I hate that I can't deny her words. I *am* weak.

When Heston attacked Nolderan and murdered my mother, I wasn't strong enough to save her. Over these past three years, I have dedicated myself to becoming the best mage I can, but despite all my hard work, I still stand no chance against Kaely. All those times we dueled inside the arena, when I thought we might be at least equals, I was so terribly wrong. With Archmage Gidston there, she was always holding back the true extent of her murderous intent, but today there was nothing stopping her from unleashing her full power against me. Even with Eliya's help, I was unable to defeat her.

And if I stand no chance against someone like Kaely, how can I protect those I love from the horrors of dark magic?

Fury courses through my veins. My blood boils like wildfire. When I squeeze my eyes shut, I can see Arluin falling at the end of that narrow street—Heston standing over his too-still body. My mother's face turning to me. Life fading from her eyes, along with the magenta glow of aether. Shadows suffocating her, swarming into her mouth and nostrils, chaining her soul to Heston's will and warping her into a wraith.

Before I can realize, aether is brimming within me, flooding from my fingers and renewing my strength.

The pain through my head, my scorched skin—they all become nothing. They are insignificant compared to the anguish scarring my heart. Even after three long years, these torturous wounds have not healed. They have only festered.

Kaely doesn't know pain. She has never watched helplessly as a monster murdered those she loves, unable to save them. And yet she dares to mock me, to stare down at me with that disgusting smugness.

My fists tighten.

Ignira.

My lips don't move as I cast the spell. The words ring through my mind, drowning out every other thought.

Flames spin from my fingers, gathering into an enormous fireball. The inferno roars through the tunnel as it charges at Kaely. Without the restriction of spell-words, the magic is wild and unbridled.

Kaely is caught off-guard. When the fireball reaches her, she has drawn no aether to her fingers.

She is entirely defenseless.

Though she screams *aquis* and fights off the flames which threaten to devour her, I refuse to let her escape so easily. We will settle this once and for all. Never again will I allow her to belittle me.

I weave fire and earth magic together into a fizzling orb of rubies and emeralds. "*Magmus!*" I hiss, flinging the spell into the stone beneath me.

My magic eats away at the rock and melts it into furious lava. I launch the molten earth at Kaely while she is still fending off my fireball.

The lava encases her and cocoons her in fire. I hear her calling out *aquir'muriz*, and then her shouts fall silent. The magma hardens into dark, polished stone.

Dread pools in the pit of my stomach.

What if I took this too far? What if I killed her?

I shake my head. Kaely can't be dead. I only caught her by surprise with my fireball. The reason I can't hear her must be because the wall surrounding her is too thick. When I stop, I'm sure I can hear her muffled shouts. She's probably buried deep beneath the rock, furiously trying to battle her way out. And if I delay, she will burst through and strike me with all her wrath.

I hurry to Eliya, who is still chained in icy shackles. I untie the violet ribbon from her mouth and press my fingers to the center of her forehead. "*Mundes*."

My spell breaks the enchantment, and the frozen chains shatter. Shards of ice heap around our feet.

Eliya stares at me with widened eyes. "Did you cast that fireball without any spell-words?"

I lift my head in a slight nod.

"Reyna!" she exclaims. "If the spell slipped out of your control, it could have killed us all! Or it could have drained all the aether from your blood!"

"I know the risks," I snap. We all do. Never casting magic without spell-words is a rule taught to every adept on the first day of our enrollment. "What choice did I have? Kaely would have defeated us. We would have both failed this trial."

Which we still might, if we linger here for much longer.

I don't wait to hear Eliya's response. I grab her wrist and pull her down the tunnel.

CHAPTER 30

As WE RUN, EACH STRIDE sends pain ricocheting through my body. Kaely has inflicted many injuries upon me, and my skin is scorched from her attacks. The wounds are worsening with every passing second. The tunnel's stone walls sway around me.

Only the determination of passing this trial and becoming a mage keeps me on my feet. I fear I will collapse at any moment. We need to finish this trial. And fast.

We say nothing as we hurry through the darkness, the glow of Eliya's illumination orb lighting our path. Our labored breaths echo through the shadows.

I don't know how much longer we have, how much farther we must run before we will reach the end of this maze. With every turn we take, I hope to see Archmage Gidston standing there. But no matter how much I will to see her indigo robes and neat platinum hair, she does not appear.

A sudden wave of fatigue crashes into me, threatening to drown me.

I clutch the nearest wall, my palms scraping over the coarse rock.

"Reyna?" Eliya says, shaking my shoulders.

I don't answer her. Patches of void eat into my vision. I feel myself falling. Eliya's hands steady me. I stop falling.

"Reyna? Can you hear me?" Her voice rings through my ears like a relentless drum. My temples throb in response.

I want to say something, but I can't. Everything requires more energy than I can give. Even breathing taxes me.

"*Conparios.*" Through my half-closed eyelids, I see violet light bursting in Eliya's hands. When it fades, a vial of ruby red liquid emerges. She tears out the stopper and presses the cool glass rim to my lips. "You need to drink. Please, Reyna."

My mouth parts. She tips the vial and sends the potion pouring down my throat. It has a metallic, alcoholic taste which fizzes on my tongue. I choke on the liquid. Some of it slides down my chin. Eliya wipes it away with the back of her sleeve.

"*Evanest,*" she says, sending the empty bottle glittering away into a cloud of aether.

The potion slips down my gullet, burning me from the inside out. Where the warmth touches, energy sparks. Adrenaline surges through my veins. Everything still spins around me, but I no longer feel weak. I push myself from the wall. My senses are so heightened that even my own breathing sounds too loud.

The potion I drank was an Elixir of Flurry, and it makes my reflexes sharper than ever. Even my thoughts are unnaturally rapid. But the potion's effects will not persist for long. It might grant me ten minutes, if I am lucky. I hope it will be enough time for us to navigate through the rest of the maze. When the elixir wears off, I am likely to collapse.

"How do you feel?" Eliya asks, peering at me.

"Fine for now," I reply, the words bursting from my mouth so quickly they jumble together into one syllable. "Let's go before it wears off."

We continue racing down the tunnel, desperately seeking the end. Now I feel no fatigue, even though I am sprinting far faster than I normally can. I seem to see the uneven peaks and troughs in the stone before they appear and leap right over them. Eliya, whose reflexes are at a normal speed, begins to fall behind. At each corner, I wait for her to catch up.

The tunnel arrives at another cave, much like the first one I faced inside this underground maze. A stone door lies at the far side, and a golden altar sits in the center. As we draw near, it gleams in the radiance of Eliya's illumination orbs. Two candles sit on either side of the altar's polished bowl. Both are lit. The conjured flames flicker, burning for eternity.

We stride past the altar and halt at the stone door. Words are etched into its surface, rippling with aether.

Before you may enter,
Look upon me with great care,
On my words and nothing more.
Only those with courage,
Dare to pay my price.

We both silently read the words and then exchange glances.

"Another riddle," Eliya says with a sigh.

"I thought you were good at them?"

"I never said I was good at them, just that you were bad at them."

I would pull a face at her, but my thoughts are too fast, spiraling out of control. The door's words echo over and over in my mind, forming a rhythm so relentless I can barely think.

Read carefully. Pay the price.

I read the riddle again and again until the shimmering letters blur. Still, I do not know what price the door demands.

"Could it be money?" Eliya muses aloud.

"Maybe," I say with a shrug, having no other suggestions myself. "So, do we just say money to the door, and it will let us pass?"

"With the riddle I faced, I had to write the answer onto the door before it let me through."

"With aether?"

"Yeah, beneath the riddle."

I take a step closer to the door and murmur *volu*. Violet light radiates from my index finger, and I use it to trace each letter of 'money' into the stone. Aether glistens where I mark the stone. But as I write each letter, the previous one disappears and fades into glittering dust.

I glance back at Eliya. "It didn't work."

Her brows furrow.

If we don't break through this door soon . . .

I banish the thought. Thinking like that won't help me solve the riddle.

"Any other ideas?" I ask.

"Maybe this one is different." She holds out her palm and mutters *conparios*. Her coin purse appears, and she hurriedly pulls it open, retrieving a copper coin. She holds it up to me, and it glints in the dazzling light of her illumination orb. An outline of the Aether Tower is pressed into the coin's metallic surface. "Maybe we need to literally pay the door before it will open."

"Maybe."

Eliya tosses the copper coin at the door. It bounces off the stone with a metallic clink, but nothing happens. She swears under her breath.

I gesture to the golden altar behind us. "Surely that wouldn't be here for no reason? Maybe try placing the coin inside there?"

With a nod, Eliya hurries over to the bowl and throws the copper coin inside. The chime of metal sings through the cave.

Again, nothing happens.

Next Eliya tries emptying the entire contents of her purse: countless coppers, several silvers, and a few gold coins. Though her offering would be enough to send the streets of the Lower City into a frenzy, the door is far less impressed. It doesn't budge.

Cursing again, Eliya scoops up all her coins and returns them to her purse.

I whirl back to the door. The aether across the riddle ripples, mocking us. "It isn't money."

"You don't say," Eliya grumbles, staring down at her coin purse. "*Evanest*." At her command, it disperses into aether.

I glare at the riddle, but it reveals no clue. "Before you may enter," I read out, wondering whether the puzzle will make more sense when spoken aloud, "look upon me with great care, on my words and nothing more. Only those with courage, dare to pay my price." Several moments pass. Despite verbalizing the riddle, I still don't know how to solve it. "What in the Abyss does it want from us?"

Eliya scrunches her face as she racks her mind. "What else would the price be? I suppose it's something we're supposed to place within the altar."

"Something that has nothing to do with wealth." I run my fingers through my hair as I think. The strands are a tangled, matted mess from the fight with Kaely. As my fingers reach the back of my head, they come across something sticky.

I pull my hand toward me, peering at the liquid on my fingers. It seems I must have hit my head hard enough to draw blood in the fight with Kaely. With the Elixir of Flurry pounding through my body, I hardly feel the pain.

The blood trickles down my finger. I stare at the crimson bead, my eyes widening. Realization slams into me.

"Blood!" I cry.

Eliya turns to me. Her expression becomes panicked as she notices the blood on my index finger. "Reyna, you're bleeding!" She clutches my shoulders, examining me carefully. "Are you all right? I didn't know you were this hurt!"

I hold the blood-coated finger up to Eliya, marveling at it. Maybe I should be concerned that I'm bleeding, but I'm far more focused on solving the riddle.

I return my gaze to the door, reading over the words once more. A grin stretches across my face, certain my guess is correct.

"Reyna?" Eliya says. "You're scaring me. Did you really hit your head this hard?"

"Don't you see?" I exclaim. "Look at the first letter of each line: *Before, Look, On, Only, Dare.* The answer is blood!"

Eliya's mouth hangs agape as she stares at the door, seeing the answer for herself. While she's busy examining the riddle, I murmur *gelu'gladis* and conjure a frozen blade. Clutching the icy hilt tightly in my hand, I stride over to the golden altar.

"What are you—"

Before she can finish, I slice the sharp edge of the frozen blade across my palm. Blood wells out from the cut. I squeeze my hand and place it over the altar, allowing several drops to splash into the golden dish.

The door rumbles, rolling upward and revealing our path.

I cast the icy blade aside, and it clatters onto the ground. I wipe my bloodied hand onto my singed cerulean robes and then grab Eliya's wrist, pulling her forth.

We are through the door even before it has fully opened, sprinting down the winding tunnels. We turn right and left, and with every corner I pray it will be the last.

Darkness clouds my vision. Even the illumination orbs behind me cannot keep it at bay. Exhaustion weighs down my legs, and intense pain burns across the back of my head. It feels like a knife is burrowing into my skull.

The Elixir of Flurry is wearing off.

My pace falters. I lean against the nearest wall, using it to support me.

"Eliya," I wheeze, "I don't think I can . . ."

Eliya stops and whirls around. She hurries back to my side, clutching my shoulders and helping me to stay on my feet. "Reyna! You can't faint. Not now."

"I feel so tired," I murmur, my eyes shutting.

She grabs either side of my face. My eyes remain closed. "Please," she begs me. "You can't give up now. We have to complete this trial."

I don't respond.

"Reyna!"

When I still say nothing, she hauls me from the wall and wraps my arm around her shoulders. "We don't know whether the trial is over yet. We have to keep on going."

Her words remind me of my purpose. Remind me that if I fail this trial, I will never become a mage.

Determination washes over me, but it is weak compared to the pain. I drag my feet forth and lean my weight into Eliya. With her help, I continue down the tunnel. Our pace is slow. I stumble over the uneven edges of the stone, almost sending us both falling over. My illumination orb fizzles out, leaving only Eliya's. The tunnel is left more shadowed and harder to navigate. Not that I can see much in my current state.

Many turns later, I feel myself slipping from Eliya's shoulders. She grips me more securely, refusing to let me go. "You must keep going."

I try, but it's becoming more difficult with every stride. The urge to rest is nearly impossible to ignore. Soon Eliya is all but carrying me through the maze of tunnels.

My senses dull. Even the intense pain numbs. I'm rapidly sinking into emptiness.

Before the darkness can claim me, Eliya suddenly shouts, "Look!"

Languidly, I lift my head. Through my partially closed eyes, I see a faint light gleaming at the end of the tunnel.

"That must be the end, Reyna! It must be!"

She picks up her pace, or at least tries to. With my weight burdening her shoulders, she doesn't manage more than a brisk walk. I do my best to lighten her load, but sleep has almost claimed me. My steps falter.

"Come on!"

Eliya heaves me down the rest of the tunnel. We burst out into the chamber beyond.

Aether crystals shine brightly. Their radiance blinds me.

When my sight adjusts, I see Archmage Gidston standing there—along with many other adepts. My vision is too blurred to identify them, but I think I see Lorea and Koby among them. The golden hourglass sits at the center of the room. Barely any aether dust is left inside the top glass bulb. I don't want to think how many minutes—seconds even—we were from failing.

"Congratulations, Ashbourne and Whiteford," Archmage Gidston says. "You have both successfully passed the Trial of Mind."

"Reyna," Eliya breathes, turning to me. "We did it. We actually did it!"

I want to rejoice with her, but numbness spreads through my body. I can no longer feel anything, not even her shoulder beneath me. All I manage is a slight smile, and then the last of my consciousness slips away.

I descend into darkness.

CHAPTER 31

WHEN I WAKE, THE COARSE stone walls beneath the Arcanium are gone. Instead, my eyes are greeted by the lavish creams and golds of my room. Mr. Waddles sits on the gilded cabinet opposite me and watches me with his glassy, black eyes.

The Trial of Mind comes rushing back to me: Kaely being consumed by my lava, Eliya hauling me down the dark tunnels. We made it out in time, didn't we? Or did I dream of Archmage Gidston congratulating us on passing the trial?

Fog shrouds my mind. Clutching my temples, I push myself upright.

"Don't move."

I turn to see my father sitting on my cushioned armchair which he has moved beside my bed. Since the curtains are closed, I can't tell what the time is.

"Father? What are you doing here?"

"You need to rest." He stares at me through narrowed eyes until I lie back down. "A healer came to examine your wounds and apply Blood Balm. She said you will be fine, but that you must sleep."

"What time is it?"

"Six o'clock?"

"What?" I exclaim, my heart skipping a beat. Wasn't I supposed to be somewhere at six o'clock? No, wait. That was tomorrow night, wasn't it? Assuming I didn't sleep for longer than I think I did. "Is it still Wednesday?"

My father peers at me suspiciously. "Yes, why?"

"Because if it was Thursday night, then my last trial would be in the morning," I hastily reply. He doesn't need to know about my date with Nolan. I don't think he would mind—and if he does, it would only be because of my Mage Trials being held this week—but I don't feel like telling him. Though we are close, we don't have that kind of relationship. If my mother were still here, I would tell her in a heartbeat. She would laugh at how I ran into Nolan and broke all of his wine bottles. Her absence leaves a gaping hole in my heart, one I doubt will ever heal.

I miss her so very much.

I stare at my hands. My father is silent. His magenta eyes don't leave me, as if he fears I will collapse again. If I do, at least I'm already lying in bed.

"What about Kaely?" I ask. As I await his answer, I chew on my lip. I don't want her to be dead. Not really. If only because it would make me a murderer.

"She was in an even worse state than you," he says with a sigh. "Archmage Calton was beside himself when they found her inside a tomb of cooled magma."

"A tomb?" My lower lip trembles, betraying my emotion. "She . . . She is alive, isn't she?"

"It will be a few days before she will be able to walk. She is lucky to be alive."

I swallow down my guilt. A few tears well in my eyes, but I blink them away and blame them on all the turmoil.

"Did she pass the trial?" I ask, not meeting his gaze.

"No, she did not."

"So, she will never become a mage now?" Once, I thought such knowledge would fill me with glee. But it doesn't. It just makes me feel hollow and heavy.

He shakes his head. "She will not. I suppose that is punishment enough for her actions."

"For her actions? What do you mean? Archmage Gidston said that the usual rules didn't apply on our Mage Trials. That we wouldn't be punished for attacking each other."

"Yes, you are right. She broke no rules. As the Grandmage of Nolderan, I cannot punish her for what she did. But she nearly killed you, Reyna. And as your father, I cannot accept that."

"Well, I also nearly killed her. And I think I did a better job at it, too. I bet Archmage Calton was furious at me, wasn't he?"

"He was," my father replies. "He also tried to have you disqualified from the Mage Trials, but Archmage Gidston reminded him that the trials do not come without risk."

"I definitely passed, didn't I?" I ask, dread knotting my stomach. "I didn't imagine Archmage Gidston telling me I passed the trial?"

"No, you didn't imagine it," he says. "Though I did hear there was little time to spare." There's a sharpness to those words.

Here I am lying wounded in bed, and he's disappointed that I completed the trial too slowly. Even though I defeated Kaely, it's still not enough.

"That wasn't my fault. If Kaely hadn't attacked me, I wouldn't have needed to navigate through the rest of the maze injured and on the brink of collapsing. It was only thanks to Eliya that I made it out."

"That wasn't how I meant it."

"Then how did you mean it?"

"As you said, it wasn't your fault, and I don't believe for a second that you would have instigated the fight."

"If I hadn't passed, would you be angry with me?"

"Of course not," he says, taking my hand in his. "When the healer was examining you, for a moment I thought . . ."

That he might lose me. Just like he lost my mother.

He says none of those words, but I know he means them. I can tell by the way his brows pinch together and his eyes stare down at our hands.

I squeeze his thumb, since his hands are much larger than mine. When I was younger, the size difference was even more astonishing.

"If it's six o'clock," I say, breaking the brief silence, "shouldn't you be working?"

"I was in a meeting when Archmage Gidston called for me, and I immediately teleported over to the Arcanium."

"What happened to your meeting? Did you return to it?"

"No," he says. "I have been here all day."

"Sorry for interrupting the meeting," I mumble. "And that you had to stay here all day because of me."

"Why would you be sorry for that?"

"You probably have far more important things to do."

"I don't have more important things than you, Reyna. But you need to rest. If you don't, you will not be well enough for your final trial on Friday."

"I'll be well enough," I reply. "I promise."

"Good," he says, releasing my hand. "Then sleep."

With the sternness in his voice, I don't argue with him. I close my eyes and sink deeper into my silk sheets and soft mattress. The gentle flicking of pages comes from where my father sits. I didn't see what book it was, but I'm willing to bet it's an exceptionally old and dusty tome. I don't open my eyes to check whether I'm correct. He would scold me for that.

My stomach growls. Apparently it's loud enough for my father to hear since he chuckles.

"You haven't eaten all day," he says. "You must be hungry. I'll go and cook something for us both to eat then."

I can't remember the last time my father cooked—using his magic, of course. He's certainly never cooked anything by hand.

"Thank you," I say.

I hear him place his book onto the window ledge and stride out the room. When the door shuts behind him, I dare to open my eyes and sit up.

After cooking us both dinner, my father resumes his vigil beside my bed. Only when Eliya arrives a few hours later does he finally leave my side. Apparently she came earlier this afternoon, but I was still out cold.

"She needs to rest," my father's voice comes from the other side of the door. "And make sure she doesn't get out of bed. The injuries she has suffered today are not light."

"Yes, I understand. I was also wondering whether you would like me to keep an eye on Reyna tonight, so you can also rest?"

My father pauses.

"You're the Grandmage of Nolderan. The city cannot run without you. I promise I will take good care of her." Eliya can sound incredibly responsible when she tries. Surprisingly.

"She will need to take an Elixir of Rejuvenation on the hour if she is to make a swift recovery ahead of Friday," my father replies after a moment.

"I will make sure she takes it."

"Good. Try not to talk to her for too long, either. She must sleep."

"Yes, of course."

"And don't let that faerie dragon into her room. I don't want it disturbing her."

"I will make sure he doesn't."

With that, my father permits Eliya into my room. She shuts the door softly behind her, and his footsteps fade away down the corridor. When he's safely gone, she flashes me an exasperated look.

"I know," I groan. "He won't even let me open my eyes. I'm only allowed to drink potions and sleep."

"I can't decide whether your father is sweet or terrifying," she says, crossing the room and sitting on the cushioned armchair beside me.

"Definitely terrifying," I reply. Though my eyes are open, I don't sit up in case he suddenly decides to return.

"How are you feeling?" she asks, leaning forward. Her eyes scan over me, lingering on the many bandages wrapped around my arms and my forehead.

"I feel fine."

"Are you sure? You didn't look so good after the trial. I don't know how I managed to get you out of those tunnels."

"Thank you for that." Tears swell in my eyes, and I blink them away before they can escape down my cheeks. "If not for you, I wouldn't have passed the trial. I don't think I can ever repay you for what you did."

"Repay me?" she scoffs. "Don't be silly. You're my best friend. Why would you need to repay me? Though if you are insisting, I certainly wouldn't say no to a bottle of moon-blossom wine. And Mrs. Baxter's finest cakes."

I laugh, and so does she. But then my chest starts to hurt, and we both stop laughing.

"I thought you said you felt fine," she says, giving me a dubious look as I clutch my chest.

"I do," I wheeze. "Or at least I did until I started laughing."

"Then don't laugh. Now I see why your father told me not to talk to you for long."

I roll my eyes.

"He's right. You need to sleep."

"I'm tired of sleeping," I complain. "I've already slept all day. What time is it even?"

"Just past nine o'clock."

"I've slept for at least eleven hours. Must I really sleep more?"

"Yes," she replies, wagging her finger at me. "You absolutely must if you are to complete the last trial on Friday. The Trial of Magic will require a great deal of strength. You know that."

"I know, I know," I huff, slumping into my sheets.

"Oh, that's right," she blurts. "Don't you have a date with Nolan tomorrow night, as well?"

Grumbling, I grab a pillow and bury my face in it. The golden tassel tickles my nose.

Eliya confiscates it. "You'll knock your bandages if you're not careful."

I wrinkle my nose at her and pull the sheets over my head.

"What's the matter? Yesterday, you were excited about it."

"Yesterday, I wasn't injured," I retort. "Nor was I excited about it."

"Were too."

"Was not."

"Come on, Reyna. It'll do you some good to have some fun for once. And that's all it needs to be. If you decide you don't like him, you don't ever need to see him again. I'll even break the bad news to him, if you want. You know I'm an expert at that. But at least see how it goes first before deciding."

"I don't think I'm in any state to have fun right now."

"You've told me twice that you feel fine. And that you're tired of sleeping."

"My father won't let me leave my bed, let alone go on a date with someone I just met."

"We have an entire day until then. And your father normally works until late, doesn't he? I'll convince him to let me look after you all of tomorrow."

I press my lips together, trying to think of an excuse she can't counter. "I'm not like you," I finally settle on saying. "I don't want a long line of broken-hearted boys pining after me."

She cackles. "It is a long line, isn't it? But you won't have a long line. At least, not yet. There would only be Nolan."

It seems nothing I can say will persuade her.

She pulls the sheets from my head and tucks the edges around my shoulders. "Anyway, you have a trial and a date to recover for, so you'd better get back to sleep."

Though I know I will be unable to sleep, I don't protest any further. Eliya glares at me until I close my eyes, and I decide that she might be even more terrifying than my father.

CHAPTER 32

"And . . . perfect," Eliya says, sliding the final hairpin into my updo. The delicate gems on the end twinkle at me in the mirror.

I glance down at myself. This time, Eliya talked me into wearing a dress even more ridiculous than what I wore to meet Nolan on Tuesday. This one is a deep mauve, with flowers embroidered into the satin. And by the gods, Eliya has pulled the corset tight. My poor breasts look as if they may burst at any moment, and the corset can't be helping my injuries. Though I've mostly healed from the Trial of Mind yesterday, I still feel rather tender. Not that I would admit it out loud.

Eliya convinced my father to attend all of his meetings today. I'm not sure what time he will come home, but I'm hoping it will be late before he does. He'll be furious if he learns that I've gone out, and if he catches me in this ridiculous dress, I will have no excuse to offer him. Eliya said she'll keep watch, but I don't know what we'll do if he arrives back before me. Maybe she'll think of a way to smuggle me into the manor without him noticing. If anyone can pull that off, it's Eliya.

My father wouldn't be wrong to be annoyed, though. I *was* badly injured, and the Trial of Magic is far more important than a date. But I also can't bear to sleep for a moment longer. At least this date gives me a reason to escape my bed.

"Don't you think I'm showing too much skin?" I ask, tearing my gaze from the mirror and turning to Eliya.

"Nonsense!" she replies, glancing over my bare shoulders and arms. Thanks to the copious layers of Blood Balm, my skin is mostly healed now. There are still some raw patches from the flames, but Eliya helped me conceal them all with illusions. The enchantment should last for a few hours. "But if you're worried about being cold, then I'll find you a shawl."

I will need a lot more than a flimsy shawl, since it's the middle of Winter, but I don't protest as Eliya starts over to my chest of drawers and rummages through them. Besides, I can simply murmur *calida* and warm myself from the inside out if I feel chilly.

"There," Eliya says, returning to me and draping a translucent pink shawl over my shoulders. "How does that look? I think it matches quite well."

I give her a hesitant nod, though the shawl doesn't hide the main problem I have with my attire—namely the excessive cleavage I'm currently exposing. "What if the corset bruises me?"

Eliya rolls her eyes. "Heavens, I didn't pull it that tight!"

"What if I can't have a normal conversation with Nolan?" I try instead.

"Why wouldn't you be able to?"

"Because what if he's too busy staring down here"—I point at my chest—"rather than my face?"

Eliya grins wickedly. "That's the entire point."

I slap her shoulder, but her laugh only grows.

"You'll thank me later," she promises me with a wink.

I scoff at her. "Anyway, I'd best get going. It's probably long past six."

"Relax," she says. "You don't want to show up too early, or he'll think you're too keen. And if you decide to break his heart, he'll be even more distraught."

Despite her words, she lets me leave my room. She follows me all the way downstairs and out the door. It's already dark outside, and the stars twinkle high above.

"Good luck," she says as I start down the few stone steps.

My stomach churns. My hands already feel clammy, and I haven't even teleported myself to The Old Dove yet. "Do you think things will go well?"

"Of course they will," she replies. "You look stunning, thanks to me."

"What if I say something stupid and make a fool out of myself?"

"Don't worry, you already made a fool out of yourself on Tuesday."

"Thanks, that really helps."

Eliya shrugs. "He still asked you out on a date, so just be yourself. Apparently he likes that. Besides, it doesn't matter what he thinks about you. What matters most tonight is your opinion of him. You're the one who needs to decide whether you like him or not. So, you have no reason to be nervous."

"Maybe that actually does help."

"Good, now go and have some fun!" She shoves me down the steps, and I almost trip over them. "But remember, we have the Trial of Magic in the morning, so don't let Nolan keep you up *all* night!"

Before I can respond, she slams the door and leaves me no choice but to continue down the steps and through the gardens.

A few faerie dragons are still tending to the flowerbeds, and when Zephyr catches sight of me, he whizzes over. His violet wings beat back and forth, and his amethystine eyes stare up at me.

"Don't look at me like that. I'm busy."

He swoops toward me and nudges my shoulder.

"I really am going to be late."

He blinks lazily at me.

I heave out a sigh and gather magic into my hands. "*Crysanthius*," I say, and the aether solidifies into glittering crystals.

Zephyr doesn't hesitate to gobble them all up, his forked tongue greedily darting out. When he's finished, I wipe my hand on my mauve skirts. Eliya would lecture me about getting faerie dragon spit all over my dress, but at least she isn't here to see. And when I peer down, the patch isn't too noticeable. Hopefully, it will soon dry.

I hurry down the gravelly path winding through our gardens, and Zephyr trails after me. When I reach the gates, I turn and frown at him.

"Zephyr, you can't come with me."

He growls in protest.

"I have a date."

He tilts his head. Though faerie dragons understand our speech perfectly well, I don't think he understands what I mean by 'date.' He probably thinks I mean the calendar kind.

"I'm meeting someone, and we're going for dinner." Only now do I realize that Nolan didn't specify where exactly we would be eating. I hope it's somewhere formal, or else I'll be extremely over-dressed. I run a hand down my face. I really shouldn't have trusted Eliya to dress me.

I'm still unsure whether Zephyr understands what I mean, since he blankly stares at me.

"Oh, and you can't let my father know I've gone out or he'll kill me. If you tell him, I won't ever conjure extra aether crystals for you again."

Zephyr swiftly bobs his head at that, his azure scales glinting in the starlight.

He thankfully doesn't follow me as the enchanted gates swing open and I step out onto the street.

When I teleport to The Old Dove, Nolan is already waiting for me outside. He leans against the paneled windows, and the tavern's wooden sign swings back and forth in the frosty wind.

Tonight he wears a vivid green doublet which matches his eyes. His black boots are as polished as always, without a single speck of dust on them. The wintry breeze tugs on his tousled golden hair.

At the sight of him, my breath catches in the back of my throat. It has only been two days since I last saw him, and yet it seems I've already forgotten how handsome he is.

I know Eliya said that I shouldn't be nervous, that tonight is about me deciding whether I like him, but I forget how to breathe when his mesmerizing emerald eyes meet mine.

"You're here," Nolan says, shattering the silence between us. To his credit, his gaze doesn't linger on my chest for long. He is far more focused on my face. Impressive, since Eliya did her best to make my breasts as prominent as possible.

I lower my eyes. "Sorry if I kept you waiting. Especially with how cold it is outside."

"No, no. Not at all." He holds his arm out to me, and I gingerly slip mine through his, linking us both together. It means that we're standing rather close, and I'm conscious of every part of my arm that touches his.

We begin down the street. A layer of frost sheens the cobblestones, and I take care not to slip. The delicately embroidered slippers on my feet provide little grip against the ice. Fortunately, Nolan's arm prevents me from sliding over the stones.

"Where are we going?" I ask.

"You'll see," he says.

"Is it a surprise?"

He chuckles. "I suppose it is."

We soon reach the end of Fairway Avenue and arrive on Lenwick Street. Nolan guides me farther into the Upper City, closer to where the Aether Tower hums above all the cobalt rooftops.

Though it's dark, it is still rather early, and we pass plenty of people on our way. Some are dressed as extravagantly as me, so no one spares me a second glance. And Nolan himself is also dressed in fine clothes. I hope that means wherever we're heading, I won't look out of place. Then again, Nolan always seems to be well-dressed.

Luckily, our destination proves to be The Shimmering Oyster, which is one of Nolderan's most luxurious restaurants. There is nowhere finer to dine than here. The guests flowing in and out of the restaurant's double doors look as though they have stepped out of a Ball. If anything, I feel underdressed compared to them.

"The Shimmering Oyster?" I exclaim, turning to Nolan as we reach the dozen steps leading up to the restaurant's entrance.

Twin baskets of ivy hang on either side of the carved doorframe. Purple azaleas add a splash of color to the green. The ivy's tendrils sway in the breeze.

"What's the matter?" he asks. "Do you not like it here?"

"No," I swiftly say. "This is my favorite place to dine." What I don't say is that I'm astonished Nolan would bring me here. The prices are incredibly steep. And hasn't he just bought a tavern? Can he really afford to take me to dinner here?

Maybe he thinks because I'm the Grandmage's daughter, I can afford to pay for us both. Maybe that's the real reason he asked me out to dinner. What he doesn't realize is that I've already spent my stipend for this month, meaning I will be unable to offer a single copper coin toward the bill. If Nolan insists on me paying, then I will have to tell the owners that my father will pay on my behalf. And then I will be in so much trouble because I should be in bed, recovering for the Trial of Magic tomorrow.

But Nolan was the one who asked me on this date, so surely he expects to pay? I know it would probably be best to clarify this with him before we sit down and eat, but I don't know how to ask politely. I should have checked on Tuesday before agreeing to come here with him. Now I fear this will end up in disaster.

"Shall we go inside?" Nolan asks, gesturing to the door.

Perhaps now would be the opportune moment to check whether he will be paying tonight, but I lack the courage to ask him. Instead I nod, and Nolan leads me up the stairs and through the open doors.

The Shimmering Oyster's interior is decorated as lavishly as I remember. Glittering chandeliers hang from the ceilings, large enough to rival the Arcanium's magnificent ones. Fine white lace decorates the tables, and small vases sit at the center of each, painted colorfully and filled with fragrant flowers. All the table legs are carved into spirals.

I haven't been here since my mother died. The three of us used to come here often, but my father hasn't suggested it over the past few years. I suppose it would feel strange without my mother with us.

Arluin took me here for dinner on the last Ranthir's Day: a day for lovers to celebrate their affections for one another. Since it was early summer, we sat out on the balcony. Tonight the balcony's doors are shut since it's the middle of winter. Though I can ward off the chill with fire magic, most guests are neither magi nor adepts.

Nolan starts over to the man behind the tall wooden stand, leading me along with him. The waiter looks up as we approach.

"Can I help you?" he asks.

"I reserved a table for six o'clock," Nolan replies.

"What's your name?" the waiter asks, rolling out his scroll and revealing a list of names scribbled across it. He holds it open with one hand and reaches for a quill with the other. He dips the nib into a pot of ink.

"Elmsworth."

The waiter pauses, scanning through his list. When he finds Nolan's surname, he strikes a line through it and returns the quill to his stand.

"Mr. Elmsworth," the waiter says with a stiff bow, "if you would like to follow me to your table."

We follow him through the restaurant. Most of the tables are full, aside from a few at the back, and the waiter escorts us to one near a large, arched window. Through the frost glazed glass, I can see the shadowed street below.

When we are seated, the waiter places a menu on our table. "Do take your time," he says. "I will return when you've had the chance to look through our menu."

With that, he turns and leaves. There's already a line of guests waiting at the entrance.

Nolan picks up the menu and holds it out to me. "Ladies first."

"Thank you," I reply, taking it from him and opening the thick, folded paper.

A variety of dishes are scrawled onto it in letters so cursive I can barely decipher what they say. My fingers drum against the table's lace cloth as I mull over the many choices.

"I really can't choose," I say, breathing a laugh. "Everything sounds so good, and they have so many new things since I last visited."

"Order as much as you want."

I glance up at him. "I can't do that."

"Why not? It's my treat."

"You're much too kind," I reply and scan over the various dishes again. In the end I decide to have clam chowder and rum-glazed salmon and hand over the menu to Nolan.

When the waiter returns, Nolan insists I order more than just a soup and main, but I decline. I don't want to take advantage of his generosity. And I feel awful for worrying that he would take advantage of my status as the Grandmage's daughter.

Another waiter soon appears with red wine and pours it into our glasses. Once he leaves, we are alone again.

Nolan gazes at me with his vivid green eyes. I instinctively reach for the menu but find it has been taken away. With nothing to hide behind, I feel terribly exposed. I wonder whether Nolan even realizes just how intensely he's staring at me.

I reach for my drink as an excuse not to meet his intent gaze. With nerves bubbling furiously through me, I almost knock over my glass. Thankfully, I steady it in time with my other hand and avoid spilling the wine all over the delicate lace tablecloth. But I suppose if I spilled it, it would interrupt Nolan's stare. Then again, I'm not entirely certain I want him to stop, as uncomfortable as it makes me feel.

"I forgot to ask," Nolan says, "how was the Trial of Mind yesterday?"

I set down my drink and fiddle with the frilly edge of the table-cloth. "All right, I suppose."

"All right?"

"Well, I passed."

"You don't look very pleased by it."

I sigh. "I almost failed."

When I dare to glance up, I catch him frowning. "Why? What happened?"

"On the trial, I fought with another adept and was badly wounded. I only made it out in time because my friend carried me through the tunnels."

"You were injured?" he asks.

"I collapsed at the end of the trial and have been in bed since yesterday morning."

"I didn't realize," he said softly. "If I had known, I wouldn't have dragged you here."

"You didn't drag me here. If I hadn't been well enough to come, I would have asked Eliya to let you know. Though you might have then thought I was using my injuries as an excuse."

His frown deepens. "I wouldn't have thought that."

Not knowing how to respond, I continue to fiddle with the tablecloth. Nolan silently watches me.

"Anyway," I say, hoping to alleviate the tension, "tell me about yourself. All I know is that you're from Dalry and own a tavern."

"What would you like to know about me?"

"Hm, maybe about your family. What did they think about you moving to Nolderan and buying a tavern here?"

Nolan pauses. "My family is dead."

"I'm so sorry. I didn't realize."

"It's fine," he replies. "My father died a few months ago, and as the only child, I inherited his entire estate. I decided to sell his property to have a fresh start here."

"Oh," I say, lowering my gaze.

Before he can reveal what happened to the rest of his family, the waiters appear with our soup.

Blue swirls are painted onto the bowls, and they look like waves rippling across the porcelain. The edges are tipped with gold and floral details are etched into the silver spoon.

We talk little as we eat our soup, and soon after we finish, our main dishes arrive. The steaming food arrives on elaborate silver plates, and the rum-glazed salmon I ordered proves to be far more delicious than I expected.

"More wine?" Nolan asks when we've cleared our plates. Less than a quarter of wine remains inside the bottle.

"It's probably best I don't have another glass, since I have my final trial in the morning."

"Of course," he replies.

Nolan doesn't finish the wine and signals to the waiter for the bill. If Eliya was here, she would lecture us about leaving so much wine.

Once Nolan has paid, he leads me back out of the restaurant and into the cool night.

Outside, it's trying to snow, and a few specks dust my hair. We reach the bottom of the steps, and Nolan holds out his arm. I take it, linking us together.

"Where to now?" I ask, my warm breath swirling into the chilly air.

"You know, I didn't think this far ahead."

"If you don't have any other ideas, maybe we could head to the fountain in the square? It'll probably be quiet now. And there are some benches to sit on."

His gaze sweeps over my thin shawl. "Won't you be cold?"

"I can conjure an aether shield around us. That'll stop the wind and the snow."

"All right," he says. "Sounds like a plan."

He begins to walk on ahead, but I pull him back. He raises a brow at me.

"You do remember that I'm a mage in training? I can just teleport us there."

"Right, of course."

With our arms still linked, I close my eyes and visualize the Upper City's square as vividly as I can. Teleporting someone else with me takes more concentration, and a lot more aether. If I'm not careful, I could end up teleporting us somewhere else in the city.

When I'm certain I have thoroughly prepared the spell, I release it. "*Laxus.*"

Magic washes over us, and we disappear into the night. My body becomes weightless, and I can no longer feel Nolan's arm around mine.

The floating sensation lasts for only a heartbeat. Then the darkness opens to the scene of the Upper City's square, sketched in vibrant purple light. Color fills the city's outline, and the buildings materialize around us.

A mermaid sits at the top of the fountain, carved from stone, and the water flows from her raised hands, splashing against each tier. Long, wavy hair covers her bosom.

We sit beside each other on the nearest bench, and there's enough distance that our legs aren't touching, but I still feel his warmth. The snowflakes fall thicker now, and I blink away the few which land on my lashes. Before more can cover us, I encase us both in a bubble of humming light.

"*Muriz.*"

Aether shrouds us and prevents snow from falling on us. Even the frigid wind can't penetrate my magic.

Nolan stares up at the shield with a contemplative expression. I can't tell what he's thinking.

I also tilt back my head and peer at the stars beyond the aether barrier. With the rippling surface, they are almost impossible to distinguish.

It takes me a few moments to realize that Nolan has lowered his gaze and is watching me. When my attention returns to him, heat floods my cheeks.

"Reyna," he murmurs, "you look lovely tonight." He lifts my hand and presses his lips to my skin.

I don't breathe. Neither do I pull away. So taken aback by the gesture, I only watch as he lifts his lips from my hand and lowers it.

But he doesn't let go. His fingers remain wrapped around mine, and we stare at each other, neither one of us blinking.

His other hand reaches for my face. His fingers trail down my cheek, tracing my jawline and then the curve of my neck. I shiver from his touch.

"May I kiss you?" His words are as sacred as a hushed prayer.

I can say nothing. The way he gazes at me—the way he touches me— overwhelms all my senses. I manage a small nod.

Nolan leans closer, leaving only a strand of distance between our lips. His fingers skim across my collarbone and over my neck. His emerald eyes settle onto my lips. He hesitates for so long that I wonder whether he has changed his mind. Whether in the next heartbeat, he will withdraw and leave my lips untouched.

But then he kisses me.

At first I freeze, unsure of the steps to this dance I have not known for so long. His lips are unfamiliar against mine but my uneasiness soon thaws, and I fall into his rhythm, kissing him back with as much certainty.

He pulls me in deeper, his fingers tangling through my hair, and I am lost to the bliss of his fervent touch. All else ceases to exist. There's only the scorch of his lips and the sting of his stubble grazing my skin.

His hand drifts from my neck, gliding over my shoulders and down my arms. My silk shawl falls loose, tumbling to the stone bench beneath us and leaving me exposed. I tremble, and he reaches for my hand, stroking my palm with his thumb. The tingle sends a dizzying rush crashing into me.

I don't know how I felt nervous about Nolan, about kissing him, because in this moment everything feels so achingly right.

When he lifts his lips from mine and ends our kiss, it feels far too soon. My breaths are uneven and heavy. Despite the aether barrier humming around us, sheltering us from the elements, I feel oddly cold. Already I crave the warmth of his lips.

His fingers return to my neck, sweeping over my skin and down my chest. Molten heat floods through me, and I wonder whether his touch will reach lower still. But he comes to a stop at the locket sitting below the hollow of my neck. He toys with it, his gaze fixed onto the silver heart.

I jerk back, pulling the locket from his grasp. The last thing I want is for the magic to pour out and the memory inside to play. For him to hear the promise Arluin made.

A flash of hurt flickers in his eyes. When I blink, the emotion is already long gone. Guilt stabs my gut. But I don't know who I am betraying.

"What's the matter?" he asks.

Maybe he thinks my pulling away means I'm rejecting him. I lower my gaze, focusing on my shawl beneath us. "The necklace was from someone important."

He frowns at me. "From whom?"

I swallow. "My . . . my mother."

I feel awful for deceiving him, but I don't know how else to explain the locket. If I speak about Arluin, I fear he will hear the affection in my voice. And that whatever is blossoming between us will never have the chance to flourish.

At least that's how I justify the lie.

"I see," he says, releasing the necklace.

We say nothing then, and I feel increasingly worse. Eventually, when I can bear it no longer, I reach for his hand. He glances up at me, surprised by the gesture. Maybe he interpreted my withdrawal as rejection.

"Thank you for tonight," I whisper. "I've had such a wonderful time."

His golden brows pinch together. "Are you sure?"

"I am," I reply, but it seems to do little to relieve his uncertainty. "I'm sorry about how I reacted just then. My mother died a few years ago, and her absence is still raw." While that's no lie, it is deceitful. To remedy the situation, I am spinning an even deeper web of dishonesty.

"It's all right. I understand."

"I would like to see you again," I say. "There will be a Ball tomorrow night in the Arcanium. Assuming I pass the Trial of Magic, that is."

"You will pass." He says those words with great certainty. I wish I had as much confidence in myself.

"I know you'll be busy working in your tavern, but it would mean a lot to me if you are able to come."

"I'll be there," he assures me.

I flash him a small smile. "Thank you."

He dips his head.

"Anyway," I say, grabbing my shawl and hauling myself from the bench. My wobbly legs manage to support my weight. "I should probably head home now."

"Of course," he replies. "Good night, Reyna. Thank you for seeing me tonight, especially after all the injuries you have suffered."

"It's not a problem. Thank you for inviting me." I draw aether to my fingers, preparing my teleportation spell. "See you tomorrow night."

With that, I drift away into a cloud of violet light, leaving Nolan and the bench far behind.

CHAPTER 33

THE CROWD ROARS WITH ANTICIPATION. The air crackles with tension.

Every seat inside the arena is filled, from the first tier all the way to the very top. It seems all of Nolderan has gathered to watch our third and final Mage Trial.

I sit on the lowest row, along with the other adepts. On the opposite side lies a raised platform where my father and his Archmagi are seated. Their chairs are so elaborately decorated they look like stone thrones. Though we sit hundreds of yards away, I feel my father's sharp gaze fixing on me, willing me not to fail.

I grip the edge of the bench, my nails scraping against the stone. I cannot fail. If I do, all I've ever worked for will be in vain.

Today, I must succeed. There is no other choice.

Archmage Gidston doesn't sit on the platform with my father and the other two Archmagi. She stands at the center of the arena. When she raises her hand, the crowd falls silent.

"We gather today to watch the remaining fifteen adepts undergo their final Mage Trial. Over the past five years, they have worked tirelessly to develop their abilities at crafting aether into spells and enchantments, preparing themselves to become fully fledged Magi of Nolderan.

"These remaining adepts have thus far proven they possess the required strength of heart and mind to graduate from the Arcanium as magi. Today, we test their proficiency with aether.

"Behold, the Trial of Magic!"

Once more, the crowd clamors with applause. My stomach tightens at the deafening noise.

Many don't gather here just to witness new generations of magi being born. They come because the Trial of Magic can be brutal. My mother forbade me from attending the trial until I joined the Arcanium, and that was only because adepts are required to watch. After all, it's the fate which awaits us all.

The Trial of Magic has the highest failure rate. Death is also not unheard of. We aren't supposed to die, but in the heat of battle, the Archmage of Knowledge may intervene a moment too late.

Over the last four years I've watched the Trial of Magic, I've seen only one adept die in the arena. And technically, he died outside the arena from his injuries. All the Blood Balm and healing potions in the world couldn't save him from his mortal wounds.

I pray I will not share his fate. At least the odds are favorable: one in approximately sixty adepts.

Archmage Gidston continues to speak, and the crowd quietens again.

"To pass this trial, each adept must complete a total of three rounds. Failing even one means failing the Trial of Magic, and they will be unable to graduate from the Arcanium. Only the brightest and most talented of our young adepts will join the ranks of the magi.

"For this first round, the adepts shall face a colossal stone structure: a golem. These constructs are bound and animated with aether.

"We now call the first adept to the arena: Reyna Ashbourne!"

I suck in a sharp breath. It's no surprise that I'm the first adept to be called. I am the only one left who has a surname beginning with 'A.'

At my name, cheers explode through the arena. My breakfast starts to come back up. I force it down. The crowd expects a spectacular performance from the Grandmage's daughter. I can only hope I don't disappoint them.

Eliya seems to sense my nerves, and she squeezes my shoulder. "Don't worry," she whispers, her voice nearly inaudible over the booming cheers. "You'll absolutely slay that golem—I know you will!"

Then she releases me, and I stand, drawing aether into my fingers. "*Laxus*," I call, and the crowd seems to quieten at the spell-word.

I glimmer away into violet light and re-emerge beside Archmage Gidston at the center of the arena.

Her narrowed eyes scan over me. I try to stifle the trembling of my hands. With the arena's terrifyingly tall walls looming over me, and the knowledge that failure will cost my entire future, a ferocious wave of nerves threatens to drown me.

"Ready, Adept Ashbourne?"

I don't know whether I'll ever be ready to face failing in front of thousands and losing everything, but I nod all the same.

"Good," she replies. "Then I wish you the very best of luck."

Her words make my gut knot even tighter.

Archmage Gidston teleports herself onto the platform where my father and the other Archmagi sit. There, she watches me for a moment, leaning over the balcony. The crowd falls hushed, eagerly awaiting her next command. It feels like a lifetime passes before she speaks again, and the thousands of faces staring down at me send terror plunging through my heart.

"Let the Trial of Magic begin!"

At her shout, the grinding of steel rumbles behind me. I whirl to see the enormous gate rolling upward. The crowd remains hushed. Everyone stares at the shadowed entrance with bated breaths.

For several beats, nothing happens. The tension is thick and heavy like inescapable fog. My heart hammers at an alarming rate.

Then comes the thundering storm. Hulking footsteps pound toward me.

The golem emerges from the tunnel, and it's so gigantic I briefly wonder whether it will collide with the gate's pointed ends. Unfortunately, it does not. Neither does its pace slow as it charges at me.

The construct is almost humanoid in appearance but is oddly disproportionate. Its square head is far too small for its mammoth body, and its fists and feet consist of monstrously sized boulders. I fear one punch or stomp would be enough to smash through the arena's dense walls. Never mind what it would do to me.

This was what killed that adept three years ago: a titanic blow from a golem's massive fists. I don't remember his name. Nor do I try. Not with the construct rushing forth.

Violet light glows between its joints, holding it together. A glittering crystal pulses in its chest, powering its every movement.

Thanks to the aether imbued within the golem, it is incredibly resistant to magic. Fortunately, its enormous size makes it slow and it's unable to cast any spells of its own. It also has a critical weakness: the very crystal which energizes it.

As the construct stomps across the arena, I prepare my first attack. Since the golem's core is formed from crystalized aether, the other four elements will be ineffective against such concentrated magic.

By the time my spell is ready, the golem is almost upon me.

"*Telum!*" I cry, unleashing a powerful blast of aether. Against the hush of the audience, my shout sounds far too loud.

My attack is precise. The spell's trajectory is perfectly on target to strike the golem's heart. To defeat it with a single blow. I bet my father accomplished such a feat during his Mage Trials.

But as my magic reaches the construct, it raises its arms and shields its exposed core from my attack. The blast of aether collides with its huge fists. Purple light ripples across the stone as it absorbs my magic. Not even the slightest chunk of rock chips off.

Despite defending itself from my attack, the golem doesn't slow its charge. It continues lumbering toward me.

Panic pounds through me. The stone construct is a few feet away. If I'm not quick enough, I will be crushed beneath its tremendous weight.

The golem swings for me.

"*Laxus!*"

Before the construct's fists can connect with my body, I fade into aether.

For a moment, everything ceases to exist, and I feel weightless, drifting through time and space. Then the ground returns beneath my feet, and I materialize several paces away from the golem. But not nearly as many as I envisioned.

I gasp for breath, shaken by the nearness of the blow. I need to be more careful. A heartbeat later, and I would have been pulverized. Or Archmage Gidston would have intervened, disqualifying me from the trial and ensuring I never become a Mage of Nolderan.

The golem does not relent. It charges for me again. This time more furiously, as if the failed attack has enraged it.

I don't have time to conjure a fearsome blast of magic or teleport to the other side of the arena. I can only summon an aether shield and leap as far back as I can, praying I will avoid the reach of its fists.

"*Muriz!*" I call, mid-jump.

The barrier spreads around me, just as the golem swings for me again. I am within its reach, but far enough away that the blow glances across my shield. It still tears through my barrier as if it's made from paper, but at least the impact is not fatal. The aether shield fizzles out, and I'm thrown back onto the ground. The collision leaves me winded and momentarily dazed.

The golem shambles forth. I don't even have the chance to scramble upright. Its immense foot comes crashing down, blanketing me with a vast shadow. I roll and barely avoid its thunderous stomp. The ground quakes and reverberates through me.

If I don't return to my feet, I will be crushed.

When I next roll away from its attack, I do so with enough momentum to fling myself upright. The construct's fist swerves toward me.

I duck, diving between its behemoth legs. I fear they will snap together and squish me between them, but this is my only chance of escape.

I emerge unscathed. With all my strength, I sprint as hard and fast as I can, desperate to put enough distance between me and the golem. To gain enough time to conjure an attack. The construct's weighty strides thump behind.

I draw upon aether as I run. When I'm certain there's enough distance, I spin and hurl my magic at the construct. *"Telum!"*

The aether blast isn't as precise as my previous, but I don't have the luxury of time. It will have to be enough.

The spell catches the golem by surprise. It raises its arms to defend itself, but it does so a moment too late.

My magic slams into its chest, meeting the pulsating crystal.

The golem falters. I hold my breath. But the stone construct doesn't come crashing to the ground.

Disoriented, it stumbles back. As the light fades, I see that the core isn't shattered. Only a slight crack pierces its surface.

I clench my fists. But there's no time to bemoan the lost victory. I can only press on, conjuring my next spell before the golem can recover.

"Laxus!"

I teleport to the far end of the arena. The stone construct hurtles toward me. This time there's enough distance for me to thoroughly prepare my spell.

Blood drums in my ears. I do my best to clear my mind and focus on the magic I'm weaving together between my fingers.

The golem is mere heartbeats from me now. The air shudders from its powerful momentum. But I hold my ground, knowing it's my only hope of defeating my opponent.

Its fists come crashing down. At that same instant, I seize the opening. Too busy attacking, the construct is unable to defend itself. And with the close distance, there's no risk of my magic missing.

"Telum!" I yell.

Aether bursts from my fingers, crackling with the intensity. My blast slams into the golem's heart.

Beneath the fizzle of my magic, I hear the core cracking. Fragments of crystallized aether rain on my face, and I shield my eyes. The glow fades from the golem's joints. It falls still, frozen mid-swing. Its enormous fists are a hair's breadth from me. I flinch at the nearness.

Before I can consider how lucky I was not to be smashed apart, the construct explodes.

I dive away. Rock hurls at me. I duck and cover my head with my arms. They bruise from some of the larger chunks.

When the barrage ceases, I straighten and stand there, gasping.

The arena erupts with applause. The rush of battle still courses through me, and I take a few seconds to realize they are cheering for me.

I succeeded.

"Congratulations, Reyna Ashbourne!" Archmage Gidston's voice rings out. The audience quietens as she speaks, hanging onto her every word. "You have successfully completed the first round of the Trial of Magic. Please now return to your seat. Lorea Bayford, if you will take your place inside the arena."

Before teleporting back to my seat beside Eliya, I stare up at the crowd towering all around me, briefly losing myself to the dizzying height and the sea of faces.

Though I have passed this first round, I must face two more before I can earn my title as a Mage of Nolderan.

CHAPTER 34

"I TOLD YOU THAT YOU'D slay it," Eliya says as I slide back onto my seat beside her.

I pull my lips into a strained smile. "It came awfully close to smashing me apart."

Eliya shakes her head. "You had it perfectly under control."

"I'm not sure I did."

"You at least looked like it."

Magi teleport themselves down to the arena where Lorea waits to begin her battle. They call *ventrez* and blow the remains of the golem out of the arena.

When the area is clear, Archmage Gidston calls, "Begin!"

Once more, the steel gate rumbles open. Lorea stands there at the center of the arena, anxiously waiting for the golem to charge out. She doesn't have to wait long before the stone construct appears.

It lumbers toward her with heavy, purposeful strides. This golem is a perfect replica of the one I faced, with a pulsating crystal powering its every movement.

Like me, Lorea focuses her attention on the construct's exposed core and blasts her magic at it. But her attack misses, and she is forced to teleport out of its reach. She repeats the same cycle over and over, teleporting around the arena and striking the golem with aether, until she eventually succeeds.

Her attack meets its target, and the crystal shatters. The golem explodes, chunks of rock bursting out in all directions. The crowd roars with applause, and then Archmage Gidston calls forth the next adept: Keion Bridwell.

One by one, the remaining adepts teleport down to the arena to fight a golem. Thankfully, no one dies and only one adept fails. Archmage Gidston had to intervene and stop the construct from killing him.

Soon, it's Eliya's turn. When her name is called, I grab her hand and give it a quick squeeze.

"Good luck," I whisper.

Eliya grins at me. "I don't need luck," she declares, lifting her chin and placing her hands on her hips. "But thanks, anyway."

With that, she teleports into the arena. She is the final adept to face the first round of the Trial of Magic.

At Archmage Gidston's shout, the gate rolls open. Eliya doesn't flinch. Nor does she gawk at the entrance, waiting for the golem to thunder out. Instead, she gathers aether into her fingers and calls, "*Speculus!*"

Two clones emerge from a flash of glittering light. Since they are all identical, I lose track of which is the real Eliya.

The construct emerges from the gate.

It pauses. Its glowing eyes scan over the three Eliyas who stand several yards apart from each other. The golem selects the middle Eliya and strides over to her, ignoring the other two.

All three begin casting. In unison, they cry out *telum* and unleash their magic. The golem raises its arms, defending itself from the attack. Its enormous fists absorb her magic. When the barrage subsides, it continues toward its chosen Eliya.

With full force, its fists swing for her. I hold my breath, praying with all my heart it's not the real Eliya. She makes no attempt to evade or defend herself. I fear Archmage Gidston might decide to intervene, disqualifying her from the Mage Trials, because there is no way of distinguishing which Eliya is real. I'm not even sure whether an accomplished mage could tell the difference.

Archmage Gidston doesn't teleport herself down from the platform. She continues to lean over the balcony as she examines the fight below.

The golem's fists slam into Eliya. She disperses into a shimmering cloud of aether.

I let out a sigh, the tension slackening in my shoulders.

I'm still unable to tell which of the remaining two is her. The construct's attention flickers between them both. Then it charges to the one on the left.

Before the golem can reach its chosen Eliya, the two of them release their spells and cry out: "*Tera!*"

Their magic crashes into the ground directly beneath the construct, carving out an enormous ditch. Though it is impervious to magic, it isn't invulnerable to the ground breaking under its feet.

Eliya flings aside the earth, and the golem crashes into the pit. It tries to scramble back out, but with its colossal weight, it is far from agile. Eliya seizes the advantage. Both she and the clone conjure another blast of aether.

By the time the stone construct hauls itself out of the hole, she has finished preparing a mighty spell.

"*Telum!*"

With the golem pulling itself out of the pit, it's left in a vulnerable position. Eliya's magic slams into it, and it's unable to defend itself from the blow.

Her spell pierces the golem's crystalline heart, defeating it. Its remains crumble onto the ground. The crowd cheers, and Eliya murmurs *terminir*. Her remaining clone disappears, and she is left alone at the center of the arena.

The applause is the loudest I've heard today—even more deafening than when Archmage Gidston announced my name. Eliya defeated the construct faster than the rest of us, thanks to her genius strategy. She deserves all the cheers which the crowd shower her with.

Eliya teleports back up into the audience and strides over to me. "Told you I wouldn't need any luck."

"You were amazing!"

She returns to her place beside me and flicks her crimson waves over her shoulder. After the fight with the golem, her hair is even wilder than usual. "I know," she replies with a wink. "I always am."

We have little time to discuss her outstanding performance. Archmage Gidston teleports to the center of the arena. Several magi are already working down there, swiftly mending the ditch that Eliya created and tidying away the golem's remains. Archmage Gidston waits until they have finished before addressing us all.

"Fourteen of our adepts have successfully completed the first round of the Trial of Magic, but they must face two more in order to prove they possess the skill required of the magi.

"We now move to the second round of this trial. Our remaining adepts will each battle four lesser elementals. To emerge victorious, they must carefully select their spells against each opponent and fluently wield all four of the elements.

"The first adept will now take their place inside the arena—Reyna Ashbourne!"

At the Archmage's command, I teleport down to where she stands. This time, she offers me no words of encouragement before returning to the platform which overlooks the arena. Behind her sits my father on his stone throne. He clasps his crystalline staff as he stares down at me. I don't meet his magenta eyes for long, and I soon turn my attention to the steel gates behind me.

"Let the second round commence!"

The gates open.

Blinding lights dart out. There are four colors in total: red, white, green, and blue.

As they rush forth, the spirits manifest into physical forms. The red light becomes a blazing salamander, the white light becomes a gigantic hawk, the green light becomes an elk formed from gnarled vines, and the blue light becomes a stallion with a mane of streaming kelp. Water ripples beneath its hooves.

The four elementals charge at me. The hawk swiftly takes the lead, thanks to its enormous wingspan.

I weave aether into fire magic and unleash the conjured flames upon it. "*Ignira!*"

The resulting fireball isn't my most ferocious, but I lack the time to make it so. I can't afford to spend too long on one enemy, or else the other three will overpower me.

My spell is enough to stop the hawk from swooping toward me and leaves it dazed. The flames feed on the air magic comprising its body. I don't stop to examine how much damage I inflict. The water stallion is already upon me.

It rears. A wave crashes forth, sweeping high over me and threatening to drown me.

"*Tera'muriz!*" I shout.

Just as the water reaches me, I wrap the ground around myself and form an earthen shield. The water slams into the rock, and I hear it churning beyond the safety of my barrier.

The wave falls silent. I shatter my shield. "*Tera'quatir!*"

The rock explodes, hurling out in all directions. It slams into the water stallion, forcing it back several paces. A large chunk also collides with the salamander which was gaining on me, gaining me a few extra moments from its sizzling flames.

When I glance back, I see the elk charging forth. Its hooves slam into the ground. Thunder rings out. The ground shatters. A bolt pierces through the center of the arena.

I fall to the right of the crack. My knees strike the ground first. My gaze briefly drifts over to the chasm. It plummets into the earth, hundreds of feet deep.

Before I can leap up, the hawk swoops at me. Its translucent wings beat back and forth, generating a terrifying force. A howling gale rushes forth, tearing through all the air in its path.

"*Ignir'muriz!*"

Flames ignite around me, and they stop the violent wind from ripping me apart. The fiery wall roars, feeding off the air magic. It grows in size until it snuffs out the gale.

The four elementals charge at me again. They come at me from all directions. I am at the center. Cornered.

I can't let them defeat me.

"*Ignir'quatir*!" I rasp with all the desperation in my heart.

My shield explodes, slamming into all four of my opponents. The hawk takes the brunt of my attack. Thanks to the damage I previously inflicted, and its vulnerability to fire, the air elemental is obliterated.

The hawk bursts apart, disintegrating into tiny fragments. Remnants of air magic descend on me like crushed diamonds. My face tingles as they land on my cheeks, but they cause no harm.

There's no time to relish my victory. Three enemies remain. The water stallion advances.

Its kelp-like tail lashes out, and its nostrils flare. A bolt of pressurized water darts toward me.

"*Tera!*" I call, carving out an enormous boulder from the ground. I launch it at the blast.

Water sprays across the arena, soaking me. The salamander's flames are momentarily doused by the splash.

The elk bows its head. Green light glows between its antlers. A giant onyx thorn springs forth. Its point glistens as it rushes at me.

"*Ventrez!*" Air magic bursts from my fingers. The furious wind tears through the thorn. Dark pieces of bark scatter across the arena.

Flames crackle behind. The salamander spews a fireball. I notice the attack too late.

I swerve back. The flames catch my shoulder, singeing my cerulean robes and scorching my flesh. I let out a sharp cry of pain but have no chance to check the wound.

The elk stomps. Green light spreads over the ground.

The earth rumbles, and vines sprout from beneath the arena. Thorns cover each tendril. They wrap around my ankles, and their needlelike points penetrate the leather of my boots. A sharp stabbing pain tells me the thorns have penetrated far enough to draw blood.

The vines curl tighter, securing their hold around me. They creep higher up my leg and press in deeper. It feels as if thousands of needles are digging into me.

I use the pain to fuel my fury. Aether boils in my blood. I unleash it as a powerful blast of air magic.

"*Tempis!*"

A vortex erupts. The sharp winds slice through the vines, and the severed remains fall in a heap of foliage. The vortex continues forth and crashes into the earth elemental. The violent winds are as sharp as blades and carve through the vines which form its body.

My spell shreds the elemental apart. Earth magic drifts from its remains in a cloud of green light. Now only two enemies are left.

Both the water stallion and the fire salamander charge at me. I stumble back. The pain shooting through my leg, where the thorns ripped through, makes it impossible to leap away.

So, I don't. I draw on my magic and wait for a moment. Then another. When both elementals are upon me, I release my spell.

"*Laxus!*"

I fade into aether. My two enemies crash into each other. The water stallion's enormous wave devours the salamander and destroys its flames. It disperses into red light, and ash scatters through the wind.

Only one enemy remains. The water elemental.

After its collision with the salamander, the water stallion is left disoriented. It takes a few seconds to recover.

I don't hesitate before launching my next attack.

"*Veitis!*"

Emerald light strikes the ground. Vines burst up, reaching for the remaining elemental. They wrap around the water stallion. It struggles beneath the vines, but their grasp tightens.

An anguished whinny pierces the silence of the arena. Then the elemental bursts apart.

Water splashes across the ground. Blue light pours out.

I glance at the puddles, gasping for breath.

The crowd roars with applause.

I've vanquished my enemies. I've passed the second round of the Trial of Magic. Only one battle stands between me becoming a Mage of Nolderan.

"Congratulations, Reyna Ashbourne!" comes Archmage Gidston's shout. "You have completed the second round. Please return to your seat until the third and final round begins."

I do as she says and return to the audience. My injuries make it hard to walk, and I hobble over to where Eliya sits. She jumps to her feet and helps me back onto our stone bench.

"Are you all right?" she whispers as Archmage Gidston calls Lorea's name. Magi teleport down to the arena and use their magic to smooth the ground, ready for her battle to begin.

"They're just small wounds." I hold out my hand and draw aether into my palm. "*Conparios.*" A vial of fluorescent green liquid appears. Even the sight of the potion makes my stomach turn, but I tear off the cork and drain every drop from the small glass bottle. The putrid slime slips down my throat. I gag, but don't let myself cough up any.

With some luck, the healing potion will work long before the third round begins. I'll have at least an hour, seeing as there are thirteen more adepts to complete the second round of the Trial of Magic.

"You only have one more round now!" Eliya exclaims, as if reading my thoughts. Her eyes gleam.

"I know," I say, clenching the empty potion vial. "One more round to go."

I pray I will pass it. Fate would be cruel to snatch away everything after I've come so close to achieving all I've ever wanted.

Lorea soon begins her trial. Magic collides as she battles the four elementals. And when she successfully completes the round, Archmage Gidston calls down the next adept.

By the time Eliya takes her turn, and the second round concludes, two adepts have failed. One girl was nearly immolated, and

Archmage Gidston had to douse the flames to save her. Another was almost strangled by barbed thorns. Both required immediate medical attention.

Then the third and final round begins. Archmage Gidston calls me down to the arena. Not once do I look up at my father. I can't bear to.

I train my gaze onto the steel gates, barely breathing as I wait for them to open.

This is it. My final reckoning.

Either I will defeat my opponent and become a Mage of Nolderan, or I will lose everything. This is my only chance. I cannot fail. Not when my future is at stake.

I'm so lost to my fear that when the gate finally rumbles open, I am delayed in noticing it.

Violet light surges out from the darkened entrance and whizzes across the arena. It comes to a halt beside me. The aether spirit swirls. Magic ripples through the air.

The surface shifts, forming a girl's silhouette. It becomes so blinding that I'm forced to shield my eyes from its dazzling radiance.

The girl steps forth, and the light fades. Her features become clearer.

Then I'm staring back at myself. Her eyes are of the same shade of magenta as mine, and her long, dark hair has even the same sheen.

It should come as no shock. I've watched this final trial unfold countless times before. The last round is always facing an aether spirit. And the elemental always clones the adept.

Staring at it is uncanny. When I summon clones of myself, they are an extension of my will. This being is separate entirely, and yet it looks completely identical to myself. It is as though I'm staring into a very real mirror.

Before I can recover from my surprise, the fake me raises her hands and sends a blast of aether hurling forth. She requires no spell-words to control her magic. That's the formidable advantage she has against me.

"*Laxus!*"

When the aether blast reaches me, I am barely fading into my teleportation spell.

I am immaterial enough that the attack continues past me. It collides with the barrier on the far side of the arena. I emerge behind my opponent, unscathed.

She spins to face me.

"*Ignira!*" I call, launching a hasty fireball at her. But she teleports away, replicating my movements.

My spell blazes through empty air and is absorbed by the arena's barrier. She reappears on the right.

It is then I realize my grave mistake.

Besides replicating my appearance, the clone can imitate whichever spells I cast. The longer I fight it, the more spells it will learn from me. After watching many other adepts undertake the Trial of Magic, I know the successful ones are always the ones who defeat it the swiftest.

That's because my opponent is a being of pure aether and can instantly restore its strength by absorbing the magic lying in the surrounding air. My power, however, will quickly deplete. I am limited by the amount of aether in my blood. Without it, I can't draw more from the air to fuel my spells. Only resting will replenish the aether coursing through my veins.

My strength is finite. The aether spirit's is not. I must defeat it before it learns too many spells, and before I tire. Only by selecting every move with great care will I achieve this.

The aether spirit conjures a fireball much like mine. Flames rush at me.

Teleportation requires much aether, and it won't inflict any damage onto my enemy. I must conserve all the magic I can.

"*Aquis!*" I instead shout. The aether in my hands turns to water magic.

I fling the bolt of pressurized water at the fireball.

The two spells collide. The water extinguishes the flames, and the remaining drops splash across the ground. Puddles glisten beneath us.

I glare at the aether spirit, and it glares back. I can see the calculating look in its eyes—in my eyes—and I know it's already plotting its next attack.

I must strike first.

"*Telum!*" I call, releasing a blast of aether. It's far from a complex spell, but it's better that way. My clone's first attack was also a blast of aether, so there's no risk in it learning a new spell.

But the aether spirit teleports away. When my blast reaches it, only empty space remains. My enemy has no need to worry about the cost of teleportation spells. Thanks to its endless supply of aether, it can cast as many spells as it likes.

Panic jolts through me.

I made a terrible mistake with my first move. I should never have teleported away. Now the aether spirit knows this spell, landing a blow on it will be nearly impossible.

I curse my stupidity. Then I whirl around, searching for where the aether spirit has reappeared. I know my father will be so disappointed with me for this foolish error.

I find the aether spirit behind me, already launching three quick bolts. Not daring to create a shield and teach my opponent yet another spell, I leap aside.

The move is far from graceful. I lose my balance and fall.

The ground slams into my shoulder at an awkward angle. I force myself upright and stagger onto my feet, clutching my shoulder.

Flames crackle. They surge toward me.

Left with no alternative, I hurriedly conjure a water shield. "*Aquis'muriz!*" I shout, drawing a bubble around myself. My haste makes the spell weak. But it's enough to cause the flames to fizzle out when they reach me.

Though the attack saved me, I've now taught it how to counter fire.

Fighting with reservation and choosing simple spells is doing me no favors. While we have only exchanged a few blows, it seems the aether spirit is already beating me.

No.

I can't let it win. Failure isn't an option. Failure means losing everything. Sacrificing my future. Shaming my father.

I must defeat the aether spirit before it defeats me.

Determination rises in my chest. I must strike it down with all the force I can muster. And quickly.

The aether spirit conjures a bolt of water.

I turn my attention to the ground and spread emerald light across the stone.

"*Tera!*"

The spell carves out an enormous boulder. I fling it forth.

The rock smacks into the water blast, and it bursts apart, spraying across the ground. Onward the boulder continues, straight toward the aether spirit's stolen face.

It conjures a water shield: the only shielding spell I have so far taught it. A terrible miscalculation. Any child knows that water is a pitiful defense against earth magic. It should have instead chosen to teleport away.

The chunk of rock tears through the water shield and crashes into the aether spirit. The boulder bursts apart from the impact. Pebbles scatter across the arena.

The blow has left the aether spirit dazed, but I haven't yet defeated it. If I strike again, I just might succeed.

None of the elements are advantageous against aether. Only aether works best against aether.

"*Telum!*" The spell-word is all but a scream as it rips through my throat. If I fail to destroy the aether spirit with this blast, I might never defeat it.

I fuel the attack with every ounce of magic in my blood. The blast of aether is ferocious as it bursts from my fingertips. The air crackles as my spell tears through it.

My magic collides with the aether spirit. Dazzling light explodes, filling the arena with its radiance. Aether dust rains over me, coating me like iridescent glitter.

It is gone. Defeated.

The audience erupts with deafening applause.

I've done it.

I've passed the Trial of Magic. The third and final Mage Trial.

I gaze up at the platform where my father sits. He is out of his seat, and so are Archmage Gidston and Archmage Lanord. My father's magenta eyes are illuminated with pride. He claps more enthusiastically and beams at me more widely than he ever has.

My heart nearly bursts at the sight.

I didn't fail. I didn't humiliate him. I made him proud.

The realization chokes me with tears.

When Archmage Gidston addresses me, I stare up at her through blurred eyes. Despite my hazy vision, I can still make out the broad smile stretching across her face.

"Congratulations, Reyna Ashbourne," she declares. The crowd quietens at her words. "You have successfully passed the Trial of Magic, the third and final Mage Trial. Let it now be known to all that you are officially a Mage of Nolderan!"

CHAPTER 35

I STARE AT THE GIRL who stands in my full-length mirror. She looks nothing like me. Her magenta eyes shine too brightly; her skin is too lustrous. If I were not alone in my room, I would believe the reflection belongs to someone else.

I have achieved all that I've ever wanted, and yet I cannot shake away the hollowness clinging to my heart. For years I imagined completing my Mage Trials, but I never gave much thought as to how passing them would make me feel. I suppose I thought starting a new chapter would rid me of the grief still plaguing my heart to this day, but its chains have only constricted tighter around me.

I believed becoming a mage would make me stronger, would prevent me from ever again being weak. But I still feel like that helpless little girl who was unable to stop Heston from murdering her mother.

Tonight, I'm supposed to be happy. Only once in my life will I graduate from the Arcanium, and I have awaited this for so long, but it feels as though a piece of me is missing—or broken—and that I don't deserve to wear the magnificent indigo robes draped over the back of my golden armchair.

My fingers play with the silver locket around my neck. A part of me considers pulling it open and watching the memory inside. But I don't. If I listen to Arluin's promise, I know I'll be reduced to tears. I must wear a mask and conceal the grief which consumes me.

A knock comes at my door.

I jolt, tearing myself from the mirror and doing my best to shed the torturous thoughts.

"Come in," I call.

The door opens to reveal my father. While I wear the most luxurious gown I can find—a dress made from pearlescent silk—he wears his usual Grandmage's robes.

He leans on his crystalline staff and beams at me with pride. "Look at you—all grown up and already a Mage of Nolderan."

I pull a smile and hope it looks more enthusiastic than it feels.

"Are you ready to leave?" he asks. "It's seven o'clock."

I take one last glance at my reflection, scanning across the delicate aether crystals hanging from my ears and then down to the pale skirts which flutter with my every move. I may not feel it, but I am a victor.

I turn back to my father and give him a nod. "Ready."

We head downstairs and through the hallway. When we pass my mother's favorite painting, he comes to a stop and stares up at it. He is quiet for a moment, contemplating the lull of the dark waves and the twinkle of the glistening stars.

"She would be so very proud of you," he finally murmurs and gives my shoulder a quick squeeze.

The painting blurs with my unshed tears, but I bite them back. I must wear a mask. If I let myself cry, all my powder and illusions will crumble apart.

I freeze my emotions into cold, hard ice and force myself to reply, "I hope so."

We continue through the hallway, and my father holds the grand doors open for me. I step outside, and the frosty evening breeze ripples through my flowing skirts. Shadows darken the blooming flowers, and water trickles from the fountain, preventing our gardens from being blanketed with silence.

My father closes the doors behind us, and we follow the narrow stone path to the enchanted gates. They swing open, allowing us both through, and clang shut once we're on the other side.

My father holds out his arm, and I take it. He draws aether into his crystalline staff, using it as a focus for his magic, and closes his eyes as he concentrates on his spell.

"*Laxus!*"

At his command, we fade away. Our forms dematerialize, and we float through the darkness until solid ground finally returns beneath my feet.

An archway is sculpted from purple light, and translucent spires rise behind it. The details grow sharper, and color fills the Arcanium's outline as it becomes real.

I let go of my father's arm and trail behind him as he strides through the archway. Many magi, adepts, and nobles flock toward the Arcanium, but all step aside to let the Grandmage of Nolderan pass.

We reach the statue of the city's founder and ascend the winding stairs. The stone walls are decorated with celebratory banners. Thousands of tiny triangular flags dance in the breeze. They are of alternating cerulean and violet hues, representing the transition from adept to mage. The transition that I myself will undergo this night.

We step through the portico, passing the many pillars which stand sentry at the entrance, and into the Arcanium's atrium.

The aether crystals which form its ceiling look even more dazzling tonight, as though they have been painstakingly polished in preparation for the Ball. There are so many people gathered inside, and everyone streams through the circular chamber. My father marches across to the entrance opposite us, and the crowd parts for him. Every head bows in reverence.

All the chairs and tables are cleared from the hall. Only four finely carved oak ones remain on the dais. Archmage Gidston and Archmage Lanord are already seated on the outer two chairs. They look up as my father strides through the wide-open double doors. His heeled boots clatter across the pristine herringbone tiles.

Three enormous chandeliers hang from the ceilings, radiating brilliant purple light through the hall. Heavy plum curtains are tucked beside each of the large windows, revealing the grassy fields at the back of the Arcanium's grounds. The arena's impressive silhouette sits in the distance.

Everyone is dressed in their finery, and the blinding aether crystals make them appear even more magnificent. Silk looks glossier; leather looks sleeker.

My father comes to a halt at the center of the hall. "We will begin when Archmage Calton arrives," he says to me. "For now, I will take my seat with the other Archmagi."

"I'll look for Eliya."

He leaves me and makes his way to the dais where Archmage Gidston and Archmage Lanord sit.

I begin my search for Eliya and carefully examine the lavishly dressed crowds. She manages to find me first.

"Rey-rey!" she exclaims, bounding over to me. "You look so pretty tonight!"

"And you look like a princess," I reply, glancing over the yellow dress that she wears. It's as though the petals of a hundred buttercups are stitched together to form her bright skirts.

"Of course I do," she replies with a grin. "But so do you."

I smile back. She takes both my hands and leans closer.

"Is Nolan coming?" she whispers.

"I invited him last night, but I haven't seen him yet. Have you?"

She shakes her head. "Maybe we should wait for him outside. It's still early, so maybe he hasn't arrived yet."

"Maybe."

We slip through the crowds, heading out the hall and through the atrium. Many more people are pouring into the Arcanium now, and descending the stairs is far from an easy task, since everyone is going in the opposite direction.

When we reach the bottom, we come to a stop before the statue of Grandmage Delmont Blackwood. He stares down at us with his unblinking eyes.

The moonlight silvers the other statues which guard the Arcanium's entrance. Behind us, music echoes from the hall. Hopefully the reason my father has ordered the enchanted instruments to start playing is because there are now so many people, and not because Archmage Calton has arrived.

"How did things go last night, anyway?" Eliya asks far too loudly for my liking. "You hardly told me anything about your date when you got home."

"I was tired."

"So you said."

When I say nothing, she raises a brow at me. "Well, what actually happened? Spit it out."

"Like I told you last night, we went to The Shimmering Oyster."

"Yes, yes, I know. But I want to know the more interesting parts. It obviously went well, since you said you invited him here tonight. So, the reason you're being so close-mouthed about it isn't because things went badly—" She cuts herself off, a devilish smirk curling onto her lips. "You kissed him, didn't you? That's the reason you won't tell me anything!"

I flush. "I didn't kiss him. He kissed me."

"I should have guessed it sooner!" She claps her hands together in delight. "So, tell me about it!"

"Tell you about what?"

"Was he a good kisser? Or was there too much tongue? Too much drool? Or did he have really bad breath? Though I suppose he must be a good kisser if you were willing to see him again."

"No, he was a perfectly acceptable kisser."

"Perfectly acceptable?" Eliya scoffs. "I bet that means he was really good."

"He was quite good," I admit.

"Anyway," she says, waggling her eyebrows, "did the two of you get up to anything else other than kissing?"

"Of course not!"

"I'm not here to judge."

"You know exactly what time I came home, since you were busy keeping watch. How would I have had the chance to do anything but kiss him?"

Eliya opens her mouth to speak, but I interrupt her before she can respond.

"On second thought, please don't answer that question. I don't want any of your stories."

"Are you sure you don't want to hear them?"

"Very sure."

She pulls a face at me but spares me from her answer.

We wait outside the Arcanium for many more minutes, but there's still no sign of Nolan and the music grows louder inside. Maybe Archmage Calton has already arrived. Maybe the Ball has already started without us.

"What if he doesn't come?" I say.

Eliya peers at me. "Why wouldn't he?"

"I don't think things went that well."

"I thought you just said he was a good kisser?"

"That part was fine. I mean after it."

"What happened after it?"

"He started looking at my necklace—"

"The one Arluin got you?"

"Yes, that one."

"He didn't open it, did he? Because if the memory crystal started playing and he heard Arluin proposing to you, then I hate to say it, but I don't think Nolan will be showing up tonight."

"Luckily, he didn't open it."

She lets out a sigh of relief. "Thank the gods for that. Did he ask who it was from?"

"I told him it was from my mother."

"Did he believe you?"

"I'm not sure."

Eliya pauses, watching as the guests ascend the stairs around us. "It doesn't matter if he doesn't show up tonight."

"It doesn't?"

"No, because you're an official Mage of Nolderan now. And that matters more than anything."

"You were the one encouraging me to get to know him in the first place."

"Just to get to know him. I thought a bit of harmless fun would do you some good. And I think it has."

I play with the locket, running my fingers across the edges of the silver heart.

I don't know whether Eliya is right, whether Nolan is helping me to set aside the past. When I think of Arluin, the burden does feel a little lighter—if only marginally so. But there's a part of me which fears closing that door means forgetting him and betraying his memory.

Eliya glances back at the Arcanium.

"It's all right," I say. "You head back inside."

"You're sure?"

"Just come and get me if they start without me."

She breathes a laugh. "Will do."

With that, she ascends the stairs and disappears inside the Arcanium.

There are fewer people outside now. It seems everyone is already in the hall, waiting for the Ball to begin. Since Eliya hasn't hurried back out, it's probably yet to start.

I shiver from the wintry air and consider murmuring *calida* to warm myself. But before I can, I glimpse golden hair emerging from beneath the Arcanium's archway.

"Nolan!" I exclaim, picking up the hem of my pearlescent skirts and hurrying over to him. "You made it!"

We come to a stop in the middle of the path, and the statues of long dead magi tower above us. A frigid wind rolls over us, but I'm too elated to feel its chill.

Tonight Nolan wears a dusky blue doublet, its sleeves finely embroidered with silver thread. His black leather boots are especially polished, and his green eyes are as vibrant as ever. It only occurs to me now how much I was worrying he would not show up. Maybe I like him more than I'm willing to admit.

He scratches the back of his head, ruffling the golden strands of his wavy hair. "I do apologize for my lateness."

"No, no," I quickly say. "You're not late at all."

Nolan scans our surroundings, lingering on the emptiness of the path. "I think I am."

"Well, maybe a little. But the Ball hasn't started, so you're not that—"

Before I can finish, Eliya reappears from the Arcanium's entrance. She sprints so fast that she almost trips over her yellow skirts. "Reyna!" she shouts from atop the stairs. "They're about to begin!"

I turn back to Nolan and shrug. "On second thought, it seems it has. Come on, we'd better hurry."

CHAPTER 36

Together, Nolan and I enter the hall. Everyone else is focused on their own conversations, and no one turns to look at us. Except for my father, that is. He stares at us from where he sits on his oaken throne at the far end of the hall, and his sharp gaze fixes on us both from the moment we step through the double doors. I don't doubt he will have many questions for me later regarding Nolan.

We don't even reach halfway through the hall before my father stands. All three Archmagi are present now, and they sit beside him on their own decorative chairs.

"*Terminir,*" he calls, drumming the end of his staff against the tiles. A wave of aether sweeps through the hall, and the enchanted instruments playing in the far corner fall silent. The floating flutes flutter back onto their chairs, and the strings of violins and cellos still.

His spell has a similar effect on the crowd. Everyone stops talking and turns to face him.

"Tonight, we welcome ten adepts into the ranks of the Magi of Nolderan," my father announces, his voice echoing through the hall. "Through successfully completing their Mage Trials, they have proven they possess the required strength of heart, mind, and magic. They have proven themselves worthy of this status.

"We now call forth each successful adept, so that we may congratulate them on their achievements and so that they may be officially granted their new position as a Mage of Nolderan.

"Reyna Ashbourne, if you will step forward."

An even greater hush falls over the crowd.

My fingers slip from Nolan's hand. I lift my chin as I stride through the length of the hall, and even when I reach my father at the dais, I don't lower it.

"Reyna Ashbourne," my father continues, "you have proven you possess the courage, the wisdom, and the power required of the magi. Do you solemnly swear that you will never waver in the face of danger, that you will obey every order issued by the Grandmage and the Archmagi without hesitation, that you will serve the people of Nolderan with all the fervor in your heart?"

"Yes, Grandmage," I reply, dipping my head. It feels strange to address my father by his title, as though he and I are not familiar, but such is tradition. There is no exception for being his daughter. I am a Mage of Nolderan first and foremost. "I, Reyna Ashbourne, do solemnly swear that I will never waver in the face of danger, that I will obey every order issued by the Grandmage and the Archmagi without hesitation, that I will serve the people of Nolderan with all the fervor in my heart."

Aether radiates from my father's fingers. He starts down the steps leading to the dais and presses his thumb to the center of my forehead. "Then from this moment forth, I hereby declare you a Mage of Nolderan."

Magic erupts, flooding through his thumb and into my body. The aether fizzes and bubbles as it reacts with that which flows through my blood. But when the magic fades, I still feel like the same Reyna I was moments before. I expected the mark of the magi to change me somehow—perhaps to make me stronger or wiser—but I feel no different. Maybe if I look in the mirror, I will find that my eyes glow with a brighter shade of magenta.

I have a sudden urge to teleport to the top of the Aether Tower and see the effect of the boon my father has granted me, but I keep my feet fixed to the hall's tiled floor. I can always try that later, after the Ball. Or maybe tomorrow. Eliya will probably want to try it, too.

The crowd showers me with applause, and then my father calls forth the next adept: Lorea.

As I step away from the dais, Archmage Calton's attention lingers on me. Though my back is turned, I can sense all the loathing radiating from him. He blames me for Kaely's failure and is unable to see that his daughter's own arrogance and hatred were her undoing. If she had focused less on destroying me and more on passing the Trial of Mind, she would be here with the rest of us as we transition from adepts to magi. I've heard no more news of her condition since Wednesday, but at least that means she's alive. Despite our feud, I have no desire for her blood to be on my hands.

I slip past the finely dressed guests and make my way back to Nolan. I've lost sight of Eliya, even though her dress is such a striking shade of yellow, but I suppose she will soon reappear when my father calls her name. Some lower year adepts I recognize from passing along the Arcanium's corridors stare at me in awe. It feels strange to no longer count myself as one of them.

"So," Nolan whispers as I come to a stop beside him. He leans toward me, and in the distant background, Lorea speaks her oath. His warm breath brushes over my ear, and every nerve within me shivers. The gesture somehow seems too private with so many people gathered around us, but it probably doesn't look as intimate as it feels. I hope I'm the only one who can tell what effect Nolan's closeness has on me.

"You're an official Mage of Nolderan now," he continues, his voice hushed. "How does it feel?"

I pause, pressing my lips together as I think. "Not quite what I expected."

"How so?"

"I don't know. I just thought I would feel different."

Nolan doesn't question me any further. We watch as my father presses his thumb to Lorea's forehead and a wave of aether rushes over her. When the magic settles, he summons the next adept.

Eliya is the last to be called to the dais, and once all ten of us have sworn our oaths and been marked by his magic, my father bangs the end of his crystalline staff against the floor.

"*Incipiret!*" he booms, and aether surges forth.

The magic swirls through the hall, twinkling like thousands of tiny stars. My father's spell reaches the instruments in the far corner, and their enchantment resumes, strings vibrating of their own accord.

People start to dance at the center of the hall. Their colorful clothes form a rainbow as they spiral and sway across the polished tiles. The chandeliers high above sparkle with violet radiance.

Nolan extends his hand to me and bows slightly. "Would you care to join me for a dance?"

The corners of my lips twitch into a light smile. "Of course. I would love to."

I place my hand on his, and he leads me to the center where everyone else is busy dancing. Nolan's arm slips around my waist, and our fingers weave between each other's, interlocking in an unbreakable embrace. I'm not sure what to do with my spare arm, and trying to decide is difficult with the dizziness sweeping over me. Standing this close to him is always intoxicating, and I'm unsure whether I welcome or fear the way he makes me feel.

In the end, I settle for resting my free hand on his shoulder, but it feels rather limp and useless there.

We step back and forth, flowing in the same gentle rhythm as all the other couples around us. I relinquish my wariness and allow the music to guide my every move.

A flash of crimson hair appears to my right as Eliya waltzes past with Koby. He must have asked her for a dance like usual, though it appears Eliya is taking the lead rather than him.

"You look lovely tonight," Nolan mutters, pulling me from my thoughts of Eliya and Koby.

I arch a brow at him. "You said the same thing last night." I regret the words as soon as they leave my lips. Though I tried to make my tone lighthearted, I worry it comes out a pitch higher than I intended. And far too accusatory.

But it seems my concerns are misplaced since Nolan chuckles, not at all flinching at the unintentional sharpness in my words. "Did I? My mistake. I can't help it that you always look so bewitching."

I flush and have absolutely no way of responding to that. When I dare to tear my attention from my clumsy feet and glance up at him, I notice his emerald eyes are scanning over my face, as if he's trying to soak up every detail.

I recall how his fingers brushed over my cheek. How he kissed me.

Then all I can think of is his lips on mine, and I take a wrong step, almost tripping over his feet. He steadies me and smooths out the movement. I doubt anyone around us will have noticed my misstep.

"Thank you," I breathe.

Nolan smiles, and his eyes continuing to sweep over me in long, lavish strokes. I try not to redden and focus on each next step, rather than the intensity of his gaze.

I'm not sure how long we dance, but I am the one who stops first. We take a break at the edge of the hall and sip on the wine served by floating silver trays. It is red wine—maybe *Sanguilus*—and not moon-blossom wine. The Arcanium could never afford to give out this much moon-blossom wine for free.

"Shall we dance again?" Nolan asks, leaning against the large arched window behind us. Condensation hazes the panels, and I imagine he must feel the glass's icy chill through the fabric of his deep blue doublet.

"What else would we do other than dancing?" I reply, setting my empty goblet on a tray as it drifts past.

Nolan's gaze flickers down to my lips and remains there for many moments. Long enough for my heartbeat to elevate, and then I feel as flustered as I did while we were dancing.

But instead of my lips, he takes my hand and kisses the back, just like he did last night.

"I would very much like to resume where we left off last night," he says softly.

With his fingers curled around my wrist, I wonder whether he can feel the wild tempo of my pulse.

When I don't respond, his shoulders stiffen. "If that was too bold, then I sincerely apologize."

"No, no," I quickly say. "I mean, it was rather bold but . . ."

I hope Nolan will say something, to save me from having to search for the words, but he doesn't. He peers at me expectantly.

"I . . . I have also been thinking about last night."

His fingers tighten around my wrist. "What have you been thinking?"

"That . . ." I lower my gaze, unable to look him in the eye. "That I would like to kiss you again." I wish I could blame my words on the wine, but the goblets are quite small and filled halfway. I've also only drank one so far.

I'm sure I sound as embarrassing as I do in my head, but Nolan smiles. His arm wraps around my waist, pulling me nearer. "I would also like to kiss you again," he whispers into my ear.

Remembering that my father is still somewhere in this hall, no doubt watching me closely, I jolt and withdraw from Nolan. "Not here," I murmur.

He lifts his head in a slight nod and then starts toward the double doors, leading me with him.

We are barely out of the hall before he starts kissing me. Luckily, this corridor is tucked away enough that there's no one around. And it's also shadowed, since all the aether crystals are turned off.

His lips are soft as they glide over mine. The cold stone wall presses into my back like hard ice, but with all the warmth pouring through me, I barely notice the chill.

Nolan's fingers weave through my hair. Then he pauses our kiss, admiring my face. His touch follows his gaze, and he gently traces my cheek, coming to a stop beneath my lower lip.

"Reyna," he murmurs, "you are the most beautiful person I've ever met."

I don't respond with words. I wrap my arms around his shoulders and pull him back to me, kissing him as deeply as I can. When my teeth graze his lips, a groan escapes him.

He pushes me harder against the wall. Now there's no escape, even if I wanted it. His every touch threatens to undo me, and all I know is that I need more of him. I can't kiss him quickly enough.

Nolan's hand slides up my waist, skimming over the pearlescent silk of my dress. He breaks our kiss, but I have no chance to protest. His lips slowly trace my neck, and his hand slips higher up to my chest. He cups the soft flesh through the thin fabric, and I can't stop myself from moaning.

A disgruntled cough sounds to our left. Nolan tears himself from me, and we both glance down the corridor. Two old magi stand there, shaking their heads at us. I suppose with how busy the Arcanium is tonight, it was foolish to think we wouldn't be caught here. Thankfully, they soon continue on their way.

"Perhaps we should go somewhere else," Nolan says when they're gone.

"Like where?" I ask. It's only as I speak that I realize how unsteady my breaths are. At least Nolan's aren't much better. "The Upper City square, like last night?"

He shakes his head. "Somewhere more private. Somewhere we won't be interrupted."

My heart drums with anticipation. I have no chance to recover before his lips are on mine. They are even softer than before.

"You could teleport us somewhere else right now," he murmurs, his fingers tracing my shoulder. I shiver. "We wouldn't even need to walk."

"Do you have somewhere in mind?"

He pauses. "How about the cliffs?"

"The cliffs?" We would be awfully secluded there, and we certainly wouldn't need to worry about anyone finding us.

Both desire and nerves ignite through me. How much further does Nolan intend to take our kiss? I don't know whether I'm ready for this step yet, but I find myself nodding all the same.

Nolan kisses my cheek as I draw aether into my fingers and wrap it around us both, preparing my spell.

"*Laxus*."

Magic basks us in violet light. We fade away, disappearing from the Arcanium's narrow corridor.

When I next blink, we are standing on the shadowed cliffs. And something cold and sharp presses into my neck.

I freeze.

A dagger.

Nolan's dagger.

CHAPTER 37

"Don't move," Nolan hisses, his voice piercing the wind. Beneath, dark waves crash into the cliffs.

"What—"

He presses the blade more firmly against the soft flesh of my neck, silencing me. "If you wish to live, then do exactly as I say."

Dread claws through my heart. The dagger's sharp edge is so close to drawing blood. If I even twitch too abruptly, the movement will send the blade slicing through my throat.

"Teleport us to the top of the Aether Tower." His voice is tempered into cool steel. "Now."

I say nothing. I only stare up at him.

"Do not make me repeat myself," he grinds out.

My heart pounds frantically against my sternum. I could teleport us back to the Arcanium, where my father will still be. But Nolan's dagger is pressed so tightly to my throat, and if he realizes I've teleported us to the place, he could kill me sooner than I could scream.

I don't dare to risk my life. I do exactly as he says.

"*L-laxus.*" My brittle voice cracks around the spell-word.

The teleportation spell seizes us both.

As we slip through the emptiness, the pressure of Nolan's dagger fades. The darkness lasts for only a heartbeat, but it's long enough for me to consider blasting him with my magic.

Then we return to the material world. Before I can cry out *telum*, I feel the cool, metallic kiss of his dagger. And all thoughts of escape are banished from my mind.

A gale slams into us and whips across my face. The Aether Tower's enormous orb of magic roars above, blinding me with its violet light.

"Good," Nolan purrs. "Now invoke a mind-link with your father and tell him to come here."

Pressure builds in my chest, squeezing the life from my lungs. I don't know what Nolan intends, just that it must involve my father.

How could I be so foolish? How could I trust Nolan? Especially when I know so little of him.

I promised myself I would never again be weak, but now my own stupidity has made me fall into this trap.

"And . . ." I begin, but my voice sounds frail and broken. Swallowing, I try again. "And if I don't?"

With his spare hand, he traces my cheek. Only minutes ago, that gesture sent warmth pooling through me. Now ice washes through my veins. And when I shiver, it is with fear alone.

"If you choose to defy me, then you will leave me little choice." His thumb sweeps over my lower lip. "And believe me, I would very much prefer not to hurt you."

"What do you want with me?" I snarl.

"Everything, Reyna. I want everything with you."

Bile burns the back of my throat. "And I want nothing to do with you."

He doesn't flinch. His fingers trail lower still, brushing down my neck and past the dagger in painfully long strokes. He comes to a stop at the silver locket and toys with it. Then he looks back up at me and smiles. "Oh, but we both know that's a lie. Why else would you take such good care of this locket? Of our promise?"

"What . . . What are you talking about?"

He lets out a sigh. "Have you really forgotten me during these three long years? Did you never think I would return for you? For us?"

Realization slams into me like a sickening punch to the gut.

"No," I gasp. "It can't be."

"You don't believe me? Let me prove it to you, Reyna. Let me show you who I truly am."

Darkness gathers in his left hand. He rakes his fingers down his face and strips away the shadows.

"*Lokriz.*"

He melts into a cloud of dark magic. A phantom hand remains, keeping the dagger fixed to my throat. The shadows swirl, reshaping. His silhouette grows taller and a little broader. Then color returns to him. His golden waves become raven curls, and his emerald eyes become gray and dead. He wears the same deep blue doublet as before, but now an amulet hangs from his neck: an obsidian skull with an icy stone plummeting from its jawless mouth.

"Have you missed me, Reyna," he says, his hand cupping my cheek, "as much as I have missed you?"

"You . . . I thought you were dead." Tears well in my eyes. They escape and tumble down my cheek.

Arluin sweeps them away with his thumb. "Shh," he murmurs, "don't cry. Of course I'm not dead. I would never leave you."

The tears freeze mid-flow. "No," I blurt, "you can't be him. Arluin . . . he would never hurt me." My attention lowers to the gnarled dagger kissing my neck.

"I don't want to hurt you, Reyna. But I must do what needs to be done—for us both. You will soon understand."

I shake my head, the movement stiff and slow to avoid the blade nicking my skin. "Where's Nolan? What did you do to him?"

My heart constricts with terror. I don't know if he is Nolan or Arluin or someone else entirely.

"There never was a Nolan," he replies. "Or at least not that you knew. I killed him months ago, long before I came to Nolderan. I knew your father would execute me on the spot, so I borrowed his face. I hoped you would still like it, even if it were not my own."

I choke. The strangled noise escapes my throat.

This must be someone else. For him to say such things and so indifferently . . .

This is not the Arluin I remember.

His brows pinch together. "What's the matter? You didn't prefer him to me, did you?"

I don't answer. I just stare at him.

"You must understand, Reyna, it was me all along. Me. Every word, every touch—it was all me."

"It can't be you," I whisper. "It can't be."

"But it is me. Your eyes do not deceive you."

I stare up at him, this man I have loved for so long. He looks just as I remember, except for his gray eyes: the mark of dark magic. I never dreamed we would be reunited like this, with a dagger pressed to my throat—

No. That's a lie. There was a nightmare once, long ago. Where I witnessed him becoming his father. Becoming what he already is today.

Blue light flickers inside the jagged stone of his amulet, moment-arily drawing my attention. When I glance back up at him, his eyes glow with the same formidable power.

All emotion vanishes from his face. His lips move, but he says no words.

I wonder whether he is preparing a spell, and I brace myself for whatever magic he will unleash. With the dagger against my throat, there will be no escape.

"Of course I will," he growls, gripping his amulet and glaring at it. "Do you think me stupid?"

After a pause, he releases the amulet. Then he turns back to me, his eyes narrowing. He grips the hilt of the dagger more tightly.

"We are wasting time," he hisses, his lip curling. Whereas before there was a chilling softness to his expression, now it is replaced with vicious cruelty. The icy glow remains in his eyes, turning them from dead gray to ghostly blue. "Tell your father to teleport here now. And tell him that if he does not come alone, then I will kill you before he can stop me."

I hesitate, still trying to make sense of everything that is unfolding. But fog blankets my mind.

He presses the dagger even more firmly against me. The force is enough to penetrate my skin. I feel a bead of blood trickling down. Fear pulses through me.

My fate lies within his hands. If he wants me dead, then I will be dead in mere instants. Long before I can scream for mercy.

"Don't test me again. Do it now."

Though my mind was beginning to suspect this may really be Arluin, now I am far less certain. I don't recognize the murderous glint in his eyes. The longing for blood. For death.

All I can believe is that if I hesitate any longer, he will kill me. The crimson line he has etched across my neck is proof of that.

I close my eyes and imagine my father in as much detail as I can: his fiery hair and beard, his bushy brows of the same auburn hue, his indigo robes with flashes of golden thread, and his glowing magenta eyes.

When my mental image is complete, I release the spell. "*Aminex.*"

My father answers immediately. "*Reyna?*" There's an urgency to his tone, or at least his projected thoughts. The last time I contacted him via a mind-link was on the night the necromancers stormed the city. When Heston murdered my mother. "*Where are you?*"

"*On . . . on top of the Aether Tower.*" Even in my thoughts, my words come out shaky.

"*Why are you up there?*"

"*Arluin. He—*"

My father doesn't wait for me to finish. He severs our mind-link before I can explain everything to him. Before I can warn him.

When I open my eyes, he's already emerging from a cloud of purple light.

His form becomes corporeal. The violent winds pull at his magnificent robes. His magenta eyes fix upon Arluin, upon the dagger pressed to my neck, and they blaze with uncontrollable fury.

"Take your wretched hands off my daughter," he roars.

Though my father's voice booms across the Aether Tower, disturbing even the relentless winds, Arluin doesn't flinch. He only sneers. "I will do as I please with your daughter. Perhaps I will kill her and raise her from the dead."

My heart stills. I try not to tremble in his grasp, try not to show how terrified I am.

"You would not dare," my father seethes.

"You don't believe I would? Then it seems I must demonstrate my sincerity."

He presses the dagger further into my skin. A cry of pain bubbles in my throat as the scratch deepens. More blood wells out.

My father blanches. "Stop!"

Arluin's hand loosens around the dagger's hilt, removing the pressure he was applying. But the blade doesn't leave my flesh. "What's the matter? Can you not bear the sight of her blood?"

His fingers graze my neck and soak up the blood pooling beneath the dagger. He holds up his hand, inspecting the crimson smear. My blood glitters under the light of the Aether Tower's orb.

"I, for one, think it is quite the remarkable sight. It is almost as radiant as she is." Arluin brings his stained fingers to his nose and inhales deeply. "Wouldn't it be a shame if we allowed all that lovely blood to spill out? What a waste it would be." I barely hear Arluin's words. His voice sounds so distant.

My father's knuckles whiten with strain as he grips his staff. "State your price."

"What I ask for in return is a simple thing."

"Then say it," my father spits.

Arluin tilts back his head, peering up at the thunderous orb of magic above us. "The Aether Tower. I want you to deactivate it. Entirely."

"You will let her go first."

"If I do," Arluin replies, his eyes glinting with the amulet's icy glow, "what reason would you have to fulfill my request?"

My father grits his teeth. "At least lower your blade."

Arluin flashes him a thin-lipped smile. His hand doesn't slacken around the dagger. "I'm growing bored of this. Deactivate the Aether Tower or watch her drown in her own blood. The choice is yours."

"Don't, Father!" I cry. "Please don't do it!"

Disabling the Aether Tower would mean rendering Nolderan defenseless. The enormous orb of magic powers the city's wards, shielding us from any external attacks.

Whatever Arluin intends, deactivating the city's defenses must be the key part of his strategy. He has gone to such lengths to carefully maneuver my father into checkmate.

Something terrible will soon befall us. I can't shake away the shadows snaking through my heart.

"Do it," Arluin urges. "I will not wait any longer."

If Nolderan falls tonight, all the blood will be on my hands. If Arluin hadn't captured me, my father wouldn't be in this impossible situation. He wouldn't be forced to disable the Aether Tower.

I need to escape. Now—before my father deactivates the orb.

Arluin won't expect me to cast magic without spell-words. I succeeded when I fought Kaely. Maybe I can succeed again.

If I harness my grief, my anger, perhaps it will be enough for all the aether in my body to burst free.

But there's no time. My father is already striding to the center of the Aether Tower. He stops directly beneath the enormous orb of magic.

"No, Father!"

He raises his staff. The crystalline surface glistens in the brilliant violet light.

Desperately, I focus my fury. On Arluin deceiving me. On him wielding me as a weapon against my father.

So many nights I cried for him. And yet, he was plotting Nol-deran's destruction.

Though I feel magic rushing through me, brimming as furiously as my emotions, it is already too late. When I unleash my explosion of aether, sending Arluin back several paces and freeing myself from his grasp, my father has already uttered the spell-word.

"*Terminir.*"

He drums his staff against the platform. The enormous orb of aether flickers off.

Without its radiance, we are cast in darkness.

The clouds are thick and heavy, suffocating the stars. The crescent moon is pallid against the shadowy haze.

Fearing Arluin will capture me again before I can escape, I break into a sprint. When I reach my father, I clutch his arm. My fingers dig into his sleeve.

"Reyna!" His free hand goes to my neck, examining the wound.

"It doesn't hurt." I wonder whether it should. The scratch is deep enough that blood smears over his fingers. But I feel numb.

Arluin straightens, having recovered from the burst of aether I hurled at him. A smirk curls onto his lips.

The city erupts.

Ghostly beams shoot into the sky, slicing through the dark heavens like sword. There are at least half a dozen, all scattered through the city. Before my father can demand an explanation, blood-curdling howls pierce the night.

The howls of the dead.

CHAPTER 38

Undead spill from the portals in a river of decayed flesh. They shamble through the streets, their stiff fingers outstretched like claws as they begin their ravenous search for the living. A horde of ghouls, wights, and wraiths engulfs the city.

This isn't like the night Heston attacked. What Arluin brings to Nolderan is a massacre.

And this is the beginning of the end.

My father's fingers tremble around his staff. Beneath his auburn beard, the veins in his neck pulse to a frantic rhythm. Upon seeing my father's fear, terror shudders through me.

"What have you done?" My father's roar cracks with horror and rage.

"I have done nothing," Arluin replies with cool indifference. "What you have done, however, is to choose your daughter over your city. You are predictable, Telric. It is no secret that Reyna is your greatest weakness."

I clench my fists. I want to shout that I'm not a weakness, nor a liability, but no words leave my tongue. Fear paralyzes me.

And even if I could speak, how could I deny Arluin's words? Nolderan's current state is because of me. I was too stupid to see through Arluin's deceit. If only I hadn't been blind to the signs: how he stared at me, how he kissed me, how he fixated on the locket last night. Now everything seems so painfully obvious. If only it were not too late.

"You will pay for this treachery, boy," my father snarls. "When your father left, I treated you as family. And this is how you show your gratitude? By taking my daughter hostage and unleashing Death Gates across my city?"

"I saved her life," Arluin hisses. "And the cost of saving her was to condemn my father, to my own future. Yet because I used necromancy to save her, you would have executed me. I was there when you murdered my father. I heard each and every one of his dying screams. You offered him no trial."

"I offered him no trial because he deserved none! He sealed his fate when he murdered my wife."

"But I didn't murder your wife. I saved your daughter by betraying my own father. Do you then claim you would have offered me a fair trial, or would you have burned me where I stood?"

My father says nothing. His hand clenches his staff so tightly the wood creaks with the force. His temple throbs.

"That is what I thought. You would blindly kill us all for the magic we practice."

"Your heinous magic threatens the living."

Arluin shakes his head. "Do you know how much I despise you, Telric, and your pathetic self-righteousness?"

Before my father can reply, Arluin raises his obsidian dagger and drags it down his palm in a jagged line. "Tonight, I will avenge the injustice my father and I have suffered at your hands."

A crimson bead wells from the wound. He gathers the shadows, and they merge with his blood.

"*Kravut!*"

Black blood spills across the Aether Tower like ink. The drops swell into an enormous worm thrice my father's height. The worm lets out a ferocious hiss, revealing rows of knifelike teeth.

Adrenaline sears through my nerves, and the numbness dissolves. Lightning energizes me to such an extent I feel as though I've consumed an Elixir of Flurry.

I will not be weak. I will not allow my presence to burden my father. I will prove Arluin wrong.

Aether floods through my veins, bubbling and fizzling as it yearns for release. I force it under my control. I bend it to my will. When my father weaves aether into flames, I do too. Fire is the most effective magic we can wield against the undead and dark magic.

"*Ignir'muriz!*" we call together. Just before the bloodworm descends on us.

Flames erupt.

Maw first, the worm plunges into our blazing wall. Its shriek pierces my eardrums as our flames devour it.

My father and I work in tandem, as though our mind-link was not entirely severed. The aether rushing through our veins is one and the same.

"*Ignir'quatir!*"

The fiery shield explodes. Flames hurl at the bloodworm.

This screech is more horrifying than the last. Even when the worm falls silent, ringing continues in my ears.

"*Ignira*," my father growls before our enemy can recover. A deadly fireball swarms from his fingers. The relentless flames slam into the worm, and it bursts apart.

Black blood splatters over us. Inky blotches stain my pearlescent dress and coat my cheeks. I wipe away the sticky liquid, but it smears further across my face. The substance shares the same abhorrent stench as the decayed flesh of ghouls.

The path to Arluin is cleared. I seize the opportunity. The frenzy of battle guides me from one movement to the next. Before Arluin can unleash his counterattack, I strike.

"*Gelu'tempis!*"

Ice shoots from my fingers. Like a firework, it explodes mid-flight. Frozen needles plunge to Arluin, their glistening points ready to rip him into shreds.

A few icicles find him. They sink into his shoulders and graze his cheeks. Where the shards meet him, they leave crimson stains in their wake.

But before my spell can inflict critical damage, Arluin wraps the shadows around him.

"*Ekrad!*"

My frozen needles bounce off his shield like hail. They clatter onto the platform.

Aether swirls in my father's hands. "*Telum!*"

The spell is quick but fierce. So much magic crackles from the blast that it shakes even the violent winds.

The aether collides with Arluin's shield. The shadows intensify into a bubble of viscous ink, concealing his silhouette. I can't tell whether my father's attack dealt him a critical blow.

I pull more aether into my grasp and prepare myself to strike again if Arluin bursts free from his shield.

The shadows ripple. Aside from that, there is no movement. Not for a long moment.

A bolt of darkness spins toward us, formed from the inky shield. The volatile magic is terrifyingly powerful—so much stronger than my father's spell.

Dark magic feeds on aether. Arluin absorbed my father's attack and corrupted it into shadows. For him to accomplish such a feat, his magic must be far greater than my father's.

I don't have time to consider the implications of this realization. The shadow bolt is already upon us.

"*Muriz!*" we both shout.

A barrier of aether forms around us. The shadow bolt pierces our shield, and we are left defenseless.

The attack isn't directed at me. It is intended for my father.

The shadow bolt slams into him, and he is thrown back. He hits the stone with a sickening thud.

"Father!" I call, sprinting toward him.

There is no visible wound, but the dark magic has left him weakened. He struggles to push himself back onto his feet.

Shadows spill from Arluin's hands. The ghastly amulet glints. It must be the source of his unfathomable strength. The skull seems to laugh at me.

Molten fury churns inside my chest. I almost burst from the relentless pressure.

"*Ignir'alas!*" I scream, channeling all my wrath into the spell.

Violent flames sweep from my fingers. They soar upward into the blazing wings of a phoenix.

Though the attack descends on Arluin at a furious velocity, he languidly lifts his head as he regards it.

"*Ekrad,*" he commands. Darkness shields him.

My fiery wings collide with his barrier. They crumble into ash. Sparks fly in the wind.

I stare at him, my eyes widening with horror. I poured all my strength into that attack, and yet he cast it aside so easily.

"*Vorikaz.*"

Arluin flings the remnants of his shield toward me. I have no chance to escape.

Obsidian chains wrap around me. Their grip tightens, squeezing the life from my chest. I can't feel even the slightest trace of magic in the air. Nor can I feel the aether in my blood.

Being cut off from my magic is as jarring as losing my sense of taste or touch.

Arluin paces toward my father, who is barely back on his feet and is significantly weakened from the shadow bolt.

Restrained by these obsidian chains, there is nothing I can do to save him.

"*Ignira,*" my father hisses, fueling his spell with all the magic he can gather. Deep lines of strain contort his brow.

"*Rivus!*"

Arluin meets my father's attack with a bolt of darkness. The two forces of magic collide, and their impact is so great it tears through the air. Wind slams into me. If not for the chains holding me firmly in place, the gale would likely throw me from the Aether Tower.

Both spells annihilate each other. But the attack cost my father much more strength.

He sways in the wind. His energy is so spent he struggles to keep himself upright.

Yet he fights on.

"*Gelu'gladis!*" He spins aether into ice magic and draws it out into a frozen sword. Blade first, he launches it at Arluin.

"*Arisga!*" A force of darkness rushes from Arluin's fingers, and it slings the sword aside. It clatters onto the stone and shatters into tiny fragments of ice.

"*Zadvuk!*"

Dark magic hurls at my father, taking the shape of an enormous hand. Shadowy fingers close around his throat.

My father chokes as the phantom hand lifts him by several feet and squeezes the air from his lungs. He tears at the spectral fingers strangling him and desperately tries to free himself. His eyes bulge from their sockets, and life drains out of him.

Though my father tries to draw on his magic, only tiny wisps of aether form—not enough to interrupt the shadowy hand.

Arluin squeezes his fist tighter. The spell chokes my father more forcefully.

He stalks nearer and raises his dagger. The gnarled blade glistens in the pallid moonlight.

"Father!" I shriek, battling my restraints. But struggling tightens the chains. They dig in so deeply that I fear my ribcage will fracture.

If only I could do something. If only I were not so helpless.

I squeeze my eyes shut and fight the dark magic which suppresses the aether in my blood. No matter how hard I try, I'm unable to sense even the faintest trace of my magic.

"Father!" I cry again. My voice falters, despair suffocating me.

My father's blood-shot eyes flicker toward me. He chokes out something which sounds like my name. His crystalline staff tumbles from his fingers. It rolls across the stone and halts at my feet. If only I could retrieve it. Maybe then I could use it to save him.

But I can't move. I can't do anything. Except watch.

Arluin stops before my father. He regards his dagger and twirls it in his fingers. Scorn contorts his lips. "Enjoy an afterlife of servitude, Telric."

Then he plunges the dagger through my father's heart.

I scream.

I scream so loudly my throat emits no sound.

My tears freeze on my cheeks.

Arluin twists the dagger. Perverted delight gleams in his eyes, still shrouded by the amulet's ghostly glow.

He tears the blade from my father's chest and holds it high. The dagger weeps crimson tears.

"Father," I gasp. "Father!" Though I call him, his head doesn't rise. It hangs lifelessly.

He is gone.

Dead.

Though my eyes witness the sight, my heart contests it as the truth.

He is the Grandmage of Nolderan, one of the most powerful sorcerers in the world. How could he be defeated?

Arluin uses the flat edge of his bloodied dagger to lift my father's limp head, and even when I see his unmoving face, I refuse to believe that he is dead. I tell myself over and over that he is not, desperate to make it true.

Darkness pours from Arluin's hands. He funnels it into my father, who remains suspended in midair by the phantom hand.

"*Arka-joud.*" Arluin's amulet glows brighter as he releases his spell.

Shadowy tendrils plunge into my father's mouth and nostrils. They seize him from within.

Arluin waves his hand. The dark magic forming the phantom hand dissipates. My father is released from its grasp.

He returns to his feet. His fingers twitch.

"Father!" I shout. "Father!"

His head turns. It tilts further over than is natural. His eyes no longer shimmer with magenta. Now the sockets are empty, filled only by the shadows swarming inside.

He snarls at me, his stiff fingers jutting out. He starts to drag his feet across the stone, but Arluin stops him. He places the blunt edge of the obsidian dagger to my father's chest and smears more blood across his robes.

My eyes fix on the wound. I want to look away, but I can't. All I can do is stare at every detail: the way the fabric is unevenly torn, the way black blood continues to seep out like ink.

"Stay," Arluin commands him. "You will not move until I tell you."

My father growls a guttural protest, but he remains still.

I barely notice Arluin lowering his dagger and pacing toward me. Only when he reaches me does my attention leave the gaping wound across my father's chest.

Arluin dismisses the obsidian chains and releases me from their grasp. I stagger. My chest heaves from the removal of the pressure, and air rushes into my lungs at such an alarming rate that my own breaths suffocate me.

The stone platform sways. I offer no resistance as I tumble.

Arluin catches me. His arm slips around my back.

I stare up at him. The icy glow has faded from his eyes. The amulet no longer shines.

"You killed him," I whisper.

The wind howls. It drowns my words.

Arluin strokes my cheek. Where his thumb touches, blood smears across my skin. My father's blood.

I should vomit at the realization—that would be the normal reaction. But I feel nothing.

"Don't worry," he says softly. "You have no reason to fear me. I know I said some hurtful things before, but I meant none of them. Of course I would never hurt you. I only needed you—your father—to believe it, or else he wouldn't have done what was required. But now, everything is nearly over. Without Nolderan, without your father, we can finally be together again."

"Arluin," I breathe, "you killed my father."

"I know you might hate me for it, at least for a while, but this was the only way we could be together. Don't you see?"

I don't blink. I continue gazing into his cold, dead eyes.

He presses his lips to my forehead. "Now that there's nothing in our way, will you marry me, Reyna?"

His kiss shatters my heart.

I am already broken, but I break even harder. Somehow the fragments of me are stronger than my entire self.

An anguished cry rips from my lips. I shove Arluin back with every ounce of my remaining resolve. My palms dig into his chest so deeply that my flesh stings with the force. But I fight through the pain. I push and push until I am freed from the shackles of his arms.

"No," I gasp, my breaths raw and heavy. "Never touch me again."

His dark brows knit together. "You no longer wish to marry me?"

"You killed him! You raised his corpse!"

"You promised you would marry me no matter what," he says quietly.

My nostrils flare. My entire body shakes.

Arluin steps closer. I lunge for the crystalline staff lying at my feet. My fingers close around the shaft. I raise it, holding it out like a ward between us. But the staff doesn't stop Arluin from continuing forth.

I shrink back. My feet meet the edge of the Aether Tower. Winds rush upward, seeking to claim me. I stand my ground. Against them, against Arluin.

"Don't come any closer!"

"All I want is you," he whispers.

I shake my head. Frantically. As if to break free from the chains of this nightmare.

He extends his hand, taking a step forth. And then another. "Come with me, Reyna."

"Never," I snarl, my fingers clenching around the staff. "I would sooner die."

"Reyna—"

There's nowhere left to run. He is almost upon me.

I turn and fling myself off the Aether Tower.

But the gales don't seize me. Arluin's fingers close around my wrist before they can.

"Let go," I growl, clutching the staff. My legs dangle in empty air. But I don't fear the height; I fear Arluin's grasp.

"No," he gasps. "I will never let you go."

Our gazes lock together. His eyes are unyielding. As are mine.

We both reach for our magic. I am first to unleash mine.

"*Ignira!*"

A fireball surges from my hand—the one Arluin holds by my wrist.

"*Okraz*," he mutters. Darkness pierces my skin.

Only when my fireball reaches him does he release me.

I plummet toward the deadly spires.

CHAPTER 39

AIR CRASHES INTO ME. I cling to the crystalline staff. The relentless winds try to prise it from my grasp, but I refuse to let go.

This is all I have of my father. I will not lose it.

Cobalt rooftops surge up to meet me. As do gleaming spires. But I have no time to fear them.

High above, Arluin melds with the shadows. In a cloud of darkness, he descends toward me.

The distance between us rapidly closes. I can't fall quickly enough.

I must do something. Now. If I do nothing, he will soon reach me.

I gather aether and craft the image of my manor's gilded gates in my mind.

"*Laxus!*"

Magic bursts from my fingers. Shadowy tendrils curl around my wrist. But I'm already fading away. The darkness seizes air.

In the next heartbeat, I'm standing outside my manor. Heavy clouds shroud the sky, and the gates glint in the stifled starlight. Now that the Aether Tower is deactivated, the enchantment on the gates is broken, and they are swung wide open.

If Arluin follows me here, the gates will do little to stop him. But with how powerful he is, even if the enchantment remained, it would provide me with little defense.

I don't know why I chose to teleport here. It offers me no advantage. It leaves me cornered.

My breaths come out in sharp bursts, and my pulse beats to a frenzied rhythm. I almost collapse in a heap outside my manor, but I know I can't. I must keep on going.

A cacophony of howls fills the night. The undead are not far. Soon they will reach this street, and I will be overwhelmed by a sea of ghouls and wights. I must escape before they do.

But before I can do anything, a sharp stabbing pain sears across my wrist. It feels as though a knife is piercing my flesh.

I glance down. There is no knife. Only an eye that has been inked across my skin. The mark of dark magic.

"Reyna," Arluin calls, his voice echoing through my mind. *"I know where you are. I can see everything."*

A tracking spell. He must have placed it on me before I fell. Now that he knows where I am, he will be here within moments.

I must run. But to where? No matter where I choose, he will find me. The eye etched into my flesh will make sure of that.

But an eye cannot see if it's blind.

I don't stop to consider whether my theory is too simplistic. I only act.

"Ventrez!" A fierce gale blasts from my fingers. It cuts through the thin fabric of my skirts.

The scraps fall to the ground. I grab them and wrap them around my wrist. My fingers are clumsy with desperate haste.

"I won't lose you. Not ever—"

I secure the knot with my teeth. Arluin's words are cut off. He doesn't speak again.

Did I succeed? Does his silence mean I blocked his tracking spell?

Even if I did, he knows that I'm here. I can hesitate no longer.

"*Laxus!*"

The gilded gates of my manor vanish. They are replaced by the Arcanium's archway.

QUEL ESTE VOLU, PODE NONQUES VERA MORIRE the carved words read. *That which is aether may never truly die.*

Chaos erupts behind me. I whirl around.

Magi and adepts stand shoulder to shoulder as they battle the rampaging undead. Necromancers are scattered through the horde, their black robes merging with the darkness.

Magic collides everywhere I can see. Ashes of aether scatter through the breeze, falling on Nolderan like glimmering specks of snow.

I push through the masses. No one turns to me. All are focused on their own enemies.

I manage three strides before a ghoul's rotten teeth snap toward me.

Using my father's staff as a focus, I draw upon aether. The crystalline surface gleams with magic, enabling me to rapidly power my spell.

"*Ignira,*" I hiss.

My scorching flames slam into the rotten carcass. It lets out an unearthly shriek as its body disintegrates into ash.

I continue through the havoc, searching for a face I recognize.

I find Archmage Gidston standing several paces ahead. Her violet robes distinguish her from everyone else still dressed in their finery. A few strands of blond hair have come loose from her usually neat bun. They dance around her in the wind.

"Archmage Gidston!" I call, hurrying over to her. Another undead lunges for me. I blast it with flames.

The Archmage finishes her fight with a wraith. Then she glances back at me.

"Reyna!" she exclaims. "Where's your father?"

I don't reply. I can't. Telling her what happened atop the Aether Tower will make it all come rushing back. For now I can only block everything out, focusing on one movement and then the next.

If I stop to think, I fear I may never move again.

Her gaze trails across to my father's staff. She must find her answer there, and in my blood-stricken face, since a shadow descends across her expression. Her lips part. No sound passes them.

This is the end. Of Nolderan. Of the magi.

Archmage Gidston's shock lasts for only a short second. A wight launches a shadow bolt at us.

"*Ignir'muriz!*" she calls, surrounding us with a wall of flames. "*Ignir'quatir!*"

The fiery shield explodes, taking the wight with it.

Ghouls swarm toward us. We stand back-to-back, battling the legions of undead. They do not relent. When one falls, another takes its place. There is no end to this storm.

"Reyna!" a shout comes from ahead.

My aether shield is so dense I can't distinguish the figure racing toward me. All I can tell is that they are among the living.

"*Quatir!*"

The barrier explodes, blasting the surrounding undead. Bone shards rain on me. Their edges graze my cheeks.

"Reyna!"

Now that my shield is gone and the nearest undead are defeated, I have a clear view of the person calling my name. Koby. His cheeks are branded red, and his breaths are labored. He barely manages to stop himself before crashing into Archmage Gidston and me.

"Koby?" I call over the crackling of flames and rattling of bones. "What is it?"

"Eliya!" he wheezes.

A ghoul lunges for him.

"*Ignira!*" I yell.

A fireball surges from my hands and hurls at the undead. It bursts into flames.

I return my attention to Koby. "What about her? Have you seen her?"

He shakes his head. "When the undead started attacking, no one could find you. Or your father. Eliya went looking for you."

My stomach knots. "Where is she? Where did she say she would look?"

"I don't know. Before I could ask, she sprinted out the Arcanium and teleported away. I . . . I hoped she was with you. Or that you had at least seen her."

I grit my teeth. "We need to find her. Now. Before it's too late."

I don't say that it may already be too late. That she may already be dead.

I refuse to believe it.

"Would she be at your house?"

"No, I came from there. I didn't see her." I pause. "Flour Power."

"The bakery? Why would she be there?"

I don't explain my reasoning. I grab his arm and draw aether over us both.

"*Laxus.*"

We fade away, leaving the Arcanium behind us.

The street we arrive on is more chaotic. With so few magi here, the undead are free to rampage. Screams of the dying and the dead fill the night.

I break into a run—heading toward the alley opposite us. To our left, a ghoul rips off the limb from a mangled corpse and gnaws on it. The undead wears Mrs. Baxter's face. I don't allow myself to stop and stare.

Koby does.

"T-that's—"

I pull him along before he can finish. He stumbles after me.

We enter the alleyway. The shadows slash across us in bold lines.

There is nothing here. No undead, no Eliya.

I inhale sharply, clenching the staff with one hand and tearing at my hair with the other.

Since she found me here, three years ago, I thought this might be where she came looking for me. But there is no trace of her.

"She isn't here," Koby says.

I scowl at him for the painful reminder.

"Where else do you think she could be?"

"I don't know," I grind out. "Stop talking."

He clamps his mouth shut. I might have felt bad, if not for the white-hot panic pounding through me. My thoughts are jumbled.

I clutch my temple. It throbs manically beneath my fingers. The stone walls spin around me. I think I might fall. But I can't. If I do, Eliya will die.

I must find her.

I break into a sprint. My footsteps thunder against the cobblestones.

"Reyna, wait!" Koby calls after me.

But I don't wait. I hardly hear his words. My blood drums too loudly in my ears.

He hurries after me. His strides are almost as frantic as mine.

I don't know where I'm running to. All I know is that I must save Eliya.

Undead charge at me from all angles. I don't stop. I carve a burning path through their ranks.

"Reyna!"

Koby's shout is drowned by my flames and my gasps. With each corner I turn, I pray I will see Eliya's crimson hair. That it will not be too late.

But it isn't Eliya I first find.

On my next turn, I glimpse a mousy brown braid fluttering in the wind.

"Kaely!" I shout. We might be sworn enemies, but right now we are allies. The fact we are living makes us so.

Except it's not Kaely that turns to me. It's something *else*.

Shadows swarm inside the wight's empty sockets. Loose bandages dangle from its arms. Scorched skin peeks out between the scraps of white cloth.

The freckles across her cheeks might be hers, but this is not her.

Koby comes to a stop beside me. He grips my shoulder. I feel him tremble.

"Reyna—" Koby begins.

I shake him off. I draw on the surrounding aether.

"*Rivus,*" the wight snarls. Its voice almost sounds like Kaely's, but deeper. And the syllables reverberate in its vocal chords.

I thrust out the crystalline staff, both my hands clasping it with strained force. "*Muriz!*" An aether barrier forms around Koby and me. It absorbs the dark magic and has power left to spare. I let it erupt. "*Quatir!*"

A wave of violet light crashes into Kaely. She staggers back.

But I have no chance to launch a subsequent attack. Three ghouls spring at us.

"*Ignir'alas!*" I call. Flaming wings crash into them. Fire devours their rotted skin and their yellowed bones.

I turn back to Kaely. Her shadowy orbs flicker between Koby and me.

"*Telum!*" Koby cries. A blast of aether races toward her.

"*Ekrad,*" she says, drawing the shadows around herself. Koby's attack bounces off her shield. "*Gavrik.*"

A storm of shadows races forth. It splits into hundreds of ravens, all with razor-like beaks.

There's no time to shield us both. I can only shield myself.

"*Ignir'muriz!*"

Flames encase me, preventing the shadowy ravens from reaching me. Their beaks stab into my fiery wall, and one by one they are obliterated.

My shield was hasty, and the attack was powerful. My flames are extinguished before the flurry ceases. The last few ravens break through my defense and tear at my dress and the flesh of my bare arms. But they inflict no fatal damage.

I glance at Koby. I don't know which spell he used to defend himself, but it appears his shield was ineffective. Long gashes mark his cheeks. His fine clothes are shredded into threads. Blood stains the rich fabric.

Kaely raises her hands. Shadows stir once more.

I also reach for my magic and pull aether into my grasp as swiftly as I can.

We both unleash our spells.

"Rivus!"

"Ignira!"

I expect my fireball and her shadow bolt to collide. But they don't. While my attack targets Kaely, hers doesn't target me.

It rushes for Koby.

I shout his name. Aether blooms from my fingers as I race toward him.

He tries to speak spell-words, but it is too late.

The shadow bolt pierces his chest.

Darkness floods through him, choking him from within. The veins in his neck throb and blacken.

My fireball strikes Kaely. She shrieks, but I don't turn to look. My gaze remains on Koby.

A strangled cry comes from his throat. His bulging, blood-shot eyes turn to me.

Then he falls. Dead.

I stare at him. My hand grips the staff so forcefully my fingers ache. I grip it even harder.

Black blood spills from Koby's chest. His unseeing eyes gaze up at the shrouded stars.

I am given no chance to mourn him.

"Rivus," Kaley calls again.

Another shadow bolt surges forth. This one is intended for me.

There is no time to speak spell-words. The darkness will tear through me before the syllables leave my throat.

Like Koby, like my father, I will be dead.

But if I die, how will I save Eliya?

Emotion smashes through the dam of numbness. A wave of fear and fury and grief engulfs me. I am helpless in its tyrannical grasp. I struggle to stay afloat, to not drown.

Magic rips through me—the pressure too great for my mortal body to contain.

An inferno explodes. It seizes everything in its path: Kaely, Koby, the undead nearest me. Stone walls heap around me. The volatile flames don't distinguish between friend or foe. They devour even the people fleeing from ghouls at the end of the street.

When the explosion is spent, I collapse. The cobblestones strike my knees, but I feel no pain.

Only ash and rubble remain. There is no living left, nor any dead. Just me.

Weariness seeps through my mind in blurry black spots. The explosion wasn't restrained by spell-words and almost burned through every drop of magic in my blood. I'm lucky to be alive. If it consumed all my aether, I would be dead.

The staff tumbles from my grasp. A hollow clatter sounds as it hits the ground. Exhaustion claims me. Like the staff, I fall.

No.

Eliya.

I fling out my arms and stop the ground from smashing into my skull.

I must find her. I must save her.

My fingers curl around the staff. I use it to haul myself upright. Once back onto my feet, I sway.

I don't hesitate for long. If I do, I will fall again.

Onward I force myself. My wobbly legs threaten to give way, and my feet are clumsy as they pound against the cobblestones. Once or twice I almost trip on the uneven edges. Determination steadies me. It keeps me from falling.

Two skeletons turn the corner. There's little aether left flowing through my veins, and there won't be more until I rest, but I must fight.

I use the smallest amount of magic possible to control the aether in the air, and I ensure the spell does not take more than I can give.

"*Ignira*," I rasp.

The resulting fireball is far from my fiercest, especially compared to the inferno which raged through the street, but it is enough. One skeleton is destroyed by the blast, while the other is crippled by it. Half its bones crumble to ash. It continues toward me, but I sprint hard and fast, and it fails to outrun me.

On the next street, a wraith turns to me and raises its spectral hands. Shadows rise.

I strike with fire before it can attack. Then I keep running.

My strength is swiftly depleting. I don't know how many more spells I can conjure—or whether my next will falter.

Three corners later, I find Eliya.

She lies slumped at a dead end, her crimson waves cascading over her face. Two ghouls stalk toward her.

"Eliya!" I shout.

The ghouls stop and turn. They race for me, ravenous hands outstretched.

Though my magic is almost spent, fury musters a fierce burst of strength.

"*Ignir'alas!*"

Blazing wings swoop into the night and dive at the undead. Flames consume their decayed flesh.

I don't watch. I continue straight through the embers. My own flames singe my tattered dress.

I lunge for Eliya and skid across the cobblestones.

"Eliya," I call, crouching beside her.

There's no reply. Her chest is so very still. Her fingers do not twitch.

With a trembling hand, I brush aside her crimson locks to reveal her heart-shaped face. Her eyes are closed. A heartbeat passes. They don't open.

I don't breathe as I press my fingers to her neck. I wait for a moment and then another, but I feel no pulse.

"Eliya!" I shriek, shaking her shoulders.

Her limp head lolls with the motion.

"No," I gasp, clutching her cheeks. They are still warm, but I feel them cooling with every passing moment. I cradle her head. "No, no, no. Wake up, Eliya. Please wake up."

No matter how much I shake her, no matter how much I plead, she does not stir.

There's no visible wound. She almost looks asleep. I tell myself that she is. I refuse to face the alternative. That I failed to save her. That I came too late.

The heavens weep. Rain drizzles over us both. Drops splatter onto Eliya's unmoving face, and they flow down her cheeks like tears. A wind blows over us, and it turns my drenched fingers into ice.

"Don't leave me, Eliya," I rasp. "Please don't leave me."

Somewhere in the far distance, chaos rages on. Deep in the back of my mind, I know I should return to Archmage Gidston and help her and the other magi and adepts defend the Arcanium against the hordes of undead, but grief shackles me in place.

All I can do is clasp Eliya and rock us back and forth, whispering her name until my voice breaks. My lips move of their own accord, calling her in an unspoken prayer.

I don't know how long passes. Time ceases to exist. There is only Eliya and me.

Soon the city falls silent and still. The streets become as lifeless as Eliya's body in my arms.

Maybe the undead were defeated. Or maybe Nolderan has fallen. Right now, I don't care which. All I want is for Eliya's eyes to flutter open. For her to laugh and tell me that everything will be fine.

I wait, and I wait. But her eyes never open. She never laughs.

A painful sob racks through my body. I clasp my mouth to stop the sound from escaping.

Footsteps echo from the adjacent street. Voices follow.

His voice.

"Have you searched the Lower City?" Arluin growls.

"Yes, my lord," a man replies in a crisp voice. "There was no sign of her."

"You searched every street?"

"Indeed. We did."

There's a pause.

"I want her found," Arluin says. "Alive."

The footsteps quicken. They grow louder as they draw nearer.

My pulse races.

At any moment, Arluin will turn the corner and find me huddled here at the end of this street. And when he does, he will snatch Eliya from my grasp and desecrate her like he desecrated my father.

He must not find me. Or Eliya.

I could try teleporting away, but I don't know where I can run that he won't find me. And I would leave a trail of aether dust behind. Then he would know that I was here.

I also cannot run. There's only one exit, and it would lead me straight to Arluin.

Instead, I focus on the surrounding stone walls and craft them carefully in my mind. I replicate every bruise and scratch inflicted by time and weather, and when my painting is perfect, I release my magic.

"*Alucinatas*," I whisper.

A barrier of aether encases me. The wall hums and ripples.

Arluin turns the corner. His black curls are like oiled crow feathers in the dying moonlight.

He marches toward me. My heart hammers in my chest.

With my haste and my fatigue, I worry the illusion won't be powerful enough to fool him. But now, I can do nothing except wait. And pray to gods who never listen.

Each footstep shoves my nerves further over the edge. The tension within me is so taut I fear it will cause my spell to shatter.

He halts three strides from me. His gray eyes scan over the wall and then the floor. Every time his gaze passes over me, my pulse beats at a terrifying tempo. My heart drums so thunderously I fear Arluin will hear it.

Unable to watch, I squeeze my eyes shut.

"I left a corpse here," Arluin says to the necromancer behind him. "Now it is gone."

I dare to open an eye. The other necromancer is built like a stake: tall and thin. Wrinkles weather his face, and the strained light reflects off his bald head.

"Corpses do have a tendency to do that," the necromancer replies. "One of the others must have raised it."

Arluin shakes his head. "No, they couldn't have."

"Then perhaps a ghoul ran off with it and feasted on its flesh."

"Perhaps," Arluin says, his eyes narrowing. "Or perhaps someone else took it."

"The girl you search for?"

Arluin clenches his jaw. "I know she's here somewhere."

"If she is a mage, she could have teleported to anywhere in Imyria. She is likely long gone."

"She has never left Nolderan before, so she couldn't have teleported anywhere off this island."

"You are sure? It has been three years."

Arluin's fists tightens. He doesn't reply.

"We have what we came for, do we not? I understand you have personal reasons for seeking the girl, but you must consider what is at stake. It won't be long before the world learns Nolderan's fate, and when they do, they will be on their guard. Achieving our ambitions will be a far greater challenge. We must strike swiftly, while they are still all unaware."

Arluin exhales deeply, his fingers running through his nest of dark curls. "Very well. Find the others. We will send our undead back through the Death Gates and then we will leave this place."

The tall necromancer bows his head. "*Farjud*," he says, melding into the shadows. He leaves in a heavy cloud of darkness.

Arluin lingers. He stares at the wall behind me. I wonder if he can sense the residue of my magic from when I defeated the undead. Or if he can sense the dark magic which marks my wrist.

I glance down. The knot remains secure and hasn't loosened in battle. I pray it will be enough.

He continues his examination. I hold my breath. A moment passes. Then another. My chest aches from the lack of air.

Finally, with one last look at the wall, he turns and vanishes down the street.

CHAPTER 40

BY THE TIME DAWN ARRIVES, the ghostly beams are extinguished and all the Death Gates are closed. Nolderan descends into an even heavier silence.

I don't know whether the necromancers have left, so I wait longer still.

The sun creeps higher through the clouds, and the heavens bleed with its emerging rays. The rain has dwindled, and wispy drops brush the crown of my head.

Minutes stretch into hours. Arluin does not return, nor do his necromancers.

Only when the sun has long reached its peak do I dare stir. While I've been sitting here, cradling Eliya's lifeless body, a small fraction of my strength has returned. It is enough to craft a teleportation spell and carry us both away.

"*Laxus*," I breathe. The sound scarcely leaves my lips, but my magic obeys my command.

We leave the narrow street and materialize inside the Upper City's cathedral, on the platform of the circular chamber. The ten major gods stare down at us. With the Aether Tower disabled and the cathedral's power line cut off, the paintings have lost their enchantment and are frozen still.

Once, when my mother's coffin laid inside this chamber, I pledged a silent promise to become powerful enough to prevent anyone I love from ever being snatched away again. Now I realize my foolishness.

Everyone is dead, and I could save no one.

I gently roll Eliya from my arms and kiss her forehead. Her skin is colder than the stone floor beneath us. Her delicate face blurs as a fresh wave of grief crashes into me.

"I'm sorry, Eliya," I choke, my voice raw and cracked. "I'm sorry I couldn't save you."

But she doesn't hear my words. She will never hear them again.

My tears patter across her icy cheeks and trail down into her crimson locks, dampening them.

When my eyes dry and I'm unable to shed any more tears, I lift my head and absently gaze out at the rest of the cathedral. Rows and rows of empty pews stare back at me, framed by the ribcage of the vaulted ceiling high above. A few are knocked over, and blood blemishes the otherwise polished ivory floor. The towering doors at the far end are both swung wide open. The street beyond is deathly quiet, rubble heaped like mounds of snow. Though much debris litters the cobblestones, there isn't a single body in sight. Only a few stains of blood that the rain has yet to erase.

I return my attention to Eliya and clasp her cold cheek. My hoarse breaths echo through the cathedral's hollow walls.

Then I stand and start through the narrow door to my left. I enter an antechamber filled with scrolls and holy relics and continue straight through. Soon I arrive at the stairs which lead beneath the cathedral. It takes longer than I expect to reach the bottom, and I hurry down the last few steps. I think all the necromancers and undead are long gone now—judging by the stillness of the city—but I don't want to leave Eliya for longer than is necessary. I can't bear the thought of her up there all alone, with the callous gods staring down at her.

The room is dark and musty. The faint glow atop the stairs provides enough light for me to make out the crystals lining the walls like sconces. Since they rely on the Aether Tower for their power, I have to draw on the remnants of my magic.

"*Iluminos.*" Though the spell-word is quiet, it shudders through the darkness.

An orb of brilliant light sweeps from my fingers. Its radiance illuminates the entire room.

Dozens of empty crystal coffins lie stacked in rows. Magic ripples across their violet surfaces.

I reach for the nearest coffin and haul it from the top of the stack. But it's heavier than I anticipate and doesn't budge, even when I shove it.

Again, I draw on the dregs of my magic, this time releasing a wind spell.

"*Ventrez.*"

A breeze blows the coffin down to knee height, and I use the spell to guide it back up the stairs.

Eliya lies where I left her. I lower the coffin to the center of the circular chamber and use another wind spell to blow her inside. The vibrant yellow skirts of her dress flutter with the magic. They look as lovely as they did at the Ball, aside from the few specks of dirt which sully them.

The coffin's purple glow reflects onto her skin and paints it with an iridescent luster. Her hair also appears as fine strands of rubies in the glistening light. She looks so beautiful and peaceful in there, and gazing at her feels like stabbing a knife through my chest. But I can't look away. I must soak up every detail and freeze an image of her in my mind so that I never forget her, even if hundreds of years pass.

I clench the side of the coffin, and my knuckles are cast ashen with the strain. Magic pulses beneath my fingers, the same magic that will preserve her until the end of time.

My eyes sting. They're too dry to shed any tears, and it feels as if they instead shed sand. I blink away the grit, but much remains.

Finally, I tear my hands from the coffin. I know I shouldn't waste my magic when I have so little left and still need to bring her down to the crypts, but I draw on the aether in my blood and use it to harness that which surrounds me.

"*Alucinatus,*" I whisper.

A single rose blooms in my fingers. Its thorns glitter in the coffin's radiance, and its silken petals are the same rich ruby red as Eliya's tangled waves.

The rose's thorns don't prick my skin as I lower it into her coffin and close her cold hands around it. The flower is an illusion and would usually wither away with time, but the crystal coffin is crafted from raw aether and will preserve my spell, just as it will preserve Eliya for eternity.

After burying Eliya inside the crypts beneath the cathedral, I return home. Since I used the very last of my magic to blow her coffin through the tunnels, I have none left to teleport back to my manor. Instead, I walk through the empty streets and stumble over the debris. Stone grinds beneath my heels. Several times, I lose my balance and my father's staff escapes my grasp. Every muscle aches as I bend to retrieve it.

I pass no one. Not even at the Arcanium, where so many gathered to battle the undead. There's no sign of anyone. Only blood and ash and streams of rubble.

The necromancers killed everyone, raised them all from the dead. Even the birds are absent. I don't know whether they flew from the horrors of last night, or whether they also fell victim to the hordes of undead.

I barely recognize where I'm walking, but my legs—weary though they are—remember the way and carry me home.

My manor's gates are as I left them, flung aside now that the Aether Tower is disabled and their enchantment is broken. The gardens are ravaged. Flowers are pulled from their roots and half the fountain is smashed apart. Water gushes across the stone path and swamps the surrounding grass.

The doors of my manor are also wide open, and one of the golden lion knockers has fallen off. It lies discarded on the lower-most stone step.

Arluin must have blasted through my manor in search of me, and he might still be here, awaiting my return. I should feel panicked by that thought, but I am too fatigued to feel anything. I stand there, hesitating for a long while, wondering whether I should run or haul myself up the stairs and into bed.

Before I can decide, scratching comes from under one of the large, rectangular planters. The trough is upturned, and mud and flowers are spilled all around it.

I freeze. Instinctively, I try to draw aether, but it fizzles out in my fingers. None remains in my veins to gather the magic in the air.

A low growl rumbles beneath the stone planter. It sounds frail and pained and very much alive. Not undead.

I don't pause. I rush over to it.

Having no magic left, I am forced to shove the heavy trough with all my might until it topples over and reveals its contents.

Azure scales glitter beneath thick layers of mud. Violet wings beat the dirt away, but one moves slower than the other and jerks back and forth, having been battered by the planter's stone rim.

"Zephyr!" I exclaim, scraping away the mud.

He doesn't respond as I lift him from the dirt. His scales are cool beneath my fingers. His usually bright eyes are dull and tired. He blinks once and then lowers his head, sinking into my grasp.

He's alive, and I'm not entirely alone.

I cradle him to my chest, hunched and trembling.

It is a while before I rise, and when I do, I carry Zephyr in my arms. We climb the stone steps and pass through the bruised doors.

Inside, my manor is as devastated as the gardens. Broken vases and ornaments are scattered through the hallway, along with glass from the shattered windows. The small circular table at the center lies helplessly on its side. All around, my mother's paintings have fallen still. I pause and gaze at the midnight seascape opposite me, the one that was always her favorite. Though I stare hard, the deep teal waves do not ripple. Neither does the powdery foam crowning their crests bubble.

I continue through the hallway and up the stairs. Shards of glass and pottery crunch on my way.

When I reach my room, I turn the handle slowly, half fearing Arluin or his necromancers are waiting for me behind the door.

But there's no one inside. The golden brilliance of my rug and curtains and sheets blinds me. I scan my surroundings a second time before fully entering, and I set Zephyr down at the foot of my bed.

He rests his head in his forelegs, and his violet wings fold across his back. The left is crooked and rests at an awkward angle.

"I'll find you some Blood Balm," I say. He doesn't look up at me. I know it isn't pain alone which causes his unresponsiveness. There's no sign of our other faerie dragons. Like the citizens of Nolderan, all are gone without a trace.

I rummage through my cabinets until I find a tin of Blood Balm. I return to Zephyr's side and perch on the edge of the bed, unscrewing the tin's lid. The scarlet substance glistens in the late noon sun. I dig my fingertips through the sticky contents and paste it across Zephyr's left wing in thick layers. At first, he flinches but doesn't shrink away.

When I finish, I screw the lid back on and place the tin onto the square cabinet beside my bed. Zephyr closes his eyes. I turn to the window and stare out at the lifeless streets. The image is distorted by the long crack zig-zagging through the glass. None of my windows are smashed, though. Not like downstairs.

I soon grow tired of gazing at the dead city and slump down onto my bed. My eyes fix onto the decorative ceiling above. But they don't stay open for long.

The claws of exhaustion drag me into darkness.

CHAPTER 41

I DREAM OF DEATH AND destruction, of blood and bone, and of aether and ash.

In my restless slumber, I flail and thrash. Sweat pools across my forehead and leaks down my back.

Then, amid the ravage and ruin, a voice calls to me.

Arluin's voice.

I jolt from my sheets and fling them aside as though they are the source of my torment. My wrist throbs. With shuddering breaths, I glance down. The mark is still bound by the scraps of my skirts. I don't loosen the knot to check.

For a moment I consider summoning a frozen blade and using it to gouge the shadows from my skin, but I don't know how deeply the tendrils of dark magic sink into my flesh. And if I do, Arluin will know I am here. Alive.

I haul myself from the mattress, and my bare feet press into the icy floor. My slippers must have loosened during my sleep. I don't search for them and continue through my room. My toes soon reach the plush rug, and I stop at the center.

Mr. Waddles watches me from the opposite cabinet. My fingers curl and my jaw hardens, and then I storm across the room and seize him. My nails claw into him and pierce his seams.

All I can see in its glossy black eyes is Arluin.

Arluin as he kills my father and raises him from the dead. Arluin as he murders Eliya and forever extinguishes her bright light.

My heart blazes with anguish and hatred. Magic, which has recovered from my rest, burns with it.

"*Ignis*," I snarl. Flames burst from my fingers. The stuffed toy duck catches fire. I watch as it withers in my grasp and crumbles across the floor.

And then I fall with it.

My fingers rake through the heaps of ash. I clench my fists, melding the fragile specks together.

From the corner of my eye, I glimpse my reflection in the full-length mirror to the left. Stiffly I turn my head and stare at myself.

My tattered pearlescent gown hangs from me like a tapestry of cobwebs. Dirt and blood smears the delicate fabric. A crusty scarlet line stretches across my neck.

I shove myself onto my feet and stagger. Everything sways.

They are all gone. My father, Eliya, Koby, Archmage Gidston, Kaely, her father, Erma, Mrs. Baxter. Everyone I can think of is dead, or undead. There is no one left but me.

I drag my gaze over to the window. Darkness envelops the city. The streets are as still and silent as before I fell asleep.

The glittering of my father's staff catches my eyes. I start over to it and lift it from where it lies discarded beside my bed. Zephyr's jewel-like eyes watch me as I walk. Until now, I didn't realize he was awake. Perhaps my flames woke him. I don't turn to look at him.

Magic vibrates beneath my fingers as I clench the staff. Across the glimmering surface, I see my father's limp head turning toward me. Shadows convulse in the empty sockets of his eyes. His mouth creases with a ravenous snarl.

I drop the weapon as though it has branded the soft flesh of my palm. It lands on the feathery mattress with a gentle thud.

Frozen in place, I gaze down at the staff, unable to shake away the nightmares which whisper across it.

My father now serves Arluin. His body will never be laid to rest. He will never slumber inside a crystal coffin. His flesh will rot upon his walking corpse until he is reduced to a putrid carcass.

No.

No, no, no.

Tears sting my eyes like acid. They hurt even more when they burst from my eyes in painfully swollen lumps.

I can't allow my father to be defiled like this. I must save him from the shackles of undeath.

My mind numbs. I stop thinking.

I force my clammy feet inside a pair of leather boots and grab the staff. Then I leave the room. Zephyr follows me down the stairs and out the manor. I don't stop him from following me. Though his wing is partially healed from the thick layers of Blood Balm, his flight remains significantly reduced. But he keeps up with me as I enter the darkness. My own pace is slow and heavy.

Shadows shroud the streets, and it's hard to discern my path. I don't summon an illumination orb, though. I let my legs lead me on and on, until they bring me to the Arcanium.

The arch looms over me. Moonlight gleams across the words etched into the stone, mocking me. Because they are all dead. All of Nolderan is dead.

I stumble through the archway. All the statues tower above me. I look none in the eye as I pass beneath them. Zephyr's wings beat behind me, rustling through the air.

I reach the winding steps and ascend them. The portico's tall pillars cast long shadows over me.

The Arcanium's large doors lie wide open. One has broken away from its hinges and leans at an awkward angle.

A crack runs through the length of the atrium's polished floor. But aside from the scorch marks and scratches across the walls, it looks no different from usual. Just deathly still.

The ceiling glows with magenta light. Like the crystals which form the coffins, it was built to eternally store aether.

I don't stare up at it for long. I take a sharp right and follow the dark path deep beneath the Arcanium. Zephyr trails behind me.

While I've never entered the Vaults—only the most senior magi are allowed inside—I know precisely where it lies. Usually the wards hold adepts and inexperienced magi at bay, but now they are broken and I am free to enter.

The heavy doors groan as I push them open.

Chests are overturned, relics spilling out, and old tomes have fallen off shelves. Bookcases lie sprawled on their backs. Like the rest of the Arcanium, the battle has left devastating scars.

I pass through another set of doors. It's within this next vast room that I notice several artifacts missing from their stands. I don't stop to determine what they were. If the necromancers seized them, they must be deadly relics.

I don't know what exactly I seek. All I know is that I will need something dark and terrible to save my father's body and soul from Arluin's clutches.

I halt before an altar with a skull floating above it. Shadows burn in its sockets. I can't tell whose it once was, but it appears to be human. Bony jaws clatter together. Zephyr springs away in fright, his antennae quivering.

As menacing as the skull might appear, it wasn't powerful enough for the necromancers to steal. That means it's of little use to me. I turn and continue through the hall.

At the very end of the Vaults lies a door formed from crystallized aether. It has no handle and when I run my fingers across its surface, I find no ridges where it meets the stone. It's just because of its shape that I suspect it may be a door at all.

I rock back onto my heels and narrow my eyes. My father would surely be able to enter. His staff is linked to Nolderan's Aether Tower, so perhaps it will also share a connection with this door.

I knock the staff against the crystal.

Nothing happens.

With a frown creasing my brow, I draw aether into my fingers and focus all the power into the staff. I weave my magic into an unlocking spell.

"*Aseros.*"

This time when I knock the staff against the door, the smooth surface ripples with energy. Then it swings open, permitting me entry. Zephyr slips through after me, and the crystal door seals behind us both.

We enter a magnificent chamber, every inch of its walls and floors carefully carved from marble. Its ceiling is crystalline like the central atrium's, though remarkably smaller, and magenta light washes over the circular room, keeping it permanently illuminated. Shelves lean against its curved walls, but they aren't just filled by books. Daggers and amulets as cruel as the ones Arluin wielded decorate the gaps between the ancient, leather-bound tomes. There are a few relics which don't exude dark magic, such as the aether-forged sword to my right. And I find a few jagged crystals lying along the shelves. But they don't shine with magenta light. Their glow is tri-coloured, and they are filled with varying shades of purple, gold, and black. I lift one and peer at it. The vibrations through my fingers are not the familiar hum of aether. Rather this stone contains all three energies: aether, light, and dark magic.

I return the strange stone to its shelf and continue my examination of the room. My fingers trail over the dusty book spines, and I lean closer to decipher their titles. There are tomes on advanced spells of the magi—some even from the enchanters of Lumaria. Or at least I think they're on moon elven magic, seeing how they're written in Elvish. I only recognize the letters of their alphabet, and not their language itself.

Other tomes are far less benevolent, and their texts contain the terrible secrets of dark magic: necromancy and demonology. I select a large one entitled *The Origins of Necromancy* and start over to the pillowy armchair in the corner. Zephyr is already curled up in the middle since it's the only chair in this chamber. I lay my father's staff against the wall and lift the faerie dragon onto my lap. He buries his azure head into the withered skirts of my pearlescent dress, licking his wounds with his forked-tongue.

I peel back the tome's leather cover—which is cracked in places—and glance through the pages.

Necromancy was not always forbidden, nor was dark magic, it begins. *In the year 558, the first corpse was successfully reanimated by Nolderan's most senior scholars, and this discovery especially piqued the interest of Korad Banwell who was, at the time, the Archmage of Defense.*

I turn to the next page. The first contains no new information. My tutors at the Arcanium already described how necromancy came to be and why dark magic is forbidden. Their explanations weren't as detailed as this tome, but the dates of experiments and the names of those overseeing them will provide me with no advantage against Arluin.

I scan over several paragraphs and then flip to the middle of the book, but it is evident this book will be of no help. With a sigh, I remove Zephyr from my lap and return the tome to its shelf.

If I am to have any hope of saving my father, I must find a way to become Arluin's equal. And swiftly. I need a weapon which will grant me unfathomable strength, or knowledge of a spell which will act as a bane against necromancy.

I suppose light magic is the greatest power against dark magic, but I'll never be able to wield it. Maybe if I studied for several decades, I would learn to use a small amount, but I would never become proficient with light magic. A fraction of the energy flows through my veins, as it does with all living beings, but my blood is dominated by aether. Those who are exceptional at casting light magic are blessed by the gods and possess souls so radiant they are like living beacons. That is why light magic is out of the question. I must resort to other measures.

Once more I continue to search the shelves. I briefly consider the crystalline sword, but I doubt it's more powerful than my father's staff. And even that failed to defeat Arluin.

No, I require something else. Something more terrible than Arluin.

My fingers stop on the spine of an obsidian tome. Chains wrap around it, binding a dark crystal to its cover. The stone is so black and glossy it looks like pitch. We magi frequently solidify aether into crystals, and it appears this substance is dark magic's equivalent. The shadows oozing from the stone confirm my suspicions.

Despite the chains, the book offers little resistance as I open it, aside from its hefty weight and bulky size.

The words *Grimoire of Demonic Incantation* are scrawled across the first page of parchment. Whoever wrote this book—I can see no name anywhere—was in a great hurry. Either that or their handwriting was awful.

The Abyss is ruled by the Void King, a being as ancient as the gods, and the most powerful Malum were created shortly after the Primordial Explosion of Aether, the splitting of light and dark magic, and the formation of the three planes of existence: the Heavens, the Abyss, and our world of Imyria. The dark energies of the Abyss continue to birth new Malum, and there also exists a second type of demons, formed from the souls of fallen mortals.

On the next page, sketches of demons are etched in black ink. They possess wings, horns, draconic wings, multiple heads and limbs, cloven hooves, claws, forked tongues, and all manner of other ghastly things. Some are tall and thin, others are short and round. Some appear humanoid, others bear resemblance to beasts. Though they are vastly different, each is as horrifying as the next.

I then come to a diagram of multiple circles—eight in total. A large one is featured in the center, and seven more are scattered around it. Some intersect with each other, while all intersect with the middle circle. The diagram almost appears to be a map, though it's unlike any I've ever seen.

My gaze reaches the short paragraph at the bottom of the page.

The Abyss is formed from eight sub-planes, with the largest ruled by the Void King. The other seven are commanded by his lieutenants, who are known as Void Princes. Each realm shares its name with its resident Void Prince, and represents the cardinal sins: Lust, Gluttony, Greed, Sloth, Wrath, Envy, and Pride. Demons value only strength and cunning, and the most powerful command their legions. These seven Void Princes risk being overthrown by rivals at any moment.

This book provides far more detail than any of my tutors ever did. All I knew until now was that the Abyss is home to the most nightmarish horrors one could dream and that it is ruled by an ancient Malum known as the Void King. But I stand against necromancers, not demons. It is doubtful any of this information will help me defeat Arluin and save my father.

Unless . . .

A nefarious idea takes root in my mind. Terrible though it may be, I don't question it. I continue flipping through the pages, until I finally reach the section I seek: *Demonic Summoning.*

These pages contain sketches of ritual circles, filled by pentagrams and triangles and other shapes. Some are complicated, others are simplistic. All are designed to summon and bind demons, though only complex patterns are capable of controlling the most powerful ones.

To summon a lesser demon, one requires three reagents: a soulgem as payment for the demon to cross the veil separating Imyria from the Abyss, a summoning circle to act as the gate through which it will enter our world, and the blood of the summoner to bind the demon to their will. The summoner also requires the true name of the demon they seek to enslave, and they must use dark magic to invoke the spell 'Kretol'morish,' followed by the demon's name. For example, if one wished to summon a demon named Norrazax, they would use the incantation 'Kretol'morish Norrazax.'

My fingers linger as I turn the page. The instructions are clear and I should in theory be able to follow the directions and summon a demon of my own, but a lesser demon will be of no use against Arluin. The formidable amulet around his neck made him powerful enough to defeat my father. I need a demon so fearsome it eclipses Arluin's strength. Maybe a Void Prince would suffice.

The thought of summoning something so vile and wicked—let alone using dark magic in the first place—chills me to the bone. It is forbidden by all of Nolderan's laws. If I summon a demon, I will break all the teachings of the Arcanium. I will be no better than Arluin and his necromancers.

But if I were only to once use dark magic to summon the demon, and if my intentions were pure, then wouldn't that make me different to them? Wouldn't my reasons make my actions justifiable? Nolderan has fallen, and my father's body and soul are enslaved to Arluin's will. I have been a mage for just one day. Without the strength of a formidable demon, how else will I ever stand a chance?

This is my sole hope, and I am desperate and broken enough to seize it.

Zephyr stirs in my lap. As I glance down at him, bitterness fogs my throat. It feels as if these thoughts are betraying him and all that I am. Despite the heavy tome in my hands, I don't think he yet realizes what I intend. I shouldn't do this, but I also can't do nothing. And if I don't do this, what else can I do?

I turn the page and then the next. The book continues to discuss the process of demonic summoning. Three paragraphs later, I arrive at a section on summoning more powerful demons—including Void Princes.

The greater the demon, the greater the price to summon it from the depths of the Abyss, the book reads. *The summoner must pay with their own blood. In the case of Void Princes, though they are summoned infrequently, the spell requires an additional reagent: the summoner's soul. This price is to be paid upon death, and the soul will be bound to the Void Prince as the Void Prince is bound to the summoner during their life. No matter whether the summoner dies within a day, year, or century of binding the demon, the price remains the same. The Void Prince will be free to do as they please with the soul, for it shall belong to them.*

At that, I close the book with a deafening thud, my breaths heavy in my ears. Zephyr looks at me and then lowers his head back onto the worn fabric of my skirts.

Summoning a Void Prince might be my only hope of freeing my father and defeating Arluin, but it also means eternal damnation. If I choose this path, I will forsake my own soul. Until the end of time, I will belong to whichever monster I summon. I will become a monster myself.

The cost is heavier than I expected. Of course, I never imagined summoning a demon—never mind a Void Prince—would be easy. But damning my own soul? It's a price I don't know whether I'm prepared to pay.

I could leave this chamber now, return the tome to its shelf and pretend I never glimpsed its contents, but where else would I go? What else would I do? Nolderan is gone, and everyone with it.

Though this path may be wicked, it offers me direction—purpose. If I decline, I will wither into nothingness. I must seize it before I lose myself.

I set the tome on the chair's arm and roll Zephyr from my legs. Once more I search the many shelves. Though this book was informative, there are still two more facts I require: the method of channeling dark magic, and the name of a Void Prince so I may call one from the Abyss. If I can learn the true name of the Void Prince of Wrath from these shelves, I am certain that demon would prove the greatest weapon against Arluin.

I find an introduction to conjuring dark magic first. In fact, there are several inside this chamber. I choose the thickest tome, hoping it will provide the most detailed explanation.

The search for a Void Prince's name takes me far longer, though I expected as much. From subsequent books, I learn that the true names of the Malum are known only to them as they come into existence. In the Abyss, names are the greatest currency, and demons may reveal the names of others to the mortals who summon them. For the demons who are not Malum and were once mortals themselves, it is their mortal name which holds power over them.

I suppose this is why I learn the name of the Void Prince of Envy first. A demonologist from a thousand years ago, before dark magic was outlawed in Nolderan, writes about her. She was Lady Eladine Pembelson of Montarra, a land annexed by Tirith long ago, and her sister who was younger and more beautiful married the Crown Prince. Jealous, she used dark magic to kill her. And then when she became the Queen of Montarra, she envied her husband and killed him too and reigned as the sole monarch until her natural death. Her soul was so wicked that the Void King took it for his own.

On the next page, I find a sketch of her. She is depicted as slender with dark curly hair, and her wings and talons and horns make her as deadly as she is beautiful.

I could summon her now, since I know her true name, but I instead continue my search. The Void Prince of Wrath must surely be the most ferocious, and if I am to sell my soul, I must choose the demon which provides me the greatest chance of defeating Arluin and freeing my father.

It takes an entire bookcase before I learn the name of another Void Prince. Though this one is still not Wrath, his description causes me to pause.

Natharius Thalanor was the greatest High Enchanter of Lumaria ever to exist, and the most arrogant. He is the only mortal evil enough to bargain his soul and the souls of his entire city to the Void King in exchange for power. He now resides over the Realm of Pride, as one of the Void King's seven lieutenants.

Unlike the book which mentioned Lady Eladine, this one provides no illustration of the aforementioned Void Prince.

I lean back against the nearby wall and reread the paragraph several times. Though it was the Void Prince of Wrath I sought, there's something about this demon which makes me linger. Perhaps it's because he was once the High Enchanter of Lumaria and wielded aether like us magi, or perhaps it's because his wickedness and ambition greatly overshadow Lady Eladine's. If he was truly that powerful as a mortal, I can only imagine his strength as a demon. Surely a demon this formidable will be enough to destroy Arluin.

"Natharius Thalanor," I whisper. The demon's name is like a prayer, a promise, upon my lips.

My mind already decided, I close the book. I could continue searching this chamber for the Void Prince of Wrath, but if he wasn't previously mortal and has kept his true name well-guarded, I may never find him. And even if I do, he may not be as formidable as the Void Prince of Pride.

I peel myself from the wall and retrieve a tri-colored shard from one of the shelves. The stone hums beneath my fingers. I didn't realize at the time, until I found sketches of the reagent inside the tomes, but this shard is a soul-gem. If my heart was not steeled with cold, hard determination, the thought of holding someone's soul in my hands might have nauseated me. Now, as I gaze at it, I see it only as a weapon.

I have my name; I have my soul-gem. Now to summon my Void Prince, I must first learn to harness dark magic.

CHAPTER 42

FOR COUNTLESS HOURS, I SIT at the center of the chamber and practice channeling dark magic. Dozens of tomes surround me in a sea of parchment and ink. In the end, I find that the first one I selected wasn't sufficient. My initial attempts are pitiful, though the subsequent aren't vastly improved. I always imagined that dark magic would come readily, given how corruptive it is, but I discover it requires much concentration.

Since there is little dark magic flowing through my veins, I must use my aether as bait to draw the shadows toward me. At first they are unresponsive, and I am required to manifest even greater quantities of my magic before the darkness is finally lured in.

It snatches the aether from my fingers and corrupts it. Then, before I can realize, the shadows are lost to the air. If I were a dark sorcerer, I would be able to snap all the dark magic back to my command, but I am not and can only use my aether to entice it.

Over and over I try, until I am quick enough to capture the shadows. Though I succeed, the dark magic is merely a faint wisp of black smoke in my fingers—nowhere near enough to summon a Void Prince from the Abyss.

It takes me a long while and hundreds of failed attempts to conjure enough. When plumes of dark energy manifest in my fingers,

Zephyr whimpers and cowers into the cushioned armchair. I extinguish the shadows and turn to him.

"I know what I'm doing is wrong," I say, "but this is the only way." Despite the cold look I give him, I find myself yet again doubting this path. But I quickly banish the thought because there is no alternative. I will summon the Void Prince of Pride and bind him to my soul, and I will defeat Arluin and save my father from the shackles of undeath—even if the cost of all that is my own soul.

I can't hesitate. I can't fail.

When I am satisfied with my ability to conjure dark magic, I return all the tomes to their shelves and replace them with pages and pages of summoning circles. I choose the most complex pattern I can find because if my chains aren't strong enough, the Void Prince will burst free and kill me before I can bind him to my soul. This particular summoning circle consists of a seven-pointed star, each of its diagonals crossing through the center and forming smaller triangles. Between each point of the stars lies a circle filled with runes I don't recognize, but I know they must be the letters of Abyssal, the language of demons.

The books state it doesn't matter what substance is used to draw the summoning circles; it may be with dark magic, blood, ink, chalk, or even aether. I choose the latter, not wishing to wield dark magic for longer than is necessary.

"*Volu.*" Violet light blooms in my hands. I kneel and press my glowing fingers to the marble floor and trace the summoning circle with as much precision as I can. A few of the lines aren't straight enough, thanks to my wobbling hand, so I murmur *terminir* and erase them all. I draw them again more carefully, and when I am certain the summoning circle looks identical to the one sketched inside the tomes, I take an obsidian dagger from the nearest shelf.

Everything is prepared. All that remains is blood. My blood.

I press the blade into my palm and hiss as the skin breaks. For a demon as powerful as the Void Prince, much blood will be required. I cut deeply enough to draw plenty and through the pain, I conjure the image of Arluin plunging his dagger through my father's heart, of Eliya lying as lifeless as a doll inside her crystal coffin. My heart hurts so much that my physical pain numbs.

When I remove the dagger and reopen my eyes, blood flows across my palm. I try not to spill any as I grasp a soul-gem and return to the center of my summoning circle.

I tighten both my fists. My left hand stings with the rawness of the wound, while my other aches from where the soul-gem's protruding edges dig into my flesh. But I care not for the pain. What I am about to do will change everything. It will grant me what I seek but cost me all I have left to lose in this world. My soul.

It almost seems a reasonable exchange. Perhaps even that I'm paying too little.

The incantation's letters flash through my mind. I studied them for so long, worried I would forget them in this crucial moment. I'm not sure how accurate my pronunciation will be, since I have never learned Abyssal, but the language forms the spell-words of the magic that necromancers wield and I have heard them speak the dark tongue many times. I hope my imitation will be close enough.

I draw aether into my bloodied hand and use it to summon the shadows. Darkness swirls in my fingers. My heart stills. I stare at the dark magic, a distant part of me questioning how I have ended up here. But I shake away that thought. Doubt will not serve me. I must sharpen my focus into a blade point.

Now that dark magic lies in my grasp, I must begin the ritual. "*Kretol'morish Natharius Thalanor.*"

I mix the shadows with my blood, and it spills like ink across the summoning circle. It bleeds into the markings of aether and replaces the violet light with thick black oil.

Nothing happens. Long enough passes that I begin to worry I mispronounced the spell-words.

Then the soul-gem disintegrates. Glittering dust falls across the summoning circle and oozes into the pulsating black lines. The markings rise an inch from the floor and spin faster and faster beneath my bare feet until they become nothing but a blur.

Thunder rings through the chamber. Instinctively, I squeeze my eyes shut—only for a heartbeat.

When I open them, the summoning circle has fallen still. A terrifying shadow looms over me. His silhouette is cast across the floor: horns, and wings, and cloven feet.

I stiffly raise my head and look upon the monster I have called forth.

He is even more frightening than his shadow. Too large for this chamber, he stands hunched over and his onyx horns threaten to impale the crystalline ceiling. Draconic wings beat back and forth, powerful enough that I am almost blown from my feet. I dig my heels into the floor and force myself to meet the eyes of this hulking monstrosity.

I can't allow it to think me weak.

His eyes glow an unearthly crimson, as do the markings which wind across the pale skin of his torso. Long, silver hair streams over his shoulders like strands of moonlight. That, and his pointed ears, assure me that I have not summoned the wrong demon. The traces of his heritage are evident beneath his monstrous horns and wings and hooves. Long ago, before demonic corruption seized him, I suspect he was beautiful like the rest of his kin. Now he is a horrifying husk.

"Who dares summon me?" his voice booms, echoing off the walls. His attention sweeps across the floor until he spots my figure far beneath him. Fury blazes in his crimson eyes.

My heart hammers with fear, with desperation. I don't answer him.

The Void Prince steps forth and his cloven hooves almost crack the marble floor. I draw away until I am safely beyond the summoning circle.

He stalks as close as he can but is unable to cross the edge of my markings. I don't know what I would have done if he'd passed through the summoning circle. All I know is that it would have ended in my death. As well as Zephyr's, who cowers behind the armchair. Too focused on the demon, I don't turn to look at him. I quickly shed the guilt which arises from the knowledge of his fear.

A low growl rumbles in the back of the Void Prince's throat. "Little mage, I will tear you limb from limb, carve the flesh from your puny bones and feed you morsel by morsel to my Void Hounds." He grips the hilt of his enormous obsidian sword, and his lips twist into a cruel snarl.

I clasp my hands behind my back to hide their trembling, but it might be in vain. I don't know whether the Void Prince can smell my fear.

Of course I wasn't expecting a Void Prince to be thrilled by being summoned to Imyria, especially not one known as Pride, but I'm paying him with the eternal damnation of my soul. It seems he has little interest in that. Perhaps I should have instead summoned the Void Prince of Envy, or continued my search for Wrath.

But it's too late now. I've already summoned him.

"Natharius Thalanor," I declare, steadying my voice and holding my head as high as I can. "I, Reyna Ashbourne, claim you as my servant, forced to obey my every command until I have freed my father from the shackles of undeath and defeated the necromancy threat which plagues Imyria. In exchange for your service, my soul will be yours for eternity after my final breath."

Unfortunately, those final words are part of the ritual. While scanning through the tomes, I did wonder what would happen if I refused to speak them, but I don't dare to alter the recommended procedure. If I do, the Void Prince could break free and destroy me. It isn't worth the risk. Not when his power is almost in my grasp.

A tendril of darkness rises from the summoning circle. It wraps around us both like thread and knots us together. Then I am as chained to him as he is to me.

The demon howls with rage. But his wrath and the dark flames he conjures are not enough to sever the cord between us.

Our souls are bound.

"I will devour your soul and ensure your suffering lasts a thousand years," he seethes.

Fear coils through me at his curse and the knowledge of what awaits me after death, but the images of my father and Eliya steel me.

I relinquished my soul, and now this demon is mine. I must not fail.

From the ashes of Nolderan, I will rise.

And Arluin pay for his sins with his blood.

EPILOGUE

JURON HATED THE NIGHT SHIFT most of all. The priestess's gentle breathing came from the door behind him: a soft, melodious whisper. Even her breathing was beautiful—torturous.

He leaned against the pillar which stood sentry outside of her chambers, and the grooves etched into the stone dug into his back. When it was only him and the darkness, his imagination always ran amok. It made him imagine a different life, where he was not her sworn protector, where she did not belong to the Mother and to Selynis. Where his sister did not call him soft between the ears for loving one who could never love him back. But he could not help his foolish heart.

Juron shifted his weight and let out a gentle sigh. His fingers played around the elegant hilt of his light-forged sword, and he felt the energy singing within. Slow and steady as a stream, with the soothing kiss of sunlight. Its presence reminded him of the priestess. She was light magic incarnate.

He shook his head and tried to sober himself from his troublesome thoughts. What use was he to the priestess if the mere thought of her distracted him from his purpose? If the only thing he could be was her guard, then he would be the best guard she could ever ask for.

Juron trained his eyes on the blunt shadows ahead and steeled his mind. He wasn't sure what time it was and how long it would be before his sister took over from him, but through the arched window, he glimpsed the ripe moon sitting full and fat like a pearl sewn into the black velvet of night. The unblemished limestone buildings of the city below stood silent and still—

A scream pierced the night.

Taria. It came from Taria's room.

Juron threw himself from the pillar and lunged for the door, shoving it open so desperately that it splintered off its hinges. He charged over the broken door without sparing it a second thought. All that mattered was Taria.

He drew his sword. Steel whispered into the shadows.

But no one else was there. The priestess was sitting up in her bed, the blankets pooled around her. The shoulder of her gossamer night-gown had slipped down, exposing her mahogany skin to the night. The moonlight silvered the soft curve of her shoulder, and he had the sudden urge to trace it. A familiar ache filled his heart.

Her white locks flowed over her other shoulder, so luminous they made the moon look faint. She stared at him with her golden eyes. Light magic poured from her like the aura of dawn. Maybe she was meditating. Though he had never seen her meditating with her eyes wide open.

"Taria?" he said gently.

The priestess did not blink. Juron paced over to her bed and perched on the edge. He nudged her shoulder, the one he'd considered tracing. He tried not to think about the softness of her skin.

She jolted to life then, and Juron almost leaped away with the suddenness. She rose onto her knees and clasped either side of his face, staring at him with unblinking eyes. This close, they blinded him.

"Taria, what's the matter?"

Now she finally answered him, her gaze clouded with the remnants of her divine vision.

"Death," she rasped, her chest heaving with the strain. "Death comes for us all."

Reyna's story will continue in...

STORM
OF SHADOWS

To learn more about STORM OF SHADOWS (Legends of Imyria, #2) and find out how to get a copy, you can visit here:

www.hollyrosebooks.com/storm-of-shadows

You can also subscribe to my newsletter so that you never miss out on new releases, giveaways, cover reveals, or other fun things (like bonus scenes!)

www.hollyrosebooks.com/subscribe

ACKNOWLEDGEMENTS

It's safe to say this book would not be in your hands if not for my sister. Writing *Ashes of Aether* broke a long string of shelved "nearly" finished manuscripts, and until then I had been starting to believe I was incapable of ever completing a first draft again (I wasn't—it was only my mindset). I did almost shelve *Ashes of Aether* twice after the second draft, but my sister convinced me to continue working on it and to bite the bullet and write it from scratch for a third time. So, thank you, Ella, for being my writing counsellor. Thank you for also being my first reader ever. I still remember you always reading my story attempts on scraps of paper when we were kids (usually on holidays, for some reason).

I also owe so much to Aimee, my critique partner. Thank you for helping me to figure out how to turn my messy "draft zero" of *Ashes of Aether* into a story with a coherent structure (oh, the pantser life). Thank you for also letting me spam your inbox with *"OMG HALP!!!"* whenever I'm having a writing emergency and helping me to brainstorm my jumbled ideas into logical plot lines. You are the best C.P. and friend anyone could ever ask for. I can't believe how far we've come over these past six years, and I'm so proud of us both. I can't wait until you also release your work into the world. I know you'll absolutely slay!

Thank you to my mum for being almost as critical as me and for reading through my third rewrite of *Ashes of Aether* when I decided to do a last-minute overhaul. Also, thank you for all your help with my Bookstagram photos!

Another thanks goes to my dad for being an even bigger fantasy nerd than me. I certainly wouldn't be writing High Fantasy if not for the fact you let me watch Lord of the Rings and play World of Warcraft at such a young age. Thank you for reading all the Harry Potter and Eragon books to me as a child (even if your voice was rather monotone, haha).

Thank you, Yazzie, for being the best beta reader any writer could ever ask for. Your suggestions are always so on point, and I can't believe how quickly you can read! I am so grateful that you were willing to read *Ashes of Aether* again after I decided to rewrite the story from scratch.

Thank you to Elle and Vanessa and everyone else who beta read for being among my first readers of *Ashes of Aether*. I hope when you read this finished version, you can see how your feedback helped to shape this story from the initial draft you read!

Kolarp Em, you helped me to think more like an artist and this story would never have reached its potential if not for your honesty. You helped me to see the direction I needed to take this story in, and I hope when you read it, you can see the impact you've had on my work. You are an incredibly talented artist, and I still can't believe how you managed to pull my ideas out of my head and illustrate them so beautifully and so accurately. I am so lucky to call you my friend.

And thank you, dear reader, for taking a chance on this story. For that, I will forever be grateful <3